OUR

DARKEST

HOUR

OUR DARKEST SERIES
BOOK ONE

SARAH BAILEY

Cover Art by Sarah Bailey

Published by Twisted Tree Publications
www.twistedtreepublications.com
info@twistedtreepublications.com

Paperback ISBN: 978-1-913217-18-1

To the most beautiful, wonderful, kind and caring soul in my life!
Sabrina.
You give me life every day. I wouldn't be where I am without you.
And neither would Rhys and Aaron.

PROLOGUE

Rhys

here's a type of love in this world which digs its way inside of you, taking root deep in your bones, latching onto every part of you and sinking deep into your soul. It tears you into a thousand tiny pieces and eviscerates your very being. That type of love is damaging, bruising, overwhelming and completely devastating.

I guess that's the type of love I was always destined to have. This love of ours wasn't meant for fairy tales or dreams. It was built to burn, wreck and ruin. It came into our lives like a storm, bringing havoc in its wake. Two souls crashed together and destroyed the world around them.

A love like ours wasn't meant to exist. It wasn't meant to grow. It wasn't meant for us. And even in our darkest hour, it was the only flame left keeping us both alive. Until that flame went out.

We crashed.

We burned.

We died.

The one I thought was my fairy tale ended up being the ultimate instrument of our destruction. And the love I once felt left me a hollow shell of myself with a cold, blackened heart.

Now in the ashes of our demise, there's only one thing I know for certain.

Aaron Jackson Parrish ruined my life.

And I'll never forgive him for it.

PART I

captivate

verb, cap·ti·vat·ed, cap·ti·vat·ing.

to attract and hold the attention or interest of, as by beauty or excellence; enchant.

CHAPTER ONE

Rhys

I never thought on the first day of school after the summer holidays I'd be cowering away from a kid twice my size. Dread seized my muscles, making them ache with tension and fear. Perhaps it might have been the fact my father was a notorious waste of space who constantly cheated on my mother and lived on the dole. No one in our estate liked him. Didn't mean I should be subject to the same ridicule. It wasn't like I'd asked to be born. Funny that even at seven years old, I understood what type of person my father had turned out to be. I understood he hated me. And I understood I wasn't wanted.

"You're going to grow up to be a little fag, aren't you? Look at you, I bet you're about to piss your pants," the boy taunted, his cruelty making me want to throw up.

I had done nothing but walk across the playground to hide away from all the other kids in my uniform, which didn't fit me properly. I didn't have any friends. An outcast in a world which had given me very little to begin with. So this was just par for the course.

"Leave me alone," I whispered, unable to speak any louder as fear froze me in place.

I got a punch in the gut for that.

"Shut up, you little fag."

I almost doubled over, clutching my stomach as pain shot through me. This kid had to be at least ten. I stared up at him blankly as I tried to ignore how much his punch hurt.

"You don't even know what that is, do you, gay boy?"

Why is he calling me that?

"I'm not… I'm not gay."

He opened his mouth to say something else when a fist flew out of nowhere and connected with his jaw. The boy staggered backwards, clutching it in pain. He swung around to see who the fist belonged to. Next to me, a boy who looked my age stood tall, his blue-grey eyes steely and his blonde hair blowing in the slight breeze.

"Go pick on someone your own size."

The kid who'd been bullying me stared at the newcomer with shock written all over his features. As if it surprised him to see whoever this boy was defending me. Then he straightened, shrugging it off like it was nothing.

"Whatever. If you want to hang out with gay boy over here, you're welcome to him." He glared at me. "I'm watching you."

He walked away, but not before I caught him rubbing his jaw. I wasn't sure what just happened, only that whoever this person was, they'd saved me. I turned to him, still holding my stomach. Blue-grey eyes stared at the retreating bully with distaste.

"You should stay away from Valentine."

I almost coughed in surprise. He'd talked to me and the bully's name was Valentine? I wanted to laugh, but the noise got caught in my throat. I didn't laugh at anything. There was no joy in my life at all. So how had this boy I didn't even know almost drag the sound out of me? I didn't like the feeling. Happiness wasn't something I happened to be well versed in.

"I didn't do anything," I mumbled.

His eyes landed on me then, the softness of his expression made me feel odd. No one except Mum had ever looked at me with any sort of kindness.

"No?"

I shook my head. He crossed his arms over his chest. He was as tall as me, but he wasn't a skinny rake like me. I suppose when you don't get fed properly at home, you end up looking like a bean pole. Some might say I suffered from neglect, but my mum tried her best. Wasn't her fault my dad kept spending all the money we got off the government on alcohol and cigarettes.

"I'm Aaron and you can thank me at any time."

I blinked. The arrogant glint in his eye made me wary of saying anything. Then he broke into a grin and slapped me around the shoulder, making me jolt.

"Kidding."

I rubbed my shoulder. As much as I appreciated him getting Valentine away from me, I was also wary of his

7

intentions. *What does this boy want?* I wasn't at school to make friends. My mum made me come. And I wanted to get away from the house so I didn't have to be around when my father started drinking and calling her names. He usually left to go out to the pub for the night before I got home.

"You're a quiet one."

Talking wasn't my strong point. I didn't participate much in class and kept to myself. Easier that way. Didn't have to explain to anyone about my home life or why some days I wondered why I even existed when I wasn't wanted in this world.

"Thanks," I muttered.

"You're welcome." He smiled. "You're Rhys, right?"

I wasn't sure how he knew that, but I nodded.

"I saw you in class. We're in the same year group."

I shrugged. Honestly, I hadn't noticed him. Then again, I didn't look at anyone around me. Sometimes I felt so adrift. I didn't tend to care who or what was in my vicinity as long as they didn't bother me. It's why I'd been a little miffed at Valentine giving me a hard time. I hadn't done anything. I kept out of everyone's way and never brought attention to myself. It's how I liked things. Blending into the background so no one could see how much I was dying on the inside.

"Am I going to have to do all the talking? I mean, I don't mind or anything, but it might get boring after a while. For you, that is. I won't get bored."

I didn't want him talking to me in the first place. Being alone was my MO. That's how it'd always been.

"Didn't ask you to talk to me."

"He speaks!"

I didn't glare at him, but I wanted to. This Aaron had started to get on my nerves. Also, why was he standing so close to me? I didn't like anyone in my personal space. It made my skin itch uncomfortably.

"Why are you still here?"

I didn't like being rude to people considering I had nothing against them. Usually. Wasn't their fault they didn't understand me. Something about Aaron riled me up the wrong way. The way he stood watching me with this expectant look in his eyes as if I owed him my friendship after he got rid of Valentine for me.

Who does this boy think he is?

"All right, I see when I'm not wanted." He tipped an imaginary hat at me. "But you know, if you ever want a friend or just to talk or anything, you can come to me. Also, if Valentine gets in your face again, I'll handle it."

With that, he walked off after digging his hands in his pockets. He looked back over his shoulder at me, those blue-grey eyes betraying a hint of confusion and sadness in them. As if he knew how much I was hurting. As if he knew I didn't want to be in this world.

I turned away, not wanting his stupid gaze or his sympathy. Just because he'd saved me from a bully, didn't mean I owed him anything.

The bell for the end of break rang. I ambled back towards the school building unable to shake the feeling my life was about to take a turn in a direction which scared me.

I didn't want a friend.

9

I didn't want someone to talk to.

And I certainly didn't want to see Aaron, whoever he was again.

CHAPTER TWO

Rhys

Within moments of sitting down in my usual spot at the back of the class, I found the seat to my right occupied. I scowled, realising Aaron had taken it upon himself to sit next to me. Usually, the stragglers sat beside me and they didn't talk to me. Guess you could say most people ignored the weird skinny kid. Not Aaron, apparently.

"Do you like history?"

I stared at him blankly.

Why is he talking to me again? Why is he sitting here? Surely, he could sit with those girls staring at him, giggling away between themselves. They're better company than me.

"You don't have to talk. Can just nod yes or no."

I wanted him to go away. Wanted not to have to deal with this kid taking an interest in me when no one else had. No one else cared enough. So why did he?

"Oh, you like history too? That's cool, maybe we can do homework together some time."

I blinked.

Is he trying to make me look stupid?

Didn't need help with my homework anyway. My mum always told me I was smart. Too smart for my own good. Probably why my reading age was so far ahead of where I should be. I read in the school library a lot last year since she couldn't afford to buy me books. The librarian, Miss Forrest, always had new recommendations for me.

"I like reading," I mumbled, hoping if I gave him something, he would leave me alone.

He grinned at me. I had a suspicion it was his goal to get me to say something to him.

The teacher, Miss Allen, started class, saving me from being pestered by Aaron any further. I spent the entirety of it ignoring his eyes on me. Funnily enough, it was a history lesson. And I didn't want him knowing how much I liked learning. How I listened and took in everything, keeping it all stored up in my head for future reference. It was just about the only thing I could be proud of, my mum said anyway. She kept telling me what a good boy I was. I didn't know if I believed her.

I actively tried to avoid Aaron for the rest of the day, but he was always there lurking like my shadow. And when I attempted to walk home as my mum couldn't pick me up today, he walked with me. Not sure she should be letting her seven-year-old son walk home alone, but I didn't exactly have a choice.

"You walking?"

I glanced at him but kept my pace, not wanting to stop and talk.

"My sister can give you a lift if you want."

I didn't respond to that either. As if I wanted him knowing where I lived.

"Rhys."

I stopped dead and turned to him.

"Why won't you leave me alone?"

He looked taken aback by my outburst and I realised my tone had been harsh. Couldn't be helped. He was getting on my nerves.

"I don't know you. I don't have any wish to know you. Just leave me be. I don't need anyone."

If only that was true. I was lonely. So lonely some days I wondered if anyone would care if I didn't exist. My mum would, but my dad not so much. He would love it if I wasn't around taking up space. I hated him. And most of all, I hated myself.

Aaron didn't seem offended by my words. He cocked his head to the side, blue-grey eyes assessing me. They looked like storm clouds right then, the grey more pronounced as if it bothered him I was being so difficult.

"Just let me ask my sister to take you home, okay? She won't mind."

I let out a puff of air.

"Fine."

He gave me a bright smile and I wanted to smile back despite myself. A stupid involuntary reaction. He indicated I should follow him with a nod of his head. I trudged along by his side, avoiding all eye contact. Why would his sister be taking him home? How old was she? Did he have any other siblings?

Why do you care?

I didn't. As far as I was concerned, I wanted nothing more to do with Aaron.

"Usually my au pair, Tamara, picks me up, but she's sick so Harriet is coming instead."

I didn't know what an au pair was, but I imagined she was some kind of nanny, which meant Aaron certainly didn't live on an estate like me. Only people with money could afford nannies.

"Can I ask why no one is picking you up?"

I felt my face grow hot. It was embarrassing my mum couldn't get me. Usually, she would, but my dad had given her a black eye in a drunken rage last night. She didn't want the other mums or teachers seeing it. Everyone on the estate knew Graham King beat on his wife and was having an affair with Maggie Polton from two doors down. My mum ignored the stares and gossip, preferring to keep to herself.

"Mum can't today." *Or tomorrow. Or the next day.*

We reached a huge Range Rover with blacked-out windows. I stared at the car wondering why anyone needed one in a city but decided it wasn't worth questioning. A woman stood by the driver's door. She looked exactly like Aaron with the same blonde hair, but her eyes were bluer.

"There you are," the woman I assumed was Harriet, his sister said.

"Is it okay if we give Rhys a lift home?"

He waved a hand at me. I shrunk back a little when she looked me over.

"A new friend?"

"I guess."

We aren't friends.

"Is Rhys' mum not getting him?"

"No. Didn't think I should let him walk home alone."

Harriet gave me the once over again.

"I'm Aaron's sister, Harriet. How about you boys get in and you can tell me where to drop you?"

Aaron opened the back door and ushered me in. I climbed in the huge car reluctantly. Why had I agreed to this? It was such a bad idea, but I didn't want to run into Valentine again, nor did I enjoy walking home alone either.

I put my seatbelt on as Aaron got in next to me. Harriet slid in the front and looked at me through the rearview mirror. I couldn't tell what she thought of me.

I told her to take me to the estate. I could walk to my house from outskirts in less than five minutes. Her eyebrow raised, but she didn't comment on it. When I glanced at Aaron, I could see the understanding in his eyes and I hated it. So what if I came from a poor working-class background? It was clear as day he didn't, judging by the car his sister drove.

I stared out the window, hoping he wouldn't try talking to me again. No such luck.

"I meant it about doing homework together," he told me quietly. "If you want."

15

Harriet had the radio on so I didn't know if she could hear us or not.

"Don't need help with it."

"Maybe I do."

Why would I care if he needed help? If he had some kind of nanny taking care of him, surely his parents could afford a tutor for him too.

"Why won't you talk to me, Rhys?"

I didn't like how he said my name with such familiarity.

"Don't like to talk."

"I just want to be your friend."

I stiffened and bit down on my tongue so I wouldn't say anything horrible to him in front of his sister. No one wanted to be friends with me. Ever. No kids on the estate and no kids at school either. My mum had got me into the best school in our catchment area since I was smart. Most of the kids on the estate went to the roughest school in the area. There'd been a lot of trouble in that school, so Mum was adamant I went somewhere decent.

"Don't need friends," I mumbled.

Aaron said nothing in response and the rest of the drive was silent. Harriet pulled up outside the entrance to the estate.

"You sure I can't drop you directly home?"

"Here's fine, thanks."

I hopped out, hoping that was the end of it until I realised Aaron had followed me. Turning, I almost sighed knowing he would not stop with this weird urge of his to be my friend.

"Did you walk this morning?"

I shrugged.

"Yeah."

"Why isn't your mum taking you?"

I didn't want to tell him. He'd look down on us. He probably already was.

"She can't."

He stared at me for a long moment.

"Be here at ten to eight tomorrow, yeah?"

He didn't give me a chance to say no, getting back in the car. I couldn't see him through the blacked-out windows. A part of me wondered what he was thinking and why he thought I'd want a lift tomorrow.

Shaking myself, I walked away as the car moved off. I hoped my dad wouldn't be home when I got in. Dealing with him would make a bad day that much worse. Having been bullied and pestered, I was done with people.

Deep down, I didn't want to acknowledge how it made me feel a little less like I wasn't wanted by anyone when Aaron said he wanted to be my friend. And I didn't want to explore the possibility I might be okay with having a friend either. Being alone was better. Being alone meant no one could hurt me like Dad hurt Mum. Being alone was the only way of life I knew. And I wasn't about to let a boy I barely knew change that. Not for anything.

CHAPTER THREE

Rhys

Was it stupid of me to be waiting for him this morning? Probably. Maybe I wanted to know if he was serious about being my friend. Surely it was all too good to be true. I'd only ever been dealt with a crappy hand in life. Even when I tried. So I stopped attempting to connect with others. It seemed such a pointless waste of time.

My dad hadn't been home when I got in, but Mum was there. She asked me why I'd got back early so I mumbled about a kid giving me a lift home. The way her eyes brightened made me sick. She wanted me to make friends. To do well in life. Little did she know the damage had already done. I wished I wasn't a part of this world on a daily basis.

I wanted to ask her why she stayed with my dad, but I knew it would be useless. My mum couldn't cope on her own. Not since she'd had me. My birth had left her permanently disabled. She had a condition called pre-eclampsia, whilst she'd been monitored closely, she'd ended up having a stroke right after I was born. It left her with spatial awareness and communication problems. Occasionally she had issues walking. My dad was technically her carer although, really, I looked after the most. She'd explained the reason behind her condition to me recently. She kept telling me I was a smart boy who could understand what everything meant.

So the fact my dad beat her sickened me. And it was why I remained. She didn't have any other family except me. Her sister had been around to help out with me when I'd been a baby, but she'd died last year. I say she died. She took her own life. Mum said Aunt Bibi had suffered from severe depression since they were teenagers. I think I understood Aunt Bibi more than I did anyone else. She couldn't take the pain any longer.

When a red Ford Fiesta pulled up in front of me, I ignored it at first as I was expecting the Range Rover. So when Aaron hopped out, I took a step back.

"I wasn't sure you'd be here. Come on, Tamara's better today."

I hesitated for a long moment whilst Aaron stared at me with those stormy blue-grey eyes of his. In their own way, they were beautiful. I could imagine him being at home during a thunderstorm with lightning striking all around him whilst the rain poured from the sky. Shaking myself, I took a step towards him which brought a smile to his face.

When we were in the car and I'd mumbled hello to Tamara who seemed quite young with red hair and blue eyes and had an Australian accent, Aaron turned to me.

"So I was wondering if you wanted to come over at the weekend. My parents are away for work so it'd just be us and Tamara."

"I can't."

It was a knee jerk reaction, but really, I had to be home for my mum. Weekends were the worst. My dad always had his friends over and they bothered Mum a lot. That's when she'd take me down to the park and we'd feed the ducks at the pond. It was our routine. Disrupting that felt like I'd be tearing off a limb.

"You sure? Tamara makes lamingtons and they're amazing."

"I have to take care of Mum."

It'd come out without me wanting it to, but his disappointed expression made me feel something. Like the last thing I wanted was his displeasure. The feeling was so alien. I never wanted to please anyone but my mum.

"Oh."

I didn't want to explain why to him. He didn't get to know about my life. No one did. No one cared. Most people pitied me and Mum. Wasn't her fault. She didn't ask to have a difficult pregnancy. She didn't ask to rely on my dad for care. Sometimes I wish he'd leave her, then I'd be her carer and we wouldn't have to deal with him. We'd be better off without Graham King.

"That's okay. Maybe some other time or after school."

Why is he so eager?

I'd barely given him anything to go on. So I didn't bother answering. Didn't want to give him false hope.

"You have really pretty eyes, you know."

I blinked.

Um, what?

I thought I had boring eyes. They were brown like my dad's. In fact, I looked like a small version of him with inky black hair and tanned skin. A fact I hated. My mum always told me I was handsome, but I didn't believe her. She loved how I'd taken after him. I didn't understand how she could still love him, but adults and love were a huge mystery to me. Why would anyone want to have a relationship with another person when all they did was disappoint you? Seemed stupid to me.

"Uh… thanks." *I think.*

What kind of boy talked like that anyway? Calling my eyes pretty. It was weird. Aaron was typically handsome, I suppose. Girls would be swooning over him when we got older.

"You're welcome."

His smile was so bright, I almost had to look away. A part of me wanted to repay the compliment, but I refrained from doing so. Afraid it would lead him to believe I welcomed his attempts to make friends with me. I didn't want the tiny bud of hope inside me to blossom. Maybe Aaron was genuine. Maybe he really did want to know me. Maybe he wouldn't judge me for where I came from. He hadn't said anything bad about where I lived despite probably knowing how rough it was. The police got called out daily. Drug dealers hung out in the alleyways behind the block of flats near my house. And the gangs were the worst. Those boys carried knives. I avoided that part of the estate like the plague.

When Tamara pulled up at the school, she got out and hugged Aaron. Her soft smile to me was unexpected.

"Laters," she said to both of us before getting in the car again.

I thought Aaron might leave me be now we were at school. I was mistaken. He walked with me to class and sat next to me again. I was beginning to see this boy wouldn't give up easily. And I wondered what it would take to get him to leave me alone. I didn't want any further disappointments in my life. I couldn't trust he wouldn't be another person to add to the ever-growing list of crap in my life. How could I convince him I wasn't worth his time? I would only be a burden. If he looked close enough, he'd see all the broken damage inside.

And that thought scared me more than anything else.

CHAPTER FOUR

Rhys

Mum was pottering around in the kitchen when I got home. I set my homework out on the table after I kissed her hello. Doing it when I got in from school gave me time to hide in my room before my dad came home. I had a new book from the school library to read. My favourites were fantasies where you could get lost in a world that wasn't your own.

"How was school?"

I looked up at Mum. She had a rolling pin out. She liked to bake when she could. Other than her black eye, she'd been doing well physically. Some days she struggled to get out of bed.

"Fine."

"You're back early again."

"Got a lift."

I wondered if I should tell her about Aaron properly or not. Didn't want her to think I actually wanted to make friends with him.

"Is this the same kid from yesterday?"

I sighed, setting my pencil down.

"Yeah."

She turned to me, her light green eyes bright with happiness.

"Do they have a name?"

"Aaron."

I only ever confided in Mum.

"Well, you can tell Aaron and his mum thank you from me."

"Not his mum who takes him. He has an au pair, which I think is like a nanny. She's Australian."

"You can thank her then."

I fiddled with my workbook.

"Tamara gave me a lift to school too. Aaron says she doesn't mind picking me up every day."

He told me today at lunchtime when he'd insisted on sitting with me. The school had an initiative to make sure all the kids got balanced lunches, so today we'd had a pasta bake full of vegetables with a side of salad. Probably the only time I actually got a proper meal. Wasn't my mum's fault my dad didn't give her enough money to buy food with.

Today it seemed he'd been generous as she had supplies to make chocolate chip cookies. My favourite. Graham was probably trying to make up for punching her in the face. Sometimes he'd be good to her, but mostly, he treated her like dirt. Not to mention how he stayed around Maggie Polton's house all the time. I didn't like her with her skimpy outfits and face full of gaudy makeup. Who knew what Dad saw in her.

"That's very kind of them. I wish I could take you myself. I feel better knowing you have someone looking out for you."

The guilt I felt at her words cut through me like a knife. Here I'd been actively trying to stop Aaron from wanting to be my friend.

"I know, Mum. It's okay."

"It's not okay, Rhys. I want you to have a better life than me. Than this." She waved the rolling pin around. "I'm sorry I can't give you more."

I got out of my chair and went over to her, wrapping myself around her waist.

"Don't. You're enough. I love you."

She stroked my hair, placing the rolling pin down and holding me.

"My sweet boy."

I tried not to let my emotions out, but they clogged up my throat. She'd been through so much to have me. I should be grateful. I should be here to take care of her.

"I want you to have someone other than me. I'm just your mum. You deserve to be around people your own age."

I wish she'd stop trying to push me to make friends. Being on my own was just fine with me. Didn't need anyone else but my mum in my life. Not now Aunt Bibi was gone.

"I don't like anyone else."

"Not even Aaron?"

I didn't know how I felt about him. Not really. He was so confident yet kind and understanding. My continual shrugging him off didn't seem to put him off me. If anything, it only made him try harder. Like he had an ice-pick and was determined to shatter the ice frosting around my blackened heart. Little did he know I was already dead inside. There wasn't any point in trying. Loneliness ate at me. Chipping away at my walls. Maybe it would be my downfall.

"He's okay. I don't know him though."

"Maybe you should try."

Or maybe he should leave me alone. That would be preferable.

"I don't want to try, Mum."

She pulled away and stared down at me. Her kind eyes were full of sadness. As if it hurt her to see how closed off I'd become.

"Rhys, we've talked about this before. You can't live in a world where you isolate yourself from everything. That's not how life works."

"You do."

She frowned.

"I'm stuck with my lot, but you don't have to settle when you have your whole life ahead of you."

I looked away, knowing she was right but hating it all the same. Hating how I couldn't make her happier. Hating how I felt responsible for making her like this. Hating how I was too young to do more to help her. I hated myself so much it burnt through me, lacing my veins with agony.

"Would it make you happy if I make friends with Aaron?"

She stroked my hair back from my face.

28

"It would make me happy to see you happy, whether or not it's by making friends. But from what you've said, it sounds like Aaron wouldn't be a bad friend to have, don't you think?"

She was probably right. My mum might have had a hard life but her instincts were always on point.

"Maybe."

I said it to appease her having no real intention of making friends with him.

"That's my boy. Now, do you want to help me cut these and I'll let you have the first one straight out of the oven when they're baked."

I nodded. I always enjoyed helping her. Homework could wait. Spending time with my mum was the only thing that put a smile on my face. I tried not to think about how yesterday Aaron had almost made me laugh. And how today he'd kept staring at me with those storm cloud eyes of his reminding me of the last time I'd heard thunder rattling our front windows.

Why was he getting in my head like this? I didn't want him in there taking up space. We didn't know each other. He meant nothing to me. What if he was being nice only to hurt me when I let him in? I didn't trust anyone other than my mum.

So why did I feel so conflicted? Why did all my thoughts keep coming back to the boy who'd rescued me from a bully? And why did I feel like I would grow to regret it if I kept pushing him away?

All of this whirled in my head as I helped Mum with the cookies. And I hated having no forthcoming answers.

Maybe you should try, Rhys. Maybe it won't be so bad. Maybe you won't get hurt.

I always got hurt. Always. Nothing would ever change that. Not my mum. Not school. And certainly not the boy with blue-grey eyes, blonde hair and a smile which made me want to smile back.

CHAPTER FIVE

Rhys

A week had gone by. A whole week where Tamara and Aaron had picked me up and dropped me off at school. A whole week of sitting next to him in lesson, at lunch and during break times. A whole week of him trying to get me to talk to him. And quite frankly, I was exhausted.

Every moment I spent in his presence wore me down until I'd become fully fed up of his constant chatter. Like how he told me he didn't think Harriet's boyfriend was very nice. Or that his parents were in America for some big launch his father's company was doing. Or that he liked gaming and would love to show me his state-of-the-art computer his dad had bought him. I gathered he came from money, but he never seemed to flaunt the fact. It was just a part of his life. He'd grown up in a world of privilege unlike me. I lived on the breadline.

We were sitting on a bench outside during break time. He'd been talking to me about how Tamara was trying to get his parents to allow him to have a pet for the past five minutes.

"Do you ever shut up?" I interjected suddenly.

He turned to me, eyes widening.

"I would if you talked back."

"You're annoying."

"You haven't told me to leave you alone again."

He was right. I'd told him that the first day we met. He'd ignored me.

"What if I did? Would you?"

"Probably not."

I crossed my arms over my chest and sat back, eying him warily. This boy didn't know when to stop. At all.

"Mum thinks I should let you be my friend. She asks me about you every day."

His eyes lit up.

"You told her about me?"

"She wanted to know who's giving me lifts is all."

I looked away before his eager expression cracked one of my walls. He was wearing me down piece by piece.

"Well, I agree with your mum."

Of course, he would. He'd been dead set on the idea of being my friend since day one.

"Still don't need a friend."

"Admit it, Rhys, you don't mind me being around you."

"Whatever," I muttered.

If I didn't want him near me, I'd have fought harder against him, wouldn't I?

"It's okay. I don't mind you being stubborn. I told you, I can talk enough for the both of us."

"No kidding."

He talked my ear off daily when we weren't in lesson. It was like having a radio blaring in my ear twenty-four-seven. Entirely irritating and yet... the more he talked, the less I seemed to mind him being there. I wouldn't tell him that though.

"Did you tell your mum I invited you over?"

"No."

Mum needed me. She'd always need me. So I couldn't go around his.

"Are you going to?"

"No."

I peered at him but he didn't seem ruffled. Why did this boy seem to think no would somehow turn into yes eventually?

"I'd like to meet your mum."

I opened my mouth to speak but no sound came out. He couldn't possibly mean that.

"I'll introduce you to my parents when they get back."

What is happening?

"Why would you do that?"

His eyes twinkled.

"You're my friend, Rhys, whether or not I'm yours."

Now I knew he was crazy. I barely spoke and I didn't encourage his advances. How could he consider me a friend?

"You're never going to give up."

"Nope. You're stuck with me."

Great. Just what I wanted. A boy who won't leave me in peace ever again.

"Don't know why you bother."

I wasn't special. Aaron was charming and confident enough he could be friends with anyone he wanted. All the girls in our class stared at him like he was a god. He should hang out with them not me. They would appreciate his company.

He cocked his head to the side. His eyes grew stormy again, the grey more defined than the blue.

"You don't see what I do."

"Oh, and what's that?"

Curiosity got the better of me. I needed to understand why he didn't just drop this.

"A boy who's crying out for someone to see him. Not the wall he puts up, but the real Rhys inside. The one who cares about his mum more than himself. The one who's hurting more and more with each passing day. I see you, Rhys, and I still want to be your friend."

I blinked. How could a fellow seven-year-old have the ability to see right through me and express it so well?

Who is this boy and where did he come from?

"You know nothing about me."

He smiled and shook his head a little.

"I know you'll keep trying to push me away and I won't stop pushing you until you let me in."

I didn't like where this was going. I didn't like him seeing me full stop.

"You'll be waiting a long time."

"That's okay with me."

He was still smiling. I didn't understand it. How could he be happy? I hadn't given him anything.

"You're crazy."

His grin widened.

"Probably, but one day you're going to tell me I'm your only friend and that will make it all worth it."

This boy was clearly mad. I wouldn't be saying that. I didn't want friends especially not him. He got under my skin in a way I hated. It was an itch I kept having to scratch. I wanted him to disappear so I wouldn't have to feel this way. Yet he was just there, making me feel everything and nothing at the same time.

"You should let Tamara drop you off at your house then we can meet your mum. I'm sure she'd like to see who's giving you lifts to school."

I didn't need him to any longer. Mum's black eye was gone. She could take me. But I didn't want to make her walk all that way with me. It was too much. At least when Aunt Bibi had been around, she'd taken me. We weren't better off without her. I think it upset Mum a lot with her sister being gone. Her little sister had been her only family other than me and my dad. I'd hardly call him that. He didn't treat her well nor me.

I wanted to say no but I knew Mum wanted to know who Aaron was. She wanted to meet Tamara. It would make her feel better about allowing a stranger to take care of her son.

"Fine," I mumbled.

I hoped my dad wouldn't be at home when we got there. And I would make my mum come outside. Didn't want Aaron seeing in our house or how I lived.

"Really?"

Why does he sound so happy about it?

"Yeah, don't make me change my mind, okay?"

"You got it."

And yet Aaron had a stupid smile on his face for the rest of the day. Like he'd won a small victory. So when it came around to home time, he was practically bouncing off the walls. I thought he was mad but it made me want to smile, seeing him so excited. I didn't. I only smiled with Mum.

I directed Tamara to the house when we got to the estate. She turned off the engine when we were outside.

"Wait here, I'll get her," I said before jumping out.

I could see the curtains twitching next door. Nat Jacob was a nosey old lady who gossiped about everyone on our street. I hated her as she was mean about Mum and her disabilities.

I let myself in the front door.

"Mum? You here?" I called.

I didn't get any answer so I walked further in.

"Mum?"

When I reached the kitchen, I found her on the floor, struggling to get back up.

"Oh god, Mum."

I was by her side the next moment. She looked pained.

"Rhys love, you're back."

"What happened?"

"I tripped over my own feet, can you imagine?"

She tried to smile but it came out as a wince.

"Mum, where does it hurt?"

"Oh, it's nothing. My ankle just got a little twisted."

I looked down at her feet. One of them had started to swell.

"That's not nothing."

I didn't know what to do. She couldn't walk on it even if I did get her up. I felt another presence behind me. Looking back, I found Aaron staring at both of us from the doorway. I told him to wait.

Why is he here?

"Can I help?"

I blinked and then looked back at Mum who was staring at Aaron.

"She fell over. I think her ankle got twisted."

Next thing I knew, he was by my side and helping me get my mum up off the floor. With both of us, it didn't take too much effort. I was too weak to lift her by myself. Aaron got her onto one of the kitchen table chairs and knelt down, checking on her ankle. It didn't look as bad now we could see it properly. Just a little swollen.

He stood up and glanced at me. I shifted on my feet as Mum stared between us.

"This is Aaron," I muttered. "This is my mum, Stephanie."

"You're Aaron? Rhys has told me a lot about you."

I felt my face growing hot, especially when Aaron grinned wide and stuck his hand out. Mum shook it, giving me a look.

"It's nice to meet you, Mrs King."

"Oh, you can call me Steph, love. I'm glad you're getting my boy out of his own head."

That made my face grow hotter. Aaron's smile was radiant. *Why is she encouraging him?*

I was going down with this sinking ship. And I couldn't find it in me to plug the holes so I wouldn't drown.

"That's okay, he's worth the effort."

These two were conspiring against me. I'd told Mum on several occasions I didn't like Aaron even though, despite myself, I did. He was hard not to like. Especially when he smiled like that and the way his blue-grey eyes twinkled whenever he was amused or saying something cheeky.

"Can I get you anything, Mum? Do you think you need to see a doctor?"

She smiled at me indulgently.

"No, Rhys, I'll be fine but you'll have to help me with dinner, yeah?"

"Of course."

There wasn't anything I wouldn't do for my mum.

"I would ask you to stay, Aaron, but I'm sure your au pair is waiting for you."

He gave a little shrug.

"Maybe another time or maybe Rhys will finally take me up on my offer to come over."

My mum gave me a stern look.

"You didn't tell me Aaron asked you. Why would you turn that down?"

I scowled, unable to help myself. She was ruining everything right now.

"You need me."

She shook her head.

"You can go around Aaron's any time you like, Rhys, you just need to tell me before you go to school."

"What about tomorrow?" Aaron piped up.

My mum clapped her hands together.

"That's a wonderful idea."

Great. Now I can't get out of it.

"Tamara will drop him home afterwards. He can have dinner with us. I promise he won't be back late."

My mum nodded and gave him a bright smile.

"I'm sure Rhys will love that."

Is she talking for me now? Don't I get a say in this?

Apparently not.

"Great. Well, I better go. I'll see you tomorrow, Rhys."

"Say thank you to Tamara for me, I'm very grateful for her ferrying Rhys around."

Aaron smiled and nodded before giving me a wink and disappearing. Mum turned to me, her expression falling.

"Rhys love, we've talked about this. You don't need to be here to help me, do you understand? That's your father's role."

"He's never here!"

She shook her head.

"You're seven. Looking after your mum is not your responsibility."

I didn't argue with her any further. She always won when I tried.

39

"You're going to go have fun with Aaron tomorrow, you hear me? No more of this 'I don't want friends' business. He seems like a very nice boy and it's rude of you to keep saying no to his hospitality."

I hung my head.

"Yes, Mum."

"Good boy. Now, have you got homework?"

I nodded and sat at the kitchen table, getting it out of my school bag. I didn't like upsetting my mum so I'd go tomorrow. I had no way out of it. If I made Tamara bring me home, Mum would only tell me off. I guess I was about to see just how rich Aaron and his parents were. And the thought of it intimidated me no end.

CHAPTER SIX

Rhys

Aaron practically vibrated with excitement all day at school. A part of me couldn't help but be swept away in all of it even if I refused to acknowledge the fact. I still didn't want to like him. Didn't want to be friends with the incredibly charismatic boy next to me whose smile lit the world on fire and he danced amongst its flames. Didn't understand how he could like me, the quiet kid who never asked for anything from anyone else. Who liked his solitude. Only Aaron didn't get that. Or maybe he did and he just didn't care about bulldozing over it and getting his way. And his way was having me over after school.

When Tamara pulled up at their house, I couldn't stop staring. It was huge. Aaron hopped out of the car and cocked his head to the side as he waited for me. I climbed out, my eyes still on the building.

"It's not our only house," he confided in me as Tamara unlocked the front door. "My parents have a couple in London and several around the world."

Inside the house, the walls were all white, which helped with the natural light streaming in through the glass windows everywhere. All the furnishings were soft and looked expensive. I barely registered Aaron telling me about the no-shoes policy in the house, too busy looking around. It was so immaculate. I'd never seen anything like it.

"Rhys?"

My eyes snapped to his and my face grew hot. I hadn't been paying any attention to what he'd been saying to me.

"Sorry, what?"

"Shoes."

I quickly slipped them off, setting them next to his on the shoe rack by the front door. He shook his head and smiled.

"I'll bring you two a snack up in a bit," Tamara told us before she walked away down the hallway.

"Come on," Aaron told me, racing towards the staircase.

I followed him more slowly, wary about being here in the first place. My eyes were drawn to the walls and how clean everything was. Nothing like my own house, which was a small two-bedroom mid-terrace.

When we reached his room, which had blue walls, he threw his bag down by the door and jumped on his bed. At home, I had a tiny room with a single bed. Aaron's was huge with blue sheets to match the walls. I carefully placed my bag down next to his and stood awkwardly.

When Aaron noticed I hadn't moved, he beckoned me over with a wave of his hand. I walked over and sat at the very edge of the mattress. It was incredibly soft and I wondered what it'd be like to sleep in a bed like this.

"You like books, don't you?"

He settled down next to me, his eyes wide and his smile wider.

"Yeah."

He waved at a bookcase in the corner.

"Do you want to look?"

I shrugged even though curiosity burnt through me. I didn't just like books. I loved them.

"Go on. I know you want to."

At his encouragement, I slid off the bed and walked over to his bookshelf. It was full of books I'd always wished I could read. Fantasies about faraway worlds with magic. I wanted to run my fingers over the spines but I was too scared of marking them even though my hands weren't dirty.

"You can borrow whatever ones you like."

I blinked and found him next to me, looking over the titles.

"I don't read much."

"You should. Books are like an escape into a world that isn't our own and even when bad things happen, you know it'll end up okay."

The words just slipped out. In the real world, things weren't okay. They were horrific and brutal. Just like the stabbing that occurred on the estate two days ago when I was at school.

"Do you want to escape from the world?"

"Sometimes."

His eyes grew sad and somehow it cut me. Sad didn't look good on Aaron. He wore his happiness and bright outlook on life on his sleeve.

"Maybe you can think of here as your escape. We don't have to be in the real world. Can just be you and me."

I swear I stopped breathing at his words. It was almost as if he saw into my soul. Saw what I was hiding. The desire not to be in this world any longer as it hurt too much.

"I only came because Mum told me I had to."

He eyed me for a moment before selecting a book from the shelf. It was the one I'd been pining after.

"Here, why don't we read this together?"

How did he know?

"What do you mean?"

He walked over to his bed and sat down. I followed him, nerves spiking in my chest.

"Well, you don't like talking so I'll read it to you."

"I can read fine by myself."

He gave me a wink.

"Oh, I know, but I can't. You can help me when I stumble over the big words. Think of it as doing me a favour."

Again. How did he know?

I swear this boy paid far too much attention to my every move and for the life of me, I couldn't understand why.

Huffing a little, I sat down next to him and he opened the book. He looked at me from under his blonde eyelashes.

"You can pretend you're not going to enjoy this. I won't be offended."

I gave him a hard stare. He really did get on my nerves with all his insisting and forcing when it came to me.

You're not exactly putting up much of a fight, you know.

As if I could try. He'd ignore me and do it anyway. Easier to give in. Besides, I would get annoyed if he said words wrong. How would he learn if I didn't tell him?

So I settled in, letting Aaron read to me and interrupting him every so often. He kept giving me these super-indulgent smiles like Mum did. As if he thought it was cute how I got worked up about things being just right.

When Tamara came up with these cakes Aaron had called lamingtons and milk, we ate them on his bed. They were pretty tasty. And after we were done, Aaron showed me around his room properly. Then he made me sit at his desk and taught me how to play a shooting game I was pretty sure no seven-year-old should be playing. It had been rather violent, but I enjoyed it, nevertheless.

Despite my determination not to have fun, I enjoyed Aaron's company the most. He was so vibrant. So full of life and laughter. And he had infinite patience with me. Even when I snapped at him, he took it on the shoulder. Never once giving me any crap back. It made it very hard to stay annoyed at him. To push him away further. Aaron was digging his way behind my walls and somehow, I was letting him.

Tamara made us roast chicken, potatoes and vegetables for dinner. I couldn't remember the last time I had a decent meal that wasn't at school. It wasn't my mum's fault. We just didn't have much and my dad wasting away his money on alcohol made it worse.

Just before it came time to leave, Aaron and I were back in his room as he asked Tamara if we could run and get something quickly.

"Okay, pick a book to take home. Then you can tell me if you liked it when you're done as long as you promise to come over again so you can help me with reading."

I shuffled my feet on the carpet. It didn't feel right to borrow one of his books. They were all in such pristine condition.

"Rhys, please... for me."

A part of me wanted to snap at him again. Tell him I'd never do anything for him. Except it was a lie. A big part of me wanted to please him. When I did that, he smiled and his eyes lit up. I'd found myself longing for those times more and more. And it got on my nerves.

"Okay," I muttered before I went over to the shelf and picked up a book I'd never had a chance to read before. One about a boy with magical powers that could get him killed if anyone found out about them. And when Aaron smiled that smile of his, his blue-grey eyes twinkling, my heart thudded in my chest and warmth spread through me.

He insisted on coming with when Tamara drove me home. We didn't talk but he watched me the entire way as if he had a hard time looking away. I didn't understand this boy at all, but somehow that was beginning not to matter. Somehow, I desperately wanted to believe him when he said I was his friend. And somehow, I wanted him to be my friend too.

CHAPTER SEVEN

Rhys

The first sign when I got in the front door that things were not well was the silence. Usually, my mum had the TV on. I'd made her up a bed on the sofa last night since my dad hadn't been home and she couldn't walk upstairs by herself. This morning I'd given her breakfast before I went to school as he hadn't been up yet. Now I knew he was home. I could feel his presence like a black cloud settling over the house.

He came out of the kitchen with a can of beer in his hand. His eyes roamed over me with disgust.

"Where the fuck have you been?"

I wanted to run back outside and hide. His temper flared between us. I held onto the straps of my backpack as if it could save me.

"A friend's house," I told him in a small, shaky voice.

Right now, I could use a friend. I pictured Aaron's smile and it bolstered me a little.

"When the fuck did you get friends?"

"At school. Didn't Mum tell you?"

A scowl etched itself on his features.

"Probably. Fuck knows. She's asleep. You should've told me she hurt herself."

Anything I said in response might result in him taking his anger out on me, so I kept my mouth shut. My dad was a mean drunk. Usually, he didn't direct his anger at me, but on occasion, he used his fists. Told me it was my fault my mother was disabled now. My fault he had to take care of her. My fault he had to go elsewhere for pussy. I hadn't understood what he meant the first time he said it. When I asked Mum, it horrified her he'd said such a thing to me. Whilst she explained what it was, she told me not to say it. It was rude to talk about girls in that way. I told her not to worry as I had no interest in girls and their pussies. I had no interest in boys either. I just had no real interest in anyone.

Graham King was a nasty man. I hated him. But what I hated him the most for was the times he told me he wished I'd never been born. I hadn't told Mum about that. It would only upset her.

"Go to your room, boy."

I hurried to the stairs and stumbled up them in my effort to get away from him. At least he'd decided not to have a go at me. It hadn't been my fault Mum fell over. I'd helped her as best I could. You could never tell what type of mood

Graham would be in when he was at home. It's why I only came out of my room when he was out or at dinner time.

I checked in on Mum before I went to my bedroom. He'd obviously carried her upstairs. She was still asleep, so I dashed towards my bedroom and shut my door behind me.

Setting my bag on my bed after flipping the bedside light on, I unzipped it and pulled out the book Aaron insisted I borrow. I stroked my fingers down the cover. Then I set it by my pillow. I changed for bed and brushed my teeth. Mum never gave me a set bedtime but it was seven already. Huddling up in the covers, I started reading, happy to get lost in the pages for a while. I was so lost in the words, I almost didn't hear shouting, but the loud noises jolted me out of the book.

"What the fuck are you doing letting our boy out so late for?" my dad's voice rang through the house.

I dropped the book down on the bed and crept towards my bedroom door, cracking it open a little.

"He wasn't out late, Grey," came Mum's muffled voice.

"He should be fucking here with you."

"He deserves a life and friends. He's just a child."

I flinched, hating they were arguing over me again because I knew what would come next.

"That little shit stole your fucking life, Steph. He should be here making sure you're looked after."

"Don't say that! Don't you dare say that about Rhys! He's our son. Our son! You should love that boy."

I heard footsteps stomping around their bedroom. Tears pricked at my eyes, but I held them back. I would not cry over Graham King. I'd never cry over that man's words ever again.

"How can I love him? He left you fucking crippled. We don't have a fucking life together anymore."

"Whose fault is that? Don't think I don't see the looks everyone gives me. Poor Steph King, her boy left her unable to do a thing. Poor Steph King, her husband can't even stay faithful. Poor Steph King, she lives with a deadbeat drunk who puts his hands on her."

"You fucking bitch."

I heard a loud thump. A tear fell unbidden. I shut my door, turned out my bedside light and crawled under my covers, burying my face in the pillow to stifle my sobs. I knew what he'd done. He'd hit her again. Just like he always did when they argued. And there was nothing I could do. If I went in there to help her, he'd hit me too. Mum warned me never to get involved. She made me promise and I always kept my promises to her. Always. No matter how much it pained me. No matter how much I wished I could stop him from hurting her.

Mum had been having so many good days recently. She'd not had issues with her speech or her movements. Her falling over and Dad beating her would surely set her back. I dreaded waking up tomorrow knowing she would have more bruises and probably not want to get out of bed. It would make it worse knowing I'd have to go to school since she never let me skip to take care of her.

I had to be a good boy for her. Do what she said so she could be proud of me. My mum was the only person in this world who loved me. No one else could. No one else wanted to. I wasn't crying over the fact my dad didn't love me. I didn't care about him any longer. I might live under his roof, but I'd lost all respect for him when he first hit Mum. He wasn't a father to me, he was a mean drunk.

It took a long time for me to stop crying, feeling stupid and weak for having emotions. I didn't like to show them to anyone. Not even Mum. Only when I was alone and I couldn't take it any longer. The pain wrecked and ruined me. Made me want to disappear. But I wouldn't. Mum wouldn't have anyone else if I wasn't here. I stayed for her. Only for her. She was my only reason for living.

And if you weren't here, you wouldn't be able to see his smile any longer.

Thoughts of that boy came without warning. Why was he in my head? I didn't want to see him tomorrow. He'd probably notice something was wrong with me. More than usual. Aaron seemed to notice everything about me and I didn't like it. I didn't like that he could see me. I hated it. It made me feel strange. And I didn't like feeling at all. Not when it came to people other than Mum.

So thoughts of him could go away. They needed to leave. Except they wouldn't because deep down, I wanted him to see me. I wanted him to ask me what was wrong. I wanted him to force me into telling him about my mum and dad. To have someone to confide in about how it cut me so deep when they argued over me. How it destroyed me when he hurt her. How it ruined me knowing he hated me as much as she loved me.

I wouldn't tell him though. Those secrets were mine to keep. No one could know about it. No one could see. If anyone knew how much he hurt her, if they knew he hurt me, then they might try to take me away from my mum. Social Services had taken a baby away from two parents on the estate as they were drug addicts. I had to be here for her. I had to. There was no other choice. So I had to keep my mouth shut. No matter how much it ached. No matter how much I desperately wanted to tell someone so they could share my burden. So they could understand why I was so quiet and withdrawn. So perhaps someone could finally see me.

Alone in bed, surrounded by the dark, I allowed myself to wish for those things I couldn't have. I allowed myself to imagine what it'd be like to have a real friend. And I let myself believe maybe that friend was Aaron. Maybe he wouldn't judge me. Maybe he'd hug me and tell me it was going to be okay. He'd be here for me. He'd keep my secrets. He'd never tell anyone else the truth.

I wished I could let him be my friend… but I couldn't. Risking everything for someone I barely knew would only end in more pain. And having had a lifetime of it, I wasn't sure I could go through more. I was already broken. If I widened the cracks, there'd be nothing left but tiny pieces of myself I'd never be able to put back together.

So I placed my wishes and hopes in a locked vault, steeling myself against the onslaught of tomorrow when I was sure he'd try to break that vault wide open. I had to stay strong. I had to be resolute.

I couldn't let Aaron in.

I couldn't.

I just… couldn't.

CHAPTER EIGHT

Rhys

I dreaded the moment we got out of the car and were alone. Kids walking through the school gates would be surrounding us, but we'd still be without another person watching over us like Tamara was as she drove.

Mum had stayed in bed this morning so I didn't see how badly my dad had beat her. I didn't dare go in their room when he was still there. Not after what he said last night. Besides, waking him up after he'd got drunk the night before was never a good idea. Graham King would hit the roof and then I'd be in trouble. Something I didn't need on top of everything else.

I could feel the weight of Aaron's stare bearing down on me. It's as if he'd zoned in on me and I would never escape. A part of me didn't want to, but I'd pushed that part in the vault. It was going to stay there forever. It belonged there.

We were at school far too soon. I slid out of the car, knowing facing him was coming.

Be strong, Rhys, you can be strong.

Could I? I felt like a weak, worthless piece of dirt most days. One who couldn't protect the only person he loved.

Aaron waved to Tamara before she pulled away. I started walking towards the gates. He caught up to me within a moment. I almost flinched, waiting for him to say something, but he didn't. He walked alongside me without making a sound. His silence spoke for him. Like a loud drum banging in my ear. It said *it's okay, I know you're hurting and I'm here if you need me.*

My heart ached. My lungs burnt. All the scenarios I'd played out in my head over and over again paled in comparison to his quiet support. And it made me want to burst into tears all over again. Made me want to reach out and let him hold my hand. I didn't. If anyone saw, I'd likely get called gay boy again and I didn't want anyone calling him that either. Kids could be mean as hell when they wanted. When they didn't understand.

I didn't care if a boy liked other boys. What difference did it make to me? Mum taught me to be respectful and that everyone was an individual and could love whoever they wanted. I just wished she didn't love Dad.

Aaron and I sat at our usual desk together. It'd become a routine. Every lesson. Like we were inseparable. We weren't, even if he rarely left me alone at school. I think he felt like it was his responsibility to protect me from bullies like Valentine who hadn't come near me since the first day of school. And secretly, I appreciated his presence.

"Thank you," I whispered.

For some reason, I felt compelled to express my gratitude towards him for not pestering me with questions this morning. His blue-grey eyes were stormy today. Whilst I disliked seeing him sad or frustrated, the colour was so striking. I stared into them as he cocked his head to the side.

"I don't know what you're thanking me for but you're welcome."

His expression told me he was waiting for me to elaborate, but I couldn't explain it to him. That just by being here, he made me feel less... alone. I didn't know how else to show him I needed him even when I pushed him away. How had this boy I'd known such a short time become so important to me? If he wasn't here, wasn't pestering me, I wouldn't know what to do with myself.

The vault cracked under the intensity of my feelings and his gaze. It cracked. How could my locked vault crack?

"I'm not going to be a very good friend to you but thank you for seeing me as one anyway."

Where did that come from? Why have you suddenly got word vomit?

Those eyes I kept needing to stare at softened. They turned into pools of pure happiness. The sight blew me away. I don't know why but it just did. He did. And then the moment was lost as the teacher started talking. I jerked my gaze towards the whiteboard, aware staring at him was probably unwise.

I felt the slight brush of fingers against mine under the table. Glancing at Aaron under my lashes, I found him smiling to himself. He kept winning every single time. Every silent battle we had. And I let him.

Another crack appeared in my vault. This one bigger and more pronounced. Aaron hadn't moved his fingers from mine. Hadn't stopped touching me. They felt like an anchor keeping me afloat. Keeping me breathing whilst everything around me tried to take me under so I'd drown. That's what kept happening to me. I kept drowning. Every time I fought to get back to the surface. Every time I took a little gasp of air as my head broke through the surface of the water, the tendrils would catch hold of my feet, wrapping around my ankles and tugging. I could never stay afloat. Never.

Until him.

Until this.

Until us.

I did something so out of character it was as if watching myself from above. Like my body moved without my say so, acting on instinct rather than command.

I caught hold of his hand, tugging it onto my leg and slid my fingers into his. I saw him let out a sharp breath, his lungs expanding in his chest. And when he inhaled again, I watched him. It rendered me completely unable to look away from the blonde-haired boy who I couldn't deny I wanted to be friends with any longer.

The vault shattered. Every thought, every feeling came flooding out. I clenched my jaw shut tight, worried it'd all spill out into the open then I'd be in trouble with the teacher for talking in lesson.

Aaron hadn't done anything. He'd barely said a word and yet I was helpless against the vortex sucking me into his sphere. Of all the ways in which I'd envisioned this happening, nothing could prepare me for the way my heart raced as he squeezed my fingers, his eyes flicking to mine and the small, secret smile he gave me.

I might not be able to confess my secrets to Aaron, but I could try to be his friend.

Couldn't I?

CHAPTER NINE

Rhys

"You haven't told me how the book is yet."

The weekend had come and gone. I'd spent it looking after Mum so hadn't done much reading except before bed. My dad had left food in the fridge and had gone to Maggie's. I was glad he hadn't been at home. Mum spent the entire time in bed as she wasn't doing well. Her speech had become impaired again, which upset me, but I tried not to show it. She had horrible bruises on her stomach from where Dad had hit her. Seeing her like that had me crying into my pillow when I tried to go to sleep. Wishing so much I had someone to share this burden with.

Aaron and I sat in the canteen, cloistered away in a corner together with our lunches.

"I'm only halfway."

"And?"

"I like it."

He nudged my hand.

"Just like?"

"What's not to like about a boy with magical powers?"

He grinned. Whilst we hadn't talked much since the day I'd held his hand in class, there seemed to be a newfound understanding between us. I didn't mind his insistence on getting to know me any longer. And it made him happy. At least, I thought it had.

"Can I ask you something?"

"I guess so."

I dug into my cottage pie, waiting for him to speak again.

"Your mum looks young."

"She's twenty-six."

Mum told me what happened to her during her pregnancy was rare. They got married when she was eighteen and she fell pregnant with me not long afterwards. Dad had been ten years older than her when they met. She told me he was good to her back then, but things had changed as I got older and he became her carer.

"Mine are in their thirties. They had me late, according to my mum."

"Are they coming back soon?"

He shrugged, fiddling with his fork.

"Tamara says yes, but they're always away for work. I don't see them much."

"What do they do?"

I knew they had a lot of money, but he hadn't volunteered any further information about them. It's almost as if Aaron wasn't keen on talking about his parents. I didn't know why, but I never pressed him on the subject.

"Dad owns a publishing house and a production studio he bought for Mum as she's a director. My grandparents come from money. I don't like going around their house. I'm afraid I'll break Grandma's Ming vases she collects."

I couldn't begin to work out exactly how much money his family must have, only it had to be a lot.

"Are they millionaires?"

Aaron laughed.

"Probably."

"And you're hanging out with me?"

He gave me an odd look.

"Why wouldn't I?"

Your parents are rich and mine are poor.

"You don't care that I live somewhere you might get stabbed if you look at someone wrong?"

He shook his head and nudged my hand again.

"No, Rhys, I don't care. I like you. The rest doesn't matter. Wait, does that actually happen? People getting stabbed?"

I nodded. A little part of me jumped for joy hearing him say he liked me. I didn't understand why when he barely knew me but trying to figure Aaron out was difficult at times.

"Mum says there are gangs in our estate. The police are always around. My street is okay though, mostly families."

He sat back, his eyes clouding over. He didn't come from my world, so I doubted he understood the dangers.

"I wouldn't want you getting hurt."

I wished I could tell him I was safe but it'd be a lie. I wasn't safe in my own home with my dad. One thing I knew for certain is I never wanted Aaron to meet Graham King. It's why I didn't mention him. Maybe he assumed I didn't have a dad. It'd be better if he thought that rather than me having to explain all the horrible things he did and said to me and Mum.

"Why? Would you try to be my knight in shining armour then?"

"You wouldn't let me."

His words made me smile despite myself. In a lot of ways, I needed rescuing. Mostly from myself. I had issues. Aaron didn't need to know about those. Didn't need to see all the damage inside, too much for a seven-year-old to have in the first place. What if he stopped liking me when he realised how much I didn't enjoy being in this world? How much I ached from the stress of taking care of Mum. How dealing with Dad was a constant struggle. And my only escape was within the pages of books.

I didn't like to remind myself he told me I could escape with him. How I wished it could be true. If I allowed myself to believe it, then reality would come crashing down to destroy it. Everything good in my life always disappeared.

I looked away, unable to stop myself from feeling my time with him was finite. That this would ultimately crash and burn. I never had anything that remained permanently.

"You're right. I wouldn't."

I felt him link his pinkie finger over mine.

"I don't like seeing you hurting."

My chest tightened. How did he read me so well? I felt like all my feelings were on show. He kept stripping back the layers and exposing my pain piece by piece without even really trying.

"Life is pain."

What are you saying? Stop talking. Don't make him think you're weird. He might stop wanting to hang out with you.

"Why do you say that?"

"You wouldn't understand."

He didn't have to live in fear of his father beating his mother. Nor his father turning those fists on him. He didn't have to hear screaming matches when Dad had too much to drink. Nor worry about what condition Mum might be in day to day.

Aaron had everything and I had nothing.

"I could try if you tell me."

I want to, but I can't.

If only things were different.

"I don't really want to talk about it."

I had to avoid the subject. I shouldn't have started down this road in the first place. What Aaron didn't know couldn't hurt him.

"Is it really so bad me wanting to help you?"

"No."

"Then why won't you let me try?"

I didn't want to tell him he'd already managed to help me in ways he could never imagine. Just having someone there gave me a tiny sliver of hope I'd never had before. No, not someone. Him. It wouldn't feel the same if it was anyone else.

There was just something about Aaron. Perhaps it was his inherent charm or maybe his dogged persistence. He had a pureness to him I rarely saw in anyone. Most people I knew were tainted somehow. Not Aaron. He had a heart of pure gold.

"If you truly knew me, I don't think you'd like me."

His brow furrowed and his blue-grey eyes turn dark.

"I'm not sure what I can say to convince you nothing you tell me will ever make me not like you."

"I'm messy and chaotic inside."

"Maybe I like messy and chaotic."

"Do you even know what that means?"

He shrugged.

"Chaos means disorder."

"I bet you just read that in a dictionary."

"So what if I did?"

I shook my head. He had an answer for everything.

"You're still annoying."

"You like that about me."

He had a point. I did. I liked everything I discovered about Aaron.

"Who said I liked you?"

"Me."

I didn't have a comeback. Mostly since I couldn't dispute what he said. I wished sometimes I didn't like him so much. It would be easier for me if I could push him away when he tried to get closer.

"If that's what you want to believe, I won't stop you."

His eyes shone.

"You like me, Rhys. You wouldn't talk to me otherwise."

"You won't leave me alone, what else am I meant to do?"

"I'm going to make you admit it one day."

I shook my head, standing as I picked up my tray. This boy would be the death of me.

"You keep telling yourself that, A."

Only when I was halfway across the canteen, I realised what I'd said.

What did you go and give him a nickname for?

Aaron's smile was so wide as he caught up with me, I could barely stand to look at it.

You are an idiot.

But I was the idiot who couldn't help falling deeper into a friendship with the boy beside me. The one I knew would never give up on me. And a big part of me didn't want to give up on him either.

CHAPTER TEN

Aaron

The moment I saw Rhys King in class on the first day of school, my heart just about stopped. My palms got sweaty and my chest ached. I imagined it was what being struck by lightning felt like. It wasn't as if I understood it fully, only I knew it was something significant and I couldn't for the life of me look away. This beautiful dark-haired boy with these dark, soulful eyes and tanned skin had my stomach in knots. And I had no clue what to do about it.

I guess somewhere in the back of my mind I'd always known I liked boys. It had never hit me more than it did that day, like a slap in the face. My eyes were drawn to him and only to him. So when I'd had the opportunity to save him from that idiot Valentine who lived near me, I took it. And ever since then, all I'd wanted to do was be around Rhys King. Every second of every moment of every day. Even if he was reluctant to talk to me. To open up to me. To even be my friend.

I kept playing the words he'd said to me over and over in my head.

"You keep telling yourself that, A."

He called me 'A'. He gave me a nickname. If that didn't tell me Rhys wanted to be my friend even if he tried to act like I was a nuisance to him, I didn't know what else would. Talking to him was impossible on occasion. He seemed to want to curl in on himself and not allow the outside world in. It made me aware of how much he hurt inside. His pain might not be obvious to others, but I saw it in his eyes. He burnt with it. And all I wanted was to understand why.

"I know what you're going to ask me," he blurted out as we waited outside the gates for Tamara.

"What's that?"

"If I can come over again."

I couldn't help smiling. Rhys didn't like me pressing the subject, so I hadn't brought it up. I wanted him to come around as much as possible. Spending time with him was the highlight of my day.

"You that desperate to hear me read to you again?"

He blinked.

His eyes are so beautiful. I could get lost in them.

"No, you suck at reading out loud."

He wasn't wrong. He'd corrected me many times when he'd been over at mine. I hadn't minded as it seemed to make him happy. Besides, I did genuinely need help. It wasn't something I excelled in. I wanted to make Mum and Dad proud next time they were home since the teachers at my last school had told them I was behind in my reading age. They'd bought a house in the catchment area so they could send me to this new school, not that they were ever at home. Mum was always away on location and Dad went with her. He could work from anywhere.

"That's why you're helping me, remember?"

He huffed and rolled his eyes. Something he did often and I thought it was cute. Everything he did was cute to me though. Especially the time he'd held my hand in class. I swear I thought my heart might burst out of my chest it was racing so fast.

I wanted to hold his hand again, but I wasn't sure he'd accept it. Not at school anyway. Boys didn't hold hands at school and we'd get picked on if we did. I'd heard Valentine calling Rhys 'gay boy' and didn't want him getting name called again. He didn't deserve to be bullied.

"Well, I can't right now. I have to be home for Mum."

Rhys kept saying he needed to be around for his mum. I had a feeling a lot of the things Rhys kept close to his heart were to do with her. She'd been nice to me when I'd met her and it made me wonder what was so wrong that he had to be at home all the time.

He didn't live in a very good area. Whilst his house had been clean and tidy from what I'd seen of it, the surrounding houses weren't in a good state. At least one had a boarded-up window. And he'd told me there were gangs and stabbings happened regularly.

I didn't care where he'd come from or his background. He mattered to me. Just Rhys. I wanted to keep him safe. To help him. Seeing him upset or sad hurt me. Even if we barely knew each other, I had a feeling about him. A feeling which wouldn't go away. Each time we were in each other's company, it grew and grew. I couldn't help wanting to be closer to him. To just hold his hand. I really wanted to hold his damn hand again.

"That's okay."

It wasn't but I wouldn't say that to him. I wouldn't tell him I wanted to be around him all the time. I wanted to hold on to him so tight and never let go.

"You sure? I want to come over and all."

It was the very first time he'd admitted it. It made my heart ache. It happened whenever I was around him. I didn't understand what it meant. Only that my heart wanted him with such a desperation it sometimes made me a little crazy. Made me want to push him to open up to me so I could be closer to him.

"Yeah, Rhys, it's okay."

Tamara pulled up, saving him from responding. We both got in the car and put our seatbelts on.

"You boys have a good day?" she asked as she set off.

"Yeah, it was all right," I replied, glancing at Rhys who said nothing.

My fingers itched to reach out to him, but what if Tamara saw? What if she told Mum and Dad? I knew she spoke to them regularly even if they only called me once a week to check in. I missed them, but it's how things had been for the past couple of years. They were always working.

Tamara was good to me. She took care of me and made sure I had everything I needed. She'd been my au pair since I was five. That's when Mum had gone back to work. Before then, it was me and her, but now things were different. I guess sometimes I didn't feel very important to them. All I did was try hard to make them proud of me. They didn't seem to notice it though. Notice me.

Thinking about them made me feel sad. And I didn't want that. Not when I had precious minutes left of the day with Rhys. I looked over at him. His eyes were fixed on the window and there was an air of discontent surrounding him. I wanted to make it better. I wanted to see him smile because when he did, it made me feel giddy.

His hand rested on the seat next to him. And I couldn't help it any longer. The urge got too strong. So I reached out across the middle seat, pulling his hand closer and lacing my fingers with his. Rhys' dark eyes got wide as he turned to me, then they fell on our hands. I had no idea what he was thinking. Touching him soothed me. Stopped the ache in my chest growing.

For the rest of the journey to his house, he stared at our hands, not saying a word. I didn't dare look to see if Tamara had seen. It didn't matter when I felt calmer than I had all day. Like I needed him as an anchor. Sometimes I felt so adrift, especially at a new school and not seeing my parents regularly.

Rhys let go of my hand when we reached his house, unbuckled his seat belt and put his hand on the door. Then he turned back and looked at me.

"If Mum is feeling better next week, then I'll come over again... yeah?"

My heart soared, but I kept my cool, smiling at him instead. "I'd like that."

He smiled. I didn't think my poor heart could deal with any more today.

"See you tomorrow, A."

He's killing me. I swear.

"See you."

He got out and I watched him walk up to his front door, unlock it and go in without looking back. I wished he'd have looked back.

Tamara set off home and I stared out of the window.

"Rhys is a quiet one."

I almost jumped at the sound of her voice.

"Yeah, but I don't mind."

"You never had trouble making friends at your last school, but not so much here. Are you happy at this one?"

The only thing about the school which made me happy was Rhys. The teachers were fine. Everything else was fine. But Rhys? He made it better. He made everything better.

"I'm fine, Tami. You can tell my parents that."

"Aaron..."

"I'm fine, honest."

"Why don't I ask Calvin and Lydia's mum if they're free this weekend? I'm sure you miss your old friends."

In all honesty, I didn't. Perhaps I would've before, but ever since I'd met Rhys, nothing else mattered but him. Being around him. Talking to him. The only friend I wanted was him. Deep down I knew he'd understand me. He had pain in his life and so did I. When he finally let me in, I'd let him in too. I'd let him see how lonely I'd been since Mum had gone back to work. I'd let him see he was the only person I'd ever felt connected with even if he was quiet, shy and withdrawn.

"If you want to."

I didn't want to alert Tamara to my mood. She'd get suspicious and then report back to my parents. I didn't want them thinking I wasn't happy at this school and taking me out of it. Then I wouldn't be able to see Rhys and the thought of it made me want to die a little inside. I already missed him even though it'd been minutes since he'd been right there.

"Good. I'll call when we get home."

I didn't want to see Calvin and Lydia, but I'd do it if it meant getting Tamara off my back. Stifling a sigh, I looked out the window again. I only had to get through the rest of today and then I'd see him. See the beautiful, broken boy who set my world on fire the moment he walked into it.

CHAPTER ELEVEN

Rhys

Mum had been feeling better for days. Her speech was still bad, but she could say yes and no, which is all I needed. She'd made up with Dad. He'd grovelled, as usual, getting her cheap flowers and chocolates from the garage down the road. There'd not been any arguments since he came back from Maggie's.

With him home, it meant I could go around Aaron's house. Hence why we were both laid out on our stomachs on the floor of his bedroom together side by side. He read to me whilst I drew. Something I liked to do but never had supplies at home as Mum couldn't afford to buy me anything. Aaron hadn't noticed me drawing him, too engrossed in the book.

"It's pol-lu-tion not pol-liton," I interjected when he said a word wrong.

"Pollution."

"Yeah."

"Why'd they put such hard words in this?"

I shook my head.

"Not that hard."

"Yeah, just 'cause you're a smarty pants, doesn't mean we all are."

I nudged him with my shoulder, which brought a smile to his face.

"Jealous much?"

His eyes flicked down to my drawing. The blue-grey got somehow brighter as he stared at it.

"Is that you and me?"

My sheet of paper had two boys holding hands, one with blonde hair and one with dark.

I shrugged, not wanting to admit it. Ever since he'd held my hand in Tamara's car, I'd felt weirdly okay with being so close to him. I didn't mind it when he brushed his hand against my arm to get my attention. And now, as he reached up and mussed my hair.

"Now it looks more like you."

The way his eyes twinkled made me swallow.

"You can keep it… if you want. I drew it for you."

Aaron fidgeted before he put the book down and picked up the drawing. He ran his fingers over the two figures.

"Does this mean we're friends for real then?"

I shrugged again. Maybe we were. I didn't know if Aaron had any other friends. He never talked about them if he did. It shouldn't make my stomach get twisted up to think of him being as close to anyone else as he seemed to be getting to me.

"Rhys."

"Yeah, okay. Don't make a big deal out of it."

He laid his hand out on the floor, palm facing up. It felt significant. If I put my hand in his, then it'd mean we truly were friends. If I didn't, I'd upset him. He'd been patient with me. Waited whilst I struggled with myself. Struggled to be open to the possibility of having a friend and it being a good thing for me. How could I upset the boy with blonde hair and blue-grey eyes who made me happy just by being there? It'd been a long time since I felt any sort of happiness.

I breathed in and slid my palm against his. My fingers slipped between his and he gripped them tightly. It gave me the impression he never wanted to let go. We stared at each other for a long moment.

"Rhys…"

"Yeah?"

"What's wrong with your mum?"

I stiffened, then wrenched my hand away like I'd been stung. Why would he ask that? I didn't think I'd ever said anything to make him think there was something wrong with her.

"Nothing." My voice came out all harsh and defensive. "She's fine."

Liar. She isn't fine. She can barely communicate with you and Dad right now.

"I didn't mean anything bad. You keep saying you have to be there for her and I want to understand why."

I shook my head, sitting up and turning my back to him, unable to look into his eyes any longer. The pain of knowing I caused her to be this way ripped through my chest. It dug its claws into me, tearing me to shreds. Dad blamed me for it. I blamed me for it. So why wouldn't Aaron? Why would he understand?

"I'm sorry, I shouldn't have asked."

I wanted to tell him even as I held back. Even as I thought he wouldn't get it. Aaron had never been anything but understanding when it came to me.

"No, you shouldn't."

My heart deflated. Who thought it would be a good idea to make a friend? All people did was hurt you, leave you or both. And it didn't make sense to me why I felt like crying. My shoulders shook with the effort of holding it all in. The emotional tornado taking up residence in my chest.

Then I felt his warmth against my back. Aaron wrapped his arms around me from behind, resting his head against mine. It shocked me so much, I didn't move or tell him to get off.

"I'm sorry," he whispered. "Please don't be mad at me. I just want to know you."

No one but Mum hugged or comforted me and she could only do it when she felt well enough. No one else had done this since Aunt Bibi died.

"Aaron," I breathed out.

"I'm here. I'm right here."

"I hate myself."

The words hung in the air between us. The truth. The lack of love and kindness, the self-blame and the words from my dad. They were all part of the recipe which signalled my spiral into self-hatred.

"Why?"

"I don't know how to explain. All I know is there's nothing good in the world for me. And no one cares how it hurts," I pointed at my chest where his hand rested, "right here."

"I care."

His words were like a balm to the bruises in my heart. I spun around and hugged him back. Aaron held onto me. He was bigger but not by much. Safe and protected were the feelings coursing through my system.

"You won't leave me, will you?" I whispered.

"Never. I promise."

Pulling back, I put my hand out, raising my pinkie finger. He immediately linked it with his.

"I swear we'll be friends always."

His eyes were so sincere, I couldn't help but believe him. This boy made me feel so many emotions, I could hardly decipher them. No matter how many times I tried to push him away, he wouldn't budge. The only option I had left would be to surrender. To give in and let this be what it was.

"I swear too."

CHAPTER TWELVE

Aaron

Weeks felt as though they melted into one another when I was with Rhys. Ever since we established a friendship, I'd been careful not to ask him any further questions about his mum. I figured he'd tell me when he was ready. Getting Rhys to admit anything was almost impossible. And now I was sulking as half-term had come around so I wouldn't see him until I went back to school. An entire week without seeing his beautiful dark eyes and the curls of his inky hair. His smile and the way he laughed.

I'd begun to realise my feelings towards Rhys weren't exactly what Tamara had called platonic. She'd explained the difference between a relationship and a friendship when I asked her about it. I told her I was curious as two people in my class had become 'boyfriend and girlfriend' but the reality was I'd become confused by my own feelings. I'd never felt drawn to my other friends in the way I did with Rhys. Never wanted to spend all my time with anyone and have it physically ache when we were apart. It didn't seem normal, or at least what I thought was normal.

I guess I had a crush on Rhys, or at least that's what I assumed after talking to Tamara. If she suspected anything about me and Rhys, she didn't say it. I hadn't told anyone I liked boys. I wasn't sure how. Even though I knew it wasn't wrong, it felt strange to admit it when all the other boys at school seemed to talk about girls. I didn't like girls that way, so it left me feeling like I was the odd one out.

I had thought about telling Rhys, but since he happened to be the object of my affections, I wasn't sure what he'd make of it. It's not like I could tell him I liked him as more than just a friend. It might freak him out.

"Aaron, your mum and dad are home," came Tamara's voice from downstairs.

I dashed out of my room. They hadn't told me they were coming. When I got to the bottom of the stairs, Mum and Dad were stood in the hallway. I looked most like my dad. He had blonde hair and blue eyes with a lopsided smile. Mum had red hair and blue-grey eyes like me.

Patrick and Kellie Parrish looked like the perfect couple who doted on their only son. At least that's the story they fed to the press. The reality was they left me with my au pair for nine months of the year whilst Mum shot TV shows and the occasional film and Dad went with her. They hadn't planned on having me. Harriet was twenty, a whole thirteen years older than me and had moved out at eighteen to live with her stupid boyfriend Ralph who I hated. He always treated me like a baby.

I barrelled my way into Mum's arms, clutching her to me. I'd missed her and the way she smelt of lavender all the time.

"Mummy."

"My sweet boy, I've missed you so much."

I'd buried my face in her stomach so she couldn't see how it scrunched up at her words. If she missed me that much, she'd be home more. And I wouldn't feel so alone.

Her hand stroked over my hair in a soothing motion. Except it didn't soothe me at all. If anything, I felt worse. They were home, but for how long? They never stayed. Always leaving me here to fend for myself without them. I loved Tamara, but she wasn't my mum. She couldn't replace the parents I had but never saw.

I pulled away and stepped over to my dad. He ruffled my hair and smiled at me before walking away into the kitchen without a word. Dad never really did affection. He reserved that for Mum. Something I didn't understand.

"Come, tell me about your new school," Mum said, taking my hand and leading me into the living room.

I looked back at the hallway. Dad wasn't coming. He didn't want to hear about how I'd been doing. It made my heart sink to the floor.

I sat with Mum on the sofa, feeling tiny and insignificant.

"So, Tamara said you've been doing much better."

"Yeah, my reading age is improving."

Thanks to Rhys. He helped me in class and at home when he came over after school. It was twice a week now on

Tuesdays and Thursdays. His mum had said it was okay. I don't know if Tamara told Mum about it or that we gave Rhys lifts to school. She knew being around Rhys made me happy.

"That's wonderful news. I'm so pleased to hear it. And have you been making friends?"

"Yeah... I have a best friend now."

Her eyes lit up. Whilst Rhys might not consider us best friends, I certainly did. He was the reason I woke up in the mornings eager to get to his so we could spend the whole day together. He was the reason I tried harder at school so I could impress him with my progress and in turn maybe make my parents proud of me.

"Do they have a name?"

"Rhys. We sit together in lesson. He's really smart and helps me a lot."

"Tamara may have mentioned him. She says he comes over quite a bit after school."

My heart stuttered, a feeling of dread sinking over me.

"Is he not allowed?"

Her eyes softened and she reached out, stroking my hair.

"Of course he is, sweet boy. If he makes you smile like that, then he's always welcome."

I hadn't realised I'd been smiling when talking about Rhys.

"He's quiet, but we have fun together. I like him better than Calvin and Lydia."

She gave me this indulgent smile as if I was still a toddler who couldn't form his own opinions.

"It's good to have lots of friends, Aaron. Not just one or two."

Our Darkest Hour

"Yes, Mummy."

I didn't want to say otherwise, even though I only wanted Rhys as my friend. No one else made me feel the way he did. He needed me. I'd made a pinkie promise never to leave him. That meant way more than a normal promise. I could never break it. Never.

Mum didn't need to know that. She wouldn't understand. Our friendship was special. I was the only one he'd told secrets to. Like the one about him hating himself. It broke my heart to hear him say it. I wanted to take his pain away. He didn't explain why but I had a feeling it was to do with his home life and his mum. Something he didn't like discussing. Now I knew better than to bring it up.

"I've got lots of plans for us this week. We're going to go to museums and do lots of fun stuff together, how does that sound?"

She looked so happy and I didn't have the heart to tell her what I really wanted was to see Rhys because I missed him. So I put on a bright smile for her.

"I can't wait."

I loved spending time with my mum but in the back of my mind, there was always the knowledge she wouldn't be here for long. She might be home as it was my half-term holidays but come the start of school next week, her and Dad would be gone. And I'd be left alone with Tamara yet again.

At least I had Rhys now. He was the balm to everything. And I couldn't wait to get back to school so I could see his beautiful face and brand it into my memory. Maybe he'd let me hug him again. Maybe he'd have missed me too.

Until then I'd enjoy my time with Mum and count down the days until I could see the boy who made my heart race again.

CHAPTER THIRTEEN

Rhys

I barely got a chance to make it out of the front door of my house for the first day back at school after half-term when a body barrelled its way into me. Two arms wrapped me up so tight, I could hardly breathe.

"Uh… A…?"

"I missed you."

My heart thumped at his admission. My arms dangled helplessly at my sides. This couldn't be happening. Nat next door would see and then it'd be all around the estate. If Dad found out how close Aaron and I had become, I might not be able to go around his any longer. Mum hadn't told him about the twice-weekly visits. For some reason, my dad didn't like me having friends. He expected me to be home with Mum all the time. Like it was my duty. Mum kept telling me it wasn't so the conflicting views bothered me. I tried not to think too much about it since I liked getting away from the estate to spend time at Aaron's.

"A, please stop."

He let go of me immediately, pulling back with a sheepish expression on his face. I wanted to hug him but not on my front doorstep. Not wanting to make things awkward, I wrapped my hands around the straps of my backpack and walked towards Tamara's car. We could talk about why at school when we didn't have ears listening in.

When we got in the car, his disappointment registered with me. It settled over us like a dark cloud. He wanted me to hug him back. It cut me, knowing I'd made him sad. He didn't understand about my dad.

You haven't told him. You should.

Telling Aaron about Graham King made my hands shake, so I tucked them under my legs. Admitting to anyone about Dad's tendency to get angry and lash out with violence worried me. He hadn't hit me in a long time, but I couldn't be sure he wouldn't. The less I did to make him angry with me, the better.

"Did you have a good holiday, Rhys?" Tamara asked as she drove.

"It was okay."

I hadn't done much other than hiding away in my room with the books I'd borrowed from Aaron or watch TV with Mum.

"Well, Aaron had fun, didn't you?"

Aaron scowled and looked out of the window with his arms crossed against his chest.

"I guess," he muttered.

"Why don't you tell Rhys about where Kellie took you?"

I wondered who Kellie was and why she was taking Aaron out.

"Mum took me to the Natural History and Science museums, we had ice cream and she got tickets to the Lion King. I got to stay up late that night."

His mum's name is Kellie. Hold on, Kellie Parrish? Isn't she like famous?

I'd heard that name before. I remembered Mum telling me she'd directed a recent adaptation of some book written in old times and how she wished she could have gone to see it in the cinema. Now I felt even more insignificant than ever. What if his parents didn't approve of me being his friend when I'd come from nothing and they were rich?

It registered with me Aaron's tone hadn't exactly been excited. He sounded... off. Like spending time with his mum wasn't something he enjoyed. It made me wonder why. He did say his parents weren't home very much.

"That sounds fun, must've been nice to see your mum."

Aaron shrugged and I noticed Tamara eying him warily through the rearview mirror.

"It was okay. I liked the museums, but it would've been better if you were there."

My heart went crazy in my chest. He wanted me there. Me. I'd never been to a museum, though I knew we'd be going to one on a school trip next term.

I wasn't sure what to say, considering Tamara happened to be staring at us with concern written all over her features.

Well, maybe it was concern for Aaron and his standoffish behaviour. I knew he was upset with me for telling him to stop hugging me.

By the time we got to school, Aaron looked like he wanted to kick the car when we got out. Everything inside me raged at the injustice of the fact that I couldn't give him what he clearly wanted. He said he missed me and it was only now I realised just how much.

"A…"

He didn't respond as we walked through the gates into the playground.

"I'm sorry."

His blue-grey eyes turned on me and the sadness in them stabbed me in the chest.

"For what?"

"You know what."

He scuffed his shoe against the ground as we came to a standstill near the main entrance.

"I don't."

I almost sighed. If we were alone, I would have come out with it straight away, but there were kids everywhere and I didn't want my home life problems aired all over the school. Kids could be mean.

"Come with me."

I took him by the arm and dragged him away towards where the bike shed sat on the school grounds, eying the area to make sure no one had seen us. When we stopped behind it, I looked up at him.

"I'm sorry I didn't hug you back. My neighbour likes to gossip and I don't want my dad finding out, okay?" I blurted out in a hushed voice.

His eyes widened slightly

"Your dad?"

I nodded. I'd gone and said it now, but I didn't want to tell him anything else about Graham King. Not all the horrible things he did to me and Mum. Not the way he grovelled afterwards to her. Nothing.

"Why does that matter? I didn't even know you had a dad."

"He is…" I thought of all the nasty words my dad used against my mum and the things he'd shout about people on our street. "…a dick."

Aaron's eyebrows shot up.

"What?"

"He might stop me from coming over to yours. Please don't ask me why."

"But, Rhys, that's not a very nice thing to say about your dad."

"He's not a nice person."

"Oh."

I knew I shouldn't say bad things about my dad to other people, but honestly, I couldn't lie to Aaron about how I felt. I hated Graham King. Hated everything about him.

"I still don't understand."

I didn't want to explain to him how my dad railed against boys liking boys or the way he'd call other people horrible names for being different. Mum said he was being racist and homophobic, but I didn't understand what those words

93

meant. She told me not to listen to him anyway and that I shouldn't be scared of people's differences as we were all human beings.

So instead of answering Aaron like I probably should've, I stepped up to him and hugged him. He seemed startled for all of two seconds before he hugged me back. I wanted to show him I didn't think horrible things like my dad. Boys hugging boys didn't mean anything. We were friends and friends could hug each other.

"Well, well, well, what do we have here? Has gay boy infected you or something?"

Aaron and I sprung apart so fast I almost stumbled backwards until he caught my arm. Then he glared at the newcomer. I turned, finding Valentine staring at us with a deadly smile on his lips.

"Get lost, Valentine. No one cares what you think. And if you go around spreading rumours about us, then I'll tell my dad and he'll fire yours."

That made me look at Aaron with confusion. Valentine's eyes flashed with fear momentarily, then he put his hands up.

"All right, all right, calm down, Parrish. No one said anything about spreading rumours."

"Really? I don't believe you. Watch yourself."

Aaron grabbed me by the arm and tugged me out from behind the bike shed. I could barely form a sentence as I looked back at Valentine, who sneered at our retreating backs.

"What was that about?" I asked when Aaron and I were in the classroom and he'd stopped dragging me across the school.

"His dad works for my dad's publishing company."

"I don't know why he has it in for me."

"He's an idiot, ignore him."

It made me wonder if Valentine and Aaron had history going on. Maybe they knew each other if Valentine's dad worked for his.

"What kind of rumours would he spread?"

"You don't know? He'd make out we're gay for each other."

I stared at him.

"Is that a bad thing?"

Aaron blinked and then his brow furrowed.

"I don't want anyone to make fun of you, it's not nice."

"They'd make fun of you too."

"Yeah, well, I can handle it."

I wondered if that was true. And I wondered why people would make fun of us for being 'gay for each other'. Who cared what other people thought anyway? It's not like it was true. Aaron and I were just friends.

"A…"

"It doesn't matter, okay? He won't say anything."

I shut my mouth, but it didn't stop me wondering why Aaron seemed so weird about the subject. He never seemed to care what people thought before, so why would he care about this?

CHAPTER FOURTEEN

Aaron

"Is that a bad thing?"

Did Rhys have any idea how confusing his question was for me? Did he not care if the other kids thought we were more than just friends? And if he didn't, did it mean he might like me that way too? Probably wishful thinking on my part. Rhys had never expressed an interest in anyone. Not girls. Not boys. He seemed closed off to anything outside the small world he kept himself locked up in. That he even let me in had been a huge deal. I could tell by the way he still sometimes kept me at arm's length even though we were friends.

It's not as if I planned to come out and tell him I liked boys. Well, more specifically him. Only him. Whenever we were together, my heart went wild in my chest. This reaction to another person was so foreign to me. I had to face facts.

My crush on Rhys wasn't going away and I'd have to deal with it.

The first time I'd realised girls weren't really my thing was when I'd met Calvin and Lydia at my old school. Lydia had been the first one to talk to me. Her golden sun-kissed skin and dark ringlets probably should've made me think she was pretty, but it wasn't her I had those thoughts about. No, it was her twin brother with his short-cropped black hair. He was the one I found myself looking at closely. Though my admiration didn't give me a strange swirling feeling in my stomach as it had done when I'd seen Rhys.

Calvin, Lydia and I had become fast friends, but it'd been obvious that Lydia *liked* me. So I tried to keep her at bay, making it very clear we were friends. And it wasn't just Lydia. Half the girls in my class stared at me. It'd been worse when I started this new school. Having them fawn over me made me uncomfortable in my own skin. On the outside, I seemed calm and collected, but inside, my self-consciousness got to me. Twisting me up in knots. Only being around Rhys kept those feelings at bay. However, the feelings he elicited were unnerving in their own way. But I'd put up with those to be close to him, even if he never reciprocated.

"See you tomorrow, yeah?" Rhys said, getting my attention with his hand on mine on the backseat.

"Yeah."

He gave me a half-smile before waving to Tamara, slipping out of the car and running up the path to his front door. I watched him as Tamara pulled away. When I first told her I wanted to help a friend by giving him lifts to and from school, she'd been a little sceptical. Then when she'd seen where Rhys lived and met him, she'd understood. He wasn't trying to take advantage of me because my mum was famous and my dad was rich. It'd all been me. My generosity towards him knew no bounds. Sometimes I wondered if Tamara gave me what I wanted to make up for the fact my parents weren't around a lot.

"Calvin and Lydia's Mum called. She wanted to know if you'd come to their birthday party next weekend."

I looked towards the front seat.

"Um, okay, I guess so."

I should go. They were my friends for two years before I'd switched schools.

"You don't sound very sure about that."

I shrugged. The prospect of going to their eighth birthday party didn't fill me with joy. Then again, nothing did if it didn't include Rhys.

"Aaron, I'm going to ask you something and I don't want you to think I'm prying or jumping to conclusions."

My skin prickled.

What's that supposed to mean?

"O...kay."

She had her eyes firmly on the road, but her hands gripped the steering wheel harder.

"Did something happen between you, Calvin and Lydia?"

"What do you mean?"

That wasn't what I'd been expecting.

"Well, you've been avoiding them and the last time you were at theirs, you seemed very... uncomfortable."

I sighed and looked out the window.

"Lydia likes me and I don't like her like that."

It seemed easier to tell Tamara that rather than the truth about why I didn't want to spend time with anyone but Rhys. Besides, Lydia *did* like me and it *did* make me uncomfortable.

"If you don't like Lydia like that, you could just tell her."

"No, I can't. That's embarrassing."

She let out a little tut, but I ignored it.

"Okay, I have another question. Do you like Calvin like that? Because it's okay if you do."

I almost jumped out of my skin. Had Tamara noticed I liked boys? I'd been so careful. Though admittedly I probably stared at Rhys way more than I should. Maybe I had to be less obvious. It would be hard, but I could do it. I'd keep my staring to when we were alone. Then I could admire him without anyone knowing about how I felt. He seemed oblivious to my crush.

"No. I don't like either of them like that. Why are you asking me? They're my friends." *Or at least they used to be.*

"I'm just trying to get to the bottom of why you don't want to spend time with them any longer."

"I just told you."

I glanced at her, noting the small furrow in her brow through the rearview mirror.

"Well okay, do you want me to tell their Mum no?"

If I did that, then it might backfire on me with my mum. She told me it was good to have lots of friends.

"No, I'll go."

"You sure?"

"Yes, Tami. I'll go. I can handle it."

Other kids would be there so maybe Lydia would be distracted. The prospect did not fill me with enthusiasm but I put on a brave face for the sake of keeping the peace. Didn't want Tamara prying any further into my feelings. Especially not when it came to Rhys.

"Okay good. I'm pleased to hear it."

No doubt she'd be reporting this to my parents. I crossed my arms over my chest and stared out the window. I didn't care if she'd told me it was okay if I liked a boy. She couldn't find out about my crush on Rhys. No one could. Least of all him. Then he might run. Everything could be ruined. I'd rather have Rhys as a friend than not at all. Without him, I felt empty. He brought colour back into my life when everything had been dark when Mum and Dad told me I was moving schools. And after they left me alone with Tamara for two years to fend for myself. Rhys was my reason to smile again. To feel genuinely happy. I wanted to make him happy too.

So I decided my feelings needed burying deep so no one could find out. I had a feeling what Rhys needed from me most was friendship. And I would never do anything to jeopardise that.

These feelings. This crush. I had to hope they'd lessen with time so I could be there for him. Be his friend. His confidant. His everything except what I really wanted the most.

And that was all of him as mine.

CHAPTER FIFTEEN

Aaron

Attending this birthday party happened to be the very last thing I wanted to do. Things between Rhys and me had been a little strained. He hadn't outwardly shown any signs of things being awkward between us but I could feel the distance all the same. As if telling me about his dad had put some kind of barrier up.

It's not like I'd asked him anything else about it. Knowing he didn't like his dad made me wonder why. What had he done to make Rhys think he was a dick? Wasn't exactly the nicest thing to think about your own parent. Then again, I couldn't exactly say mine were the best parents in the world either. I had a feeling what Rhys was going through would be much worse than what I experienced.

Tamara knocked at the front door, which Lydia and Calvin's mum, Polly duly answered.

"Aaron! It's so lovely to see you."

"Hi, Mrs Sani."

She ushered both of us in. Lydia and Calvin's dad, Tayo, was Nigerian. He'd come to the UK and met Polly years ago. I liked their parents, they were always nice to me.

Tamara promised she'd come in with me so I didn't have to stay long. My behaviour definitely concerned her, but not so much she'd tell my parents. She popped the presents down on the table set up in the living room before following me out into the garden. There were tons of kids and their parents which made me feel awkward but I wouldn't show it.

Saying hi to some of my old school friends, I made my way over to where Calvin was watching his sister in the bouncy castle their parents had clearly hired.

"Happy birthday, Cal."

Calvin grinned and gave me a wink.

"All right, Aaron?"

"Yeah, all good. Lyds looks like she's having fun."

He snorted.

"She begged Mum for this."

Several kids were bouncing with her looking like they were having the time of their lives.

"Let me guess, she went to Tayo and asked him."

Calvin laughed. Their dad doted on her. His little princess. Polly tried not to spoil them, but clearly, no expense had been spared for their party.

"Busted. Mum was so mad but Dad went ahead anyway."

I watched the kids, not saying a word. Maybe in the past, I'd have been right in there in the thick of it. These days only the prospect of seeing Rhys got me excited.

"You're quiet."

I shrugged.

"Just thinking."

Calvin ran his eyes over me. It'd been the same way when I'd last seen him and Lydia. Life had changed drastically for me. Mum was away more and the loneliness hit hard. Maybe I'd become more withdrawn too. Not wanting to express my feelings any longer.

"You ever going to tell Lyds you aren't her Prince Charming?"

"What?"

"Come on, Aaron, I'm not stupid. She adores you."

I looked away as my face grew hot.

"And? I can't stop her."

"Girls are dumb, they can't even tell when boys don't fancy them."

Maybe not all girls but Lydia hadn't got the message. She kept staring at me like she worshipped the ground I walked on.

"What do you know about girls?"

"Well, dur, I live with one. It's gross. She's all Aaron this, Aaron that. She cried when you didn't come back to school."

A horrible feeling settled in my stomach. Lydia needed to get over it. And I needed to be clear I didn't like her in that way.

"Not my fault, Mum thinks this new school is better for me and I think so too."

Calvin nudged my shoulder.

"Yeah?"

"Yeah. I met a new friend. He's cool. Likes reading."

"You hate reading."

I grinned.

"It's not so bad. Rhys gets so excited about books, can't help but find them interesting too."

Before Calvin had a chance to answer, Lydia came rushing up to us having got off the bouncy castle.

"Aaron!"

"Hi, Lyds, happy birthday."

I didn't have time to object to her hugging me.

"Missed you," she whispered in my ear.

I stiffened. Letting her down gently would be hard, but I had to.

She pulled back and rocked on her feet.

"Wanna come bounce?"

I shook my head. The very last thing I wanted to do was upset my stomach, which was already in knots.

"Come on, Aaron… for me."

Be strong.

"I'm okay here with Cal."

Lydia pouted.

"Leave him alone, Lyds. If he doesn't want to go, you can't make him," Calvin said rolling his eyes.

She crossed her arms over her chest, glaring daggers at her twin brother.

"Shut up, Aaron can tell me himself."

I almost sighed. Lydia could act like a spoilt brat at times.

"Oh look, Tami's waving at me."

I practically ran away from the two of them, glancing back to find Calvin laughing and Lydia looking incensed. Tamara wasn't even in the garden but I had to get away. The very thought of having to tell Lydia I didn't like her in that way made my skin crawl. Telling anyone I wasn't into girls made me sick. It wouldn't bother Calvin but I didn't think Lydia would understand. Better to not have that confrontation. I had enough of those at school with Valentine trying to bully Rhys. I hated that idiot. He kept trying to insert himself into my business. Just because our dads knew each other, didn't make us friends. Besides, I didn't make friends with bullies.

A little while later, I'd just filled up a paper plate with food when Lydia cornered me by the dining table.

"Hey, Aaron."

"Lyds."

"Are you avoiding me?"

I blinked.

"No."

"You sure? It feels like it."

"I'm really not. You just seem busy, I mean it is your birthday party."

She put a hand on my arm. I stumbled back immediately, not wanting any physical contact between us. Lydia couldn't get the wrong idea.

"See, you won't even let me near you. What's going on?"

"Nothing. I swear."

Her eyes narrowed to slits.

"Did... did you meet someone at your new school?"

My heart pounded in my ears.

"Huh? No, why would you ask that?"

"Cal said you had a new friend. Is she prettier than me?"

I almost choked on my tongue. Why on earth would she automatically assume my new friend was a girl?

"Um, I can't really say if *he* is or not."

Lydia looked like she'd hit the jackpot.

"He? Oh… then you don't have a girlfriend."

I shook my head. As if I would ever have one.

"No girlfriends. Rhys and I are just friends."

"I'm glad you've made a friend, must be weird being somewhere new where you don't know anyone."

I shrugged and fiddled with my paper plate.

"It's okay. I don't mind it. The teachers are nice and I'm doing better with my schoolwork."

Lydia knew that's why my parents made me change schools. They wanted the best for me.

"So definitely no girls you like?"

"No, Lyds, I don't like any girls." *At all, whatsoever.*

"Good, that's good… you know I was hoping—"

"Lydia, time for cake," called Polly from the kitchen.

I breathed a silent sigh of relief when Lydia gave me an apologetic look and scurried away. No doubt she was about to ask me if I liked her and I'd have to say no. That conversation would not go well.

I was thankful she didn't manage to corner me again before I left the party. Tamara talked the whole way home with me giving one-word answers. At least that was over with. Maybe I could tell Rhys what an absolute disaster it had been at school on Monday. My heart warmed at the thought of him.

I couldn't wait. Most kids wouldn't look forward to school. Not me. I relished every moment. It meant I could be close to him.

My heart sank again when I realised it wouldn't be the end of things with Lydia. I would have to tell her, eventually. But perhaps I could put off seeing them again for a while and hope in the meantime she might transfer her affections elsewhere. Because I would never feel the same way. Especially not when the person who held all of my attention was everything I could've ever hoped for in another person. And so much more.

CHAPTER SIXTEEN

Aaron

R hys was unusually quiet when we picked him up on Monday morning. His eyes fixed on the window outside as he hid his hands under his legs. Tamara chatted away about the weekend but I don't think he was listening. I had planned to tell him about Lydia until I'd seen his face when he got in. Something happened over the weekend and I could put money on it being bad. He might normally be quiet and reserved, but he was never completely silent and uncommunicative with me. At least he hadn't been since we'd established we were friends.

Even when we got to school and walked to the classroom, he wouldn't meet my eyes nor say a word. We sat at our usual desk near the back. He began to pull out his things. I watched him for signs he would talk, but he seemed to be ignoring me.

"Rhys…"

"Yeah?"

"What's wrong?"

"Nothing."

It didn't look like nothing. His eyes were haunted. My heart shrivelled at the sight of it. He only ever let me in a little way. I kept finding myself slamming into his walls at every turn. Being his friend was almost impossible at times, but I reminded myself he'd open up, eventually. He'd allow me access to the deeper workings of his mind when he learnt to trust me completely. I just wished it'd happen faster.

"You look unhappy."

He flinched.

"You see too much," he muttered, turning his face from me.

Every time we took a step forward with each other, we always took four steps back. I steeled myself. No matter what, I'd get him to talk to me. To open up because I couldn't not. Rhys had to stop hiding. Didn't he know I'd do anything for him? I'd keep each and every one of his secrets. I'd hold him when it all got too much. I'd just damn well be there for him whenever he needed me.

"I just want to help you."

"You can't help me, Aaron. No one can."

The note of despair in his voice and the fact he'd used my full name made my stomach sink to the floor. This wasn't like him. Not the Rhys I'd come to know since the beginning of term. What happened at the weekend? What could've possibly gone so wrong to make him want to shut me out completely all over again?

"Don't say that. It's not true. I can if you let me."

His expression darkened and his fists clenched in his lap.

"You don't understand. You can't possibly... it doesn't matter. Just leave me be. I can't talk about it. I won't talk about it."

The way my heart fractured at his words had me almost clutching my chest. Pain drove through me. Not for myself, but for him. For the boy I couldn't help but be drawn to. I wished he'd let me carry his burdens. I wouldn't give up on him. I couldn't. He needed someone. I'd made a promise to never leave him. And I intended to keep it.

I placed my hand on his forearm to reassure him I was here even when he insisted on trying to push me away. The next thing I knew, he'd flinched back, pain etched across his features.

"Rhys...?"

"Don't," he whispered.

I didn't allow him to run from me. Before he could object, I pulled up his school jumper and found several bruises across his wrist and up his arm.

"Who... who did this to you?" My voice was barely above a whisper so as not to alert anyone else who might be lurking nearby.

He tugged his arm away from me, hurriedly pulling his jumper back down. His dark eyes were full of heartache. The realisation he was likely being abused slammed into me like a million shards of ice hitting my chest.

"Who's hurting you?"

He shook his head, clutching his arm to his chest and staring down at the desk. Nothing could prepare me for seeing it. The evidence of something worse than I could've ever imagined.

"I can't."

"You can, please, you can trust me."

Who would I tell? If he needed me to keep it a secret, I would. I'd never betray him. I couldn't.

"Stop asking, A, please. Just stop. Not here. Not now. I can't tell you now."

The pain in his voice made the ice shards in my chest dig deeper. I wanted so much to put my arms around him and take it all away. Keep him safe. But what could I do? I was a seven-year-old boy. Nothing I said or did would change his life for him.

"When?"

He dropped his arm and his hands shook in his lap. We couldn't go back to before I'd seen the marks on his arms. The bruises. He couldn't keep hiding the truth from me. He knew it. I knew it. It would only be a matter of time before he told me what was really going on at home. Why he kept telling me he had to look after his mum. And why he'd called his dad a dick.

The only logical conclusion I could draw was this had been his dad. It made me sick to my stomach to think anyone could hurt him let alone his own father.

"Tomorrow," he whispered. "At yours… when no one else can hear us."

He finally met my eyes. The promise in them had my heart slamming hard against my ribcage. Rhys wanted to open up.

He wanted to trust me. I'd prove to him how worthy I could be of his trust. I wouldn't let him down.

The teacher came into the room and started asking us to settle down. I turned towards the front of the room, but not before slipping my hand over his in his lap.

"A," he breathed.

"I know. I'm here. I've got you," I whispered. "I promise."

Tomorrow I'd learn exactly how dark and difficult his life was. And I wasn't sure I could prepare myself for the secrets he'd reveal. But whatever they were, I'd help him through it. I'd fight by his side forever.

That was the day I knew it wasn't just some kind of stupid crush. No... I cared about Rhys far more than that. No matter how hard he fought against it, we had a connection. It ran deep in our veins and it couldn't be undone. I'd be his sword and shield, just like the warriors in the books he liked. I'd go to war for him. Fight by his side. And I'd do it because he was the only person I could see myself next to for the rest of my life.

Is this what adults call falling in love? Because I'm pretty sure I love Rhys King more than life itself.

I didn't care what it was called. All I knew was Rhys and I were meant to be even if he didn't know it quite yet.

CHAPTER SEVENTEEN

Rhys

The weekend had been hell on earth for me. I'd debated going into school, but Mum said I had to even though she was confined to her bed again. And now I had inadvertently allowed Aaron to see some of the damage Graham King had inflicted on me. All because I'd tried to stop him from hurting Mum again.

I could still hear his shouting echoing in my ears and the awful things he'd said to the both of us. And the very worst part of all? He'd come back the next day, grovelling at Mum's feet and begging for her forgiveness. It was never me he apologised to. Only her. He didn't care how much he hurt me even though I was his son. His own flesh and blood.

I didn't understand how she could keep forgiving him even after he hurt both of us. We'd be better off without him. He should leave Mum and go live with Maggie Polton since he spent enough time around her house anyway. But Mum said we couldn't survive without him. I hated how she couldn't see our lives were much worse with him around.

Aaron and I climbed the stairs in his house, making a beeline for his bedroom after Tamara brought us back after school. I'd promised him I'd reveal the truth today even though I really didn't want to. What would Aaron even think anyway when he found out my dad was an abusive dick? Would he judge me like I did myself? Perhaps he'd understand why I hated myself so much.

He closed the bedroom door and popped our snacks on his desk after we'd waited downstairs for Tamara to make them so she wouldn't interrupt us. I took a large gulp of my juice to settle my nerves before putting it down next to his. Aaron walked over to the window and stared out at the houses surrounding us.

"It was your dad, wasn't it?"

I swallowed hard. It shouldn't have come as a surprise he'd worked out that much. I had told him Graham King was a dick.

"Yes."

"Why… why would he hurt you?"

"He hates me."

Except the explanation wasn't quite as simple as that. So I walked over and looked up at Aaron. His blue-grey eyes had darkened significantly. It was more than just a storm brewing in them. It was as if they were the raging sea, the swell rising, ready to smash ships against rocks and drown their occupants. I could barely breathe, my lungs constricting from the intensity I saw there. It wasn't directed at me. No, Aaron's ire was for my dad, but he didn't know the full story.

"Why?" came his voice, all hard and full of repressed anger.

I took his hand, linking our fingers together even though I was scared of revealing the truth. Aaron made me feel safe in a way I'd never experienced before. His confident attitude had drawn me in and his insistence on not letting me run. Even if I had, he'd still be there, pushing me to open up to him.

He sucked in a breath, his eyes flicking down to our entwined fingers. Then he let it out, his fingers shaking with the effort. I didn't understand his reaction, but I chose not to read into it too much.

"Come."

I pulled him over to his bed and made him sit down next to me, keeping our fingers locked. Having his touch kept me grounded. I stared hard at his hand, wondering why he made me feel so peaceful and comforted.

"When Mum had me, there were complications… she suffered a stroke after I was born and it left her with permanent disabilities. Sometimes her speech is impaired and she has trouble with walking and movement. She has good days and bad ones. That's why I have to look after her."

"Rhys—"

I put my other hand up, stopping him from saying a word.

"You need to let me finish… please."

I met his eyes, finding so much compassion in them, it made tears prick at the corners of my own. I blinked them back. Allowing myself to get emotional wasn't something I could afford if I was going to tell him the truth. The whole sorry truth of my tragic and desolate life.

"Graham… my dad… is her full-time carer. At least, he's supposed to be. He spends more time at the pub with his friends or at Maggie Polton's, two doors down from us. He expects me to take care of Mum as he blames me for the way she is. Because having me caused her to have a stroke. He blames me for everything. That's why he hates me, A, but it's worse than that."

My hands shook as I stared into Aaron's eyes and saw the abject horror in them. I wasn't sure if it was directed at me or about my dad. Didn't matter. I had to press on. I'd promised him an explanation.

"I don't remember when exactly he started hitting Mum. I just remember the screaming matches, the slamming doors and the stamping of feet. I remember him coming back from the pub, drunk and getting into arguments with her over me. Every time something went wrong, it was always my fault because I'd ruined Mum's life by being born. Her condition started worsening every time they had a fight and when I saw the bruises he left on her, I realised what was happening."

It killed me on the inside. Knowing my dad took out his anger at me on her. His anger at the world for having landed him with a son who'd ruined his wife's life.

"The first time he hurt me, I'd tried to stop him from punching Mum in the face. He backhanded me, then he gripped my arm so hard and shook me, it left bruises for days afterwards. He screamed in my face, swore at me and called me worthless. He said he wished I'd never been born. That it was my fault he has to… *fuck* other women. All I could smell was the alcohol on his breath. It makes me sick every time."

I didn't like using bad words as Mum told me not to copy him, but I knew what the word *fuck* meant. It didn't take a genius to realise he had sex with Maggie Polton because Mum couldn't give him that any longer. Nor that their fights had got worse after Aunt Bibi killed herself. A part of me didn't want to remember how Graham used to look at her with that disgusting leer in his eyes. So I knew why Aunt Bibi ended it even if Mum had told me something different. I knew why because Aunt Bibi and Mum had looked a lot alike.

"He only hurts me when I try to save Mum from him. So she told me I had to stay in my room. She made me promise, but I couldn't on Saturday. He was shouting so loud, I heard the neighbours banging on the walls telling them to shut up. I went downstairs and found him with his hands wrapped around Mum's throat. I threw myself at his back and hit him until he let go. He grabbed my arms and threw me across the room. Then he hit me in the stomach again and again until I was sobbing and couldn't breathe properly. That's when Mum pulled him off and kicked him out of the house."

Gingerly, I pulled up my school jumper and shirt with my free hand, showing Aaron the bruises across my skin. They'd turned a dark purple and were yellowing around the outside. The agony in Aaron's eyes damn near broke me, but I pressed on.

"He came home the next day grovelling like he always does. Mum took him back like she always does. She can't get out of bed at the moment. He's been taking care of her, but it won't last. It never does. They'll get into another fight and it'll happen all over again. I wish she'd leave him. He does nothing but hurt us. Mum keeps saying we can't survive without him. I don't believe that. If he wasn't in our lives, then Mum wouldn't have so many bad days. She wouldn't have to struggle and be in pain. Her medication would work properly. Everything would be better if Graham left us. But she doesn't see that…" I faltered, swallowing down the lump in my throat. "She says she loves him, but I don't. I hate him… but most of all… I hate myself because I can't protect her. I caused all of this by just existing."

I looked away from Aaron, pulling my jumper back down and staring at our hands. The simple fact he'd not let go made my heart thump violently in my chest. I didn't want to meet his eyes again. Whilst I felt relief at unburdening myself to him, fear also gripped me at what he'd think. What he'd say to everything I'd told him. He lived such a privileged life with his rich parents, a big house and could never want for anything. Here was me, living on a council estate where you could get stabbed for looking at someone the wrong way with an abusive dad and a disabled mother. Aaron and I came from completely different worlds. Would he still stand by me now he knew the real extent of my tragic life?

Except Aaron didn't say a word, he let go of my hand and edged closer before gently wrapping his arms around me. I sat there for a long moment, unsure of how to take him hugging me.

"A?" I whispered.

His arms around me tightened as he buried his face against my neck. I felt his breath fluttering over my skin, making it prickle.

"It's not your fault."

I almost stiffened.

"What isn't?"

"Any of it. Your dad is wrong. He shouldn't hurt you or your mum. You did nothing wrong, Rhys. Nothing at all. You are so special and I won't let anyone else tell you otherwise."

My heart couldn't take his words. Those tears which I didn't want pricking at my eyes started falling. They dripped down my cheeks, falling off my chin and landing in his blonde hair. I'm not sure Aaron cared since he didn't pull away. His hand stroked up and down my back in a soothing motion. It made me choke out a sob. I'd had no one to talk to about this for so long. Aaron had come along, smashed through all my defences and shown me how much I needed him in my life. How much I needed... no... craved his friendship, his kindness, his care.

When he finally pulled back, he reached up and wiped away my tears with his thumbs before his hands circled my face. He leant towards me and rested his forehead against mine. I swallowed hard, my lungs constricting in my chest at his closeness.

"I made you a promise that I'd never leave you. I'm going to make you another one. I promise to listen, to be here and to care for you for as long as we live. I'll never let you go, Rhys. Never."

"Never?" I echoed.

"Never ever."

All I could see was his irises glinting at me, the blue-grey of his eyes so pronounced this close up. It struck me how beautiful Aaron was inside and out. It was really no wonder half the girls in our class swooned over him. They didn't get to see this side of him though. The complete openness of his expression. They didn't get to see him laugh so hard, he snorted and choked on his own breath. I made him laugh that much. Only me. And it made me feel like I was on top of the world.

A part of me felt incredibly possessive over Aaron. I wanted those things to be mine and mine alone. I didn't want anyone else to see him like this. The very thought of it loosened my tongue and made me confess something I'd only just realised as I said it.

"You're my best friend, Aaron. I know you're my only friend, but you're still the best."

He opened his mouth and closed it again, his eyes growing so soft, I almost couldn't take it. Such a contrast to how angry he'd been earlier.

"You're my best friend too, Rhys."

The moment the words left his lips, it cemented something so deep inside me, I would be hard-pressed to tear it out. Aaron meant more to me than any other person ever had. He'd given me something no one else could. A place free from judgement or excuses. He let me tell my story without once looking at me like I was damaged or wrong. He accepted me for the way I was. Not even Mum did that sometimes.

My hand left my lap and curled around his face, mirroring the way he held mine.

"Thank you for understanding. You have no idea how much that means to me. I need... I need you, A. You're like the light in my darkness. I don't know what I'd do without you."

Aaron sucked in a breath, his eyes growing wider and flicking down to my hand. He stared for a long moment before his eyes turned back to me. He didn't meet my eyes, instead, their sole focus was on my mouth as if he couldn't believe the words which had come out of it.

"I'm right here," he whispered. "You have me. Never forget that."

I don't know why, but something in his voice told me there was so much more to his words than I could comprehend or even begin to understand. The only thing which mattered was Aaron hadn't run from me. He'd stayed despite knowing how messed up my life was.

I dropped my hand from his face before pulling his from mine. I noticed the slight disappointment in his eyes before I pressed forward and leant my head against his shoulder, wrapping my arms around his back.

That was the day our bond with each other became a permanent fixture in our lives. Nothing could change us. Nothing would stand in our way. Not whilst we had each other.

I vowed to myself to be stronger. To withstand the agony and pain my dad inflicted on my mum and me. Because I knew

Aaron would be there for me if and when I fell apart. He'd put me back together piece by piece just by being him.

Aaron was my saviour.

And my downfall.

PART II

infatuate

verb, in·fat·u·at·ed, in·fat·u·at·ing.

to inspire or possess with a foolish or unreasoning passion, as of love.

CHAPTER EIGHTEEN

Aaron

Ten Years Later

Rhys sat out with his head tipped up towards the sun, basking in the warmth as his chest rose and fell with each breath. A bead of sweat gathered on his upper lip, tempting me to lick it off him. My eyes feasted on the boy in front of me and he had absolutely no idea. His eyes were closed, his posture completely relaxed. He was only like this with me. Completely open and unashamed in his own skin. And fuck, it was just about the hottest sight imaginable.

Rhys had morphed from a skinny seven-year-old into a well-defined, tall and incredibly handsome seventeen-year-old. Growing his hair out so it sat in beautiful dark waves whilst still keeping the back and sides cut close to his head. And don't even get me started on the fact he was currently shirtless. It was like having every wet dream I'd ever had rolled into one watching him bathe in the rays of the sun as the two of us sat in the park away from the families with their picnics and teenagers hanging out smoking and drinking on the benches.

The good weather had only made his tanned skin darker. I looked pasty next to him even though I'd got a slight tan. It was the beginning of the summer holidays. Six weeks until we had to go back to reality and I hated the thought of it. Going back to school meant not seeing Rhys every day. As close as we'd grown over the past ten years, when it came to us starting at secondary school, my parents had decided to send me somewhere closer to our house. It meant Rhys and I had been separated. Something I hated with a passion. I knew it bothered him too, but perhaps not quite as much as me.

We still tried to see each other most days regardless of my parents' attempts at putting a stop to our friendship. I didn't care what they said or thought about Rhys. He was my best friend and the boy I'd been in love with since we were seven. Ten whole years of pining after him hadn't dampened my feelings. They'd only grown stronger with the passage of time.

Of course, my parents had no idea how I felt about Rhys deep down, nor that I wasn't straight. I couldn't imagine telling them. Not least because my dad expected me to live up to his standards. His expectations. I didn't think having a gay son would be good enough for Patrick Parrish. Especially not when his son was in love with a boy who grew up on a council estate with an abusive, drunk, unfaithful father and a disabled mother.

I'd made promises to Rhys when we were seven and I intended to keep them forever. It felt like him and me against the world most of the time. We relied on each other. He was there for me when my parents pressurised me and I let him crash at mine whenever his dad got too much, something which had increased with an alarming frequency over the past few years. Graham and Rhys didn't get on at all. In fact, the moment Rhys turned sixteen, he'd told his dad if he laid a hand on Steph ever again, he'd kick the shit out of him. Something Graham had taken seriously, but it didn't stop the arguments and screaming matches.

"Pass the water, will you?" Rhys' voice filtered over, startling me out of my thoughts.

I picked up the bottle next to me and tossed it to him. He sat up and caught it, grinning at me. That grin could stop my damn heart. And it did. Every. Single. Time.

He unscrewed the cap and took a long draw from it, his throat muscles working and making my mouth water. To say I hadn't imagined his throat working around my dick would be a complete and utter lie. If he knew how many times I'd fantasised about us naked together as I lay in bed with my hand wrapped around my cock, he'd probably hate me for it.

Rhys had never expressed an interest in anyone. Whilst the boys and girls around us coupled up, started sleeping together and got into all sorts of drama, the two of us had remained very much single. Neither of us had even kissed anyone, let alone lost our virginity.

Rhys didn't know I was attracted to boys. It's not as if I'd deliberately kept it from him. We never talked about the subject of who we liked, as strange as it sounds. It was always about us. Other people didn't seem to exist when we were in our own little world. We knew everything there was to know about each other, yet I literally had no idea whether Rhys was straight, gay or something in between. And asking after all this time didn't feel right.

He screwed the cap back on the water, dumping it next to him and laid back against the grass with his hands tucked under his head. The urge to crawl over him and plant kisses down his bare chest made me look away. I didn't know why it was worse today, but this felt like absolute torture.

"Mum wants to know if we'll pop round for dinner tonight."

I blinked and turned back to him.

"Will Graham be there?"

"No. Him and Mum argued last night. She's kicked him out again, but fuck knows how long that'll last."

This had been the way of things for the past year. Steph kicked Graham out every time they fought and he always came crawling back a week later after spending time with one of his mistresses. Since Graham had stopped beating her, Steph's health had improved. She had more good days than bad, something I knew gave Rhys a sense of peace.

"Then sure, that'd be nice."

Rhys opened his eyes and smiled before grabbing his phone and typing out a message to his mum. Graham didn't like my friendship with Rhys almost as much as my parents hated it. He thought I was stuck up because I came from money. Little did he know I hated being known as the rich kid. Having money didn't make you any happier. If anything, it made me miserable. My parents were so obsessed with keeping up appearances because of it. And the fact my mum was a famous director so they couldn't escape the public eye.

Harriet, my sister, loved the attention. But me? I hated it. The only saving grace was my mum putting her foot down with my dad when it came to me. She said if I didn't want to be subjected to all the media crap that came with their careers, then she'd respect it. They didn't talk about me in interviews or allow photos. It would all change after I left school. They'd already told me exactly where I had to apply for university and when I'd got my degree, I'd start at my dad's publishing house, Johnstone & Parrish. I didn't have a choice in the matter. They'd made up their minds about my future and that was that.

"You sure you don't mind?"

I smiled at him.

"I never mind, Rhys, you know I love Steph's cooking."

He threw his phone down in the grass and moved closer to me, settling himself down on his side with his head propped up by his hand. His closeness made my senses come alive.

"You're the best, you know that?"

"Uh, yeah, you only tell me like *all* the time."

He smacked my arm.

"Shut up."

"Never. You can't shut me up even when you try."

I followed that up by nudging his nose with my finger, something I knew he hated me doing. He grabbed my hand

Sarah Bailey

before I could retract it and pinned it next to my head, leaning over me with an amused glint in his dark eyes.

"You're terribly irritating when you want to be."

My heart stuttered in my chest, my eyes finding his lips and wishing I could kiss him or even that he'd kiss me.

"You love it really."

"Oh yeah? We've talked about you living in delusional land. I. Hate. It."

His smile took away the sting of his words.

"You wouldn't know what to do without me and my irritating mouth driving you up the wall."

There was one way he could shut me up, but I'm not sure the thought of it had ever crossed Rhys' mind. He'd never thought about sticking his tongue down his best friend's throat like I'd been doing ever since I'd hit puberty. And honestly? I'm not sure what I'd do with myself if I found out he had been imagining it. Probably faint.

Rhys wasn't flirting with me. This was how we were with each other. Thick as thieves. Constantly giving each other shit. The fact he'd pinned my hand down wasn't anything new either. Rhys and I had always held hands and hugged each other when we weren't around anyone else. I'd never questioned it because I liked it so much.

"All right, gay boys?"

Rhys let go of me immediately and glared at the newcomer. I turned my head, finding Valentine and his friends a few feet away with cans of cheap beer in their hands. He was three years older than us and still very much an arsehole.

"Get fucked, Valentine," Rhys practically growled.

Rhys might have cowered away from the guy when we were kids, but when we grew up, he refused to take any shit off anyone. Especially not Valentine Jenkins.

"Ooh, still touchy as ever. Anyone would think you're ashamed of your hardon for Parrish."

If anyone should be ashamed, it was me. I shouldn't be having all these feelings regarding my best friend. I shouldn't pine over him and wish we could be more. Rhys deserved better than that from me, and yet my stupid hormones went wild whenever he was near me. Making me want things I could never have.

Rhys got up, flexing his muscles as he took a step towards Valentine.

"Aaron and I don't need your shitty attitude ruining our afternoon. Go bother someone else… unless your face wants to meet my fist, then, by all means, keep going."

It didn't escape my notice Rhys never seemed to make a big deal out of Valentine accusing us of being gay for each other. Like he didn't care if anyone thought that about us. It made my heart soar. If I ever worked up the courage to tell him I liked boys, he would be fine with it. I'd have to keep the part about me liking… no… loving him to myself.

"Oh yeah, you think you're a hard man, do you? Think you can fucking take me?"

"Valentine, leave off, hey?" I said quietly. "We were just minding our own business here before you came over so don't start something unnecessary."

He looked down at me for a long moment with an odd expression on his face before huffing, "Let's go, guys."

He walked away and his friends trudged after him, glancing back with disgust on their faces. That was exactly why I didn't tell anyone about my sexuality. Too many people in this world gave you shit for just being yourself. It's not like I asked to be gay or anything.

"That guy is a fucking idiot," Rhys ground out through his teeth as he sat back down next to me.

"Too right."

"He really winds me up. Like who the fuck cares if we're gay or not. Why does it matter so much to him? He needs to grow the fuck up."

I stared at him. The anger in his dark eyes and the little furrow between his brows.

"You don't care if people think we're together?"

"No, why would I? It's not like it's true and even if it was, it's not their business."

I ignored the way my heart thumped against my chest at his words.

"You're right, it's not."

He turned to me, the anger dissipating from his eyes. God, I loved his eyes. I could drown in them. Drown in him. My eyes raked down his chest again, wanting to run my fingers over the hard planes of his stomach and lower.

"I only ever care about what you think, A. As long as we're good, nothing else matters."

"We're always good."

My eyes flicked straight back up to his as the guilt ate me away on the inside. I should not be looking at my best friend like I wanted to eat him up. Nor thinking about how much I wanted to tear his clothes off, pin him down and take him ruthlessly. I swallowed hard. The one thing I'd banned myself from imagining was having sex with him, and yet the images kept playing over and over in my mind on repeat. So when he reached over with his hand and brushed my hair back from my eyes, I just about died.

"You're cute when you get all serious."

"W…what?"

"You and these dimples." He poked my cheek. "It's totally why those girls over there keep drooling and giggling as they stare at you."

I blinked, unable to take in what he was saying right then because Rhys noticed I had dimples and said I was cute.

Jesus, Aaron, calm down. He doesn't look at you as anything other than his best friend.

"What girls?"

He pointed over my shoulder. I turned to look at them. There were five sitting out on a blanket in barely-there tops and shorts. The sight of them did nothing for me. They started nudging each other the moment they realised I was looking at them. I turned back to Rhys as fast as I could, not wanting to give any of them the wrong idea. Except that was a bad idea too as Rhys' chest was right in my face. And he was laughing.

"Jesus, A, you look like a deer in headlights." He patted my shoulder. "Don't worry, they're not coming over here… unless you want them to."

"Fuck no," I said far too quickly.

He laughed harder.

137

"Oh boy, you're going to break all their hearts. They'll be sobbing into their pillows tonight. Boohoo, Aaron Parrish is so hot but he won't look at me, whatever will I do?"

"Oh, shut up. They're staring at you with your shirt off."

He shrugged and laid out flat on his back, his eyes still full of amusement. And I, unashamedly, stared at him just like I'd accused those girls of doing.

"Don't care. They can look all they want. Not interested."

"Are you even interested in anyone?"

"No. Girls are too much drama. Besides, I have you, why would I need anyone else?"

I tried and failed not to be affected by his words. He did have me, but he didn't realise that meant more than just me as a friend. He owned my heart. I couldn't deny it. I wanted Rhys so much, it burnt a hole in my chest. Except I couldn't ruin our friendship by telling him. So instead of saying what I wanted to, I gave him a smart comment because that's the only way I knew how to deal with this.

"What? You're seriously telling me you wouldn't say yes if one of them offered themselves up to you on a silver platter? Are you sure you're a teenage boy, Rhys? Because you're sounding like a nun right now."

He reached over and slapped my arm.

"Fuck off. I'm not a fucking nun. Honestly, just because I don't want to get with a random person doesn't make me some kind of prude. It doesn't work like that for me."

"Then tell me, how does it work?"

I watched him for signs this line of conversation was making him uncomfortable.

"I don't know. I just don't feel that kind of way about anyone I've met. I can't explain it... maybe I'm broken or something."

"You're not broken. Maybe you've not met the right person yet."

He shrugged.

"I told you. I don't need anyone else but you, A, so it doesn't really matter anyway."

I decided to drop it, not wanting to push him any further. His confession gave me pause. If Rhys didn't like anyone he'd met, then what the hell hope was there for me?

My heart sunk.

There was none.

None at all.

CHAPTER NINETEEN

Rhys

Aaron was unusually quiet on the drive from the park to my house. His parents had insisted on him learning right after he turned seventeen and he'd passed his test just before school ended. It came in handy. Before he got his licence, we'd had to take the bus to see each other since his parents were never around. Tamara, Aaron's au pair, had left when he turned ten and then they had another girl, Maritza, take care of him until he turned sixteen. At that point, they decided he could fend for himself, although his sister checked in on him from time to time.

"Do you think Mum's made cottage pie?"

Aaron lifted a shoulder in a shrug, his lip quirking up. I wouldn't put it past her considering she knew it was Aaron's favourite. She absolutely adored him, but then again, who didn't? Everyone was drawn to him like a moth to a flame. But he didn't seem to care about all the girls drooling over him. Though, honestly, I think it had more to do with the fact Aaron didn't seem to be into girls at all. He'd never said anything to me about it. Then again, we never discussed girls, boys or relationships. Except for today. That had been weird. Really fucking weird.

I hadn't expected him to ask me outright who or what I was interested in. And I hadn't been lying when I told him I couldn't explain it. When we overheard other boys talking about how they'd love to bang some chick, I couldn't relate to it. I'd never looked at a girl or a boy for that matter and been attracted to them. It wasn't like I didn't have sexual urges because fuck did I, but no one made me want to take them to bed. At least no one I should want.

I shook myself as Aaron pulled up outside my house. He turned to me, his blue-grey eyes glinting.

"I bet she's made apple crumble and custard for dessert."

"She spoils you."

He grinned and then got out of the car. I jumped out and made sure he locked the doors. You could never tell with people around here. They'd nick anything they could get their hands on.

We walked up the path and I unlocked the front door.

"Mum?"

"In the kitchen, love."

Aaron and I walked down the hallway and into the kitchen, finding Mum sitting at the table with a smile on her face. I kissed her cheek, letting her ruffle my hair.

"My beautiful boy."

"Mum," I grumbled, pulling away as I stuck my hands in my pockets and moved towards the stove, checking the oven. I smiled when I saw I'd been right, she'd got a cottage pie on the go.

"Hello, Aaron."

"Steph, how are you?"

I popped my head back up in time to see him kiss her cheek too.

"I'm well. Rhys love, will you set the table for me?"

"'Course, Mum."

Aaron took a seat whilst I got the cutlery out of the drawer and the plates from the cupboard.

"You boys been up to anything fun today?"

"Just at the park sunbathing," Aaron replied. "All the girls were drooling over him."

I scowled at him as I popped the plates on the table and got some glasses.

"Shut up, they were looking at A, not me."

Mum smiled, her eyes twinkling.

"Don't be so modest, love. I bet they were looking at both of you."

I scoffed, grabbing a bottle of Pepsi out of the fridge and popping it on the table. Aaron put the plates and cutlery out before pouring us all a glass.

"A and I don't need girls, Mum. They're drama."

She laughed, shaking her head as Aaron bit his lip.

"You've told me enough times you only need each other."

I tapped my nose.

"Exactly."

It didn't escape my notice Aaron's cheeks went red at my assertion. I turned away and opened the oven, checking on the food.

"Should be done, love, if you want to get it out."

I grabbed the oven gloves and pulled it out, setting it on top of the stove. It smelt amazing. Then again, her cooking always did. Now Graham had a job down the local supermarket, we weren't so hard up for money. I was just glad he wasn't here right now. It'd likely end up with me telling him to piss off because he'd got drunk again. There was hardly a time he was at home and sober.

Mum, Aaron and I ate and laughed together. She always loved having Aaron here. If only my twat of a father wasn't around all the time, then we'd be here more.

When Aaron went to the bathroom, I turned to her.

"Is he gone for good this time?"

Mum looked down at her hands. I knew the answer before it even came out of her mouth.

"You know it's not that simple, love."

"It could be. We could get more help from the government and you could get a proper carer rather than him."

She shook her head. Mum didn't like handouts even though it wouldn't be one. It'd mean we'd be getting away from Graham and his bullshit. Mum deserved so much more than him.

"I don't expect you to understand."

She always said the same thing.

"No, I do understand, Mum. I want you to be happy and you're not when you're with him."

Before she had a chance to answer, Aaron came back and dropped in the chair next to me, slapping my shoulder.

"Please tell me there's pudding."

Mum smiled and nodded to the fridge.

"There's cheesecake. I know you boys love your puds."

"Yes!"

I rolled my eyes as he jumped up to sort it out. His eyes met mine and I saw understanding in them for the briefest of moments before he opened the fridge.

By the time we'd both eaten huge slices and Mum had a little one, Aaron was complaining about how full he was and I kept poking his stomach. He slapped my hand away, scowling at me.

"Leave off."

"If you keep eating like that, you're going to get all soft and doughy."

"As if. Unlike you, I run three times a week."

I laughed. By running, he meant getting on the treadmill whereas I used his parents' home gym to do weights. Meant I wasn't scrawny any longer. I'd started exercising to put on some muscle so I could defend Mum from Graham better. I enjoyed it, so I kept it up. Probably why I spent more time at Aaron's than my own home as well as avoiding Graham like the plague.

"You staying home tonight, love, or you going back with Aaron?" Mum asked as Aaron and I got up to do the dishes.

I glanced at him and could immediately tell by the shift in his blue-grey eyes he hoped I'd stay with him. Aaron couldn't exactly hide a lot of things from me. I could always tell his mood by the colour of his eyes.

"Going back with A. He promised me a movie marathon, including popcorn."

"Don't remind me, I don't think I can eat any more tonight."

"Ha, whatever, you eat like a horse."

He nudged my shoulder with his as I ran the tap and squirted the washing up liquid in the bowl. I washed up whilst he dried, the two of us repeatedly nudging each other which almost ended up in me splashing water all over him. By the time we were done, Mum had retired into the living room.

"Thanks for dinner, Steph, it was lovely."

He dropped a kiss on her cheek.

"You're welcome. Don't keep my son up too late."

"You sure you're okay here by yourself, Mum?" I asked as I leant down to kiss her too.

She stroked my cheek before I pulled away.

"Of course, love. You go have fun. Don't mind me."

A part of me felt bad, but the other half knew Mum wanted me to live my life. It was our last year of school after this summer and I hoped to get the right A-Level grades so I could do graphic design at university.

On the way back to Aaron's, we discussed what films we wanted to watch and as soon as we got in, I went into the kitchen to dump the popcorn in the microwave.

"You want to watch downstairs or in my room?" Aaron asked from the doorway.

"Your room. I don't want to carry your arse to bed when you fall asleep."

He shot me a dirty look before disappearing upstairs. I shook my head. Nine times out of ten, he fell asleep during films and I always had to wake him up. He got grumpy whenever I did that, so one night, I'd hauled him over my shoulder. He'd woken up and asked me what the fuck I was doing. I'd dumped him on his bed and tucked him in, telling him if he was going to fall asleep like a baby, then I'd treat him like one. He'd called me a cock for that and kicked me out of his room. I usually slept in one of the guest rooms anyway when I was around his.

I took the popcorn upstairs and found him already laid out in shorts with his shirt off. Dumping the bowl down on the bed, I tugged off my t-shirt. I jumped on the bed next to him and dug my hand in the popcorn, stuffing some in my mouth.

"You sure you want a *Die Hard* marathon?"

"Fuck yeah. Let's watch some explosions."

He rolled his eyes before pressing play. The two of us spent the entire first film making fun of Alan Rickman's accent and guzzling the entire bowl of popcorn.

"Hey, open the window, it's fucking hot in here," he grumbled as he loaded up the next film.

I hopped off the bed and opened the windows.

"Take your shorts off then if you're too hot."

"Maybe I will."

I rolled my eyes and got back on the bed.

"Don't tell me you sleep naked when I'm not here. Is that why I'm always in the guest room?"

147

"What? No! Never!"

He said it a little too quickly and with alarm in his eyes.

"All right, calm down. I was joking."

His eyes roamed over my bare chest and my skin prickled. I didn't know why I kept having that feeling lately whenever I caught him staring at me, which was far more often than he realised.

"Going to get a drink, you want one?"

"Yeah, whatever you're having is fine."

He got off the bed and trudged out of the room. I laid back with my hands behind my head and stared up at his ceiling, trying to work out why every time Aaron and I were all alone like this, all I wanted to do was be much closer to him. When we were in public, I kept an appropriate distance, but as soon as we were behind closed doors, it was the way it had been when we were younger. Sometimes we'd hold each other's hands and hug a lot. It didn't feel weird or wrong. Being around Aaron was the most natural thing in the world.

Maybe I'd realised we were growing up and only people in relationships held hands and cuddled. Aaron and I were just friends. I didn't want us to change. Aaron was the only person I needed. He and I shared an irreplaceable bond.

"God, it's still fucking stuffy," he grumbled as he came back in the room with two glasses of iced water, popping them on the bedside table. "Going to put the fan on. Can't sleep like this."

"Who said anything about sleeping?"

"You and I both know I'll be out like a light half an hour into this."

I grinned, watching him flip the fan on and get back into bed. I handed him a glass and he put the next film on.

True to his word, Aaron fell asleep half an hour in. I turned the film off and lay there watching him. He looked so peaceful, as if he didn't have a care in the world. And I let my eyes roam across his perfect washboard stomach, taking in the light smattering of blonde hair right above the waistband of his shorts. It really didn't take a genius to work out why everyone was so enamoured with him. He was beautiful. Like he'd been carved out of marble by the gods.

I shook myself and got up off the bed, walking over to turn out the light. For a minute I contemplated going to the guest room. Something inside me wanted to be close to Aaron. So I turned around and got back into his bed. It was too hot for sheets, so I lay on top of the covers like him. And even though he was fast asleep, I reached over so I could entwine our fingers together. That simple touch helped me drift off despite the heat. I was safe next to him. I'd always be safe with Aaron, his beautiful blue-grey eyes and big heart. Always.

CHAPTER TWENTY

Rhys

I surfaced from a deep sleep, feeling groggy and in need of a drink. Why the hell was it so hot? And why was I awake? As much as I loved summer, it could also be stifling in the city. I swear we had the windows open and Aaron put the fan on last night so it should not be this hot.

I blinked, grumbling at the bright light burning my eyes. When I attempted to move, I found the reason I was roasting in my own skin. Aaron had curled himself around me in the night, his arm slung over my waist and his hand was very close to my morning wood. Not only that, I felt his pressed against me.

What the fuck?

I went very still, afraid of waking him up. It's not as if either of us could help it. I just needed his hand away from my dick. And I didn't want him getting embarrassed either.

This had never happened before. Whenever I fell asleep in his bed, he hadn't hugged me in our sleep, let alone wrapped himself around me, holding me close like he never wanted to let go.

What did I do? Move his hand? Wake him up?

I felt stupid and ridiculously horny at the same time. Being at Aaron's and in his bed meant I hadn't jacked off in a couple of days. This was my best friend, for fuck's sake. I should not be having this dilemma. We'd grown so close, we were completely comfortable around each other no matter the circumstances. Right now, I felt so far out of that zone, I had no idea what was up or down. The fact I could feel his hard dick against me wasn't something I'd ever prepared for.

"A… going to need you to wake up now," I grunted because there was no fucking way I could deal with this alone.

Except apparently hearing my voice in his sleep only made him cuddle me closer, his hand dipping lower and brushing against me. I almost died on the spot. Having anyone touch me other than myself was strange in itself, but it being him set all kinds of alarm bells off inside my head.

"Aaron, wake the fuck up," I all but squeaked at him.

He shifted against me.

"But you're so comfy," he mumbled sleepily.

Not helping. Your damn hand is touching my dick.

"You're not."

"Don't be so grumpy."

Did he have any idea what was happening right now or was he fucking with me? I wouldn't put it past him. He'd fucked with me on many, many occasions, but it had never involved us up close and personal with each other like this.

"You'd be grumpy too if you woke up with a furnace cuddling you." *Not to mention how my dick keeps twitching like crazy right now.*

He moved again and I practically choked on my breath. His body was pressed so tightly against mine, I would've had no idea where he ended and I began if I wasn't so very aware of his cock digging into me.

"Mmm, go back to sleep."

I couldn't believe what I was hearing. For a minute, I lay there in shock. How could he not know? It was pretty fucking obvious to me. Then I couldn't take it any longer.

"Aaron, if you don't get off me in ten seconds, I will throw you and your *hand* out the window."

He lifted his head from behind me.

"What do you mean my ha… oh shit."

He snatched his hand back away from my dick then he was off me and scrambling backwards until he almost fell off the bed. I flipped over on to my back, watching him silently.

"Holy shit, I'm so sorry. I had no idea." He scraped his hand over his face. "Jesus, I didn't mean to. Rhys, I really didn't…"

I put a hand up.

"It's okay."

Except it wasn't. His eyes fell on me and mine were on him. He seemed to be out of breath. There was also a clear indication of his arousal. I could only imagine what he was looking at. Neither of us spoke because what the fuck could we even say? This was weird, wasn't it? And why on earth could I not drag my eyes away?

I swallowed, knowing I had to do something. Anything to stop the weird feeling in my chest and my stomach… and lower. Forcing myself to sit up, I waved a hand at him.

"You were asleep and it's involuntary anyway, so don't worry about it."

He let out a nervous laugh.

"Uh, yeah, totally."

When his eyes darted away, I saw the lie in them. I didn't know how I felt about that, but given how uncomfortable he looked, I decided to drop it. Jumping up off the bed, I turned away and adjusted myself.

"I'm just going to… uh…"

I didn't finish my sentence, quick walking out of the room because this was fucking awkward and I didn't know what to do. Locking myself in the bathroom, I leant my head back against the door and took a few deep breaths. When I looked down at my dick, it was still hard as a rock.

"For fuck's sake," I muttered.

I pulled my shorts and boxers off before flipping on the shower, turning it to lukewarm since it was too hot for anything else. As I stood under the spray, my mind kept fixating on what just happened. On the feel of his very warm, hard body against mine. My hand pressed against the shower wall, body tensing as I tried to control my wayward thoughts.

Stop. Stop thinking about it. Do not think about what it would feel like if he had wrapped his hand around your cock just like you're doing now.

I shuddered, unable to help myself. Unable to prevent the raging cocktail of alien feelings brewing up a storm inside me.

Is this what lust and desire is meant to feel like?

I didn't have a fucking clue. All I knew was the urge to come pounded inside me and I could no more control the feeling nor stop it. I panted as I stroked myself. The memory of his touch played over and over in my head. I turned around, banging the back of my head against the wall to dislodge him from my brain, but nothing worked.

"Fuck," I breathed. "Fuck."

What the hell is happening to me?

I could see it now. Pinned to his bed staring up at him whilst he ground into me, sweat painting his chest and stomach, his eyes rolled back in ecstasy and bliss.

"Aaron," I whimpered as I erupted, the intense sensations slamming into me over and over until I could hardly hold myself up.

As the shower washed away the evidence, then came the crashing wave of sickening disgust. How could I think about him like that? How could I have a fucking wank over my best friend? It was all kinds of wrong. Everything about it felt so… wrong. I wanted to place the blame on me being horny as fuck. I wanted to so desperately, I pushed aside all the other emotions threatening to burst through.

It doesn't mean anything. It doesn't. You can't. It's not okay. You just needed to get off. That's all. That's it.

I was so fucked up. Why would I have those feelings towards him, of all people, when I never felt that way about anyone else?

155

I dragged a hand through my hair and forced those thoughts away. Dwelling on it wouldn't help me. Especially not when I had to go back out there and act normal. Act like he'd not touched my dick and made me feel things I'd never experienced before.

I could do that. For the sake of our friendship. I could. I had to. There was no other choice. Because ruining my friendship with Aaron would destroy me.

CHAPTER TWENTY ONE

Aaron

I sat there staring at his retreating back as he walked out of the room. There was absolutely no controlling my erratic breathing nor the way my heart pounded in my chest. And especially not how hard I was right then.

Holy shit. What the fuck just happened?

The last thing I remember was falling asleep during the film and then waking up to find myself wrapped around Rhys after having a vivid dream of the exact same scenario. Except in my dream, neither of us had been wearing clothes and I'd been… I stopped that line of thought immediately. I couldn't go there again.

Oh fuck, I touched him. I actually touched him.

No wonder he looked at me so strangely and then bolted from the room like I was a leper or something. I flopped back against the covers, folding a hand over my eyes and groaning.

Rhys and I had slept in the same bed countless times when we were kids. It's only in the past few years, we'd stopped doing it as if we'd both silently agreed after we'd hit puberty it was no longer an innocent thing childhood friends did. So why had he not gone to the guest room last night?

My chest ached with the need to make this all go away. I didn't want it to change our friendship or ruin anything. I could continue to live with the guilt of knowing I'd broken all the rules of our friendship by falling in love with him ten years ago. It's all that mattered. Keeping him close whilst also keeping him at arm's length. I couldn't live without Rhys. Couldn't fucking breathe if he wasn't there. So I'd told myself repeatedly, if I couldn't have him in the way I wanted, then I'd settle for having him as my friend. Having that part of Rhys was better than nothing at all.

I heard the shower flip on and groaned again.

Well, that's just fucking great. Now I know he's naked and that's… that's… fuck.

I raised my hand from my face and stared down at my cock. The memory of it pressed against the curve of his behind made it twitch. For so many years, I'd stopped myself short of fantasising about being inside him, but now I couldn't prevent the tidal wave of lust coursing through me. I wanted it so much, it fucking burnt. No one else made me feel this way. No one at all. And trust me, I'd fucking tried to look at other boys the way I did Rhys. I'd tried and failed.

I loved him. I was so fucking in love with Rhys King. All of him. Tearing him out of my heart would be utterly impossible. He'd buried himself so deep, latched onto every part of me as if his soul had banded around mine. I thought it might go away and I could write it off as a stupid childhood crush. Did it fuck! Every day it grew and grew until he'd infected my entire being.

I rubbed my chest, trying to stifle the wave of pain which came from knowing I'd lied to him for ten years. Every day those lies built until the guilt tore me apart on the inside.

It was that pain and guilt which thankfully drowned out the images in my head and finally made my dick go soft. I grabbed the glass of water on the bedside table and downed the rest of it. It was stale and warm from having sat there all night, but it quenched my dry mouth some. Then I got up and threw some clean clothes on.

I hadn't realised the shower shut off because if I had, then I'd have known he'd come back in here since that's where his clothes where. The moment he walked in with only a towel on, I froze on the spot. My eyes watched the water drip down from his wet hair and trail its way along his chest towards his stomach. I swallowed when my eyes hit the edge of the towel resting on his hips. All that pent-up lust I'd managed to get rid of came rushing back.

"I… I'm going to make breakfast, you want anything?"

His eyes were on mine, narrowing until they were almost slits. Rhys read me like an open book. The uncomfortableness of what happened between us hung in the air.

"Sure, whatever you're having is fine."

The word *fine* echoed in my ear. Nothing about this was fine. Nothing at all.

159

"Okay," I mumbled, looking away and walking past him, careful to avoid touching his bare skin.

I didn't know how to go back to before we'd woken up entangled together. Shouldn't it be something we could laugh off as a stupid accident?

I trudged downstairs, pulling open the fridge when I got to the kitchen. I grabbed the bacon and orange juice, dumping it out on the counter. Picking up the frying pan from the hanger, I popped it on the stove and turned the gas on. Next, I filled the kettle and stuck that on before grabbing plates, glasses and bread. I buttered four slices, then chucked the bacon in the pan.

The methodical way I went about making breakfast calmed my warring mind. It was the only way to get this shit out of my head. I was so lost in it, I barely registered footsteps behind me. A warm body pressed against my back as Rhys leant over my shoulder and stared down at the pan.

"Oh, you are a lifesaver. I'm fucking starved."

My body shook with the effort of trying to keep my emotions in check when he wrapped an arm around my chest and leant his chin on my shoulder.

"We're okay, A. Let's not make this shit into a bigger deal than it should be."

I let out a shaky breath.

"Yeah."

He gripped me tighter, pressing his face against my neck which made my pulse go wild.

"I need you and me to be normal," he whispered against my skin. "I *need* this to be normal. You forget I can't be without you?"

"N...No."

How could I ever forget it? The two of us were the world to each other. He ended where I began and vice versa.

"Then answer me this one question."

"Anything... you know that."

I would live and die for him. Rhys was the only person I needed more than life itself.

"As much as I hate bringing the prick up, you never deny it when Valentine accuses us of being gay. So I need you to tell me if it's true or not. Are you?"

I swallowed and leant my chin on his head. I'd never admitted it out loud to anyone else before. Tamara had suspected it the entire time we'd known each other, but she'd never pushed me to tell her.

"It doesn't matter to me either way," he continued. "It'll never make me see you any differently or care about you any less, if that worries you at all."

Reaching up, I laid my hand against his and squeezed it. I'd never been able to deny Rhys anything before. And I wasn't about to start now.

"Yes," I croaked out, my voice all shaky. "I am."

He kept his arm around me for a long moment and the only sound was the bacon sizzling in the pan. His breath fluttered across my skin, then he was gone, walking over to the kettle and pouring the water into the two mugs I'd set out.

"Don't burn the bacon."

Is that it?

I shook myself and flipped it over because as much as I loved crispy bacon, I didn't dig burnt at all. Eying Rhys out of the corner of my eye, he seemed relaxed and utterly unaffected by my confession. Did I ever really think he'd react otherwise? Rhys wasn't the type to judge me for anything. He'd accept it all no matter what.

When I finished our breakfast, complete with ketchup, I set both plates on the kitchen island. Rhys sat on one of the stools, having poured us both orange juice and made tea. I took a seat next to him and stuffed my sandwich in my mouth, watching him do the same.

"What do you fancy doing today?" he asked when he'd swallowed his mouthful. I tried to tell myself I hadn't watched his throat working, but it was an absolute blatant lie.

"Getting the fuck out of this place."

He raised a dark eyebrow. His damp hair curled on top of his head in those delicious waves. I struggled to control the urge to run my fingers through it nor to not think about how I'd grip it in my fist whilst I covered his body from behind.

Just cut it out already.

"And go where?"

"I don't know. We could go for a drive." Then the perfect idea occurred to me. "Let's go down the coast, hey? It's a nice day. It'd be like a road trip."

"What like Brighton?"

I nodded. We could go on the pier and play in the arcades like we had done when we were kids and Tamara took us down there for the day.

"Yeah, like old times."

He leant over to me with a twinkle in his eyes.

"And overspend on Daddy's credit card?"

I grinned.

"Like he gives a shit."

My dad might not do much for me other than demand I follow the path he and Mum had set out, but he had given me a credit card without a limit when I'd turned sixteen. Not that I ever went crazy with it. It was for me to live on since they had left me to fend for myself after they let Maritza go.

"You're on."

"Eat up and then we'll get going."

If there was any way for us to go back to normal, it was to do something fun and reckless together. Going somewhere no one knew us and we could be just Aaron and Rhys. No expectations. No parents. Nothing.

So despite the shit from this morning, I felt excited and full of nervous energy. Rhys and I were going to have the best day. I could feel it in my bones.

CHAPTER TWENTY TWO

Rhys

O n the drive, we'd rolled the windows down and blasted music out of the speakers, singing out of tune at the top of our voices. We'd stuck our arms out the windows, laughing as if nothing weird had happened between us this morning. As much as I tried to forget it, I couldn't. Especially not now he'd admitted the truth regarding his sexuality to me. It opened up entirely new possibilities I wasn't comfortable thinking about.

The two of us walked along the beachfront with Mr Whippy ice creams in our hands, grinning to each other. The beach was packed with people drinking, sunbathing and some braving the sea. It reminded me of more innocent times when we were young, running along the pebbles with Tamara chasing after us.

"You've got ice cream on your nose," Aaron said, pointing at me.

"What?"

I looked down to find him painting some on there with his finger. So I dug my finger in mine and dabbed it on his cheek.

"Oh no, my finger slipped."

He slapped my arm and wiped it off as I brushed my nose with my hand. When our arms dropped, our fingers brushed together sending a strange jolt up my arm. Aaron had always been the only one except for my mum I accepted any kind of physical contact from. Mostly it made me uncomfortable with someone I didn't know. Not with him though. So having these weird feelings extend to small touches bothered me somewhat.

"Dick," he muttered.

"You started it."

"Mmm, and I'll finish it if you're not careful."

I moved my ice cream away before he could make a grab for it, knowing exactly what he intended. Then I wrapped an arm around his shoulder, hugging him closer. He let out a long breath, his body almost melting against mine.

"What should we do now?"

"We totally need to go change up all this money I have burning a hole in my pocket and play the 2p machines."

"And lose it all before we win anything?"

"You know it."

We raced each other up the beachfront towards the pier, trying not to drop our ice creams. A few people stared at us, but neither Aaron nor I cared. Here we could be whoever we wanted. And right now, we were choosing to be two teenage boys having a laugh with each other.

We'd finished our ice creams by the time we got up to the pier and Aaron changed up our coins.

"You think your dad will notice the charges?" I asked as he dropped pennies into the slot whilst I leant up against the glass.

"He doesn't check up on me. That would require him actually caring what I do outside of getting good grades."

Patrick Parrish was a certified arsehole. He looked down on me as if I was a piece of dirt on his shoe and hardly treated Aaron any better. I was glad his parents rarely showed up. Too busy jet-setting around the world now Kellie Parrish was an in-demand director. Her fame had blown up over the past few years, making her a household name. They never talked about Aaron to the media so anything we did together wouldn't get reported on. Aaron had grown up without the spotlight on him because the only good thing Kellie had done was to maintain his privacy.

"I'll try to make sure we don't get arrested for dumb shit since he's not around to bail us out."

Aaron scoffed and rolled his eyes.

"As if. We've never even nicked sweets from the corner shop."

I grinned. Aaron and I were good boys. Probably too good. We never got into trouble if we could help it. The only time we'd gone to the headmaster's office when we were at primary was because Valentine had socked me in the jaw for being in the way. Aaron had almost got suspended for defending me. He'd kneed Valentine in the balls and I'd had to stop him from kicking the prick in the stomach whilst he was down. From then on, his parents had told him if he ever did anything like that again, they'd rip him out of school. It was shit when they sent him to a different secondary to me. A blatant move to stop us from hanging out so much. Pity for them, we'd found our own ways to, regardless.

"Goodie two-shoes Aaron and Rhys are too innocent for such atrocious acts."

"We'd have got in so much trouble with my dad."

"You would. He'd have more excuses to hate me because you know I'm such a bad influence on his son."

I turned towards the machine next to his and started dumping coins in when he didn't respond. I hadn't done anything other than be born to poor working-class parents and live on a shitty council estate. If those were my only crimes then it was absolute bullshit. Fuck Patrick Parrish and his haughty attitude. He thought he was better than me having come from money. No, he was a conceited arsehole who thought money and status ran the world. He didn't give a shit about Aaron's feelings or what he wanted to do with his life.

"You're not a bad influence. You're the best friend I could ever have. The only friend."

Aaron had other friends before me, but once we met, we became inseparable. No matter how much his parents encouraged him to meet other people, he ignored them, giving all of his attention to me. He told me once it was because I'd given him all of me and it meant more to him than anyone else ever could.

"Lucky for you we promised we'd be best friends for life."

I saw him smiling out of the corner of my eye. And those dimples I'd wound him up about yesterday were pronounced. I felt bad about it now considering I'd been taunting him about girls when he wasn't interested in them at all. So many things about him made sense now in light of his confession. The way he'd be very polite towards the girls in our class when we were at primary but never gave them the time of day. How he'd laugh it off whenever anyone talked about them in a sexual context. And I never brought it up as I didn't know what to say. I didn't feel any kind of way about boys or girls.

I felt broken sometimes. Like I wasn't normal because I didn't experience attraction. Not how I'd heard it described by others anyway. It wasn't until today. This morning. When my best friend had touched me. And then it all became very, very clear even if I'd tried to deny it. That word. Attraction. Finally made fucking sense to me.

So why the fuck did it have to be him who made me feel it?

I shoved those thoughts back in the box they belonged in. I'd told myself already, Aaron and I were friends. Nothing more.

"The luckiest," he whispered, nudging my shoulder with his.

Reaching up, I ruffled his hair which made him scowl and shove me, almost knocking my cup of 2p's out of my hand.

"Hey, careful."

"Would serve you right."

He smoothed his hair back down, perfecting the windswept look he seemed to keep these days. His blonde hair glinted in the lights of the arcades, his blue-grey eyes shining as he glanced at me. Those damn eyes. The window to his feelings, his emotions, his soul. And what a fucking beautiful soul it was.

"We going to finish up here and go on the teacup ride?"

"Hell yes," he replied, slamming more pennies into the slot in a rush.

I laughed and shook my head. Even though it was for kids, neither of us cared. Aaron's enthusiasm for everything had always been infectious.

The two of us quickly went through all our coins, winning very little before he took me by the hand and dragged me out the arcade and down towards the rides. I swallowed hard when he didn't let go of my hand, glancing back at me with excitement written all over his features.

He bought us some ride passes before we lined up, grinning the entire time like this was the most exciting thing we'd done in forever. The ride attendant gave us sceptical looks before we got on, but we ignored him. We laughed as it went around and around, egging each other on to spin faster. I'm sure we would have got kicked off if a child hadn't started crying about wanting to get out of the teacup and their parent had to pin them down in the seat.

Aaron rested his head on my shoulder when our laughter had died down, glancing up at me with wide eyes.

"What?"

His lip quirked up at the side.

"Just remembering all the times we made Tamara go on this over and over."

"She hated it."

"So true, we drove her crazy. It's a wonder she ever brought us back."

"She wanted to make you happy."

His eyes grew sad and it tore at me. Aaron had been really cut up when Tamara left to go live with her boyfriend as he'd asked her to marry him. He'd really loved her. I lifted my arm and wrapped it around his shoulder, tugging him closer.

"She never cared about us being inseparable, not like Mum and Dad do. They're arseholes about it."

"Didn't stop us though."

"Nothing ever could. Don't care what they say. Me and you are forever."

"Forever," I echoed, feeling the word tug at my heart.

CHAPTER TWENTY THREE

Aaron

I t'd got late, like past ten. The sun had set finally almost an hour ago. Rhys and I hadn't wanted to leave. The two of us spent the day in the arcades and rides on the pier before we'd laid out on the beach together with bottles of Dr Pepper and watched the beachgoers. Then we'd got fish and chips for dinner. It'd been the best day we'd had in a long time.

The two of us strolled along the promenade away from the bars and clubs where it was quiet. We could hear the sounds in the distance but I focused on the sea crashing against the pebbles.

"Did you manage to get sunburn? I thought you put enough cream on," he said, prodding my arm which stung a little.

"You know I'm a pasty white boy, unlike you."

"Aww, poor baby. Don't worry, I promise to lather you up in after-sun when we get back."

I shivered at the thought of his hands all over me.

"I can do it myself," I muttered.

No need to have temptation knocking at my door. Especially not after this morning. That would be a complete disaster in the making.

"You sure you can reach everywhere?"

"Oh haha, fuck off."

I shoved him and he shoved me back. I nudged him in the ribs so he retaliated by grabbing me around the neck, pushing me down and digging his knuckles into my head.

"Get off," I grunted, trying to push him away whilst laughter bubbled up from my chest.

"You know you can't take me. Don't even know why you still try."

"Rhys!"

It only made him dig his fingers in harder. I grabbed him around the waist and pinched his side, making him squeal. He tried to pull away, but I held on tight, digging my fingers into his ribs until he let me go. I rubbed my head whilst he rubbed his side.

"Are we even now?" I asked, watching him warily.

"Fuck yeah, that hurt."

I stuck my tongue out at him and strolled away with my hands in my pockets. He caught up to me quickly, wrapping an arm around my shoulder and nudging his head against mine.

"It's so much more peaceful out here. Not like at home. We can even see the stars properly."

He pointed up at the sky. I tipped my head back, watching them twinkling above us. There was still a ton of light pollution, but it wasn't as bad as London. Even so, we could see so many up there in the sky and it struck me how beautiful it all was.

"Pretty."

He dropped his arm from my shoulder and grabbed my hand, dragging me towards the pebbles.

"What are you doing?"

I shivered. Now night had fallen, it was getting cold.

"Just come on."

I let him drag me down the beach. He stopped and practically threw himself on the stones, laying back with his hands under his head. I stared at him for a long moment.

"Rhys?"

He patted the stones next to him.

"Lie down and look at the sky with me."

"Are you sure that's comfortable?"

"Aaron, just do it."

How could I say no? Especially not when he used my full name. I lay next to him, propping my head up with my hands. The pebbles dug into my back and were cold, but I ignored it. If I was with Rhys, it didn't matter. I'd go anywhere and do anything with him.

The gentle lap of the waves and the tide were the only sounds we heard for several long minutes. Rhys was right. It was peaceful. And we were all alone here, far enough away from the main drag of the promenade. No one would disturb us.

"You remember when we made that stupid pact when we were eleven and your parents decided you weren't going to the same secondary as me?"

His voice startled me, breaking through the silence.

"The one where we promised if we were ever separated permanently, we'd run away together and live our lives out by the ocean?"

"Yeah, that one… I don't know why we made it. Not like we've ever been separated. You promised you'd never leave me."

"I won't."

I had no reason to. I felt as though I would die on the inside if I wasn't with him. Maybe that's how you were supposed to feel when you loved someone as much as I did him. Letting go of Rhys wasn't an option.

"And we made it because we were scared my parents would find a way to keep us apart for good."

The day I'd realised they were trying to stop me from spending time with Rhys, I'd run away from the house and caught the bus by myself. We'd hauled up in his room, hugging each other until my mum had come to get me. I think that was the day she realised the lengths I'd go to be near Rhys. So even though I'd been grounded for two weeks, the moment my incarceration had been lifted, I begged Maritza to take me around Rhys' house. And when she drove me there, the two of us had sat out in his overgrown back garden and made that pact.

Rhys reached over and grabbed my hand, entwining his fingers with mine.

"Too bad for them we were wise to their intentions."

I swallowed, my skin tingling where our hands were joined. As much as I wanted things to go back to normal after this morning, I wasn't sure they could. Something between me and Rhys had shifted. I could see it when I looked in his dark eyes. There was a layer of emotion I didn't recognise. And I'd thought I'd seen Rhys display every emotion imaginable to me.

"At least your mum likes me."

"As if anyone could not like you, A. You're like Prince Charming on steroids. People flock to you... don't think they can help themselves."

Wasn't the first time he'd said something like that. I couldn't see it myself. I didn't do anything special other than being nice to those around me. A little kindness went a long way in this fucked up world. What was the point in being mean and nasty? Didn't do anyone any favours, least of all myself.

"Valentine hates me."

"No, he hates me. He just tolerates you. There's a difference."

"He's a prick."

"Too fucking right. I wish that prick would fuck off permanently. Why he even still seeks us out is a mystery."

Who knew? His dad still worked for mine, but I'd long since made it clear I wanted nothing to do with his son. Especially after I got in trouble for kicking Valentine in the balls. Prick deserved it a thousand times over.

"He likes to torment us for sport."

"Still think he should grow up. He's twenty years old. Surely he's got better shit to do."

"That would imply he has a life, which he doesn't."

Rhys winced.

"Ouch!"

"He's a waste of oxygen."

"A cretin."

I snorted, laughter bubbling up from my chest and spilling out.

"Are we coming up with shite insults for him now?"

"Hey, that was a good one. He is a fucking cretin."

He slapped me with his free hand on the shoulder so I slapped him back. Next thing I knew he was practically on top of me, his fingers digging into my ribs as he tickled the shit out of me.

"Ah, fuck, stop it," I almost screeched.

"Not until you admit it was the best insult ever."

"Fuck no!"

Rhys only tickled me harder. I tried to push him off me, the two of us struggling for dominance which only had us both laughing and gasping for breath after a few minutes. It's at that moment we both heard the rumble of thunder and then the heavens erupted.

"Fuck!"

The downpour was torrential within seconds. Lightning streaked across the sky, lighting up the sea as the storm raged above us. Rhys got up, unsteady on his feet and put a hand out to me. He dragged me up when I put my hand in his and the two of us ran hand in hand towards the promenade, both laughing as the rain drenched us to the bone.

"Jesus, this wasn't fucking forecast."

We reached the wall and huddled next to each other, shivering, the rain continuing to hammer down around us.

"We're going to have to run back to the car."

Rhys stared at me as I rubbed my arms. His dark eyes held something which made me swallow hard. My clothes were plastered against my skin as were his. His dark hair had fallen in his face, driving me to want to push it back. I couldn't help staring because I'd already seen him wet this morning after his shower. And the memory of being pressed up against him surfaced, making me very aware of how close we were standing.

Even though we were both cold, his breath came fast and his hands fisted and un-fisted at his sides. My eyes went to his mouth and the urge drove through me. The urge to press against him. To feel him everywhere.

"A..." he breathed out.

Hearing my name on his lips. Watching him say it. It had me in knots. Absolute fucking knots. I couldn't do this any longer. I couldn't pretend. My heart hammered so hard against my chest, drowning out everything else.

I wanted Rhys King so much, I could no longer think straight.

My hands came up, gripping his face before I pushed him back against the sea wall. He stared at me, eyes wide and breathing as erratic as mine.

"Aaron..."

The way he said my name this time drove me. It was almost like a plea. A desperate all-consuming plea.

And there, with lightning flashing around us, thunder rumbling in the distance and the rain pouring down hard, I pressed forward, planting my mouth on his and sealing away anything else either of us had to say.

CHAPTER TWENTY FOUR

Rhys

The pounding of my heart echoed in my ears over and over. Aaron kissed me. Aaron had actually kissed me. His hands were on my face. His mouth on mine. His body pressed against me. I had no idea what the fuck was happening or how we'd even got here. It seemed so surreal. There we'd been laughing and joking with each other. Then the fucking downpour started and now this. Us. Kissing. Because I wasn't standing there doing nothing. No, my mouth was moving against his as my hands came up and gripped his waist because I felt like I was capsizing and needed something to hold on to. Desperately.

I didn't even know if we were doing this right either. Neither of us had kissed anyone before. And I had no idea why I was kissing him back. Why wave after wave of lust drove through me, stealing away all of my self-control.

His hands gripped my face harder, pushing my head back against the wall as if he didn't want me to go anywhere. As if I could. My limbs felt paralysed. My whole body drowned in him. In Aaron. My fucking best friend.

The next thing I knew, he'd pulled back, putting inches between us, staring at me with wide eyes. As if he couldn't believe he'd just kissed me. And I'd kissed him back. His eyes flicked down to my mouth and back.

I don't know who moved first this time, but our mouths fused together again. And our hands grasped each other like we couldn't get enough.

"Rhys," he moaned against my mouth like a prayer.

The rain continued to beat down on the pavement, but it was like neither of us noticed. He felt so warm against me despite the cold. I wanted him closer. I needed it. Needed him.

His tongue pressed against the seal of my mouth, demanding I give him more. The moment I relented, it was a clash of tongues and lips. Messy and completely insane. Perhaps we'd both lost our minds. Today had been so full of emotions. From this morning where he'd made me feel things I shouldn't about him by accidentally touching me in his sleep. Me masturbating over him in the shower and the sense of nostalgia I'd felt all day as we traipsed around Brighton. So who the fuck knew what was up or down any longer.

All I knew is Aaron felt very right against me. That was up until I realised I was getting hard and so was he. The painful reminder we were supposed to be friends. Best friends didn't kiss each other. Best friends didn't cling to each other and lose all sense of control. Best friends shouldn't be rubbing their hard cocks against each other.

So I shoved him back away from me, breaking that insane kiss and our bodies grinding against each other.

"What the fuck?" I ground out.

He blinked. The rain had plastered his hair against his head. No doubt we both looked like drowned rats with swollen mouths right then.

"I… I… I don't know."

"No, seriously, Aaron, what the fuck was that?"

I shouldn't be getting pissed off at him. I'd actively participated in the kiss, but I couldn't deal with the emotions rushing through me at an alarming pace. I couldn't cope. Nothing about this was anything but complicated. And we couldn't be doing this. Kissing each other. It was just plain fucking wrong.

"I don't know."

"You don't know? You kissed me!"

He took a step back, putting his hands up.

"I know."

"That's not a fucking explanation. Why? Why would you…? You're supposed to be my friend. What the hell is wrong with you?"

He flinched, rubbing his hand over his arm.

"I'm sorry, I… I don't know what just happened."

I ran my hands through my wet hair. The cold seeped into my bones, making me tremble. Us standing in the rain wasn't helping this situation one bit.

"Stop saying you don't know. What made you think it was okay to kiss me, huh? Like I don't get it, A. I don't."

I didn't want him to think I wasn't okay with him being gay. So no matter what, I would not bring it up. It wasn't about that anyway. This was about him kissing me out of the blue.

Did he like me in that way? And if so, how long? God, how fucking long had he harboured secret feelings towards me?

The thought of it made my stomach roil in protest.

"I'm sorry," he whispered. "I'm sorry, please don't hate me."

I could hardly stand to look at him right then. Seeing the abject misery and agony in his eyes cleaved me in two. I couldn't stand the pain I saw there. The last thing I'd ever wanted to do was cause him pain.

"Let's just fucking go. I'm cold and… and I want to go home."

I wanted to be alone to process this. To try to understand what happened. The two of us were never supposed to kiss. Never. It didn't work like that, did it? We were friends. Best friends. We had been for ten years and yet Aaron had thrown fucking acid all over it by kissing me. By turning our friendship into something else. Something I wasn't remotely prepared for.

"Okay," he replied in a small voice, looking like he wanted to throw up.

I couldn't stand to see him that way, so I turned and started walking back the way we'd come. It took us fifteen minutes to get back to the car. We'd been absolutely drenched by the rain so Aaron whacked the heating up high before we set off.

"Rhys—"

"Don't. Just don't. I don't want to talk about it."

I didn't know what the fuck to say. He'd not told me why and at this point, I wasn't sure I wanted to know either. It didn't help that it kept replaying in my head over and over again. The press of his body against mine. The way he'd taken complete control despite being the smaller of the two of us in terms of body mass. We'd become evenly matched in height over the years since I shot up when I'd turned fifteen. It reminded me of the way I'd thought about him in the shower this morning. How I'd wanted him to pin me down and take me. I looked out of the car window, trying to shove those images away from my brain. This whole thing was absolutely fucked up on every level.

By the time we pulled up at my house, it was almost midnight. Mum would be in bed by now and she probably expected me to crash at Aaron's again. I hadn't told her where we were going today. She'd got used to me disappearing for days on end to avoid Graham.

My hand was on the door handle when his voice made me freeze.

"Rhys, we need to talk about what happened."

I turned my head towards him, meeting his eyes finally. Those blue-grey eyes which had the ability to destroy me with one look. And it was the exact look he had in them right then. My heart burnt a hole in my chest. I wanted to crush him to me and shove him away in the same breath.

"No. No, we really don't, A. I don't know why the fuck you even entertained the idea that was remotely okay nor do I

185

really even give a shit right now. Just… just stay away from me."

It broke my damn soul to say those words. I turned away, but not before I saw his heart break in front of my eyes. I had the door open and was out of the car, slamming it shut. As I strode away towards the house, I heard the other car door open.

"Please, Rhys, please don't walk away from me."

I stiffened but kept walking, digging my house key out of my pocket.

"Rhys, please, let me explain."

I didn't want to hear it. I didn't want him to tell me he had feelings for me. I didn't want him to ruin our friendship. The can of worms he'd open up with that… well… we wouldn't be able to stuff them back in again.

"Rhys!"

"Go home, Aaron."

I unlocked my front door, wrenched it open and slammed it shut behind me. Then I slid down it and scraped my hands across my face before I buried it in my knees.

"What the fuck?" I whispered.

My entire world collapsed before my eyes. Aaron kissing me? Well, that had just fucked with me completely. But that wasn't everything… not by a long fucking shot. No, the icing on the cake? I'd kissed him back. And I had no fucking clue how to feel about any of it at all.

CHAPTER TWENTY FIVE

Aaron

I spent the night tossing and turning, kicking myself over and over for the stupid decision I'd made. Rhys was right to be angry. Right to be pissed off and refusing to talk to me. And yet it didn't stop the pain radiating out of my chest and destroying me from the inside out.

Why did I do it? And why did it feel so goddamn fucking right?

I don't even know how I got home last night. Tears had blurred my vision the whole way, streaming down my cheeks as I drove. Probably good it was late and the roads weren't busy. As soon as I got in the house, I stripped off my still damp clothes and jumped in the shower, letting the hot water warm me up. And wash away the horrific beauty of the kiss and his touch from my skin. I'd thrown myself in bed after, not bothering with clothes and hugged the pillow where he'd slept the night before to my chest. It smelt of him. And it made me break down all over again, sobbing into it, the noise echoing in my ears.

When my tears dried up, I put my fingers to my lips. The memory of his against them assaulted all my senses. Heat blossomed across my skin. It had been everything and more. Electrifying me. Bringing vivid colour into my world. Making me feel alive.

My first ever kiss had simultaneously been the very best and absolute worst experience of my life. Kissing Rhys King was like kissing a god. Getting shouted at by him for it afterwards annihilating me.

After everything we'd been through together, I should've known better than to spring it on him like that. He deserved better. So much better. I should've told him the truth. That I loved him. And I wanted to be more than just his friend. But no, instead of calmly explaining my feelings towards him like the rational adult thing to do, I'd gone with my hormones and thrown myself at him.

What a fucking idiot.

I had no idea what time it was when the doorbell went. Groaning and scrubbing my eyes, I got up, feeling dead on my feet as I pulled on a t-shirt, boxers and a pair of shorts. I trudged downstairs wondering who the hell was disturbing me. When I wrenched the door open, my heart dropped out from underneath me.

"R…Rhys?"

He ignored me, pushing past and flying into my house. I barely had a chance to blink before I rushed after him, shoving the door shut.

"Rhys!"

"I came to get my shit, that's it. We are not okay, Aaron, not okay at all."

He stomped up the stairs with me trailing after him.

"We need to talk."

"No, we really don't."

When we reached the landing, I grabbed his arm and spun him around to face me. He looked at my hand like it'd scorched him. The dark circles under his eyes had me thinking he must not have slept either. It shattered my already broken heart further. I'd caused that agony. I'd done this to us.

"Please let me explain."

Shaking me off, he strode away towards my room. Half his stuff he'd left around here was in there and the rest in the guest room.

"Rhys, just two minutes, please."

"No."

All I knew was I had to stop him leaving. Had to stop him walking out the door on us. On our friendship. On ten years of us being together like we were supposed to be. Because fuck, Rhys and I were meant for each other and I didn't care what anyone else had to say about it. He was it for me. He always had been. No one else could ever replace the boy in front of me.

I stood in the doorway of my room, watching him pace about grabbing various items of clothing. I took a deep breath.

I had to be a man and own up to my feelings towards him. There was no other way I could get him to stop this madness.

"Rhys… I love you."

He froze in place, his entire body going rigid at my words.

"What did you just say to me?" he choked out, his voice vibrating with repressed emotion.

I didn't want to say it to his back again so I stalked into the room and rounded him. His eyes were so dark, they were almost black. He blinked when I came into view. I got up in his personal space, forcing him to meet my eyes.

"I love you."

His mouth opened and closed like he couldn't believe what I'd said.

"You asked me why yesterday. Why I kissed you. That's why… I'm in love with you."

His eyes flicked down to my mouth and then back up to my eyes. The silence between us widened until it felt like he would never speak. I couldn't read his emotions like normal. He'd locked all of it down tight.

"Fuck you, Aaron," he practically spat before turning away to walk out of the room.

I couldn't let him do that. The reason being I'd felt his desperation when he'd kissed me back last night. I felt every ounce of need pulsing inside him because I knew Rhys like the back of my damn hand. I wouldn't allow him to walk out on us as, on some level, he wanted me too. And he had to damn well face up to it.

I curled my hand around his wrist and tugged him back. Reaching out, I grabbed his other wrist and shoved him towards the wall until his back hit it. Rhys could easily overpower me and put a stop to this but for some reason, he didn't. He stared at me wide-eyed whilst I pinned his hands to the wall by his head and leaned in close.

"You do not get to walk away from me again, Rhys, you hear me? Do not fucking walk out on us."

He swallowed then nodded slowly.

Why did this make me feel so… good? I should be dying on the inside and to some extent I was, but having him pinned against the wall, him allowing me to be in control when he didn't have to stirred my senses. Before I knew what I was doing, I'd ran my nose up his cheek causing him to let out a little pant. The noise the same as last night when I pulled back the first time our lips had fused together.

"I love you."

"Stop saying that," his words tumbled out on a ragged breath.

"Why? It's the truth. Does it scare you? Does me loving you make you afraid?"

"Yes."

His body trembled. I could feel it where my hands were holding his wrists. And I wanted to make his fear go away. Remind him of why the two of us never had to be afraid of each other.

"Tell me why."

"You're my best friend, A. This isn't how it's supposed to happen. I told you yesterday I needed us to be normal. And then you bloody kissed me, now everything is fucked up. I'm a mess and I can't do this. I just… can't. I… I'm so confused."

I let go of one of his hands so I could stroke his cheek. He didn't move it. He kept it there as if I was still pinning him down. As if he was afraid taking it away from the wall would mean it landed on me. I pressed my cheek to his free one, needing his touch so badly. Needing the physical connection between us.

"You kissed me back."

"I know."

"You don't have to be scared. You're safe with me. You always have been. I promised you I'd never leave, that I'd protect you. Let me be here for you. Let me be your shield and cover you when you're feeling lost and in the dark. Let me take care of you. You need me as much as I need you. So don't fight me."

He shuddered. I knew what he needed. What both of us needed. We were exhausted and wrung out from what happened. So I did what I had to. Pulling him away from the wall, I walked him over to my bed. Rhys stared at me as I pulled his t-shirt off him followed by his shorts. I pushed him down on the bed, making him kick off his flip-flops. Then I tugged off my clothes, leaving us both in boxer shorts. I got in bed next to him, covering us with the sheets before I cradled him against my chest, stroking his hair and feeling sleep drag at my senses.

"What are you doing?" he whispered.

"Giving you what you need. Go to sleep, I'll keep you safe."

The moment I felt him relax was when I knew he'd given in. No matter how angry, confused and upset he was, he still needed me. His arm curled around me, his hand resting on my back. I kept stroking his hair until his breathing turned steady and even, fluttering across my chest with the rise and fall of his ribcage.

"I've got you," I whispered against his hair as I buried my face in it. "I love you. I love you so fucking much. Please don't leave me. Please don't let go of us. I'll beg if I have to. Just stay right here, Rhys. Stay with me forever… and let me love you."

CHAPTER TWENTY SIX

Rhys

I didn't know what came over me when I got up this morning. Just the driving need to put an end to this torment inside me. It built and built until I couldn't think straight any longer. Sleep hadn't come at all. Not even after I had a long, very hot shower and fell into bed, feeling like absolute shit. A huge piece of me had gone missing and I knew exactly where to find it. Maybe it's why I'd jumped on the bus at some stupidly early hour of the morning and gone over to his. I'd told myself I needed my things as an excuse, but it wasn't true. I wanted to see him. Aaron was the very air I breathed into my lungs time and time again.

He was right. I needed him. It was only now I realised how much. Now when everything was a mess. My feelings and emotions were all over the place. I didn't understand myself. Didn't understand this sudden wave of attraction and need I felt towards him.

Why is it him? It makes no sense. I've never wanted anyone. Not like this.

I needed him to take it away for me. To be my shield like he said he'd be. I sure as hell couldn't sort out the complicated mess by myself. And I couldn't process what he'd said either. The part where he'd told me he was in love with me. That just about broke my already fractured mind completely.

I woke up still pressed against his chest, our bodies so tightly joined together I didn't know where I ended and he began. Turning my head up, I found his eyes closed with his lips parted, breathing steady. I don't know what came over me when I reached up and brushed the pads of my fingers across his bottom lip. Perhaps I needed to remind myself they were real and they'd been against me yesterday, kissing without restraint. With so much passion and fury it almost burnt me to a crisp despite the fact we'd been standing in the pouring rain.

This beautiful boy who'd befriended me. Who'd torn me out of my locked cage and set me free. Given me everything. He saw me as something more. He… loved me.

My fingers were still on his lip when his eyes opened. Those blue-grey eyes stealing my ability to breathe. His hand captured mine, holding it in place before he kissed the pads of my fingers one by one. My heart slammed against my ribcage. All of my senses became attuned to him. To the way he looked at me as he did it. Daring me to stop him. The heat simmering in them set my blood on fire.

He pulled my hand away from his mouth, not stopping for a second as he slowly bent his head down towards me. I sucked in air, unable to move or stop what was about to happen. He gave me all the time in the world to do so. Each inch of distance he closed felt like an eternity. Letting go of my hand, his closed around my face right before his lips pressed to mine.

Everything about it was soft, gentle and completely overwhelming. His eyes were still open, staring into mine. His tongue snaked out, licking, sucking and nibbling my bottom lip in a manner so sensual, I almost died on the spot. And I couldn't prevent the whimper from escaping my throat either.

The noise made me bold. My hand tangled in his hair, pulling him closer so he'd kiss me harder. Kiss me the way he had done last night. I needed him to drown out the chatter in my head. To show me what it meant to be loved by him. To piece together all the broken pieces of me. God, I just fucking well needed him. So desperately. I wanted Aaron to do things to me. To… *take* me.

My eyes fluttered closed. The rushing noise of my blood pounding surrounded me. The sensation of his mouth moving against mine, his tongue delving into my mouth and devouring me only made my fingers tighten in his hair. Everything about Aaron was hard. His body a solid force against mine, his edges digging into me. And I revelled in it. The feel of him. The touch of him. The taste of him. I let myself be open to the possibility in that heated moment between us. His teeth grazed against my bottom lip, sending sparks running down my spine.

"A, please," I whispered on a shaky breath.

In response, he only kissed me harder. I wasn't sure what I even wanted from him. What I was asking for. He seemed to know. He seemed to recognise whatever I was begging for. The hand around my face drifted down my shoulder, stroking along my bare side, making me shudder. Sinking between us, he flattened it against the hard planes of my stomach. Why did his touch make my skin burn? Why did everything about him drive me absolutely fucking crazy?

The moan erupting from me when his hand dipped below my boxers and circled itself around my cock scared the life out of me. It sounded so guttural. So unlike me in every single way. Not least of all because I hadn't noticed how hard I'd grown from kissing him.

"Rhys," he groaned, his hand slowly stroking up and down my dick, making my toes curl. "Touch me."

The command in his voice made my nerve endings go haywire. And the feeling of his cock thrusting against my hip as he stroked me had me losing all sense of rationality.

"What?" I spluttered whilst he kissed his way down my jaw.

His tongue curled around the back of my ear, making me twitch.

"Touch me."

I had a pretty good idea of where he wanted my hand. Even so, it terrified me. He might be touching me, but I didn't know if I could reciprocate when all my feelings were so tangled up. My hand left his hair and ran down his side, curling around his hip, encouraging his thrusts against me. His hand tightened around me, stroking harder as if he knew exactly how to drive me higher.

"Those sounds you make are so fucking sexy. Do you like this? Huh? Do you want me to make you come? Tell me, Rhys. Tell me to make you feel good."

The only response I could come up with was another whimper which had him panting in my ear. Something about the noise only made me harder. My cock pulsed in his hand. All my pent-up lust had spilt out all over the place. There was no denying it. Aaron turned me on. Especially this side of him. The demanding one. Pushing me beyond my limits and forcing me to open up to him.

"Please."

"Say. It."

"Make me come, A," I whispered, almost unable to believe I'd uttered those words aloud.

"With fucking pleasure."

Next thing I knew, he'd tore his hand out of my boxers and pulled them halfway down my thighs. Then he grabbed my hand and shoved it inside his clothes, making me curl it around his cock. I trembled at the feel of him.

"You're going to touch me. I don't care if you're scared. Fucking do it, Rhys. Do as I say."

Whatever side of Aaron this had dragged out, I had no idea, but the way he spoke to me only made me harder for him. So I did as he commanded. It's not like I didn't know how to stroke a dick considering I'd done it enough times to myself. He moaned and took mine in hand again. Then he captured my mouth and kissed me so hard, I thought I might stop breathing.

Nothing else mattered right then except the driving need to get us both off. It consumed me. My fingers tightened around his cock, stroking harder and making him moan in my mouth like I gave him everything he needed in life. My body felt so hot. The desire raging inside choking me.

"Rhys, fuck, yes, fuck, I'm so close."

His encouragement against my lips had my heart tightening and my cock throbbing harder against his touch. If he was close, I was basically there. Nothing could hold it back.

"Aaron!"

My eyes rolled back in my head, body tensing as I erupted all over his hand and my stomach. I could hear him panting against my mouth, his breath coming out in spurts.

"Jesus, I love you," he whimpered.

I felt hot ribbons of cum spurting all over my fingers, making a mess inside his boxers. Him shuddering against me, his body losing all control as he came right alongside me.

Neither of us said anything. The only sound in the air was our laboured breathing. Our eyes fixed on each other. That blue-grey was so harsh right then as if his loss of control with me made him wild. The sight of it made my heart do backflips in my chest. Searing into me with such an intensity, my soul drowned in him.

We released each other at the same time. The sticky mess on my hand didn't bother me so much. It's what we'd done that had me pulling away from him, tugging up my boxers and swallowing hard.

"What… what the fuck was that?" I whispered.

He blinked then his eyes turned sad and it killed me.

What did we just do? Have I lost my sanity?

"Rhys, please don't freak out."

My heart thumped. My chest caving in as the reality of the situation crashed over me. I'd let my best friend kiss me. Let him make me come whilst I touched him too. Made him fucking come.

Oh fuck. Fuck. Fuck!

"Don't… don't freak out? You… you expect me not to freak out?"

He tried to reach for me but I tore myself away, almost falling out of the bed. I threw the sheets off and scrambled up. I reached out with my clean hand, ripping tissues from the box on his bedside table and wiping off the evidence of what we'd done together. I could feel his eyes on me but I couldn't look at him. I couldn't fucking take it.

"Don't shut me out… that's not fair."

"No, don't do that. Don't tell me it's not fair and don't bloody well tell me we need to talk about this either. Jesus, Aaron, we just… and you… and me… fuck."

I threw the box of tissues at him and bolted from the room. Considering I wasn't dressed, I slumped down on the top step of the stairs, putting my head in my hands. That was not how I wanted any of this to go. We should've had a fucking conversation about what he'd confessed to me. There should've been no kissing. No touching. No getting each other off like two fucking animals in heat.

I felt him beside me a minute later as he sat down and leant his head against my shoulder. No part of me felt it necessary to push him away. If anything, I needed his presence because the war going on in my head had my stomach twisting and my hands shaking.

"I know you're scared. I know this is confusing and not what you expected. Trust me, I understand. I never wanted to feel these things about you, but I do. And on some level, you feel them about me too. So I'm going to sit here with you whilst you freak out."

"How are you not freaking out?" I whispered.

He let out a soft chuckle.

"I've had a long time to get used to it. To come to terms with it."

"How long?"

I wasn't sure I wanted to know, but something in the way he said it gave me pause.

"Ten years."

I swallowed. The finality of it hit me. Aaron had always loved me. He'd always felt this way towards me. And I honestly couldn't say I blamed him for never saying a word about it. He knew me. The way I was. My tendency to bolt when things got too hard or when I freaked out so much I couldn't cope with it.

"That long, hey?"

"Yeah… that long."

"Well, fuck."

What else could I say? I could get mad and throw all kinds of accusations about how he'd lied to me but it wouldn't change anything. Besides, I wasn't angry. Not really. It wasn't him having those feelings about me which was the issue here. It was my feelings towards him. The confusion they'd brought on.

Am I gay?

Not that it changed anything if I was. I just didn't know for sure either way. How could I when the only person I'd felt attracted to was sitting next to me? You'd think being a teenage boy I'd have taken the time to explore those things by watching porn or something, but it didn't seem like a big deal not knowing. Until now. Now it seemed like a huge fucking deal.

"I don't know what this means, A, and I don't mean you liking me. I mean for me. I don't know what it means for me."

"In what way?"

I dropped my hands from my face and stared at the floor.

"I told you in the park, I don't feel attracted to anyone. Not like the way people describe. You know I don't like being touched by strangers. It makes me uncomfortable. It's part of that. The only people I feel comfortable with are you and Mum."

I sighed, rubbing my face with one hand.

"Whenever boys at school talk about girls, it's all about how their tits make them hard or whatever, but I don't get that. I don't feel it. Objectively, I can see how girls and boys are like physically beautiful, but I don't want to have sex with any of them. I don't feel those sorts of urges towards other people."

I hoped I was making sense because I didn't feel like it. My thoughts were messy and jumbled, but I had to try to explain why this was so fucking weird for me. Why I didn't feel normal. Why I couldn't understand how when I was with him, I felt those urges.

"Because of that, I don't even know if I'm straight or gay or something in between. It never mattered. At least it didn't until… well… you."

I dropped my hand and turned to him. His expression was neutral, but I had to face him when I said this. I had to do it for my own fucking sake.

"You make me feel, A. Just you. Yesterday when you touched my dick by accident, it confused the shit out of me. Especially when afterwards, I couldn't get it out of my head and in the shower… well, you know…" My face felt hot, but I pushed on. "I got myself off thinking about you, then I got so fucking scared when you kissed me. Scared it would ruin everything between us. You are my lifeline in this world, I can't live without you. So I don't know what this means. I don't know why it's you, but it is and… and… I'm scared of what that means. For me and for us."

He reached up and stroked my cheek, making me shudder.

"You don't have to figure it out alone. You have me. No matter what this means for you or us, you always have me."

He dropped his hand and put his arms out for me. It took me a second before I let him enfold me in them, pressing my face into his neck and breathing him in.

"It doesn't bother you I don't know my own sexuality?"

"Why would it? You're a big idiot if you think that would ever matter to me. My heart belongs to you, regardless. *I* belong to *you* just as *you* belong to *me*."

The truth of his words settled over me.

"A…"

"Mmm?"

"I think I have to be a little bit gay if I'm into you."

For a second I thought he might take it the wrong way, but then his shoulders shook and laughter bubbled out of his chest.

"Just a little?"

I nodded which only made him laugh harder. I smiled against his neck, feeling the tension between us dissipate.

"You're a fucking idiot sometimes, you know that?"

"I made you laugh though."

His fingers tucked under my chin, forcing my face up towards him. His blue-grey eyes twinkled as he leant closer.

"Mmm, I suppose you did."

There was no hesitation on his part as his lips brushed against mine. And there was none from me either as I kissed him back.

CHAPTER TWENTY SEVEN

Aaron

I watched Rhys out of the corner of my eye, both of us sat up on stools tucked into the kitchen island. Considering we'd not eaten, I'd whipped up huevos rancheros for lunch. Something Maritza had taught me to cook. All of my skills in the kitchen came from her. She told me she was preparing me for living on my own. Little did I know that would come when I turned sixteen. To be honest, it didn't bother me since Rhys was around here most days.

We seemed to have reached some kind of equilibrium earlier. Whilst he'd freaked out over the fact we'd touched each other intimately, I did not expect what he offloaded on me next. Honestly, it would never bother me how he identified, but I hadn't realised how badly it affected him. How confused it made him feel. My heart fucking died in my chest at how miserable and broken he sounded over the whole thing. Even more so because it was his confusion over his feelings towards me which caused his distress. And whilst he'd let me kiss him again after he talked about everything on his mind, I wasn't sure what we were now. Where we stood with each other. Or whether it was even a good idea to ask.

"How are we going to work it out?"

I looked at him. His eyes were intent on his food but his brow was furrowed.

"Work what out?"

"What I am."

I should've known that's what he meant.

"Um, I hadn't really thought about it yet."

For me, it was easy since I'd always felt attraction towards boys and not girls. Yet he didn't feel sexually attracted to anyone.

Except you that is. He admitted his attraction towards you.

He wasn't incapable of feeling attraction and desire, it just didn't happen the same way for him as it did for other people. I could work with that… somehow. I didn't want him feeling like he was broken or abnormal. Rhys was such a fucking beautiful person inside and out. He didn't have to be like everyone else. He only needed to be himself. I loved him exactly the way he was.

"How did you know?"

"What? That I'm gay?"

He nodded. I realised it was the very first time I'd called myself gay out loud. It didn't feel weird saying it to him. Maybe it would be telling anyone else. I couldn't imagine attempting to tell my parents. What a mess that would be.

"I've always known on some level. I was never confused about it. I just knew I liked boys and you're the only person who knows that about me."

A grin split his face and he nudged my shoulder.

"Because I'm special?"

"Yeah... *special.*"

"Fuck off."

I stroked his cheek which only made him smile harder.

"You are special to me."

"A..." he breathed, his eyes flicking down to my mouth.

The cord between us tugged hard. I resisted it because I didn't know if it was a good idea for me to kiss him again. Not when everything between us was so up in the air. Besides, I'd told him I'd help him work this out and kissing him wouldn't make that any easier. I didn't want to confuse him any further than he already was.

"Eat your food, special boy."

I saw the disappointment in his eyes but I turned away and dug back into my own food so it couldn't hurt me more than it already had. He had to realise how much I wanted him by now. This was for his own good even if I really, really wanted to fucking well kiss the shit out of him.

"Fine," he muttered and picked up his fork again.

It didn't stop him reaching over and stroking his free hand down my thigh, leaving it resting on my knee. I almost choked on my mouthful at the sudden contact. And my heart stopped at the next words out of his mouth.

"I thought we could watch porn together."

I swallowed my food, trying not to lose the plot completely over Rhys' sudden boldness.

"What?"

"Well, I figured maybe seeing it might give me a hint, you know."

"And you need me for that?"

He gave me a searching look.

"You said you'd help me."

"Yeah, but not by watching porn with you."

It's not as if I hadn't watched it myself, but the thought of being next to him whilst it was on made me have all sorts of dirty thoughts. Ones about him and me naked together. Would I be able to control myself? I certainly hadn't been able to earlier. Not when he'd looked up at me like that with his fingers on my lips. The need in his eyes damn near killed me. So I'd kissed him. And he hadn't pushed me away. Hadn't said no. Then one thing had led to another.

I shut those thoughts right down before my dick got hard from the memory of his fist wrapped around it.

"Is that too weird for you? Like watching girls I mean. I'd understand if it is."

"Jesus, Rhys, no, I don't care about that."

I'd watched straight sex to make sure I really wasn't into girls. Whilst it didn't do anything for me, I didn't find it gross. Besides, I'd do anything for Rhys, but I didn't think this would be a good idea.

"Then what?"

"Do you think putting us in a situation where both of us might get turned on is really the best way to explore your sexuality?"

He was silent for a moment, his fingers squeezing around my knee.

"Oh. I didn't really think of it like that."

He chewed on his bottom lip, distracting me entirely since I wanted to be the one chewing on it.

For fuck's sake. Is he doing this on purpose? Making me want him so much I lose all fucking control?

Now I knew what he tasted like, I wanted more. I wanted everything. But I couldn't have that. For his sake, I had to silence those urges. Keep them on lockdown. One way of doing it was taking that damn lip out of his mouth. So I reached over and tugged his chin down, forcing him to stop.

"Don't do that."

He blinked.

"Do what?"

"Bite your lip."

His eyes fell on me, brows furrowed.

"Why not?"

I stuffed another forkful in my mouth to save myself from answering despite his gaze burning into the side of my head.

"A? What's going on? Are you okay?"

I swallowed and mumbled, "It makes me want to kiss you."

Glancing at him, I watched his eyebrow raise. My face felt hot all of a sudden. Talk about fucking awkward. It's not like he didn't know I desired him. I felt weird about admitting it out loud like that.

"And that's a problem?"

I let out a lengthy sigh.

"Yes, it is." I waved my fork at him. "I can't be confusing you any further whilst you're working this shit out. I don't want you getting all mixed up over it and thinking you have to do stuff with me if it's not what you really want."

He was about to open his mouth when I stopped him.

"I want you to want me because you actually do, not because you're confused."

He pursed his lips. I thought he might drop it, but he leant over instead, his breath dusting across my ear.

"I'm not confused about you."

"Yes, you are. I'm not going to kiss you again, Rhys. I shouldn't have earlier."

As hard as it was for me to say it and not act on the way I felt about him now he knew, I had to stay strong. Rhys needed to get his shit straight. I wouldn't be the one who made things harder for him. I loved him too much for that.

"If you say so," he whispered before his lips trailed along the shell of my ear.

I was about to tell him to cut it out when he pulled back, dropping his hand from my leg and going back to his food.

"Should we catch a movie later?"

I blinked at the sudden turn in conversation.

"Um… sure."

"Cool."

When I looked at him, his expression wasn't remotely perturbed. If anything, he looked happy. I decided it was best not to press the subject. I wasn't sure what else he expected me to do after his confession that his attraction to me confused him. Perhaps I should have been more concerned about why he'd been so quick to drop it. And his newfound boldness with me. In fact, I should have been really fucking concerned about it. Pity for me, I had no idea what was going through that beautiful mind of his. Absolutely no fucking idea at all.

CHAPTER TWENTY EIGHT

Rhys

I understood why Aaron had told me he wouldn't kiss me again. It didn't mean I had to like it. Because I didn't. Despite freaking out over everything between us, knowing he loved me and wanted me regardless made it all easier to deal with. Whether I was straight or gay, didn't change my feelings. I wanted to explore them. With him. Specifically. So now I was on a kissing ban, I felt extremely put out by it.

I could be confused about who I was attracted to all I wanted. Aaron was still Aaron. And I was still me. We didn't need labels or terms to know we belonged with each other. That hadn't suddenly changed because he'd confessed he loved me and I wanted him to show me exactly how much.

When we got to the cinema, I insisted on getting seats in the back. He hadn't batted an eyelid over it but he should've. The place was almost empty given it was mid-afternoon and we'd picked a film which had been out for weeks. It only worked in my favour.

I watched him more than the actual film for the first half an hour. The way he sipped his Pepsi and stuffed his face with popcorn. We never shared because despite what Aaron said, he was a greedy little shit who'd eat the entire tub in one sitting. I'd learnt that early on so always got my own.

The seats at the back were those plush ones you paid extra for. He looked entirely relaxed, his legs spread out in front of him inviting me to admire every inch of his hard body. He dumped the popcorn in the seat next to him and stretched out further. I swallowed at the sight. It gave me ideas. Too many ideas.

What would he say if I crawled between his legs right now and ran my fingers up his inner thighs? Would he pant like he had done this morning in bed? Would he stop me?

No one else was in this row. There were maybe ten other people scattered across the seats below us. And this film was boring as fuck.

I didn't know what was up with me. It's like kissing Aaron had opened up a whole new world of possibilities. I wanted to experience everything. What every groove of his body felt like under my fingertips and perhaps my tongue. I wanted to touch him again but this time draw it out slowly so I could see him come apart in front of me… because of *me*.

Since when did you get so horny over your best friend?

This wasn't exactly like me. I didn't get all worked up over another person. Sure, I had the urge to pound one out on a regular basis because what seventeen-year-old didn't. But I never had 'wank bank material' as those idiots at school liked to call it. It was just a physical release.

Did I hit my head too hard against the sea wall last night when he kissed me or something?

Aaron flipped a switch on inside me and I couldn't fucking well turn it off. All of this shit was directed solely at him. It was all about him. The way he laughed. Smiled. Our bond which only seemed to grow stronger with each passing day. How I felt safe and wanted. Comfortable in my own skin. Except I was far from fucking comfortable right now. Not when I was itching to touch him. Not when thoughts of what we'd done earlier made me hard all over.

"Watch the fucking film, Rhys," he hissed, startling me.

My eyes flicked up to his face finding him staring right back at me as if he could read my thoughts in the dark.

"Can't," I whispered back.

"Why not?"

"You're right here looking all sexy and shit. I can't pay attention."

I swear to god he spluttered at my whispered words. Aaron didn't get flustered often so to see it now even in a dark cinema was a sight to behold. And just to fuck with him some more, I reached over and ran my finger down his bare arm resting next to us. He grabbed his drink with his other hand and sipped at it. I could tell he was trying not to look at me or respond to what I'd said.

His self-control must be impeccable considering he'd had feelings for me for ten years. For some reason, I wanted to see him lose it so he'd pin me down and have his wicked way with me. When he'd done it this morning, shoving me against the wall and ordering me not to walk out, I couldn't help the thrill of excitement it elicited despite the emotional turmoil both of us were going through at the time.

I wouldn't be like this with anyone else. Not least because I didn't feel things towards them the way I did with Aaron. My emotions were so intrinsically linked to him. We had a deep, intense connection with each other as best friends.

Continuing to run my fingers up and down his arm, I watched him shift in his seat. He ran his hand down his thigh as if getting increasingly agitated by my touch. It was a wonder he hadn't told me to stop. Clearly, he didn't want me to.

Did he crave me? How much would it take to get him to break his stupid kissing ban?

I shouldn't be thinking these thoughts or even trying to push his buttons. Using my knowledge of him to my advantage like this. So why did I do it anyway? Why could I not stop?

I turned in my seat, leaning my head up against the back of it. My fingers trailed higher up his bicep and across his shoulder. I could feel his eyes on my fingers, watching their progress as they dipped down his collarbone and lower. His hand gripped the armrest as if to stop himself from reacting. Except his reaction was clear to me. The part of his mouth. His fist clenching on his thigh. He wasn't the only one getting turned on.

You're being bad and he's going to lose it with you if you're not careful. He's already shown you how dominant he can be. Is that what you want?

Some part of me must do as my fingers were on his stomach now, so close to the hem of his jeans. Before I could go any lower, he snatched my hand up and held it away from him, his eyes burning into me. If I could see him properly right now, I knew the grey would be more pronounced. A storm was brewing and I was about to get completely swept away in it.

"Come with me," he hissed.

He stood up, tugging me with him as he quick-walked down the aisle and the steps. I was hard-pressed to keep up with him. We were out the doors and striding towards the toilets a moment later. I swallowed hard when he dragged me in before shoving me into a cubicle and locking the door. The moment his eyes met mine and I saw the hard edge to them, I knew I was in trouble. Big fucking trouble. He pushed me against the wall with an arm across my chest, pinning me down.

"What the fuck are you playing at?"

"You know what."

"No, Rhys, I really don't. Is this some kind of game to you? Because if it is, it's not funny."

It stung a little that he'd think I'd be playing games with him over this.

"Of course it's not a fucking game, A."

His eyes searched mine for a long moment.

"I already told you, we're not doing this until you work your shit out."

I raised an eyebrow.

"No? So you're not happy to see me then?"

His eyes flicked down to where he'd pressed himself against me.

Yeah, that's right, Aaron. I can fucking feel how much I've turned you on.

"You are such fucking trouble," he muttered.

I bit my lip forgetting he'd told me not to this morning. His arm against my chest pressed down harder as if he was contemplating doing something he shouldn't.

"You love that I am."

Taunting him probably wasn't the best idea I'd ever had. Not when I knew exactly what might happen when I did.

"I hate that you're right."

His arm left my chest and he dropped to the floor. Fingers dug into me as he tugged at my clothes. I stared down at his blonde head, swallowing hard at the sight of my best friend on his knees for me. The moment his fist wrapped around my cock as he freed me, I let out a shaky gasp. Then those blue-grey eyes of his flicked upwards towards me. I froze in place, unable to stand the heat and desire radiating from them. It licked across my skin as I watched his tongue slide out and trail its way up my length before swirling around the crown.

"Fuck," I panted out.

His hand ran up my stomach, holding me against the wall. As if I'd be going anywhere right now. I doubted my legs' ability to hold me up. Especially not when his mouth covered me.

Had I remotely been expecting him to go down on me? Hell no.

We stared at each other whilst he took me deeper. His eyes told me I'd pushed him too hard and now he was going to punish me for it. Punish me with pleasure. Because absolutely nothing could prepare me for the warm wetness of his mouth.

It took him a few minutes to find a rhythm since he'd not done this before, but it didn't bother me in the slightest. Hell, Aaron could practice on me any time if it felt this good. His hand worked me from the base whilst his mouth suctioned over the head of my cock. His tongue bathed me, making me tremble.

"Aaron," I moaned, trying to be as quiet as possible in case someone else was in here.

I couldn't help wrapping my hand around the back of his head, my fingers digging into his scalp as he only sucked harder. And by god those fucking eyes. The taunting satisfaction in them did things to me. It got increasingly difficult to drag oxygen into my lungs. The sensations were too overwhelming. Too much.

"A, I can't… going to… fuck."

He didn't stop despite my words. It's as if he wanted me to come in his mouth. So when the first wave hit, my head fell back against the wall and I closed my eyes, letting it take me under. He didn't falter whilst my cock spurted in his mouth over and over. And when I was spent, he licked me clean before readjusting my clothes and tucking me away.

I slumped against the wall, my eyes still closed as my legs struggled not to buckle underneath me. I felt him rise up and his hands connect with the wall by my head. He leant in close, his breath fluttering across my cheek.

"Is that what you wanted?" he murmured. "To make me lose control... because if so, it fucking well worked."

"Maybe," I whispered, my hands reaching out and curling around his hips, dragging him closer.

I opened my eyes and stared at him. He pressed his forehead against mine, letting out little harsh breaths as he struggled to regain his composure after what just happened.

"What am I going to do with you?"

"Give in."

His eyes darkened.

"Is that so?"

I nodded, hooking my fingers in the loops of his jeans so I could keep him right there. He let out a sigh and I knew immediately I still had an uphill battle convincing Aaron I wanted him. Perhaps I should be putting my efforts into working out my sexuality, but my brain was consumed by thoughts of him instead.

"You don't get it, Rhys. I can't go through this if it's an experiment for you. It already hurts enough as it is so don't do this to me if it's not real, okay? You'll break my heart."

My chest ached at the seriousness of his tone. Breaking his heart would kill me.

"Okay, A. I'll sort my shit out first. I promise."

It wasn't an experiment for me at all, but if he needed me to work out how I identified before he took me seriously, then I'd do that for him. I'd do anything for the boy in front of me. He was my beating heart. My damn fucking soul.

"Thank you."

"Anything for you."

And I meant it. Now I had to do some soul searching. Some real, genuine soul searching. Perhaps some research too. Surely, I couldn't be the only person in the world who didn't experience attraction like normal people, could I?

CHAPTER TWENTY NINE

Aaron

I swear Rhys was trying to kill me. Actually trying to kill me. If not with those hauntingly beautiful dark eyes of his, then it was with his damn fingers and mouth. The way he'd teased the shit out of me in the cinema drove me fucking insane. And somehow, he got what he wanted despite how determined I'd been not to touch him in the ways I desperately wanted to. It's not like I intended to shove him against a wall in the toilets and drop to my knees for him. I don't know what the fuck came over me.

Hell, that had been the hottest experience of my life. The overwhelming sense of need lancing across my skin as I saw his cock up close for the first time. It made my damn mouth water. I'd acted on complete instinct, taking him in my mouth and driving him to distraction. I'd got off on the power it gave me over him. Seeing him tremble and pant whilst trying not to moan had been incredibly sexy.

Whilst I'd quite happily do it again and again as long as we both breathed air, the crushing weight of knowing I could be Rhys' way of experimenting all but destroyed my enjoyment of it. I was not an experiment or a toy. He couldn't play with my feelings. I'd made it crystal clear to him and I think he'd finally got the message. He needed to work out what was going on with him. Only then would I consider him wanting me as real. Right now, that boy was a mess of emotions and feelings. Us being intimate wouldn't give him clarity. I had a feeling it would only confuse him more.

I let him out the cubicle when we'd both calmed down, ignoring the look the man standing by the urinals gave us when we walked out. In the toilets at the cinema is not where I imagined giving my first blowjob, but when it came to me and Rhys, all bets seemed to be off. It'd been nothing like I imagined and everything I needed. The feel of him. The taste of him. It'd driven me wild. The desperation and need between us stifling in the small space. As if years of pent up lust had overflowed and there was no holding back. I restrained him and Rhys surrendered. Just like the way I'd always imagined he would.

As we moved back towards our cinema screen, the very last person either of us wanted to see stepped into our path.

"Well, well, if it isn't my two favourite gay boys."

I almost groaned. Why did Valentine Jenkins have to be everywhere we went? I'd be convinced he was deliberately following us around if I thought he had any brain cells to plan such a thing. The prick had a habit of showing up when we least wanted him to. Like right now. After that intense moment between us. Here he was, calling us gay all over again. And quite frankly, it wasn't far from the truth given what happened in the toilets.

Rhys stiffened at my side and my eyes flicked down to his hand to see him clenching his fist. Then the very next moment he relaxed, his posture growing languid and suddenly his fingers entwined with mine. A sharp tug brought me closer to him.

"Oh, we're your favourites, are we? Who'd have thought? Did you hear that, A? Valentine likes us."

The man in front of us spluttered, staring down at our joined hands with a confounded look on his face. His friends behind him looked at us like we'd grown two extra heads.

"What? No, I don't fucking like you."

Rhys nudged my shoulder, a grin flashing across his face.

"Oh, I think he's just jealous."

"J…jealous?"

"Of me and A here, and how free we are to be open with our affections. Clearly, you want what we have. Now, excuse us, we're missing the rest of our film."

Rhys tugged me away, leaving Valentine and his cronies staring after us.

"What the fuck was that?" I whispered as we quick-walked towards our cinema screen.

"That was us playing him at his own game."

I shook my head as Rhys pushed open the door and pulled me inside before I had a chance to glance back at our childhood bully. We traipsed back up to our seats, but who the hell knew what was happening in the film anymore. To be honest, I hadn't been paying as much attention as I should've been. Not when Rhys' eyes kept boring a hole in my head.

He seemed particularly quiet as we sat back down. Did he regret what happened? Did it make him uncomfortable now it was over like it had this morning after we touched each other?

Stop worrying. He'd have told you if it was an issue.

I didn't like the weird vibe I was getting. I hadn't rejected him if that's what he thought. Hell, I wanted him to work his shit out so fucking badly. If he did that, there might be a possibility, a chance his feelings towards me were very real. And we could explore it together. He could be mine. *All* mine. The thought of it made my heart slam hard against my ribcage. I wanted that outcome so much, it threatened to choke me. Free rein of his body. The ability to touch and taste him with nothing holding me back. To love him in the exact way I'd dreamed of. Well, shit, it would be heaven. It would make me the happiest damn person in this world.

Still, right now, I had a feeling Rhys was a bit sore after what I said to him. And I didn't want that. We were still best friends regardless of the sexual turn our relationship had taken. I always comforted Rhys when he was feeling out of sorts.

When I lifted my arm, put it around him and tugged him half across the armrest, he stared up at me for a long moment. I couldn't see him properly in the dark but I knew he was questioning what I was doing.

"I know when you need me," I whispered.

He settled his head against my shoulder and wrapped an arm around my waist without saying a word. And he stayed that way for the rest of the film even though it was probably not the most comfortable position for him.

When we walked out of the cinema together, I turned to ask him what he wanted to do now, but I found him watching me already.

"Do you mind taking me home?" He rubbed the back of his neck. "I should probably see Mum whilst Graham isn't around."

I didn't want to call him out, but I knew it was an excuse. He didn't want to be around me any further today. I saw it in his eyes. And maybe it was for the best. I only complicated things for him. I hated it. Hated I'd forced this mess out into the open by kissing him last night.

"Sure, no worries."

This time as I drove, he tapped along to the music on the radio, nodding his head as the houses and streets passed us by. I had to wonder how he was really feeling, but I didn't ask the question. Rhys needed to process and I had to let him.

Before he got out as I pulled up, I put a hand on his arm.

"Are we okay?"

His eyes met mine and the emotions swirling inside them threatened to undo me.

"We're good. I'll text you, yeah?"

He shrugged off my hand and got out without waiting for a response. My senses prickled as I watched him walk up the path towards his house.

Everything in his expression wrecked me.

Everything.

We were not okay.

We were most definitely not okay at all.

Fuck.

CHAPTER THIRTY

Rhys

I wasn't sure what Aaron expected from me right now. He'd told me nothing else would happen between us whilst I worked my shit out, but then he still wanted things to be normal. They weren't normal. Not at all. How could they be?

I scrubbed my hand across my face as I shut the front door behind me. He was usually the first person I talked to when I was feeling all kinds of crazy. It being him I was going crazy over meant I couldn't do that.

I trudged along the hallway and poked my head into the living room as I could hear the TV going. Mum sat with her hands crossed over her chest watching a daytime TV game show.

"Hi, Mum, do you want a tea?"

"Ooh, that'd be perfect, love, thank you."

Before she could question why I was home, I continued along to the kitchen, filled the kettle and flipped it on. Maybe I should talk to her about it. Mum always told me I could tell her anything. I don't think she would care if I suddenly came out as gay to her. Not that I knew if I was or not. I mean, I had some idea considering how hard I got thinking about Aaron and his beautiful physique. It wasn't the only issue at hand here though. There was also the whole thing with me not feeling sexual attraction in the way other people did.

I pulled my phone out, typing in a search to Google.

Why don't I experience sexual attraction?

It came up with a ton of different hits. I clicked on the first article which talked about asexuality. The attraction I felt towards Aaron was raw and completely overwhelming so I didn't think I was asexual. The kettle boiled. I stuffed my phone back in my pocket, not being any the wiser to why I felt the way I did. After making tea for both me and Mum, I took the mugs into the living room, handing one to her before I took a seat on the sofa.

"You okay, love? I thought you'd be out with Aaron."

I almost flinched at his name. Of course, she'd bring him up. Aaron and I were rarely without each other, especially during the holidays.

"I was."

She raised an eyebrow. I sipped my tea and swallowed hard.

"Are you two okay?"

Aaron wasn't the only one who could read me like an open book. Mum tended to do it too.

"Yes and no."

Her stare burnt into the side of my head as I looked down at my mug.

"What's happened, love? Did you fall out?"

I shook my head. If only it was that simple. Nothing about me and Aaron was simple any longer. What happened had blurred the lines between friendship and more. There would be no going back no matter what.

"I don't think I'm normal, Mum."

She reached over and stroked the side of my head where my hair was cropped close to my scalp.

"What makes you say that?"

Talking to my mum about sexual attraction or my lack of it? Yeah, that was a new one on me, but what other choice did I have.

"Normal people are attracted to other people, like, you know, they want to sleep with them. I don't feel like that... ever. I don't know if I like boys or girls because I never thought to work it out. It never mattered until now."

Her fingers continued their path along my head.

"That doesn't make you not normal, sweetheart. Lots of people get confused about that stuff. It's okay if you don't know."

It used to be. Until yesterday. Until Aaron kissed me. Until he touched me and made me want him. Now my entire relationship with him hinged on me knowing who I am. The pressure I felt was intense and unyielding. I wanted things between us to be okay and they really weren't.

"It's not though. I need to know."

I looked up at her, finding her expression full of compassion which made my heart ache. Mum never made me feel like I was stupid or wrong for anything I did.

"Does this have something to do with Aaron?"

"How did you know?"

She smiled.

"Because I'm your mother and the two of you are inseparable. You always have been."

I sighed and sipped my tea again. I couldn't exactly tell her about all the physical stuff we'd done. That would be embarrassing as hell.

"Aaron kissed me last night," I mumbled.

"And how did that make you feel?"

I rubbed my face.

"Weird, I guess. It scared me. Wait… why don't you sound surprised about that?"

She chuckled and shook her head.

"Aaron looks at you like you hung the moon, love. It didn't take much for me to put two and two together."

Why didn't I know that?

Probably because I didn't want to see it. Aaron was the first and only friend I'd ever had. He understood me. Was there for me when everything got dark. He saved me from myself. I was confident and secure because of him. Except now I was far from confident about who I was. At least parts of me anyway. I'd not changed who I was deep down just because I didn't know my own sexuality.

"I'm terrified of losing him, Mum. He's everything to me."

Her hand stroked down my cheek. I hadn't shaved this morning so I'd already grown a rough patch of stubble. It'd started growing in when I turned sixteen. Since then, I kept it under control, but some days I forgot. Like today. I'd had other things on my mind. Like Aaron.

"Tell me what happened, sweetheart."

"I have all these feelings for him… feelings of attraction which I've never felt before. It was like a switch flipped, you know. One minute he was Aaron, my best friend, and the next, I wanted more. But how does that even work? I don't like strangers in that way and I don't even know if I'm… gay."

Mum's expression almost killed me. She had so much understanding in her eyes.

"And the worst part is everything is weird between us. He told me I had to work it out and that he'd help me do it, but he won't let me explore with him. I do understand why. He loves me and he doesn't want to get hurt if I decide I don't want him like that."

Saying it out loud made it so real. My heart felt tight. How could I ever have thought it would be okay to push him? He didn't need that from me. This was such a fucking mess. I desperately wanted to apologise for my behaviour today. Aaron deserved so much better from me.

Mum took my mug from me and popped it and hers down on the coffee table in front of us. She wrapped her arms around me and tugged me against her chest, stroking my hair.

"Oh, Rhys love, I imagine he's just as scared as you. It'll be okay. You two will work it out."

"I don't know how to work out what I am."

She pulled away and gave me a searching look.

"Have you tried looking it up online?"

"Not properly."

"Maybe you should."

"Maybe."

Mum cupped my face.

"I just want you to be happy. I hope you know I love you no matter what. And I know Aaron loves you too. Whatever the outcome, he won't abandon you."

Out of everything, Aaron leaving me scared me the most. I needed him to survive.

"Thanks, Mum. Guess I needed to get that off my chest."

"It's okay, love. I'm here whenever you need to talk."

I kissed her cheek before picking up our mugs and handing hers over. The two of us sat watching TV together whilst I finished my tea. There didn't seem like much else to say. I knew what I had to do.

"Should I start on dinner?" I asked when I'd downed my tea and looked at the time.

"There's a pizza in the freezer."

I nodded and got up, taking our mugs through into the kitchen. I turned the oven on before washing up and getting some plates out. Then I leant against the counter and pulled out my phone. If I wasn't asexual, there had to be another explanation. I spent the next ten minutes searching various terms online whilst waiting for the oven to heat up. I put the pizza in the oven, setting a timer before I clicked on another article. My eyes scanned down the description and hit on a word which gave me pause.

Demisexual.

As I looked at the definition, something about it clicked into place for me. I had no interest in strangers, at least not sexually. There was one person in my life I had a strong emotional bond with whom I'd started to feel attracted to. I couldn't test out the theory as much as I'd like, but it felt right. It wasn't that I never wanted to have sex because, clearly, I did considering how much I'd liked touching Aaron and my fantasies about him. I just didn't find someone attractive on that level unless I knew them and felt something towards them.

"Holy shit."

There's a term for it. I'm not the only one who feels this way.

I didn't think I'd have some random lightbulb moment about it. Seemed too simple, yet I knew this is what I was. Nothing else I'd read resonated with me in the same way.

So I could explain the attraction thing. It did not, however, tell me what my sexual orientation was. That required further research and something I wasn't prepared to conduct in the kitchen. Not sure I could explain it away if Mum came in and I had porn on. I had no idea how else I'd work that part out. I knew I wasn't straight. Not when I desired Aaron like nothing else. So I supposed it was a toss-up between gay, bisexual and perhaps even pansexual.

Why are there so many different options?

I hated how complicated this felt.

I rubbed my face and checked the timer I'd put on. A few more minutes until the pizza was ready.

"Mum, do you want to eat in the living room?" I called.

237

"Please, love," came the response.

At least I had something to tell Aaron now. Some way of explaining why I didn't feel attracted to people in the same way as he might experience it. And I hoped he believed me.

Now was not the time though. We both needed to cool off. Even so, I felt like perhaps he might think I was upset with him when I wasn't. So I tapped out a message so he'd know I was thinking of him.

Rhys: Miss you x

I wasn't sure if he'd even respond to it when I saw he'd read it. Minutes ticked by and I got nervous. Was that a stupid thing to say? It was the truth. Even though it'd been a couple of hours, it felt like an eternity. I sounded stupid. I really did. Telling him I missed him. What the hell was I even thinking? Why did I have to be so awkward?

Quit overthinking it. You're not helping yourself here, Rhys.

I took a breath as the timer went off for the pizza. Dropping my phone on the counter, I got some oven gloves and pulled it out. Then I set about cutting it up and putting it on two plates. I grabbed a couple of glasses of water and took Mum's through to her. When I came back, I picked up my phone, finding a response. My stomach twisted, but I steeled myself and opened it.

Aaron: Do you?

Did he think I was lying? God, when did everything between us become so crazy?

Rhys: I always miss you. Things being weird doesn't change how much I need you.

I tapped my fingers on the counter, knowing I should take my pizza through, but wanting a reply. When I didn't get one, I sighed and picked up my plate, stuffing my phone back in my pocket. I wanted things between Aaron and me to be okay. They just weren't. And a few words in a text message wasn't going to change that.

I'd promised I'd work my shit out and I really was trying. So maybe I should give him space until I'd done that. As much as it killed me, the thought of being away from him for any length of time, I'd do it for both our sakes.

I sat with Mum whilst we ate, watching this detective show she loved. I'd just finished my food when my phone buzzed repeatedly. Placing my plate on the coffee table, I pulled it out, staring down at the series of messages which were still coming through.

Aaron: No matter what you decide, I'm always here for you.

Aaron: Always. I promise.

Aaron: I can't stand this. I feel like I'm going to lose you and it's killing me.

Aaron: Do you have any idea how much I love you? You're everything to me. I can't live without you.

Aaron: FUCK! Now you're going to think I'm crazy. Please ignore this. I want you to be sure and you need time for that.

Aaron: I'm sorry. Please don't hate me.

I could hardly breathe picturing him right now. Agonising over it all. And it broke something so deep inside me. My Aaron was hurting like crazy and I couldn't do anything about it. I couldn't tell him it was going to be okay. Not until I kept my promise to him.

Aaron: I need you to know it would destroy me if you don't want this with me for real, but even then, I would never abandon you.

Aaron: I'm yours. All yours. You have all of me. There's nothing left I can give you. So I'm begging you, please don't break me by walking away.

I couldn't take it any longer. This was absolutely ruining me.

"I'll be back in a sec, Mum," I said in a rush before getting up and bolting from the room.

I had my phone against my ear the next moment, listening to the ringing sound as I ran upstairs and shut myself in my bedroom. When he answered, I started talking before he could even get a word in.

"I'm not leaving you, A. I would never... I can't..."

The thought of it made tears well in my eyes and my chest burn.

"Please trust me when I tell you I have no intentions of walking away. You're still my best friend."

He didn't speak. I slumped down on my bed, scrubbing a hand across my face.

"Aaron, you are my world. My whole entire universe. I can't live without you either."

I heard his breathing but nothing else. If I was there right now, I'd wrap him up in my arms and hold him to me like my fucking life depended on it.

"Say something," I whispered. "Please say something."

The choked noise I got in response made my heart fracture. How could this be happening to us? It didn't have to be this way, did it?

"I don't want to be just your best friend," he whispered, his voice laced with pain and I could tell he was crying. "I want to be your everything like you are mine."

"A..."

"I want to hold your hand, kiss you, hug you, make love to you. I want you to be mine, Rhys. Do you understand what that means? I want it all."

My throat got all tight. My lungs constricted in my chest.

"I can't go back. You have to tell me if this is real... when you're ready... when you know."

I wanted to tell him it was real. But I hadn't kept my promise to him. I hadn't worked it out yet. Not fully. So even though it wrecked me, I couldn't give him the reassurance he desperately wanted right then.

"I promised you I'd work it out, A. I'm doing it for you and myself, so please give me a little more time."

"Okay," he whispered, sniffling.

"Are you going to be okay?"

"I have to be."

"Aaron—"

"I'll be okay… I should go. Say hello to Steph for me."

Then he hung up. My hand fell from my ear. I stared at the wall. Aaron and I had never fallen out before. And it fucking well sucked. I mean, we hadn't really fallen out. This was something else entirely. I just couldn't explain it.

All I knew was understanding myself was key to fixing this. So for Aaron, I was going to find out for sure either way. Because the person I cared about most in the world was dying on the inside. And only *I* could make it go away for him.

CHAPTER THIRTY ONE

Aaron

hen Rhys told me to give him a little more time,
I hadn't expected not to hear a word from him
for three days. Not being able to hear his voice or
see his face made me feel so alone. I couldn't count the
number of times I'd ended up in tears at the thought of him
never coming back to me. He promised me he wasn't leaving,
but having no contact gave me anxiety. Had me questioning
everything. I wanted him back. So fucking bad. I'd do
anything to have him right here next to me.

I'd spent all my time in the same shorts and t-shirt in bed
watching shit TV with junk food. It reflected my mood.
Desolate and deeply unhappy. There was nothing worse than
feeling like you'd fucked up the only good thing in your life.

When the doorbell went, I thought it might be the delivery
guy since I'd done an online food shop. Trudging downstairs
without even fixing my appearance, who cared what a stranger

thought of me, I opened the front door and stared at the person on the threshold like I was seeing things.

Is it really him?

Rhys had a fresh haircut, making him ten times more attractive than ever. His dark eyes were full of life and... happiness. He had two carrier bags with him and his own bag slung across his back. He looked me over and raised an eyebrow. Those beautiful damn eyebrows. I must be mad because everything about Rhys was attractive to me, even the little scar he had on his pinkie finger from where he'd almost sliced it off whilst cutting an avocado once. He'd had to get stitches for that. I remembered sitting in minor injuries with him like it was yesterday.

I can't believe you're here.

"Wow, you look like shit... you going to stand there gawking or you going to let me in?"

I stepped back on automatic, unable to comprehend what I was seeing or hearing. Rhys walked in, taking the door from my hand and closing it behind him. His eyes met mine for a moment before he shook his head and walked through into the kitchen. I followed him, unable to help myself. I'd been starved of his presence for three entire days.

"Have you eaten?" he asked as he popped the bags on the counter.

"No."

He turned to me, eyes roaming over my body.

"When did you last shower?"

"Um..."

When had I?

He shook his head again and stepped towards me, putting a hand on my shoulder. His touch scorched me, making me shudder involuntarily.

"Go upstairs, shower and put some damn clean clothes on, A. You look like you got dragged through a hedge backwards. And here I thought you were meticulous about this stuff."

He turned me around and shoved me out of the kitchen.

What the hell is going on?

I turned slowly, staring at his back as he walked towards the counter.

"Rhys…"

"Take your time, don't come back until you're clean and looking like a normal human being."

I wanted to ask him so many questions, but instead, I turned away and trudged upstairs. Doing what I was told seemed like the easier option. Talking to him made me nervous. He appeared to be fine, but what did that even mean? What was he going to tell me? Had he worked everything out? Was it why he'd gone on radio silence for three days?

Shaking myself, I went into the bathroom and turned the shower on. After I'd stripped my clothes off and stood under the spray, I couldn't help my anxiety rising all over again. Did he not realise how fucked up I'd got over this entire thing? How much I needed him? He'd left me hanging for three days. Three fucking days.

What is wrong with you? You told him to sort his shit out. You can't be annoyed about him doing what you asked him to.

I ran my hands through my wet hair, needing to get my head on straight. Rhys would give me an explanation. I knew that. It's why he was here. I just didn't know what the fuck the outcome would be. It's what worried me the most. I had no idea if I could go back to us being friends after sharing those kisses and touches with him. It would decimate me. I'd do it as this was Rhys and I'd rather die than be without him completely as dramatic as that sounded. He made me that way. He made me want to bow down at his feet and worship every inch of him.

I don't know how long I stood there under the spray, letting it wash away all of my insecurities, anxieties and doubts. When I went down to him, I had to keep my cool and listen to what he had to say.

Him being here acting like nothing is wrong can only be a positive thing, right?

I washed thoroughly before I got out, wrapping a towel around my waist. Leaning against the sink counter with both hands, I stared into the steamed-up mirror, my reflection all blurry.

You have to do this. For both of you. Stay calm. Stay cool. You can do it.

I wish I felt more confident than I sounded in my head. Shaking myself, I dried off before going into my bedroom and pulling on some clothes. I ran my fingers through my damp hair, trying to style it as best I could so it wouldn't look insane after it air-dried. Most of the time, I used a hairdryer, but getting down to see Rhys felt far more important.

I took a deep breath and went in search of him. When I reached the kitchen, he hummed as he sat at the kitchen counter on his phone. He looked up, finding me standing in the doorway. His eyes roamed over my skin, a slight furrow appearing in his brow. It cleared after a moment. Then he set his phone down and popped off the stool, shoving his hands in his pockets.

"Hungry?"

I nodded, unsure of what to say to him. I hadn't eaten today, which was stupid of me.

"Your food got delivered. I put it away for you." He waved a hand at the cupboards. "Go sit in the dining room. I'll be there in a minute."

I blinked. We never ate in the dining room. In fact, that room only got used when my parents were home. Which was like… never. I wanted to question it, but the look in his eyes told me not to. Told me to do what he'd said. And for once in my life, I decided to let him dictate this.

Backing out of the kitchen, I took a few steps down the hallway and walked into the dining room. When I took in the scene in front of me, I bit down on my lip to stop myself from losing it completely. He'd set two places at the end of the table. In between them were candles which he'd lit and a single daisy sat in a vase. Propped up against it was a card with my name on it.

What has he done?

A part of me wanted to hold out hope it meant everything between us was real, but the other side kept telling me it was all far too good to be true.

I padded towards the table and pulled out the chair, planting myself in it. My fingers reached out, grasping the card and running over my name. I flipped it over and opened the envelope. As I pulled it out, I saw it had a watercolour heart design on it. I found myself getting choked up without knowing what I'd find inside. Setting the envelope on the table next to me, I opened the card and stared down at the handwritten words.

Aaron,

I'm sorry for everything which has come to pass over the past few days.

I'm sorry for leaving you in the dark and making you think I would disappear from your life.

I'm sorry for not knowing who I was when you confessed your feelings to me.

I'm sorry for pushing you away when you needed me the most.

But what I'm not sorry for, what I will never be sorry for, is you and me.

What I'm trying to say, to articulate, to make you understand is…

I am yours.

Forever.

Rhys

A single tear landed at the bottom of the card. I hadn't realised they'd started falling as I read the words over and over again.

I am yours.

Did that mean what I thought it did? I couldn't bear it. I needed to ask him. Needed to see his face and know it was real and true. I was about to get out of the chair when I found the card plucked out of my fingers and placed in front of me on the table. Then two arms banded around my chest as he hugged me from behind. His cheek came to rest against mine.

"I know what you want to ask," he whispered. "It means exactly what you think it does."

My words got stuck in my throat and my only response to him was a choked out gasp which turned into a sob. He let go of me and came around the side of the chair before forcing me to turn to him. I watched him squat down on his haunches and take both my hands in his. There were so many emotions in his dark eyes, ones I could read and ones I couldn't.

"I've done a fuck ton of soul searching and research over the past few days and it's only led me to one conclusion. Who I am, what my sexuality and sexual orientation is doesn't really matter a whole lot when the only person in this world my heart beats for is right in front of me. The thing is, Aaron, the big thing is… I'm sort of in love with you and I'd like to think that is the most important discovery I made from us being apart."

I swallowed hard, trying to hold back the tidal wave of emotion battering me at his words.

He's in love with me?

"But I promised you I'd work out what the fuck I am and I think I've done that. So you're going to have to give me a minute to explain it to you."

249

He rose from his haunches and let go of my hands. Reaching out, he tugged the chair from the end of the table towards him and set it down in front of me. He sat down and took my hands again, squeezing them as if he knew I needed his touch to ground me.

"First of all, I'm pretty sure I'm gay because you know, girls really don't do it for me. Like at all. And I'm sure you don't want to know how I worked that out, but I can tell you if you want."

I shook my head. I could imagine how he'd gone about it without needing an explanation after he'd asked me to watch porn with him.

"However, that's not all. I told you attraction for me doesn't work in the same way as most people. I'm not asexual as I definitely desire sex... with you specifically, but we can get to that later. But I'm also not like regular person sexual either. It's an in between thing for me. The term I found I most identify with is demisexual."

I blinked. It's not like I hadn't heard the term asexual before, but demisexual? It was new to me.

"It essentially means you don't experience sexual attraction unless you have a strong emotional connection with another person. It has nothing to do with my orientation, but who I feel sexually attracted to. So when I was confused about why I suddenly felt desire towards you, it's because of this. I need an emotional bond to form before I can feel physically attracted to someone. I don't know if it'll be the same for anyone I form a bond with since the only reference I have for it is you. That said, considering I'm into guys, I doubt if I got close to a girl, I'd want to sleep with her."

He searched my face for a long moment.

"Am I making sense, A? You're going to have to give me some indication that you're understanding and taking in what I'm saying."

It took me a hell of a lot longer to process what he was telling me than normal. I hadn't been sleeping well without him and my emotions were running riot inside me. Somehow, I had to answer him. So I latched onto the one thing which had made my heart go wild the moment he said it.

"You love me?" I whispered.

That made him smile. The sight of it almost broke me in half.

"I see I should have saved that part for last."

"Rhys…"

He let go of my hands, leant forward and cupped my face, wiping away my tears with his thumbs.

"I am madly in love with you, Aaron Jackson Parrish. So please stop looking at me like I'm a crazy person because, you know, a guy is going to get a complex in a minute."

The only thing I could do was let out a choking sound which made his eyes grow concerned.

"Jesus, come here, you idiot." He let go of me, grabbing my shoulders and tugged me towards him so my face landed on his chest. "Anyone would think I just told you a puppy died with the way you're staring at me."

I clutched his t-shirt, holding onto him for dear life as I felt like I was drowning.

"Rhys."

"Shh, I know, A, it's a lot for you to take in," he murmured, stroking my still-damp hair.

I broke down entirely and sobbed into his t-shirt. He held me, not once making me feel ridiculous for crying all over him like a big fucking baby. When I got hold of myself, I pulled away and stared up at him. He brushed my tears away again, watching me with a pensive expression on his face.

"You know, I was going to ask if I could kiss you, but you're a snotty mess."

He reached over and grabbed a napkin from the table before wiping my face with it. Then he leant his forehead against mine, cupping my cheek with one hand. I couldn't believe it. This boy. This beautiful boy had told me he loved me and he was mine.

"I've missed you."

"I'm here now, A. I'm right here."

I couldn't hold back any longer. Everything inside me wanted him so much, constricting my lungs and making my heart get tight. My hand landed on his shoulder before I pressed my lips against his. At first, it was soft, the relief I felt at knowing he cared for me in the same way driving me. Then it became heated and desperate, as if both of us couldn't get enough of each other. He tugged at me and I pulled at him. Lips and tongues clashed in a battle of who needed who more. I don't know how, but I ended up in his lap, straddling his legs as I held his face and kissed him harder. Lost in the sensations and feelings wreaking havoc through my body.

"I love you," I said between kisses. "Only you. Forever."

My hands were at the bottom of his t-shirt, attempting to pull it from him. He moved back and put his hand on mine, stopping me in my tracks.

"Hey, hey, easy now. Did you think I set this out for nothing?" He waved at the table. "I'm feeding you first, A, then you can have me any way you want me."

"Any way I want you?"

His eyes grew heated.

"Let me put it another way, you can make love to me. I want you to."

I thought I might die from his words. The very idea of being inside him giving me heart palpitations. I didn't want to wait, but I was also hungry. And if I wanted him in my bed for the rest of the day, then we both needed fuel for that.

"Okay."

I nuzzled my nose against his before slipping from his lap and sitting back in my chair. He smiled before getting up and setting his chair back where it should be. As he disappeared back towards the kitchen, he stroked a hand along my shoulder. It felt like a promise of things to come.

I sat there staring at the candles and the daisy in the vase, trying to process everything.

Is this actually real?

Had Rhys King just told me he loved me and he wanted me to make love to him?

Holy shit, does this mean we're together now? Like is he my boyfriend?

I could ask him when he came back with food. All I knew is my heart was full and I'd literally just got everything I wanted in life.

Him.

Rhys King.

And I would never let go.

CHAPTER THIRTY TWO

Rhys

To say the last three days without Aaron were torture was an understatement. I wanted to see him, but I knew if I did, then we might be back at square one. I couldn't take any chances here. Not with Aaron. Never with him. I wouldn't play with his feelings. Not least because the conclusion I'd come to is that I loved him. Working out my sexuality paled in comparison to that revelation.

I'd never taken any time to examine my feelings towards Aaron until this had forced them out into the open. And some fucking feelings they were. At first, they'd scared me. The depth of my need and desire towards him. It hadn't started in the last few days. I'd been falling in love with Aaron for years. I just hadn't known it because I thought these feelings I had towards him were natural to have about your best friend. Except you shouldn't want to kiss and have sex with your friends. And you certainly shouldn't want to spend the rest of your life with them. Belonging only to them. Forever and always.

So now, having him on top of me, kissing me like I was the very air he needed to breathe. There was nothing else like it.

The last hour whilst we ate had been filled with longing glances, small touches and conversations about what I'd done for the past three days. Aaron had asked me all sorts of questions about being demisexual after he'd got over the *I love you* business. I wasn't an expert, but I tried to explain how I felt the best I could. He'd accepted it, he was just curious about how it worked. It meant he would never have to worry about me wanting anyone else. I couldn't imagine being as close to another person the way I was with him.

"Rhys," he moaned against my mouth, his hand roaming down my side, clutching me to him. He ground into me, both our cocks rock hard already.

The moment we'd got upstairs, he'd pulled me to him as if his desperation had reached fever pitch, but I stopped him from kissing me. I'd brought my bag up with me so I set it on his bed and grabbed a couple of things from it, placing them on his bedside table. When he'd looked at them, his face had gone bright red. Since I was pretty sure he hadn't expected to be in this position, I'd bought supplies before I'd come over. Porn had opened my eyes about sex, as well as my own research. If we were going to sleep together, I wanted to know what the hell I was doing.

We didn't need to have a conversation about what they were or why I'd got them. Lube and condoms made it very clear where this was heading.

"Aaron, I want you," I groaned when his lips trailed down my neck.

"I want you too, so fucking badly. You make me so hard."

I could tell but hearing it from his lips made my cock throb. His hands trailed under my t-shirt, stroking across my stomach. His touch was both teasing and sensual.

"You'll go slow with me, right?"

His head popped up, blue-grey eyes full of arousal but also concern.

"Are you sure about this? I'm scared I'll hurt you."

Reaching up, I cupped his face as I smiled.

"You do know what to do, right?"

"Well yes, theoretically. I just mean we don't have to like have sex yet."

"You don't want to?"

His eyes widened.

"No, no, trust me, I do." His fingers continued their path along my stomach, making me tremble. "Maybe we should work up to sex is all."

I saw the uncertainty and hesitation in his eyes. Dropping my hand, I ran it along his shoulder.

"Would that make you feel better about it?"

He nodded. Didn't he know I'd do anything to make sure he was happy and comfortable? The two of us could work it out together.

"Anything for you, love… now come here and kiss me."

The smile which graced his face damn near killed me. He leant down and kissed me, his fingers pushing up my t-shirt.

"I'm your love, am I?" he murmured against my mouth.

"You have a problem with that?"

"No... because I'm going to call you my boyfriend."

My heart rate kicked up a notch, my body heating further from that word. Boyfriend.

"I'm more than okay with that."

His hand came up, his fingers tangling in my hair as he kissed me harder, his tongue darting between my lips. I lost myself in him, my hands curling around his back, keeping him locked to me. Our hips ground together, desperately seeking the friction between us.

I heard the distinct sound of the front door slamming shut. I froze underneath him as a voice floated up from downstairs as we hadn't shut the bedroom door.

"Aaron?"

He pulled back, staring down at me with horror on his face.

"Aaron? Are you home?"

"Fuck," he muttered. "What the fuck are they doing here?"

All my pent-up lust felt like it had ice thrown all over it. Aaron's parents were home. The last two people I wanted to see... well... ever. Being around them was awkward since they made no secret how much they hated Aaron and I being friends.

"They didn't tell you they'd be back?" I asked.

"No."

He got off me and sat up, running his hands through his hair as we both heard footsteps on the stairs.

"Aaron?" came Kellie's voice again.

"In here, Mum."

I scrambled into sitting position, smoothing my hair down and adjusting myself so it didn't look like we'd just been kissing and dry humping each other. Unable to see myself, I don't know how successful I was. Aaron stood up and walked towards the door, meeting his mother on the threshold.

"Oh, there you are, sweetie. Your dad and I are home for a few days."

Aaron's back stiffened and I knew for a fact he wasn't happy about it at all.

"You didn't tell me you were coming home."

"Oh well, it was a spur-of-the-moment thing," Kellie said, waving her hand at him before her eyes fell on me. "Oh… hello, Rhys, I didn't see you there."

"Hello, Mrs Parrish."

She looked at Aaron again, her disapproval at my presence written all over her face. Aaron looked back at me, irritation painting his features. He did not want them here. And neither did I. Especially not since the two of us were about to get each other off. Something I wanted with a desperation it bordered on fucking madness.

"Well, I thought the three of us could go out to dinner, how does that sound?"

Aaron looked back at her with a frown.

"The three of us?"

"Yes, sweetie."

259

"I'm kind of busy right now."

She looked between us.

"Busy? With Rhys? I'm sure he won't mind going home now. You two have the rest of the summer to do whatever it is you've been doing."

I watched Aaron's fist clench at his side. We'd been apart for three days. I minded a fuck load. It was meant to be my time with him. And I was sure he felt the same way.

"Actually, Mum, I mind. A lot. You and Dad can't just turn up unannounced and expect me to change all of my plans for you."

I had to put a hand to my mouth to stop myself from snorting in shock. Aaron rarely said no to his mum and never to his dad. He must be more pissed off about this than I realised.

Kellie looked taken aback and incensed at the same time.

"Well, I'm sorry if your parents wanting to spend time with you is such an inconvenience for you, but I'm not taking no for an answer, Aaron. We have a table booked for later."

Aaron crossed his arms over his chest.

"Fine, if you and Dad insist then I'm sure you won't mind me bringing Rhys with."

Kellie stared at him for a long moment, but Aaron stood his ground as if daring her to say no.

"We'd love to have Rhys along too. I'll see you both downstairs later, shall I? No later than six."

"Yes, Mum."

She turned on her heel and strode away. Aaron watched her before shutting his bedroom door and banging his head against it.

"For fuck's sake."

"A, I don't want to go to dinner with them."

"And you think I do?"

He turned and trudged over to me before throwing himself on the bed and burying his face in my chest. His arms came around me and he let out a huff.

"I fucking hate them sometimes. Why the hell did they have to come home?"

I stroked his hair, knowing I'd go along anyway no matter how much the thought of spending an entire dinner stuck with Patrick and Kellie Parrish made me feel sick to my stomach.

"Because they're determined to cockblock us."

He was silent for a moment before his body started shaking with laughter. I grinned since it was the truth.

"It's okay, A, we can always resume later… oh shit, you don't think she saw the condoms, do you?"

He lifted his head as his laughter halted.

"Shit, I hope not."

He scrambled off me and grabbed the items, shoving them in his drawer. Then he sat back on the bed and put his head in his hands, groaning.

"This is the worst!"

"Well… the worst would be if they'd come home and you were balls deep inside me. This is just kind of shit."

He reached out and slapped my arm. I could see the blush creeping up his neck.

"Don't say stuff like that. You'll get my dick hard again... god, Rhys, how are we going to deal with them all evening? I can't do this shit. I just want to stay up here in bed with you."

I leant over and rubbed his shoulder.

"We don't have to go downstairs until six, so why don't you come here and we can watch TV and cuddle, yeah?"

He grumbled but crawled up on the bed and sat next to me up against the headboard. I wrapped an arm around his shoulder, grabbing the remote off the bedside table.

"Fucking cockblocking parents," he muttered.

I held back a smile. Aaron and I had all the time in the world to be intimate with each other.

"Someone's impatient."

He looked up at me.

"And you're not?"

I bit my lip, watching his eyes flick down to it and spike with heat. The raging storm brewing in those blue-grey depths made flames lick across my skin.

"Don't do that."

"Do what?"

With no further warning, he leant forward and sucked my bottom lip into his mouth before biting down on it. I whimpered in response, finding myself growing hard all over again.

"That," he groaned. "Don't do that... fuck."

His hand wrapped around my head and he kissed me, deep and hard until I thought we'd never come up for air.

"Don't tease me right now," he murmured as he pulled away. "I'm this close to pinning you down and shoving my dick in your mouth to shut you up."

I stifled the urge to bite my lip again, knowing it would drive him crazy.

"Why don't you?"

He scowled and sat back, hugging my arm to his chest.

"Because my stupid parents are here and they don't know I'm gay nor that we're together. I don't trust Mum not to come back up here. So we're going to have to keep it PG... for now."

"And later, after dinner?"

His eyes darkened.

"All bets are off... and trust me, I plan to put that mouth of yours to good use."

Even though I really didn't want to go to dinner with Aaron's parents, the thought of what he'd do to me afterwards made the inevitable suffering we'd both have to go through worthwhile.

I can't fucking wait.

CHAPTER THIRTY THREE

Aaron

I hated my parents. I full-on hated them right now for coming home and ruining my afternoon with Rhys. Ruining my entire damn week. It was bad enough I'd gone through three days of absolute hell and heartache. To finally get what I wanted, which was me and Rhys together, only to have my parents cockblock me… well, that was the icing on the shit cake.

Having to sit in an expensive restaurant whilst my dad seethed quietly, looking at his phone and Mum pretended everything was fine was not my idea of fun. Especially not when Rhys looked like he wanted to throw up. I don't know why they even bothered coming home any longer. The two of them weren't exactly parents of the decade. They cared more about my sister than they did me, especially now Harriet was getting married to fucktard… I mean… Ralph. They'd been together for so long, I wasn't sure it'd ever happen. But no, he popped the question two months ago. My sister hadn't stopped gushing over her 18carat rose gold diamond engagement ring.

"So, how was the end of term?" Mum asked after we'd ordered.

Rhys had looked at the menu and asked me what on it was normal food when my parents weren't paying attention to us. I'd pointed out everything I thought he'd like. My poor boyfriend was completely out of his element here. He kept glancing around the room, looking like he wanted to be anywhere else. I felt shit for dragging him here with me, but I could not deal with my parents on my own today. Not after everything I'd been through. I needed Rhys here to ground me. Especially since they'd interrupted us earlier and all I wanted was him right now.

"Fine, Mum."

I didn't have much to say about school. The teachers said I was on target to get the right grades for university. Rhys had been helping me with English since he was also taking it, so it's not as if they had anything to worry about on that score.

"And you, Rhys, how's school going? If I remember correctly, you want to do graphic design."

Rhys glanced at me before answering.

"All good, Mrs Parrish. My teachers are happy with my progress."

I nudged him.

"Don't be modest, he's top of all his classes."

One of Rhys' most attractive qualities was just how smart and talented he was. I'd been harassing him to draw me for

266

years, but he always said no. Perhaps now we were together, he might agree to it. I'd quite happily pose for him, especially if he wanted to draw me naked. I tried not to think too hard on that subject whilst in the presence of my parents.

"I guess so," he mumbled, his ears going red.

Fuck, that's the most adorable thing ever.

"That's lovely. I know you've always helped our Aaron here."

Dad snorted from next to Mum and she glared at him. He was being rude as usual. I ignored him, putting my hand on Rhys' thigh under the table since we were sitting across from my parents so they wouldn't see. He covered it with his own, squeezing my fingers to reassure me he was okay.

"Patrick, do you have to insist on working right now?" Kellie hissed as she leant over to him. "This is supposed to be a nice meal with your son."

He sighed and put his phone on the table, levelling his gaze directly on me. I almost flinched from the steely look in his blue eyes.

"Are you going to get your predicted grades, Aaron?"

"Um… I think so."

"And university applications, are you going to start on those?"

I shifted in my seat.

"Yes, Dad. It's my plan to do it over the summer."

Patrick Parrish was a no-nonsense man who wanted everything done his way. We'd clashed over it on more than one occasion, but these days it was easier to do what he told me. The only thing I'd ever stood my ground on was my friendship with Rhys. No matter how hard he tried to break us up, I'd never give way.

"Good. I expect you to let me know when you've done it."

He picked up his phone, dismissing me and the rest of the table. I noticed Mum giving us a tight smile before staring at the side of my dad's head.

"Jesus, this is painful," Rhys whispered.

"You're telling me," I whispered back.

I knew it was going to be bad, but the tension in the air was so thick, it was unbearable. Wanting to make an attempt at salvaging the situation, I glanced at Mum.

"Why are Harriet and Ralph not joining us?"

"Oh, they're attending a charity gala tonight. They're coming over for tea tomorrow."

I almost rolled my eyes. What fun. An afternoon with fucktard and my sister. I absolutely hated Ralph. He was stuck so far up his own arse, I'm surprised he didn't shit rainbows.

"Have they set a date yet?"

"Well, you know Harriet wants a spring wedding, but Ralph's parents are insisting on June. I told her, darling, you do not have to listen to them, it's your big day. I'm just so excited. It will be such a big affair."

The thought of Harriet's wedding to Ralph Bartholomew Mountbatten the Third made me want to run very, very far away. No doubt the fucking tabloids would flock to get the scoop on it. And his parents? I couldn't stand their snooty attitudes.

I glanced at Rhys who bit his lip as if he was trying not to snort. Big mistake. I wanted to bite it again. I wanted to nibble him all over. Now I was allowed to have dirty thoughts about him, they seemed to be running rampant. The longer I went without being able to satisfy my intense desire to have sex with him, the more I craved it. Craved him. I wanted to experience it for the first time with him and only him.

When his eyes turned to me, he immediately released his lip and smirked. The little shit knew what he was doing to me. I squeezed his thigh, making him jolt.

"Yeah, it's very exciting," I finally replied to Mum with fake enthusiasm.

She didn't seem to notice as she started off on what she and Harriet had already begun planning for the wedding. I rolled my eyes at Rhys discreetly whilst nodding and making appropriate noises to Mum. Of course, she'd rather talk about my sister than my life. This is how it always went with her. It was either that or talking about her latest film. Honestly, having a parent who directed for a living was not at all glamourous.

By the time dinner was over, Rhys and I were bored to tears of listening to all the antics from her latest film set and what colour napkins Harriet wanted. Honestly, I didn't get what the big deal was between pale blue or green. Just have white napkins and be done with it. Dad had ignored us the entire time, which I wasn't unhappy about. I could do without his snide remarks.

Rhys and I sat in the back of my dad's car, itching to touch each other but refraining from doing so in front of my parents. He kept looking at me with those dark eyes, taunting me with their blatant invitation to undress him. I was so intent on watching him, I almost didn't notice my parents were not driving home.

"Where are we going?"

Mum looked back at me with a frown.

"We're dropping Rhys home."

I opened my mouth to retort but saw my dad looking at me in the rearview mirror and snapped it shut again. If I objected, we'd get into a fight and I really didn't want to deal with that shit right now. Time to sit back and shut up no matter how much I wanted Rhys in my bed tonight.

Rhys and I looked at each other. I could not put the sinking disappointment and frustration I felt into words. His eyes told me it was okay, but it didn't feel okay at all. After everything we'd been through this week, I didn't need my parents here fucking it all up.

I refused to let them stop me from getting out with him when they pulled up outside the estate. Dad wouldn't ever drive through what he termed the shithole where Rhys lived. Walking around the car, I stood in front of him, wanting so much to kiss him.

"Guess I'll see you after they've gone," he said, rubbing the back of his neck.

"I'm sorry."

His eyes softened.

"Don't be. I know what they're like."

"No, Rhys, I'm sorry you had to deal with them at all. They suck." I glanced at the car, knowing they were likely pissed at me for taking too long. "Text me when you get in, okay?"

"I will." Then he leant closer and lowered his voice, "I love you."

I stifled a smile.

"Love you too."

He turned and ambled off towards the estate, glancing back and giving me a wink, which made my heart thump. I got back in the car, barely getting the door closed before my dad drove away. It took a minute before he glanced back at me, his expression full of irritation.

"I do not understand why you insist on hanging around that boy. He is nothing but trouble."

"Patrick, don't do this tonight," Mum said, putting her hand on his arm.

"No, Kellie, Aaron is going to be eighteen next year. He needs to focus on school, not get distracted by someone who is clearly a bad influence over him."

I stared at him, my heart sinking to my feet. It wasn't the first time he'd had a go at me over Rhys and it wouldn't be the last. But I'd had enough of it. Rhys was my boyfriend now and I wasn't going to let my dad continue to put him down.

"Really, Dad? For your information, the only reason I get good grades is because we study together and he helps me when I'm struggling. So don't you sit there and tell me he's a bad influence when you and Mum are never home."

"Aaron! Do not speak to your father like that."

"Why not? He seems to think it's okay to disparage Rhys every chance he gets just because he lives on a council estate. Why don't you tell him to stop being such a judgemental arsehole instead of having a go at me for defending my best friend who has literally done nothing wrong?"

I think I shocked both my parents into silence. Right then, I didn't care. They'd showed up here without telling me, made us go out to dinner with them and were now keeping me from spending the night with Rhys.

They shared a look between them, but neither responded to my outburst. I had no idea what would happen when we got home. They could try to ground me or something but considering they wouldn't be around to police me for long, it wouldn't make a difference. No matter what they did, I wouldn't let them stop me seeing the love of my life.

It was high time they got the message.

Rhys was my past, my present and my future.

He was the one.

CHAPTER THIRTY FOUR

Aaron

*L*ast night was awful. I'd sat up in my room listening to my parents shouting at each other for almost an hour. Neither of them had spoken to me about what I said to them. In fact, they had ignored me when we got in. I wasn't sure what else I expected when the only time either of them ever took an interest in me was when it came to my future.

I'd got up before them in the morning and snuck out of the house, not caring I was meant to be back in the afternoon for tea with Harriet and fucktard. They might have kept me from Rhys last night but there was no way in hell I'd stay away today. I even left my car at home so they wouldn't suspect I'd caught the bus.

By the time I got to Rhys' house, I was so desperate to be with him, my hands started shaking. We'd texted a little last night, but I hadn't wanted to tell him about what happened in the car. He seemed to be distracted. I imagined he was drawing as usual so I hadn't told him I was coming.

I rang the doorbell. The last person I'd been expecting opened it. Then again, I shouldn't really be surprised considering how many times Steph took him back after kicking him out.

"Hello, Mr King."

"Oh… it's you," he replied, disdain dripping from his lips.

"Is Rhys home?"

Graham looked me over with obvious disapproval but stepped back to let me in.

"He's in his room."

I inched by him. Whilst I didn't think Graham would do anything to me, I still didn't like him. Not when I knew exactly what kind of shit he'd pulled with Steph and Rhys over the years.

"Who is it, Gray?" called Steph from the living room as Graham shut the door.

I walked along and stuck my head around the door.

"Hi, Steph."

Her face lit up at the sight of me.

"Hi, love. Rhys will be pleased you're here."

I saw the twinkle in her eye and wondered what on earth Rhys had told her. Had he mentioned what happened between us? He hadn't told me, but then again, we'd been a little preoccupied with each other.

"Yeah… I'm just going to…"

She smiled knowingly. Graham walked past me with a scowl as I pulled away from the door. Deciding it was better not to say anything else, I sped walked over to the stairs and climbed them. I didn't bother knocking, just opened the door to his bedroom and shut it behind me.

Rhys sat at his desk, his hair messy as if he hadn't bothered styling it this morning with his headphones stuck over the top of it. His brow was furrowed as he concentrated, his hand brushing across the graphics tablet I'd bought him for his birthday. He'd worked part time at a local corner shop for an entire year to save up for his laptop so I'd wanted to get him something he'd find useful to go with it.

My eyes dropped to his back. He was shirtless, just sat there in shorts with the window open as it was already getting hot. Seeing him like that made my chest ache with longing and a stirring happened in my own shorts.

I padded towards him, knowing he couldn't hear me over his music. He almost jumped out of his seat when I wrapped my arms around him from behind and kissed his neck. Turning in his chair and sliding his headphones off his head, which he dumped on the desk, he stared at me before smiling.

"Shit, you scared the crap out of me."

Before he knew what was up or down, I was in his lap, my hands curling around his face and my lips against his. I needed him. Urgently. It didn't take him long to get on board with the program. His hands tangled in my hair as I ground against him.

"Rhys," I moaned into his mouth. "I want you, now."

He pulled my face from his and stared up at me, face flushed and eyes darkening with heat.

"Want me how?"

Gone was my hesitation from yesterday, I knew we should go slow, but fuck if I wasn't so ready for this. I ran my nose up his, bringing our faces close together.

"I want inside you."

His breath hitched.

"You want to fuck me, Aaron?"

The deep rumble of those words slid across my skin, making me hotter than ever. It sounded so crude and aggressive, but I didn't care. The way I wanted him right now was not gentle, sweet or even tender.

"Fuck yes."

"Then take me."

I was out of the chair and tugging him up the next second. I pushed him against his desk, kissing him without restraint. My hands gripped his hips, dragging my own against him as my dick hardened to the point of pain. I held his hands down on the desk as I kissed my way along his neck before trailing my tongue across his chest.

"A, fuck, please."

"Do you have what we need here?"

"Yes, in my drawer."

I groaned, wanting to worship him for having the foresight. My lips trailed along his ear before I bit down on the lobe.

"Do you want me to fuck you?"

He shuddered, hips arching into me and grinding his cock against mine.

"Yes," he whimpered. "So much."

I couldn't wait any longer. I needed him naked. I needed me naked. And I needed inside this beautiful boy who had my heart in the palm of his hand. Pulling away, I stared into his eyes, seeing all the desire I felt reflected back at me. It wasn't just that. There was love there. A deep-seated love which threatened to drown us both.

"Rhys…" I choked out. "I need you to know before we do this… you… you are my one. My only one. I will never love anyone else. Not like this. I'm yours completely. Now and always. No matter what."

His expression grew so fucking tender it almost killed me.

"I know, we belong together, A. You're my soulmate."

I let go of his hands, dug my fingers into his hair and kissed him. His hands came around my back, clutching me to him. The desperation and love seeping from both of us made the air thick with tension. When I pulled away, his lips were glistening, his chest rising and falling rapidly. He'd never looked so beautiful. I couldn't get over it.

"Get naked and lie down."

He smirked which only made me want to kiss him all over again, but I had more pressing matters at hand. Like preparing my boyfriend to take my cock for the first time. I stepped back so he could move. He slipped out from the desk and walked over to his single bed. It would have to do because there was no way I was waiting any longer.

I walked over to the door and slid the lock into place. Rhys had installed it years ago so Graham couldn't barge into the room. And right now, neither of us needed any interruptions.

As I approached the bed, I tugged off my t-shirt and shorts, toeing off my trainers in the process as I watched Rhys lay back against the covers in all his glory. He slid open the bedside table drawer and fished out the lube, chucking it on the bed. I raised an eyebrow when he shut the drawer again.

"I don't want anything between us," he said, his voice pitched low. "I want you as you are… skin on skin."

I fingered the hemline of my boxers.

"Are you sure?"

"You are the only person I want this with, A, so I'm sure."

I knelt on the bed and crawled over him.

"I love you."

"I love you too."

His hands reached for my boxers and I let him pull them off me, leaving us both bare. We took a moment to look at each other. His hands ran down my chest and circled my hips. His thumbs traced lines along them, making me shiver.

"You're perfect," he whispered. "I've always thought you were, but now… now I know for sure."

My heart went wild in my chest. He was perfect too. Everything and more. And he trusted me with this. Trusted me to take care of him. Leaning down, I gave him a lingering kiss before I sat up and grabbed the bottle of lube.

He moved his legs up, bending them at the knee, giving me access to him. I swallowed hard and shifted down the bed a little. I'd wanted our first time to be just like this. So I could see his face as I slid inside him.

Leaning down, I ran my tongue up his cock, making him let out a little moan. Then I flipped the cap and squirted the liquid over my fingers.

"Have you touched yourself here before?"

He bit his lip as he stared down at me.

"A little... when I knew it's what I wanted from you."

"So if I do this... you're not going to jump."

I ran my coated fingers across his hole, making him shiver.

"No," he panted.

With my free hand, I wrapped it around his cock and stroked him. He seemed pretty relaxed, but it didn't stop me being scared I'd hurt him.

"Don't look at me like that, I'm not fragile."

The reassuring look he gave me prompted me to slide the tip of my finger inside him. He let out a breath but put his hand out to indicate he was okay. I slid it deeper, almost choking at the heat and tightness of him. I could only imagine what he would feel like around my cock.

"More, don't hold back on me," he moaned as I worked my finger inside him.

It made me wonder how many fingers he'd used, but if I thought too hard about any of this, I might blow my load on his covers rather than inside him. My dick was hard and throbbing. I tried not to rub it against the sheets to relieve the ache. So I gave him another finger, making him wince a little, but he told me not to hold back.

After a few minutes of stretching him out, I added a third. He panted, his body undulating in front of me as if he couldn't get enough. I was still stroking his cock, which throbbed restlessly in my hand.

"Aaron, please."

"Does it feel good?"

"Yes, god… I won't lie, it burns too, but I don't care."

I kissed his inner thigh, knowing if he wanted me to stop, he'd tell me. His eyes were on me, the lust dripping from them making me harder than ever. His hands curled around the sheets, fisting them as if he was trying not to grab me. I kept thrusting my fingers inside him, stretching him further because I sure as hell didn't want to make this an unpleasant experience for either of us. He moaned and struggled against me as if he couldn't control himself the moment my fingers brushed up against his prostate.

"Please, please, god, A, I want you in me."

I pulled my fingers from him and sat up, hoping he was ready now. Popping open the cap again, I liberally applied it to my hand before stroking it into my cock.

Holy shit, I'm about to lose my virginity to my best friend.

Rhys was more than that. He was the love of my life. He was the only one I ever wanted to give this part of me to. Reaching down, I grabbed one of his discarded t-shirts off the floor and wiped off the excess lube from my hand.

I held onto the back of his thigh with one hand and guided my cock to his hole with the other. He stared at me, eyes dark with arousal. He wanted this as much as me.

"Ready?" I whispered, almost unable to get the word out.

"Make love to me, A."

After all our talk about fucking, it seemed so at odds, but it's what we were about to do. Make love to each other.

I pressed forward, finding a little resistance until my cock slid into him. He let out a grunt and I bit down on my lip so hard, I almost tasted blood. Nothing could prepare me for the intense sensation of his heat wrapped around the head of my cock. I almost came on the spot, but I gripped the base of my cock hard to stop the pounding need to erupt.

"Rhys… you okay?"

I don't know how I managed to get those words out but seeing his closed eyes and the tense expression on his face concerned me.

"Give me a sec."

I needed a damn second too, so I could compose myself because everything about this was fucking heaven and we were only just getting started.

When he opened his eyes and smiled at me, relief flooded through me.

"Okay, you can keep going."

I wanted to kiss him then and I would once I'd worked my way inside his tight heat.

I went slow as hell, giving him time to adjust with each inch I fed him. My whole body was burning up from the strain of holding back. When I was halfway inside him, I pulled my hips back and thrust in again, needing to move a little to relieve the ache inside me. I applied more lube, to make sure he was comfortable. Watching his expression change every so often as he tried to adjust to the new sensation, I attempted to gauge if he was okay.

"Rhys…"

His eyes popped open and widened when he took in my face. He reached out a hand to me and I leant over so he could cup my face.

"I'm okay, A. I promise… keep going."

I pulled back again, pushing deeper with the next thrust. He let out a little pant. The damn noise making me crazy. He moved his legs higher so I could lean over him. I let go of his thigh and planted my hand by his head. As I built up a slow rhythm, he lifted his head from the bed and kissed me, nibbling on my bottom lip. I groaned, the feel of him overwhelming me. This whole thing was nothing like I expected. He felt so fucking good. So… everything.

He wrapped a hand around my neck and tugged me closer, kissing me harder.

"A… fuck," he moaned. "Fuck me."

It was if he gave me permission to give it to him and I couldn't help it any longer. I thrust deeper, loving the way he gripped me. The tightness and the heat. He felt incredible and I really fucking hoped he was enjoying himself too.

"Yes, god, Aaron, don't stop," he panted, his head falling back against the pillow.

His hand dug between us and he gripped his cock, stroking it as I gave it to him harder. We lost ourselves in each other. Moaning and grunting with each thrust. I wasn't going to last much longer.

"Fuck, I don't think I can hold on," I panted, gripping his hair in my fist.

"So close, A… shit… coming!"

I felt hot streams splatter both of us and it set me off. I groaned as I emptied myself inside him, revelling in the way he tightened around me with each spurt of his cock. The moment his hand fell away from between us, I all but collapsed on him, completely out of breath and utterly spent.

I don't know how long it was before I felt him kiss my cheek, his hands stroking up and down my back. His touch soothed me in so many ways.

"I love you," he whispered.

I shifted, putting my hands on the bed and shoving myself up. Then I slowly and gently pulled out of him, sitting up on my knees. I watched him for a moment, trying to gauge his feelings, but he gave nothing away.

"Was… was that okay for you?"

"Yeah, A, it was."

"You sure?"

He smiled at me, his dark eyes lighting up.

"I can see I'm not going to get away with a vague answer. It was uncomfortable at first, but then it felt good… more than good. Besides, I just came all over the both of us so I think you have your answer there."

I shook my head and smiled. Then I went to try to lie down next to him in the cramped space but he sat up and stopped me.

"You mind if we like clean up first before cuddling? I'm all sticky."

I couldn't help snorting.

"We're going to have to make a run for the bathroom."

"Shit, I hope they didn't hear us. I almost forgot they're both home."

We got up off the bed, him wincing a little, but his hand on my arm reassured me he was okay. The two of us cleaned up as much as we could with a t-shirt first before pulling boxers on. We made a dash for the bathroom, me cleaning up thoroughly first before leaving him to.

When Rhys came back in his bedroom, he curled up against my chest, stroking his fingers down my side.

"Was that everything you hoped it would be?"

I wanted to ask him the same thing.

"It was more."

He kissed my chest as I stroked his hair.

"I love you, Rhys… like fuck loads."

I felt him smile against my skin.

"Oh, I'm aware… I felt all your love when you came in me."

I couldn't help sniggering and I had a feeling he meant to make me laugh.

"You're an idiot."

"Maybe so, but you love me anyway."

My arm tightened around him and I kissed the top of his head.

"I do. I'm going to love you forever so you better get used to it."

His fingers stroked along my stomach.

"Same goes for you, A, you're mine for life."

There was no question about it so I didn't even try to deny the simple fact.

I was Rhys' and he was mine.

CHAPTER THIRTY FIVE

Rhys

A aron had spent the past half an hour of us lying on my bed together pestering me to draw him. So here I was, my personal sketchbook and pencil in hand, sat on my desk chair whilst he laid out on my bed in a pose that was straight up from *Titanic*.

"I'm not drawing you like that."

I dumped my book on the end of the bed and got up. He let me move him into a more appropriate position where he wasn't fully on show considering he'd refused to put clothes on. Not that I planned on showing anyone else this sketch, but Aaron naked? That was mine and mine alone to see. If I sounded a little possessive, it's because I was. Every inch of his glorious body was one hundred percent mine. A body which had utterly claimed and tamed me not too long ago. I tried not to shiver at the memory of him inside me.

"You don't want to draw this?" he asked, pointing at his dick.

"You're a perv, A. No, I'm not going to draw your cock."

He grinned and I retreated to the chair before he could say anything else. I picked up my sketchbook, eyed him for a long moment and then I began. He sat there quietly for five minutes, just watching me whilst I outlined him, making sure I got everything in proportion.

"Why didn't you want to draw me before?"

I rolled my eyes.

"I don't now, but someone is insisting."

I could sketch people and had to do fine art as part of my A-Levels, but I preferred a more comic book style of art. Aaron didn't know I'd drawn him a thousand times over, but just as a cartoon version of him. I had an entire series of them as part of one of my GCSE Art and Design projects. Something I'd never shown him. Maybe I would now we were together. Then he'd see how long I'd been fascinated with him. It's only I hadn't realised my fascination was really because I had feelings for him. Deep-seated and visceral emotions which intrinsically linked me to him.

"Am I not pretty enough for you to draw?"

I snorted.

"You're plenty pretty, Prince Charming. Why do you think I keep winding you up about girls swooning over you? Too bad for them you're mine."

"I've always been yours."

I smirked. If only I'd known, but then again, would I have been so accepting of all of this if we'd been younger?

"If I'm Prince Charming, are you my damsel in distress?"

I raised one of my shoulders in a shrug.

"You did save me so I guess so."

I didn't look up to see his expression as I was busy trying to get his eyes right.

"Rhys…"

"Mmm?"

"I didn't save you… I just helped you save yourself."

If that's the way he saw it, it was his prerogative. In my mind, he had saved me. He'd forced me out of my shell and helped me grow into the person I was now. I'd never stop being grateful to him for sticking by me this whole time.

"Oh, the ladies are going to be swooning even more when they hear that. A modern-day feminist Prince Charming we've got here."

"Fuck off."

I grinned, glancing up to find him scowling.

"No frowning, love, did you forget I'm trying to draw you after you begged me to?"

His expression cleared but not before he stuck a finger up at me. I raised an eyebrow until he settled back down and became still again.

"Okay… *babes*."

I shuddered. I hated that word and he knew it.

"It turns me on so much when you call me that, *baby*."

"Really? Can't see you getting hard from here."

"Someone wore my dick out."

He snorted.

"I doubt that. I bet if I came over there and ran my tongue over it, you'd be hard in seconds."

I shifted in my seat, trying to shove the mental image away. Trying and failing.

"Whatever, tease."

He started to move, but I put a hand up.

"Don't you dare, I'm trying to finish this damn sketch so sit there and shut up."

His smile was absolutely radiant. That boy knew exactly what he was doing to me.

Little shit.

I was going to get him back for it. And I had just the plan once I was done with this drawing.

Thankfully, he stayed still and silent whilst I finished up. I sat back and admired my work for a moment, making sure I'd caught his likeness. Then I signed it and set it aside on the desk. His brows turned down immediately.

"You not going to show me it?"

I crawled onto the bed and forced him down on his back. Aaron might like to be in control most of the time, but I was determined to make him lose it.

"Later, *baby*."

Leaning down, I ran my tongue along his pec before circling his nipple. He let out a choked moan. He tried to reach for me, but I pinned his hands down on the bed. Aaron's eyes widened, the grey more pronounced than the blue as heat radiated from them.

"No."

That single word made his breath hitch. He'd had plenty of time exploring me. I wanted to touch him this time. My fingers itched to be on his skin. I leant down again, trailing my tongue along the grooves of his stomach. He shuddered and twitched, sucking in air as he tried to contain his reaction.

Oh, Aaron, seeing you struggle with your need to be in control is so fucking sexy.

There would be no containing this. His dick hardened before my eyes as I continued my torturous path across his stomach with my tongue. His skin was soft but his edges were all hard muscle. I loved every inch of him. His dips and curves.

"Rhys, please," he moaned.

The sound was so delicious. I never thought I'd hear him beg like this.

"What was that?"

"Please."

"Use your words, *baby*."

He let out a strangled moan as my tongue skimmed the head of his cock, tasting his salty pre-cum for the first time.

"Fuck you, don't call me that."

I chuckled, moving away which only made him let out a little whine in protest. He strained against my hands pinning his to the covers, but I didn't let him up. No matter how much he liked to be in control, I was still stronger than him and he knew it. Probably why me submitting to him drove him wild. The trust between us was immeasurable.

"Do you want me to suck your cock or not? If you don't stop struggling against me, I'll quite happily keep teasing you."

His eyes were a raging cocktail of lust and need.

"Please."

"Then keep your hands right here, got it?"

He nodded, biting down on his lip. I released his hands slowly, making sure he was going to keep still before I gripped his cock. Considering I hadn't done this before, I was nervous, but the need to bring pleasure to my Prince Charming outweighed my doubts. I ran my tongue up his shaft, eliciting another moan from him. His hands fisted in the covers, making me smile. My poor boy wanted so much to control the narrative.

I stroked the base of him as I wrapped my lips around his head. He was hard yet soft at the same time. I revelled in the feel of him against my tongue, throbbing with need. Keeping my teeth sheathed, I took more of him, running my tongue along the underside of his cock as I did so.

"Fuck, Rhys."

It took me a few attempts to find a natural rhythm, but he didn't seem to mind in the slightest. His hips bucked as I sucked him, his knuckles going white in the covers. The little gasps and pants escaping from his lips fed me. His eyes were so dark and stormy, making my cock throb in response. I swear Aaron could make me hard as fuck with a single look. His eyes just did something to me. They had done since we were seven, except now the sexual edge to our relationship only made me want to stare at them all the more.

"Please, god, faster," he begged before letting out a garbled cry, his hands releasing the covers and digging into my hair instead.

I reached up and grabbed one, shoving it back on the bed. Releasing him, I raised an eyebrow when he whimpered in protest.

"What did I tell you?"

He released my hair, fisting his hand against his stomach instead, giving me a mutinous look. I adored how much he hated and loved this in equal amounts. I could see it in his eyes.

"You're mean," he grumbled.

"I can show you mean if you want," I retorted, squeezing the base of his cock.

He jerked upwards, whining again.

"Please don't, I'm sorry, please make me come."

"Only if you beg."

I licked up his cock which made him buck once more.

"Rhys," he whimpered. "This isn't fair."

"All's fair in love and war, Prince Charming."

He slammed his fist down on the bed and groaned as I took him in my mouth again.

"Please, god, I can't take it. Please save me from my own personal hell, only my knight in shining armour can rescue me from this torment."

I tried not to laugh with my mouth full of his cock. If he was my prince, then I was definitely his knight who'd stand by his side and protect him through thick and thin just as he'd done for me over half our lives.

"Rhys," he choked out as I went faster, knowing he was close to erupting.

And when he did, he trembled all over, crying out without words as he planted his fist against his mouth to stop the loud noise. The taste of him made me shiver. I could do this forever with him. Drive him crazy with need until he came. There was no sight quite like it.

He closed his eyes, his chest heaving as he lay there on my bed, utterly spent. I swallowed hard after releasing him before I crawled up his body and kissed his cheek. He wrapped an arm around me, forcing me to lie on him. I stroked his face, watching the beautiful boy I'd driven crazy smile lazily.

"You are undoubtedly a troublemaker, *knight*," he muttered.

"You complaining, *prince*?"

"Fuck no. Now, show me this drawing. I want to see if you've made me all sexy and shit."

I rolled my eyes. In my view, he was always sexy so it wouldn't matter how I drew him. Hopping off the bed, I grabbed the sketchbook and handed it to him. He sat up and stared down at my drawing of him. Gently, he ran his fingers over it, his eyes growing soft.

"This is… amazing."

I shrugged and sat back in my desk chair. If I had more time, I'd have highlighted all his finer details, but I didn't want to spend too long on it.

"You can keep it… it's yours."

His eyes flicked over to me.

"You sure?"

"You wanted me to draw it, so you get to keep it. Besides, I have others."

His eyebrows shot up.

"What?"

I grinned and bit my lip which only made his eyes darken.

"That damn lip," he muttered.

"Come here and I'll show you."

He got off the bed, snagging his boxers and pulling them on. I spun around in my chair and reached up, grabbing another smaller sketchbook from my shelves above the desk. Then I handed it to him as he sat on the edge of the bed closest to me.

"What is this?"

"Was part of my GCSE project."

He opened it to the first page where I'd drawn him as a comic book character, complete with blonde hair and blue-grey eyes. He flipped through the book, his brow furrowed.

"You never told me."

"You've always been my muse, A. I just didn't want you getting big-headed over it."

He reached out and smacked my arm.

"Hey, what was that for?"

"Keeping this shit a secret. It's fucking incredible, Rhys."

My face grew hot at his compliment. I'd always known he liked my art, but to have him like this was a whole other level of pride for me.

"Yeah well, that's why I did so well."

"I'm not surprised. Honestly, you should do this shit for a living."

I didn't want to draw comics or anything like that. It was my hobby. Graphic design is what I aimed for, then I could get myself a good job and perhaps freelance one day so I could be my own boss. Aaron knew all about my aspirations. It's why he'd bought me a graphics tablet for my birthday.

When he finished flipping through the book, he placed it down next to him and levelled his gaze on me. His eyes were so soft and tender, full of his love and affection for me. Then he dropped to his knees on the floor and crawled between my legs as he spread them wide.

"What are you doing?"

The little smirk he wore told me nothing innocent.

"Someone just drove me crazy with his very talented mouth… now I'm going to drive him wild right back."

"Is that so?"

His fingers were at the hem of my boxers, peeling them down.

"Oh, it is most definitely so, *knight*."

My head fell back against the chair as Aaron proceeded to show me how much of a knight I was to him. I could do this forever with him.

And I just hoped when we said forever, we really meant it.

PART III

annihilate

verb, an·ni·hi·lat·ed, an·ni·hi·lat·ing.

to reduce to utter ruin or nonexistence; destroy utterly.

CHAPTER THIRTY SIX

Aaron

The past four weeks had gone by in a blur of days out with Rhys, watching movies, sunbathing and sex… a whole lot of sex. It's as if once we'd taken that final step, we couldn't keep our hands off each other. I swear being inside him was the sweetest damn ecstasy. The way he submitted to me completely had me so hard all the time. We were already inseparable before but being together like this had only brought us so much closer together.

I'd whined about us going to the park today, but it was so fucking hot outside, neither of us wanted to pass up the opportunity to relax in the sun. Currently, we were hiding from it underneath a large oak tree. Rhys sat against it, sketching, whilst I dozed with my head in his lap. It's why I didn't hear footsteps until they were almost upon us.

"Hey, Rhys," came a feminine voice from above me.

I opened my eyes and found a group of girls I didn't know had approached us.

"Um, hi, Becky," he replied, shading his eyes to look up at them.

They must go to his school or live on his estate since I hadn't seen them before.

"How's your summer going?"

"Good, yours?"

She fiddled with her blonde hair, nudging the grass with her foot. I almost rolled my eyes. Clearly, someone had a bit of a crush on my boyfriend.

"Yeah, been good. Me and the girls have been keeping busy. Hey, you heard about the party on Friday?"

He blinked before shaking his head.

"No."

"Olly Trenton is throwing it. You should come."

Rhys and I didn't do parties. They were usually full of underage drinking and people hooking up. Definitely not our scene.

"Um…"

"Come on, Rhys, you never come out. The girls and I'll be there. It'll be fun."

Rhys looked down at me and I could tell he wanted to roll his eyes. That's when I think the girls finally noticed me. One of the girls behind Becky gave me a shy smile and flicked her black hair back.

"I can text you the address… just say you'll come."

Rhys bit down on his lip. I almost died on the spot. That fucking lip of his. Always drove me crazy. And he damn well knew it.

"You can bring your friend." Becky indicated me with her hand.

Rhys popped his sketchpad and pencil down before stroking a hand along my hair.

"You mean my boyfriend."

All the girls looked stupefied for a full minute. I fought not to laugh. They clearly had no idea what to say to his statement. Then Becky coughed.

"Yes, you can bring your... boyfriend too."

He looked down at me again.

"Do you want to go, *prince?*"

Going to a party didn't exactly fill me with excitement, but maybe we'd have a good time. Especially since we were apparently being open about our relationship. I could dance with him. The thought of it made my skin tingle.

"It could be fun," I said, smiling up at him.

"See, Rhys, even he thinks you'll have a good time," Becky chimed in. "Also, hello, boyfriend."

Rhys looked contrite.

"Sorry, this is Aaron. Um, I go to school with Becky." He then pointed at the other girls. "That's Jemima, Dotty, Pen and Kiki."

The girls all exchanged hellos with me. Rhys never talked about anyone he went to school with. I wondered how well he knew these girls.

"When did this all happen?" Becky asked, waving at us.

"Recently… um, we've been best friends for years," Rhys shrugged.

"Oh my god, that's so cute. Isn't it, girls?"

They all murmured words of encouragement. I felt like we were in some kind of circus show with the way they were looking at us with such curiosity. We weren't some kind of commodity. Just two boys in love.

"You don't go to school with us, Aaron, do you?"

I shook my head.

"No, but Rhys and I went to primary together."

"Oh well, we'd love to see you at Olly's party. Maybe we can get to know the boy who's stolen quiet Rhys' heart."

My face grew hot. Rhys looked plain uncomfortable as he rubbed the back of his neck.

"Yeah, okay, Becky, we'll come… just text me when, yeah?" he said in a hurry.

She grinned at him and nodded.

"Sure thing… well, enjoy your afternoon, boys. Don't forget to put on sun cream."

Becky gave us a wink and the girls giggled before they all sloped away. Rhys banged his head back against the tree.

"Jesus Christ, I do not want to go to fucking Olly Trenton's party."

"No? You just agreed to it."

He dug his fingers in my shoulder.

"Shut up. I wanted to get them off my back. Those girls have been trying to get me to come out with them forever."

I raised an eyebrow.

"You never said."

He shrugged, picking up his sketchbook again, but I wasn't done talking about this.

"Why would I tell you about some girls trying to hit on me all the time? It's not like I've ever been interested in Becky or her friends."

I sat up and stole his sketchbook so he'd have to pay full attention to me.

"It's that you didn't tell me about them at all."

He frowned.

"They're just girls from school, A. Why would it matter?"

"She has your number."

He reached out and stroked his hand down my thigh.

"Are you jealous?"

"Huh? This isn't about me."

His mouth curved upwards. I didn't have a chance in hell when he ripped the sketchbook out of my hands, threw it down next to us and launched himself at me. His hands pinned mine in the grass as he straddled my hips.

"You are!"

"Shut up."

He leant down and ran his nose along mine.

"My prince is so cute when he's jealous."

"Fuck off."

Any attempt I made at dislodging him would go unheeded. Rhys was stronger than me.

He planted a kiss at the corner of my mouth, melting me from the inside out.

"There's no competition. I already have the hottest boy all to myself. If anything, they should be jealous of me for that."

"The hottest?"

He nodded, planting another kiss to the side of my mouth.

"Mmm, my sexy prince who I can't stop touching no matter how hard I try."

He kissed me properly then, forcing his tongue in my mouth and devouring me whole. My hands flexed against his, wanting to be buried in his hair. We'd never kissed in public before, nor been so overt about us being together. Rhys didn't seem to care. In fact, he was grinding against me, which made my cock perk up.

"*Knight*," I whimpered against his mouth.

He was going to make me damn hard in a public park. This wasn't how I envisioned this afternoon going. As he pulled back, I noticed a pair of feet nearby out of the corner of my eye.

"You two make me actually physically sick," came the voice of the one person I had zero interest in seeing.

Rhys sat up, releasing my hands and glaring at Valentine who was, for once, by himself. He had his hands stuck in his pockets and a disgusted look on his face.

"Oh no, I'm so sorry we offended your precious sensibilities, *Val*." Rhys pressed a hand to his chest in mock horror. "Why don't you fuck off if two guys kissing makes you so sick?"

I hoped Rhys wouldn't move off me. He must know he'd got me at half-mast with all his kissing. Definitely did not want to give Valentine further ammunition to berate us with.

"You two should not be fucking doing that in public. It's wrong."

His eyes flicked down to me, roaming across the expanse of my chest. I felt entirely exposed and not in a good way.

Why the fuck is there heat in his eyes? Am I actually seeing things?

He blinked the next second and it was gone, replaced by an intense loathing, making me think I'd imagined the whole thing.

"Just go away. No one forced you to come over here."

I'd just about had enough of him now. His constant taunts were exhausting.

"You need to get the fuck over yourself, Valentine. Rhys and I don't give a shit if you don't want to see us kissing. We're not harming anyone. It's a free fucking country. So if I want to kiss my boyfriend in a park, I fucking well will. Got it?"

He blinked, his mouth dropping open almost comically. Then he shook himself and glared at us.

"Whatever," he spat before turning on his heel and walking away.

"Fucking prick," Rhys called after him.

He climbed off me and sat back against the tree again, picking up his discarded sketchbook. I sat up on my elbows, cocking my head to the side. Valentine had unnerved me. I didn't like the way he'd looked at me at all.

"We should go to Olly's party, then we can shove it in that prick's face some more," Rhys muttered.

"You sure you want to go down that path?"

We'd never deliberately gone out of our way to piss Valentine off before, but some part of me wanted to get my own back on him for all the years he'd tormented us. And I think Rhys had reached his limit too.

"Yeah, fuck it. Let's go have fun, eh? If it sucks, we can just leave… and fuck instead."

He winked, which only made me grin. I pointed at my dick.

"What about now? You got me worked up."

His eyes landed on it and he bit his lip. I stifled a groan.

"Take me home then, *prince.*"

CHAPTER THIRTY SEVEN

Rhys

The moment we got through the door, Aaron was on me, pressing me back towards the stairs. His hands grasped my arse, squeezing and making me harder than ever. I wanted him so badly, every part of me ached. It was as if our appetites for each other were utterly insatiable. The past four weeks had been a blissful haze. I never wanted it to end.

"Damn it, *knight*, you get me so fucking hard," he grunted against my lips as we stumbled upstairs together, both of us unwilling to stop touching one another.

We hadn't stopped calling each other by those stupid nicknames. If anything, they'd stuck.

"Good thing I want you just as much then, isn't it?"

He groaned, hands grasping at my clothes as if he was going to tear them from my skin. I wanted to feel him in me. His body against mine. The sweet ecstasy of his cock driving into me over and over. It hadn't taken us long to work out what the other liked. The way Aaron looked at me spoke volumes. He wanted it rough. And I would let him take me the way he needed.

We stumbled into his bedroom together, hands tangled in each other's hair as we kissed without restraint. He bit down on my bottom lip, making me whimper in anticipation. The moment we reached his bed, he shoved me down on my stomach and tore my clothes off my legs. I helped him along by pulling my t-shirt off.

He walked away, ripping open his bedside drawer and grabbing the bottle from there. Then he was behind me, running his hands down my back. I could hear his laboured breathing and feel his eyes burning into my skin.

"Aaron, please."

His hand ran up my neck and into my hair as he gripped it tightly in his fist.

"You want my cock, do you?"

"Please."

"Want me to pin you down and fuck you until you're coming all over yourself?"

My only response was to whimper as his fingers brushed against my hole.

"Mmm, yes, you do, my little *knight*."

I shivered, bucking against him as he slid a lubed finger into me. How we discovered dirty talk turned us both on? One night whilst we were curled up on the sofa watching a film, I started whispering in his ear about how I wanted him to fuck me. I swear Aaron had been rougher than ever when he got me upstairs. And I loved every minute of it.

Aaron worked me until I was a panting mess beneath him, begging him to give it to me. When he pulled back, I whined in protest, desperate for him already.

It made me feel so fucking good earlier to show Aaron off as my boyfriend. It'd come naturally, telling Becky and her friends. Because everything about Aaron and me together came naturally. We were meant to be. I knew it deep in my heart. In my fucking soul. Aaron was my one and only.

I looked back at him. My heart thumped hard against my chest watching him undress. The way his muscles flexed with each movement. I could stare at Aaron all day. He was the most beautiful boy I'd ever known. From the moment we'd met, I couldn't take my eyes off him even if I'd fought so hard against us becoming friends. He had that way about him. He drew everyone around him in with his charm and charisma. Probably why I felt possessive. He was mine and I wanted to make sure everyone knew it.

"What's that smile for?" he asked, stroking his fingers down my spine when he'd stripped.

"You make me happy."

The fire in his eyes dimmed a little, his expression growing softer. Only I saw this side of him. When he was open and unreserved with his affection and desire for me.

He leant over and kissed my shoulder, his tender caress so at odds with his rough treatment from a few minutes ago.

"You make me happy too."

He kicked my legs open wider, stroking his fingers across my lower back.

"You're perfect," he whispered before pulling away.

The pop of the cap signalled foreplay was over. A minute later I felt him against me, his hand gripping my hip. I grunted when his cock slid inside, the stretch making me crazy. He neither went too fast or too slow, feeding me inch by inch so I could have time to adjust. When his hips pressed against my behind, I gripped the covers below me as I knew what would come next.

His hand ran up my back and curled into my hair, gripping onto it. Pulling his hips back, he thrust inside me again, the force of it making me moan. Aaron wasn't gentle with me at all. I didn't want him to be.

"Don't stop, *prince*, please."

The hand around my hip tightened. The way thrust into me had me rubbing against the covers, making my cock throb. At this rate, I wouldn't even need to touch myself. He knew exactly how to work me up until I exploded. He adjusted his angle slightly so he could hit my prostate. I choked out a moan.

"That's right, little *knight*, you're mine."

Aaron was possessive of me too. Hearing him tell me that made me tremble. And it only prompted him to fuck me harder. My knuckles went white in the sheets as I held on for dear fucking life.

"Aaron!"

I'd make a complete mess of his sheets if he wasn't careful.

"Close?"

"Yes," I choked out, trying desperately to hold back, wanting the feeling to last because there was nothing like this. Nothing at all. Everything about sex with Aaron had me needing more. So much more.

He pulled out of me and flipped me over, shoving me on my back. Hands were on my thighs, pushing my legs back, then he was inside me again. The expression of pure bliss on his face set my body alight. His blue-grey eyes had me drowning in their heat and intensity.

"I want to see you make a mess of yourself."

The angle was perfect, knocking against the right spot again and again. Nothing could stop this and I hadn't even wrapped my hand around my cock. The first wave hit me all at once.

"Oh fuck."

Aaron's eyes were on me as I came, crying out and straining against him as he continued to fuck me into submission. Fuck me so I knew I was his completely. The mess on my stomach only made him wilder. His thrusts growing erratic and his breathing laboured and uneven.

"Rhys," he moaned, his hands around my thighs digging in as he erupted abruptly.

I loved watching him when he came. His head thrown back, his eyes closed and his mouth slightly parted. Aaron in the throes of ecstasy was a sight to behold. Him at his most vulnerable moment. Nothing sexier than that.

His eyes opened as his head dropped and he licked his lip.

"Satisfied?" I asked, grinning.

"More than."

He leant over me, running his tongue up my chest and neck until he met my jaw, then he kissed me. My hands curled into his hair, holding him to me so he couldn't escape.

"My *prince*, I'll do anything for you," I murmured.

I felt him smile before his tongue drove between my lips. No doubt I loved this boy to death. He was my sun, my oceans and my storms. The one who made me feel alive.

He pulled away and let me up so I could get cleaned up in the bathroom with him. The two of us laid out on his bed afterwards with the windows wide open and the fan on in our boxers. The entire house was roasting hot. Aaron put the TV on and had brought up a pitcher of ice water along with glasses.

"I swear to god this heat is making me sleepy all the time," I complained, as I sipped my ice water.

"Or I'm just wearing you out with sex."

I snorted.

"Okay, also that."

"You sure you want to go to this party on Friday?"

I'd had a message from Becky whilst we were on our way back to Aaron's with the details.

"Yeah, why not? Can't do us any harm to get out more."

He reached over and stroked my hand.

"True."

I turned my head towards him. His brows were turned down and his expression wary.

"What's wrong? You don't want to?"

"No… it's not that." He lifted his shoulder in a shrug. "I just got a really weird vibe off Valentine earlier."

I raised an eyebrow.

"What kind of vibe?"

"I don't know, Rhys, he looked at me strangely. Not with hate like usual. Maybe I'm seeing things. He was acting weird though."

"He's always acting fucking weird. I'm sure it's nothing, A."

He didn't look convinced, but he smiled at me. Nothing concerning Valentine was ever good.

"We don't have to go to the party... he'll be there, guaranteed."

He shook his head.

"No, we should go. It'll be fun."

I didn't know if I believed him but decided to drop it. We were both hot and bothered right now. No point getting into an argument or anything.

It was just a stupid party.

What's the worst that could happen?

CHAPTER THIRTY EIGHT

Rhys

The heady beat pumped out of the speakers someone had brought over. Sweaty bodies crowded around us, drinks in hand whilst they swayed to the music. Some had their hands in the air. Some were grinding against each other obscenely. Others were so high off the drugs one of Olly's friends had smuggled into the house, they barely knew what was up or down any longer.

My fingers were hooked into Aaron's belt loops whilst his arms were wrapped around my neck. The two of us gazed at each other, moving in tandem to the music. Almost lost in our own little bubble. Neither of us were drinking, but it hadn't stopped us having fun. Getting to be with him like this was a high all on its own. I'd take this any day over an artificial one.

Aaron's eyes held a promise for later. His hand curled around my neck, pulling me closer so our foreheads touched. My eyes flicked down to his lips, wondering if he might kiss me. A cheer went up around us as the next song came on and someone bumped into us when the dancing became ever more vigorous.

"Want to get some water?" I all but shouted at Aaron.

He nodded, releasing me so he could take my hand instead. I turned and battled my way through the bodies given I was the bigger of the two of us. My hand tightened around Aaron's, keeping him locked to me. It was a little quieter in the kitchen, but not by much. One entire side of the counter was filled with various bottles of booze and mixers. We'd seen the inside of the fridge earlier, filled to the brim with beer. Outside in the garden beyond were huge buckets full of ice with beers too. Everyone had been encouraged to bring a bottle or two. I'd heard Olly's parties were legendary and this just proved it.

Aaron grabbed some plastic cups and filled them both with water, handing one to me. We were both hot and sweaty from dancing. I leant up against the counter and he stood next to me, leaning his head on my shoulder.

"I'm glad we came."

I glanced down at him.

"Yeah?"

"It's nice not to hide who we are, you know."

I nodded slowly. Aaron hadn't admitted his sexuality to anyone but me before everything happened between us. Now we'd both come out to everyone here without having to say a word. Our closeness with each other made a statement. And no one seemed to care. Wasn't like we were the only queer couple here. I'd seen a couple of girls sucking face in the corner and others getting handsy with each other.

We'd told my mum about our relationship. She'd been over the moon, especially since she knew how much it'd eaten me up inside. Seeing me and him find happiness together gave her everything she'd ever wanted for me. Graham likely knew, but he hadn't said anything to me. We'd barely shared more than two words since he'd come back after Mum kicked him out. Me being gay probably made him hate me even more than he already did. I didn't care what he thought. He'd lost the right to be my parent the moment he started hitting me and Mum.

"You sure it's not because you get to touch me up without breaking public decency laws?"

Aaron snorted and shoved me.

"Shut up."

"What? I see those looks you've been giving me."

"Can you blame me?"

I waved a hand at myself.

"Oh, you'd like a piece of this?"

He grinned up at me.

"Always."

I leant down towards him.

"You think anyone would notice if we disappeared for a little while?"

Heat flickered in his blue-grey depths as I stared at him.

"Can't wait until later?"

I bit my lip, knowing what it did to him.

"Oh I can, but I'm not sure about you."

He straightened and took my cup off me, placing both of ours down on the counter. Then he took my hand and dragged me out into the hallway. We had to push through the bodies littering the corridor and the couples making out on the staircase. There was a line for the bathroom, but we by-passed it, heading down the corridor. Aaron opened a door at the end, checking inside before tugging me in. He pushed me up against the door, closing it with a loud click. We seemed to be in a pink bedroom, which was only illuminated by a nightlight.

"Um, are you sure this is a good idea?" I asked, waving at the surroundings whilst he ran his hands down my sides.

"Not like anyone will find out."

His fingers worked the buttons of my jeans open as his mouth landed on my neck, licking, kissing and sucking my skin. I let out a little pant, knowing it wouldn't be long before he had his mouth wrapped around my cock.

"But this is a kid's bedroom, A."

Probably Olly's younger sister's room. It seemed so wrong to be defiling the place in the way we were about to. According to Becky, his parents had taken his younger siblings away to the Caribbean for three weeks, but Olly hadn't wanted to go.

"Close your damn eyes then."

I flattened my palms against the door and did as he said, feeling him drop to his knees and his hand pull my hardening cock from my boxers. No more protests fell out of my mouth when he licked his way up my shaft.

"*Prince*," I whimpered the moment his mouth closed over my cock.

He hummed in approval, making me twitch. No matter how many times he went down on me, I always wanted more. It's not as if we always had sex. Sometimes it was just this and sometimes a handjob. Any type of sex with Aaron set my blood on fire.

The deeper he took me, the more I fought against making too much noise. My hand curled into his hair, but I was wary of messing it up. He knew exactly how to draw this out until I begged him to let me come. Tonight, it wasn't about that sort of game between us. He wanted me to come quickly. I could tell by the pace he set. His hand curled around the base of me whilst the other was lower, brushing against my hole and making me shiver.

"Aaron," I panted. "Going to…"

He merely sucked me harder and that was it. I groaned, spurting wildly in his mouth with my release. My eyes were still closed and my chest heaving when I came down. He cleaned me up and put me away, rising to his feet and cupping my cheek. Then I felt his lips against mine and I opened. I could taste myself on him as he kissed me.

"Better, *knight*?" he murmured.

"Mmm."

Anytime Aaron's hands or mouth was on me, everything felt better. I cupped the back of his head and kissed him deeper. I smiled when he pulled away, his blue-grey eyes full of unrepressed emotion.

"Want me to repay the favour, *baby*?"

"I'm going to let the fact you called me that slide."

I reversed our positions in the blink of an eye, pushing him up against the door and running my hand over where his cock throbbed in his jeans.

"Why? You want my mouth on you that much?"

"Please, *knight*."

He knew I couldn't resist him. I wasn't in the mood for taunting. Not after he'd made me come. Didn't take me long to work open his jeans and drop to my knees. The moment his hands wrapped around my head, I knew he wanted to be in charge. I let him, opening my mouth wide so he could sink his cock deep inside. He groaned, his hips thrusting forward as he began to fuck me. I really got off on letting him take control. Aaron's dominant streak had me surrendering to him every single time.

"Rhys," he moaned as I gagged slightly around his dick when he pressed right up against the back of my mouth.

I gripped his jeans, holding on whilst he thrust harder. My eyes flicked up to his, watching the way his mouth parted, signalling he was close. When he erupted, his grunt echoed in my ears. The salty taste of him made me tremble. He pulled his cock out of my mouth and smirked. The satisfaction on his face made me grin back.

I tucked him away and rose to my full height, stroking his face with my hand.

"We're kind of sick for doing this in here."

He laughed and shoved me away before opening the door. We stumbled out and ran slap bang into the very last person we wanted to see.

"I knew this party was going to suck," came Valentine's voice as he stared at the two of us with no small amount of disapproval.

"Oh, why? Because we got invited?" I retorted as I felt Aaron stiffen next to me.

Valentine's eyes narrowed.

"What were you two doing in there?"

I snorted and took Aaron's hand. As if I'd tell him we'd just gone down on each other in a kid's bedroom.

"None of your fucking business."

I shoved past him, dragging Aaron along with me. Valentine had dampened my mood entirely. I could feel his heated stare at our backs.

"What a dick," I heard Aaron mutter behind me.

"You're telling me."

We made our way back downstairs and into the crowd dancing. The two of us got lost in the beat for a while, but it didn't feel the same any longer. So when Aaron told me he was going to get in line for the toilet, I went into the kitchen to get a drink.

I'd just started making my way back into the living room when someone shoved my shoulder as they walked by, making me spill my entire cup of water all over the place. Feeling more than a little bothered, I turned to find Valentine glaring at me.

"Watch where you're going, gay boy."

I don't know why his statement made me see red. Perhaps it was the number of times he'd called me that. Or maybe I was done being bullied. Either way, my temper got the better of me. I threw the empty cup on the floor and glared at him.

"You were the one who knocked into me."

"Whatever."

He turned to go, but I grabbed him by the shoulder and shoved him against the wall.

"I've fucking had enough of your attitude. I don't know what your problem with me and Aaron is but you need to back the fuck off, right? So what if we're gay, it's not a fucking crime. Get over yourself, you absolute prick."

He shoved me off him and started getting up in my face.

"Watch what you say to me, King."

"Or what? You going to hit me? I've done fuck all to you, Valentine. Fuck all."

"You're damn fucking right I'll hit you, cunt."

I pushed him away from me, not wanting to get into a fight even though rage coursed through me.

"You hit me, I'll just hit right back. You think I'm fucking weak, huh? Just fucking try me. Guaranteed I'll hurt you far more than you'll ever hurt me. Back off and stay away from me and Aaron, got it? Or I'll fuck you up."

Valentine tried to take a swing at me, but I stepped back, narrowly avoiding his fist.

"Hey, hey, guys break it up," called someone from behind Valentine.

He kept coming at me, but I backed away, putting distance and bodies between us.

"I'm going to fucking kill you," he roared.

Two guys grabbed hold of Valentine and held him back.

"You fucking try it, dickhead. I'll rain down hell on you if you dare come at me," I called to him. "You better watch yourself."

I was so done with this place and this prick. Before anyone could say anything else, I turned and pushed my way through the crowd. I forgot all about the fact Aaron was here. Frustration and anger pumped through my system, making me want to hit something or someone.

As soon as I got out the front door, I took a deep breath and stared up at the night's sky. The sun had set a couple of hours ago. It was probably after midnight by now. Time I got out of this place. I didn't want to be around anyone until I cooled off. So I took off, walking down the road and turning into an alley at the end. The moment I got into a small park that opened out beyond it, the oppressive air of the party started to leave me.

Fucking Valentine.

The prick had ruined my entire evening with his bullshit.

Aaron would be wondering where I'd run off to, but right then, I couldn't bring myself to text him and let him know. I wanted to calm the fuck down first. Otherwise, I might do something I later regretted. Valentine wasn't worth it. I should've ignored him instead of making a scene in front of everyone.

At least I didn't hit him.

Famous fucking last words because this evening wasn't done shitting on me just yet. Not by a long shot.

CHAPTER THIRTY NINE

Aaron

I heard raised voices in the hallway as I fought my way back downstairs. A moment later, I saw Rhys shoving his way through the crowd and walking out the front door without turning back. My heart got tight wondering what happened. I turned to the person next to me.

"What's going on?"

The guy glanced at me with wide eyes.

"Oh, didn't you see? Valentine Jenkins got into it with Rhys King again. That guy really has it out for King."

My heart sunk to my feet. I needed to go to my boyfriend. He'd likely be angry and understandably so. Valentine had put a damper on our evening. Having him get up in our faces right after we'd got each other off had been particularly unpleasant. Valentine had a way of rubbing Rhys up the wrong way.

I didn't bother finding out what was said. No point when it was probably nothing good. I fought my way through the rest of the bodies and got out the front door myself. Looking up and down the street, I couldn't see him.

"Fuck," I muttered, running my hands through my hair.

I pulled out my phone and fired off a text.

Aaron: Where did you go?

I didn't get an immediate response nor did it look like he'd even read it. Deciding not to wait, I trudged off in the direction of the park nearby, knowing Rhys might have gone that way to cool off. I made my way down the alley at the end of the road, shoving my hands in my pockets.

"Where do you think you're going?" came a voice from behind me.

I stopped, glancing back to find Valentine standing a few feet back from me. Why on earth had he followed me out here? I hadn't seen him when I'd left the party.

"What do you want?"

He started towards me, making me feel uneasy.

"Came to fucking finish what I started with your idiot boyfriend."

I turned fully, frowning.

"What is your problem with me and Rhys?"

He laughed, the sound sending a chill down my spine. I took a step back, wanting to get out of the dark alleyway and into the light at the end.

"Oh, Parrish, I don't have a problem with you. It's him."

I frowned and took a further step backwards.

"Sure seems like you have a problem with me."

326

He shook his head, giving me a smile which did nothing to make me feel any less nervous. I glanced behind me. A few more steps and we'd be under the streetlamp. I didn't like the shadows around us. They made everything seem far more sinister.

He struck then, launching himself towards me and shoving me up against the wall before I had a chance to run. He had a few inches on me so I had to crane my head up slightly to look him in the eye.

"The only problem I have is with you making fucking gooey eyes at him. You've been obsessed with King since we were kids."

"So what? It's not your business."

I tried to shove him off me, but he pressed down harder on my chest.

"I think you'll find it is. If that little prick hadn't come along, we'd have never fallen out. You were too busy protecting him to notice anything else."

I blinked, unable to comprehend the meaning behind his words. Why would he care about us being friends? I'd never liked him. The first time our parents had introduced us, he'd sneered at me. A black mark against him in my book. He was an absolute prick who'd not grown up at all in the intervening years.

"What kind of deluded bullshit have you got knocking around in your head? We were never friends."

He used his free hand to trace a finger down my cheek. The gesture made my skin crawl as did the look in his eyes. I didn't want to believe what I was seeing. Not one bit.

327

"Liar. You weren't meant to be his. And I fucking hated you for it. But I hated him more. Hated the two of you for making me feel like this."

I swallowed hard, not wanting to ask what he meant as I had a pretty good idea already.

"I like girls," he ground out. "I love pussy... but you... you fucking make me crazy."

What the actual fuck?

"I'm not gay. I fucking swear it."

I tried to move again, wanting to be as far away from this man as possible and the desire flickering in his eyes. He held me tighter against the wall, leaning towards me until his breath hit my cheek.

"It's not fucking gay if I stick it to you. That fucking King took you away from me. I'm taking you back."

I struggled harder against him.

"Get off me!"

"Oh no, no, no, Aaron. You're fucking mine."

"I'm not, you psycho. Get off me. I don't want this."

He laughed. He actually laughed. The sound made my body tense up.

"Oh, you do. You really fucking do. You've been taunting me for years."

I shook my head. Whatever he thought, he was wrong. I'd done nothing of the sort. I'd stayed away from him as much as possible. It was him constantly getting up in mine and Rhys' faces, not the other way around.

This was the most fucked up situation I'd ever been in. I should have run when I saw him.

"Get off, Valentine. I'm not fucking around."

He pulled away, giving me precious inches, but it wasn't any good. The next thing I knew, he'd grabbed me, flipped me over and pressed my front against the wall, pinning my hands to it.

"Here's what's going to happen. You're going to take it like the pussy boy you are. Just like all the girls I've fucked. It won't be any different from them. It won't make me fucking gay."

My entire body froze on the spot. I didn't know how to get out of this. Not when he held me down with such a force, my face dug into the brick wall he'd pressed me against. It hurt and I was in no doubt if he went through with this, I'd be in for a lot more pain.

I don't want this. Not with him.

The only person I'd ever consider letting fuck me would be Rhys. We'd never talked about it since we'd fallen into our roles with little hesitation. He had my heart and he could have that part of me if he wanted. I certainly did not want to give it over to Valentine. Especially not like this. The very idea of being forced horrified me.

"No. You can't! Stop it."

"Oh yes, I fucking can, Parrish."

I felt his body press against me and his cock harden on my behind. It sickened me all the more. No way in hell I'd let him rape me without putting up a fight. I couldn't allow this to happen. It would break something inside me.

"Now you better shut the fuck up and take it like a good little pussy boy."

No, no, no. This cannot be happening!

He let go of my hands so he could unzip his jeans. I felt him fumbling behind me and took the opportunity to make my escape. Dropping my arms, I bent one and elbowed him in the gut. He let out a grunt and I did the same with the other side. He loosened his grip, giving me some wriggle room. I shoved hard against him. He took a step back. I didn't want to give him a chance to recover. I pushed off the wall and spun around. I could see the shock in his eyes. So I shoved him hard again, forcing him backwards.

"You fucking prick," I almost shouted at him. "Stay the hell away from me."

I didn't care any longer. His intentions made me ill. This prick would've raped me without a second thought. My hands came up one last time as he fumbled with his clothes, trying to adjust himself so he could come after me again.

The next moments happened in slow motion. Valentine stumbled backwards, catching himself on the top step of the stairs behind him that led down to the canal. The moment he lost his balance, he let out a yelp, putting his hands out to grab hold of something but it was too late. I watched him fall backwards and heard the sickening crunch as his head slammed down on the steps below. It didn't stop there. He rolled down the steps, falling in a heap at the bottom.

I put my hand to my mouth, running towards the steps and staring down at the body at the bottom.

"Valentine?"

There was no sound or movement from him. Had the impact knocked him out?

What the fuck did I just do?

"Valentine!"

I stumbled down the steps in a hurry. This wasn't meant to happen. I'd only wanted to get him away from me.

Shit!

When I got down to the bottom, I knew things weren't good. Blood had already pooled by his head.

"Valentine?"

Leaning down, I tried to feel for a pulse at his neck. There was nothing. I staggered back, putting my hand on my mouth again. Was he dead? He couldn't be. I hadn't meant to. It was an accident.

My body shook violently, my hand trembling against my face. My whole world crumbled before my eyes. The idea of anyone finding out I'd accidentally killed Valentine making me want to throw up. I backed away to the wall next to me, pressing against it to hold myself up.

"No. No. He's not dead. He can't be."

I couldn't deal with this. Nothing felt real. How could this happen? All Rhys and I had wanted to do tonight was to have some fun. How had I ended up like this?

Rhys.

My chest ached. I needed him. He'd know what to do. He'd help me. Rhys and I would go to the ends of the earth for each other.

With shaky hands, I pulled my phone from my pocket and dialled his number.

"Hey, *prince*… I'm sorry I ran out of the party. You ready to head home?"

The sound of his voice broke me. I let out a choked moan.

"Aaron? Are you okay?"

"No," I whispered, feeling tears welling in my eyes.

"What's happened?"

My free hand flattened against the wall behind me as my legs tried to buckle under the onslaught of feelings rushing through my body.

"I need you."

"I'm coming. Where are you? Still at the party?"

The concern in his voice destroyed me.

"No... the... the canal path."

"Okay. I'll be right there, okay? You going to tell me what happened?"

I couldn't bring myself to say the words.

I think I killed Valentine.

"Just come, please. I can't do this, Rhys. I can't."

My legs gave out. I slid down the wall, not caring about the concrete grazing my skin.

"Hey, hey, you can. I'm on my way, I promise."

"Hurry."

I couldn't hold the phone up to my ear any longer. My hand dropped onto the floor below me. I could still hear Rhys' concerned voice, but nothing seemed to register with me any longer.

I killed someone. How could I do that?

I tried to remind myself it was an accident and Valentine had been attempting to rape me. It didn't matter. The guilt ate me alive. I couldn't move from the spot I'd found myself in. Rhys had to get to me. I needed him. I couldn't survive this without him.

Hurry, Rhys... please.

CHAPTER FORTY

Rhys

The panic in Aaron's voice spiked my anxiety. What the hell just happened? Why was he on the canal path? It wasn't like I'd gone too far when I'd left the party. I'd found a bench in the park and sat down, staring up at the sky whilst I calmed my warring soul.

"Aaron? Can you hear me? You still there?"

He wasn't talking any longer. I couldn't help the sickening feeling coiling in my stomach. Something terrible had happened to him. The knowledge of it sunk into my bones, making me run up the path towards the alley where the stairs to the canal were.

The moment I reached the top of them, I froze, staring down at the scene below me. I hung up and stuffed my phone in my pocket. There was a body slumped at the bottom. Beyond that, I could see another person huddled against the wall.

"Aaron?"

When he didn't answer, I hurried down the steps, not wanting to look at who was on the ground at the bottom. When my eyes fell on the body, the whole world tipped on its axis.

Why the fuck is he here?

I didn't have time for this. The most important person was Aaron. I rushed over to him, crouching down and putting my hands on his shoulders.

"Aaron?"

He slowly raised his head, looking up at me.

"Rhys," he whimpered.

"Hey, hey, I'm here. It's okay."

He reached for me, his hands grasping at my clothes and tugging me closer.

"I killed him. I killed him, Rhys."

"What?"

"Valentine is dead. I killed him, it was an accident. Oh god!"

He broke down into wracking sobs, burying his face against my chest and clutching me for all he was worth. I stroked his hair on automatic, trying to comprehend what he'd said.

"What do you mean you killed him?"

"I... I... I pushed him... he... he... he fell and now... he's... he's... he's dead."

My boy was completely distraught and honestly, I didn't know how to take what he'd told me. Why would he push Valentine down the stairs? Aaron didn't like to get into altercations with anyone unless someone had pushed him beyond his limits.

"What did he do to you?"

Aaron sobbed harder. I wanted to check on Valentine to see if he was actually dead like Aaron had said, but my boyfriend held on too tight.

"Hey, it's going to be okay, A. I promise. I'm right here."

"No," he moaned. "No, it's not. He's dead, Rhys, dead!"

I held him, letting him cry on me whilst I rocked us back and forth. How could I soothe him enough to get him to let go? We couldn't stay here like this. We needed to deal with the situation.

"I just want to check on him, okay? We'll need to call the police and an ambulance."

"No! You can't! Rhys, no."

I pulled away slightly. Aaron looked up at me, his face completely void of all colour. The fear in his blue-grey eyes made me hesitate.

"What happened, Aaron?"

He swallowed back a sob as more tears dripped down his cheeks.

"He... he... he tried to rape me."

If the prick wasn't dead already, I'd have killed him myself. Except I couldn't afford to lose control right then. Aaron was relying on me to sort this shit out. I could see he was in no fit state to do anything.

"Stay here."

He let me go, but I could feel his reluctance to do so. I rose to my feet and walked over to Valentine. I looked down at him. His chest wasn't moving and his eyes stared up at me, glassy and unblinking. I squatted on my haunches and felt for his pulse at his neck. There was no movement or activity. I put my hand close to his mouth, unable to feel any breath against it.

"Shit," I muttered.

Aaron was right. Valentine was dead. And he'd tried to rape my boyfriend. The entire situation made me feel like throwing up. I swallowed down my reaction and rose back to my feet. Then I tugged my phone out of my pocket. We had to get the police here and we could explain what happened. It was an accident. I knew Aaron. He wouldn't have done this on purpose.

"I'm going to call 999 now, okay?"

Aaron scrambled to his feet and lunged for me, grabbing my phone.

"No!"

"Hey, what's up with you? We can't leave him like this."

"Do not phone the police. Promise me. No one can find out about this, Rhys. No one. I can't... they won't believe me. How could they? It will look like I did it on purpose."

I frowned. He hadn't. If Valentine had been trying to hurt him, then it was self-defence.

"No, it won't. I know it'll be hard to talk about, but they'll believe you. Aaron, this is for the best. They'll know what to do, okay?"

He shook his head, holding my phone out of my reach and backing away.

"No. Promise me you won't tell anyone about this."

338

I saw the seriousness in his eyes. He was scared out of his mind, but we couldn't walk away without telling someone.

"Aaron…"

"No. Do you not understand? My parents, they'll call them. What if they don't believe me? What if they think I did it on purpose? Rhys, they'll kill me and use it as an excuse to break us apart. You know that. They don't want me around you. No one can know. No one."

I blinked. His parents would go absolutely crazy if they found out Aaron had got in trouble with the police. It would ruin their perfect image if it got out. And he was right. Patrick would use any excuse to ruin my friendship with his son.

I didn't know what to do. For Aaron, I'd go to the ends of the earth. This, however, wasn't something I could have ever anticipated.

"Promise me, Rhys, please."

The panic in his voice and on his face made the decision easy. It was simple. I loved Aaron. I'd always kept his secrets just as he kept mine.

I took a step towards him.

"Okay. I won't tell anyone. I promise."

The relief in his eyes had my heart in knots.

"We need to leave before someone else comes along."

He nodded. Then he turned around, picking his phone up from the ground before handing me back my own. I took his hand and he let me lead him back up the stairs and out into the alleyway. We'd caught the bus here from mine, but in all honesty, Aaron wasn't in a fit state to be around anyone. We could walk back to his from here. He didn't live too far from Olly's place.

As we walked through the park together hand in hand, I wasn't sure if I should ask exactly what Valentine did or not. I glanced at Aaron to find tears still running down his cheeks. So I pulled him off the path to the side and tipped his face up, wiping away his tears with my thumbs.

"I know it's hard, but I need you to hold it together for me, okay? Just until we get back to yours. If you keep crying like this and someone sees, I can't protect you. When they find his body, they'll appeal for witnesses if they suspect foul play. Do you understand?"

He nodded, sniffling. Then he reached up and wiped his face with his t-shirt.

This secret was now on both our consciences. Aaron might have accidentally killed Valentine, but I was an accessory to it. By calling me and not the police, he'd set us on this path. So now we had to stick together. I'd keep his secret even if it meant I had to lie about it. I'd give my fucking life to protect him.

"You good?"

"Yeah," he whispered, reaching for me and curling his arms around my neck before pressing his face into my shoulder. "I just need a second."

I wrapped my arms around him and kissed the top of his head. He could have a moment, but we needed to get as far away from here as possible. I tugged him off me and took his hand, pulling him back onto the path.

It took us half an hour to walk back to his. Neither of us spoke. We saw a few people out and about, but some of them were drunks so they'd likely not paid much attention to who we were. It made me a little paranoid, but I couldn't let on to Aaron about that. He was shaken up enough already.

When we got into his house, I took him upstairs and stripped the two of us down to our boxers. Then I put him to bed before I went downstairs to get us both a drink. I could only be glad Patrick and Kellie weren't home, but they were due back in a couple of days according to Aaron. They wanted to talk to him about his last year at school, apparently.

I took the glasses upstairs and set them on the bedside table. Crawling into bed, I wrapped my arms around Aaron and held him close to my chest. He wasn't crying, but his breathing was a little erratic.

"Do you want to talk about it?"

"What's there even to say?" he replied, his words muffled by my chest.

"Aaron…"

There were plenty of things for him to say. Like first of all, why the fuck would Valentine Jenkins try to rape him? I thought the guy was straight. It didn't make any sense whatsoever. Then again, nothing Valentine did could ever be called rational. He'd spent far too much time bullying us and generally being very homophobic.

"It was horrible, Rhys. I was so scared."

I held him tighter, reassuring him I was right there and would listen to everything he had to say.

"He followed me from the party and pinned me against the wall... then he started spouting all this stuff about how he hated you for stealing me away from him. He kept saying shit like it wasn't gay if he fucked me like a girl... he said I drove him crazy. I kept telling him to get off me and stop, but he wouldn't listen."

Rage boiled inside me, but I kept a lid on my temper. He was dead now. There wasn't anything I could do.

"He had me pinned against the wall with my back to him. I could feel him, and it terrified me, Rhys. I didn't want that. Not with him."

I stroked his hair, trying to soothe him as his body shook in my arms. Valentine trying to take that from Aaron made me sick. No one should be forced.

"When he was trying to get it out, I elbowed him in the gut twice, which gave me enough room to shove him away. I couldn't stop pushing him... it made me so angry, but he lost his footing on the top step and fell backwards. I didn't mean to kill him. I didn't mean to. It was an accident. An accident!"

"Hey, hey, A, I know. You didn't do it on purpose. It's okay. It wasn't your fault. You didn't know he would trip and fall."

"You believe me?"

Nothing in this world would make me not believe Aaron. He might have kept his feelings a secret from me, but he'd never lied about anything else.

"Yes, of course, I do. I know you. You are the gentlest soul deep down inside. You'd never hurt someone without cause, and I know you didn't mean to do this. He was trying to hurt you. You acted in self-defence."

He nodded against my chest. Whilst I still thought we should've phoned the police, I understood Aaron's fears. Now I would protect him from anything that happened as a result of this. You did that for the person you loved. And I loved Aaron more than life itself. He'd rescued me all those years ago. It was my turn to rescue him.

"I was trying to protect myself."

"I know you were."

I kissed the top of his head. He raised it from my chest, watching me with a storm brewing in those blue-grey eyes. Reaching up, he stroked his fingers across my face as if memorising the contours of my cheekbone.

"I love you."

"I love you too, A."

"Thank you for being there. I don't know what I'd do without you."

"You never have to find out."

My lip curved up at the side, remembering he'd said something similar to me when we'd been kids. If I had my way, I'd hold on to Aaron forever no matter what he'd done.

He moved closer until our noses brushed.

"I want to give it to you... what he tried to take from me."

I didn't have time to register exactly what he said. His lips landed on mine, his fingers curling around my neck and anchoring me to him.

Does he mean what I think he does?

We'd never talked about reversing roles. It's not so much I didn't want to top Aaron. It never occurred to me to ask. I was happy with how we were.

I tried to pull away so we could have a discussion about it, but he held onto me. Not wanting to use any sort of force on him after what happened, I reluctantly let him kiss me until his lips trailed down my jaw.

"Aaron—"

"Please, Rhys," he whispered, planting more kisses along my jaw. "It's my choice. I want you to fuck me."

I flinched, which made him freeze. The thought of doing that right now did not sit well with me at all. Especially not after what he'd just gone through. Aaron was clearly in a fragile emotional state. I wasn't going to take advantage of him. Ever.

He moved back, staring at me with misery and rejection written all over his face.

"You don't want me like that?"

"What? No. What makes you think that?"

"You flinched. Is it because of him? Am I not good enough anymore?"

I cupped his face, preventing him from running away. He looked like he was about to bolt.

"No, Aaron, don't do that. This has nothing to do with him." I wasn't going to say his name again. "I don't not want to do that with you. You've just been through a traumatic experience. It's about that. I wouldn't feel right about it. I love you too much to ever do anything when you're vulnerable and hurting. Do you understand?"

He stared at me for several minutes. I let him, knowing if he thought about it for long enough, he'd see I was doing this for his own good. If he still wanted me to when he'd slept and calmed down, we'd discuss it then. For now, I wasn't going to let him take that step when he might later regret it.

"I'm sorry, Rhys," he whispered.

"There's nothing for you to be sorry for." I stroked his cheek with my thumb. "I understand why. He tried to force you and you want it to be your choice."

His eyes told me everything. He wanted to be the one to decide when and if it happened. And he wanted it with me. He trusted me with that part of him. I would never betray his trust.

"I think we should try to get some sleep now, okay? Things will feel better in the morning."

He nodded and curled up against my chest again. I held him until he fell asleep, his breathing even and steady. I wasn't sure things would be better in the morning. We had Valentine's death hanging over our heads. I had to hope nothing would come back to bite us in the arse over it.

Wishful thinking, I know.

CHAPTER FORTY ONE

Aaron

or the first few minutes after I woke up, I felt nothing but peace being wrapped up in Rhys' arms. There, I was warm and safe. He'd protect me through thick and thin. My knight in shining armour. Then I remembered last night. And I trembled as the waves of guilt and self-loathing hit me like a sack of bricks.

"Aaron?"

A sob erupted from my lips. Rhys' arms tightened around me, his face pressed against my hair.

"Shh, it's okay, just let it out, *prince*."

His voice made tears fall. I couldn't handle it. I'd killed someone. I'd done it. Valentine was dead because of me. I might not have done it on purpose, but it didn't make me feel any better. It didn't make what happened go away. I'd have to live with the knowledge I'd caused someone's death for the rest of my life.

"It's all my fault," I whimpered.

His hand stroked down my back.

"It was an accident. You didn't mean to."

I clutched him harder. Rhys was my only anchor, keeping me afloat so I didn't drown in my fucked up emotions. How did anyone handle this? Almost being assaulted was already enough. To have someone's death on your hands on top of it made it one hundred times worse. Even if Valentine had tried to rape me, didn't mean he deserved to die. It's the last outcome I'd ever wanted.

Then there was the fact I'd forced Rhys into promising not to tell anyone. I saw his reluctance last night. He'd wanted to go to the police. How could I? They wouldn't believe me, not about Valentine's attempt to assault me. People didn't report rape, so why on earth would I report an attempted one? Especially not when my attacker had ended up dead. Didn't matter if it was an accident. It didn't look good on me. I'd pushed Valentine. He'd tripped because of me.

"I'm sorry, I'm so sorry I dragged you into this," I sobbed, unable to prevent those words from spilling out of my mouth.

"You needed me, Aaron, and I was there for you. Don't you know by now I'd do anything for you?"

"What if we get questioned by the police? What if they find out we were at that party?"

He pulled me away from his chest and stroked my face. His dark eyes were so full of compassion. I felt it then. The sheer depth of his love and devotion. It held my heart in a vice-like grip. This beautiful boy I'd loved over half my life was my saviour, just as I'd been his when we met.

"What part about anything do you not understand? I will keep your secrets. I will lie for you. I made a promise. I won't break that, not for the world. We're in this together. You and me. Forever. I love you, Aaron. I love you more than life its-fucking-self. This secret, I'll take it to the grave no matter what happens. No one will find out from me. Not even the police. Okay?"

I nodded. Reaching up, I ran my fingers across his bottom lip, needing to touch him to keep from breaking down entirely.

"I was scared last night. I'm still scared. And I hate that I've put you in this position. It's not fair of me."

He was about to open his mouth, but I pressed my fingers against his lips, sealing away his words.

"No, let me finish. When… when he tried to assault me, all I could think about is how I'd never be able to choose the person I wanted that with if he went ahead with it. I wanted it to be you. I still want it to be you. No matter what happens, the only person I'll ever want is you. No one can eclipse you in my heart. So when I tell you I hate putting you in this position, I mean it. This is my responsibility. It's on me."

Asking Rhys to keep a secret this big weighed heavily on me. Everything could go spectacularly wrong. Rhys' unwavering loyalty to me could be our downfall. He'd wanted to go to the police. He wanted to fix this for me. It couldn't be fixed. The damage was already done.

"I wasn't just scared they wouldn't believe me about it being an accident, but about the attempted… rape too. It made me feel weak, someone being able to overpower me like that and take away my choice… so to have the police not believe me… that would kill me. They'd have asked me all sorts of intrusive questions and there's not even any evidence he assaulted me. It's my word against a dead man's. Do you really think they're going to believe me? A boy who's not even out to his parents. What do you think they'll say when I tell them a straight guy tried to rape me? It sounds implausible even to my ears."

I dropped my fingers from his mouth. Rhys didn't look at me with anything but understanding. It made me feel worse. Everything I'd said sounded like an excuse. A justification for why I'd dragged him into this shit situation.

"It doesn't matter that he's bullied us for years. They might think I did it out of revenge, pushed him down those stairs because I snapped. The risk of them not believing me is too much… the odds are not stacked in my favour."

"You're right. They're not."

We might live in a more tolerant society, but people like Valentine still existed. I almost felt sorry for him. He clearly hadn't come to terms with his sexuality, or maybe he just got off on the power trip. Didn't matter. I couldn't feel sympathy for a man who'd bullied me and tried to force himself on me. He'd not been remorseful. He'd blamed his feelings on me and Rhys when none of it was our fault. We hadn't done anything other than exist and both happen to be gay.

"I wish I never had to ask you to keep a secret like this."

"I know, but I was never going to leave you in the dark all alone without me. You saved me all those years ago, it's about time I got to save you back."

I couldn't help smiling.

"My *knight*, I love you."

He leant down slowly and I almost sighed when our lips met. The kiss was so soft and loving, a far cry from the passion usually pulsing between the two of us. When he pulled back, I took his hand and linked our fingers, staring up at how well they fit together. Rhys and I were meant to be. Nothing could break us. Not even this.

"I still want you to be my first… and only one," I whispered.

I didn't blame him for refusing me last night. Rhys had my best interests at heart. He never wanted to hurt me. Didn't mean I wasn't sure I wanted him inside me. If anything, I was more so this morning. I trusted him with everything.

He remained quiet for a long moment, his dark eyes assessing me. I felt open and exposed, but Rhys would never take advantage of me. He was my safety.

"Okay, but we're not going to fall straight into it. Just as you wanted to work up to sex with me, I want the same with you."

"Are you sure you even want to do this at all?"

He smiled, which set my heart at ease.

"Trust me, A, I have no issues with topping you even though I've not done it before. We might not have discussed it, but I've never been against it."

My hand tightened in his.

"I want you to experience what I do when I'm in you."

His expression grew concerned.

"Is that the only reason?"

351

"No, I mean, when I thought about us having sex before we got together, it was always me on top, but now, I want to feel you. I want to know why you enjoy it so much."

His teeth dug into his bottom lip. The sight of it made my pulse spike. The urge to bite his lip drove through me. I'd never been able to resist him when he did it.

"As long as it doesn't mean you won't keep fucking me."

I raised an eyebrow. As if there was any chance of that happening.

"I'll never not want that."

He pressed his forehead against mine and closed his eyes. For the first time since last night, a little part of me felt at peace next to him. No doubt my guilt over Valentine wouldn't go away any time soon, but I had Rhys to help me through it. He would make sure I didn't fall apart. He'd keep me together.

"You are the best thing that ever happened to me," I whispered.

"So are you."

Now more than ever I knew how lucky I was to have found him. To have this love we shared. The deep, everlasting type of love people wrote poems and songs about. Even if everything else went wrong, I'd always have him. The love of my life. My soulmate.

We'd make it through together.

CHAPTER FORTY TWO

Rhys

Aaron and I had spent the past few days hauled up in his room. He'd gone through too many lows to count. When he cried, I held him and told him it'd be okay. Especially when we'd seen the news. There was a report of a body being found, but the police hadn't released many details yet. It stressed Aaron out further, but I kept telling him we had to be patient. Neither of us knew what would happen whilst they investigated it. I had to be the calm one for him, even though my worries escalated daily. The worst one being what if they suspected foul play? We had just left him there. It did look suspicious as fuck. So who knew what would happen. I was sure they'd start questioning people soon. And it was only a matter of time before they found out about Olly Trenton's party.

I had a feeling in my gut. This would not end well. Whether they found out Aaron and I were there or not, something would happen. I just wasn't sure what.

His parents were due home tomorrow, so it was our last night together alone for at least a week. Then we only had one more week left before school started again. I wasn't looking forward to it at all. Having spent the entire summer with Aaron, it'd feel weird going back to only seeing him a few times a week. I'd miss the fuck out of him.

"What are you thinking about?" he asked, stroking his fingers down my bare chest as we both laid out on his bed after stuffing our faces with pizza for dinner.

"Don't want the summer to end. We won't see each other as much."

He rested his head on my shoulder. Aaron had been particularly clingy since the Valentine incident, but I put it down to his fragile state of mind. Besides, I wasn't going to complain about my boyfriend wanting cuddles and affection. I happily gave it to him.

"We'll still study together though, right?"

"Course."

As if that was in any doubt. Aaron needed my help more often than not. I'd never minded. It kept his parents off his back when he got good grades.

"Then we'll see each other all the time."

"Mmm, true. Want to watch Netflix or something?"

He shook his head. I looked down at him. His blue-grey eyes had that twinkle in them. One I knew all too well.

"I want you to…" He swallowed. "I'm ready to…"

He'd been growing more insistent about the sex thing. I don't know what the rush was, but Aaron really wanted me to take his virginity. Don't get me wrong, I wanted to, especially after we'd spent the past couple of days with him on his back and me testing the waters. The misgivings I had were about his state of mind. I didn't want him to freak out or anything after Valentine had tried to force him. And I had worries about my own ability to make it feel good for him.

"A, we talked about this."

He sat up and stared down at me. Whilst he didn't look annoyed, his expression made me aware he wasn't happy.

"Stop treating me with kid gloves already, Rhys."

"I'm not. Is me worrying about your well-being a bad thing?"

He frowned.

"No. I just wish you'd trust me."

"I do."

"Then why won't you?"

I rubbed my face. Getting into an argument with him over sex was my idea of hell right now.

"I'm scared I'll be shit at it or you won't like it or I'll hurt you. That's why. You're so confident about all of this. I'm not... I mean, shit, Aaron, I only realised I'm gay weeks ago."

He took my hand, pulling it away from my face and holding it in his. I hadn't told him about my fears since I wanted to be the strong one for him.

"I've been putting too much pressure on you."

I raised up on my elbow.

"That's not what I'm saying. I just don't want to do it wrong."

He eyed me for a long moment, his expression almost contemplative. Then he dropped my hand and pointed at the headboard.

"Sit up there."

I raised an eyebrow.

"Why?"

"I understand your fears and I don't want you to be scared, so I'm going to make it easy for you."

I still wasn't sure what he meant, but I pushed myself up and got settled back against the headboard. Aaron straddled my lap and cupped my face with both hands. His eyes grew darker and more intense when he leant closer. My cock thickened the moment he sucked my bottom lip into his mouth, his teeth grazing along it. Honestly, it didn't take much to get me hard when he touched me.

I knew he'd felt it when he started grinding against me. My hands wrapped around his hips, encouraging him. Kissing him. Touching him. It helped me get lost in the sensations and feelings. I'd always been more comfortable when he took control as much as I loved teasing him.

His hand dragged down my chest, making me moan in his mouth. Mine curled around his behind, squeezing as I became aware of what he was trying to do. Get me out of my head so I stopped worrying. Having him on top of me certainly did that.

He pulled away so he could tug our clothes off. As he kissed me again, he tugged open the bedside drawer with one hand. Then he slapped the bottle of lube into my hand, making it clear what he wanted.

"Aaron…"

Pulling back, he cupped my face.

"All you have to do is prep me."

I nodded, not wanting to press the issue any further. I had to accept he wanted this. Trust he would stop me if he wasn't enjoying it. So I did what he asked of me, watching him pant and close his eyes. His hands gripped my shoulders. The sight of it only made me harder. My fears started to dissipate. I wanted this. To be buried inside him. To feel the way he did when he fucked me.

"Rhys, more," he moaned.

I slipped a third finger inside him, stretching him out further. He started to grind against me again as if he needed the friction.

"You want it, *prince*?" I murmured, leaning closer and running my cheek across his.

He let out a whimper, the sound like music to my ears, making my confidence grow in swathes.

"You going to sit on my dick, huh?"

"Yes," he hissed.

I slipped my fingers from him, grabbing the tissues and cleaning them off. Aaron picked up the lube and coated my cock in it. I held it for him as he adjusted our position slightly. My eyes were on him, making sure he was okay as he lowered himself on my cock. The moment I slid into him, I let out a harsh breath, not at all prepared for the overload on my senses. Aaron's fingers dug into my shoulders where he was holding onto me.

"Fuck," he breathed.

"You're telling me," I muttered.

His lips curved upwards before he took a deep breath. I laid my free hand on his thigh, not to push him down, but needing to hold on to him somehow.

He took it slow, sinking down on me inch by inch and stopping to let himself adjust. I couldn't believe it when I was almost fully inside him. The feeling was unlike anything else. Hot and tight. The urge to thrust raced through me, but I held back. I'd meant what I said. I didn't want to hurt him.

"You holding up okay there?" I asked when I noticed his eyes were closed.

"It hurts more than I expected it to."

Exactly what I was worried about.

"Do you want to stop?"

He shook his head, opening his eyes and staring straight into mine.

"No… I just need… movement."

Not letting me say anything else, he gripped my shoulders harder and rose up before sliding back down. I let out a grunt and him a little moan. My hand tightened around his thigh. This felt so good. He felt fucking amazing. Now I got it. Why he wanted inside me. Why he enjoyed fucking me so much.

"Fuck," I ground out. "You're so… tight."

He bit his lip, moving a little faster.

"You're not exactly small."

I snorted, unable to help myself.

"Is that why you didn't want to do this before?"

He slapped my chest.

"No, I happen to like the size of your cock."

"Just as well I like yours too."

He smiled before kissing me. I curled my hands around his hips, guiding him into a better angle for me as he continued to ride my dick. He moaned in my mouth, so I assumed I'd started to hit the right spot. Now I knew he was okay, I really wanted to fuck him. Perhaps not in quite the possessive and rough way he did with me, but I wanted to set the pace.

"*Prince*," I murmured. "I want you on your back."

He pulled away, a smile spreading across his face. A moment later, he slid off me and laid back against the bed. I was right there with him, spreading his legs and pushing them up. Applying more lube before I slid back inside him, I felt like I was in heaven. I leant over Aaron and kissed him whilst I started to thrust inside his tight little hole.

Fuck me, I had no idea it would be this good.

"Harder," he moaned, his hands grasping at me.

I obliged, slightly adjusting the angle again. His fingers dug into my skin and his moans grew louder.

"Yes, yes, fuck, like that, *knight*, don't stop. Fuck, don't stop."

No way would I be doing that. I could do this all fucking night. My hand slid between us and wrapped around his cock, stroking in time with my thrusts. It only made him beg me more. That sped up my impending climax. The sensations ran up my spine. I wanted him to fall apart with me.

"Rhys, god, fuck me."

His blue-grey eyes burnt with need. Telling me how close he was to snapping. And when he did, I followed him off the edge. My eyes almost rolled back in my head as the bliss overtook everything else.

I tried not to collapse on him when I came down, but my limbs shook with the effort. So I pulled out of him and flopped down on the bed, trying to catch my breath.

"That was…" I started.

"…kind of amazing," he finished for me.

I grinned, happy he'd enjoyed it as much as me. He'd spent long enough harassing me so I'd have felt like shit if he'd not.

"Please tell me you're okay with watching Netflix and chilling out after that."

He snorted.

"Sure, after we clean up."

I felt content and happy when we got back from the bathroom. We curled up under the covers together and put a show on. Aaron wrapped himself around me, resting his head on my shoulder whilst I stroked his arm absentmindedly. Nothing felt as good as this. Being with him in the aftermath of sex.

For the rest of the night, I didn't think about the events of a couple of days ago. I almost forgot it even happened.

And that was my first mistake.

The second was yet to come.

CHAPTER FORTY THREE

Rhys

*S*aying goodbye to Aaron before I went home was painful. His eyes had been full of agony, as if being without me physically pained him. I didn't want to hang around his parents any more than I had to. They'd been polite enough to me, but I knew how much Patrick hated me being around his son. Especially after the last time I'd seen him. Aaron had fessed up about what happened in the car after they'd dropped me home. I'd appreciated him coming to my defence, even if it had fallen on deaf ears.

When I got in, I was happy to find Graham wasn't home. Mum was in the living room so I took a seat on the sofa next to her after kissing her cheek.

"I didn't expect you home," she said, turning down the volume on the TV.

"Aaron's parents are back for a week."

She nodded in understanding. I'd told her all about them and their dislike of me. Our parents had never met in person and I could only be glad of it. Didn't need Patrick looking down on them more than he did already.

"How's Aaron?"

"He's okay."

Her brows turned down.

"Don't tell me the two of you have fallen out again?"

"Huh? No, we're good."

I was not going to tell my mum about the fucking party and the shit with Valentine. It'd set me on edge enough as it was. Not being close to Aaron right now made me nervous. Mostly for him. I didn't want anything to go wrong.

"Pleased to hear it. You should bring him around for dinner soon."

"Yeah, I will do... just not when Graham is here."

Mum pursed her lips but didn't comment on it. She understood why. Graham did not approve of my relationship with Aaron in the slightest. She'd told him about it and he'd gone off on a rant about how gays shouldn't have rights. And it'd only made him hate me all the more. I'd known having a gay son would only piss him off. The number of times he'd railed against anyone who was different from him didn't bear thinking about. Probably a good thing Mum hadn't tried to explain to him I was demisexual too.

Besides, Graham and I had barely exchanged more than a few words over the past few weeks. We kept out of each other's way. Just as well I only had a year left of school then I could go off to university. I had no plans to stay at home to attend, regardless of where I got accepted. As much as I loved my mum, putting up with Graham was more aggravation than it was worth.

The doorbell rang. I started to rise, but Mum put a hand on my arm.

"I'll get it."

"You sure?"

"It's probably one of the neighbours."

She gave me a smile, getting up and walking out into the hallway. The front door opened and voices filtered down the hallway.

"Good morning, ma'am, I'm PC Lambert and this is Detective Sargent Mandrake. Are you Mrs King?" came a deep voice.

"Yes, can I ask what this is about?"

"Is your son home, Mrs King?"

"Rhys? Yes, he's here."

All of my limbs locked up. The police were here. It meant they knew something about me being there that night. The night Valentine died. There could be no other explanation.

"Would we be able to come in? We need to speak to your son."

"Um, yes, of course."

I had no idea what they were going to ask me or what they'd discovered.

Fuck. Fuck. Fuck.

Mum came back in the living room, her eyes full of concern. I wanted to reassure her, but I couldn't. She was followed by four police officers. It was at that point I knew this would not be just them questioning me.

I had to protect Aaron at all costs. Whatever happened next, I would keep silent about his involvement.

I stood up from the sofa as one of the officers approached me.

"Rhys King?"

"Yes."

"I'm Detective Sargent Mandrake. I'm afraid I'm here to inform you I'm arresting you on suspicion of the murder of Valentine Jenkins, which took place on the evening of the fourteenth of August. You do not have to say anything, but it may harm your defence if you do not mention when questioned something which you later rely on in court. Anything you do say may be given in evidence. Is that understood?"

I swallowed hard. Arrested. I was being arrested. How the fuck had this happened? I had nothing to do with Valentine's death. I'd merely helped Aaron leave the scene. Yes, it made me an accessory, but I hadn't murdered him. His death was an accident. If anything, it was a manslaughter charge, not murder.

Fuck.

"Yes, sir."

"As you are under the age of eighteen, you have the right to have your guardian with you. Would this be your mother here?"

The officer indicated my mum with his hand. I glanced at her. Mum's eyes were wide with shock and horror. I had to think quickly about this and remain calm no matter how much my heart pounded in my chest and I felt sick to my stomach.

"Yes. Is it okay if she makes a phone call to my father first? We need to let him know as my mum has a disability and he's her carer."

I actually wanted Mum to call Aaron. I hoped since I was being reasonable with them, they would allow this.

"Of course, I understand."

I looked at Mum again. She hadn't moved from her spot.

"Mum?"

She shook herself.

"Yes, of course, I'll just get my phone. I left it in the kitchen."

I gave her a significant look.

Please call Aaron, not Graham.

I wasn't sure if she got the message I was trying to convey or not, but she gave me a nod before disappearing from the room. I looked at the officers, not knowing what to say. Obviously, I wasn't about to say anything incriminating, but considering I hadn't killed Valentine, it didn't matter.

How on earth would I get through this shit? I'd never been in trouble with the police before. And this wasn't some kind of minor crime. This was serious. They suspected me of murder. Of all the scenarios I'd imagined, this hadn't been one of them. If anyone should be arrested, it was Aaron. Why would they suspect me? I hadn't done anything.

Then I remembered I'd had that huge argument with Valentine in front of everyone at the party. And most of the kids there knew Valentine had bullied me for years. Did they suspect I had an altercation with Valentine after I stormed out? This couldn't be good. Everyone had seen me leave but had they noticed Aaron? Probably not.

I had to keep my boyfriend safe. If the police didn't know he'd left the party, then I'd keep it that way. I'd told Aaron I'd lie for him and would never tell the police. It didn't mean I was going to take the fall for this. They couldn't pin a crime on me I hadn't committed. Not unless they had real evidence. And I hadn't left any of that behind as far as I remembered.

They had to have something if they'd gone so far as to arrest me. I wondered what it was. No doubt I'd find out soon enough when we got to the police station.

This sucked. Why had this come down on my head? The only thing I'd done was to protect Aaron when he asked me to. I didn't deserve this shit. My feelings were tangled up inside me. I couldn't admit to them I'd been there after Valentine had died. No, I just had to tell them I left and walked home. People had seen Aaron and I together, hadn't they? How could I keep Aaron out of this entirely?

What a fucking mess!

Mum came back into the living room and walked straight over to me. The officer didn't object to her wrapping me up in her arms. I leant down so she could hold me properly. She pressed her mouth up to my ear.

"I called Aaron," she whispered. "Please tell me you didn't do this."

I shook my head. This wasn't my fault. None of it.

She called Aaron. It will be okay. At least he knows. He'll do something. I hope.

Then she let me go and the officer stepped forward. He looked a little sympathetic as he took out his handcuffs. I put my hands out towards him, willingly accepting my fate.

Don't break down. Stay strong. You can do this. They won't pin this on you if you tell them most of the truth.

I had to hope they'd believe me as they led me and Mum from the house. The neighbours were looking on. The police showing up on the estate wasn't an unusual occurrence. Arresting me, however, was. Old Nat Jacobs' curtains twitched. I was surprised she hadn't popped her clogs yet. The woman was in her nineties. No doubt she was shaking her head over all of this.

They pressed me down into the backseat and allowed Mum to sit next to me. I looked over at her, worried about what she was thinking. She had to know I'd never hurt another soul. I couldn't ask her what she'd told Aaron or what he'd said. It would put everything at risk. I hoped he wouldn't come and try to save me by turning himself in. Not after we'd covered up what he'd done. It would look worse on both of us. Better for me to be in this situation where I could tell them I hadn't been involved. That was the truth. I hadn't pushed Valentine down those stairs.

So even though I'd have to lie to them about my knowledge of Valentine's death, I could at the very least, tell them I hadn't killed him. It wasn't me. It was Aaron.

And no matter what, I'd protect him. I wouldn't let the police find out what he'd done. Aaron was my world and owned my heart. I'd be his knight in shining armour and save him from a fate he didn't deserve. I'd save him from everything by sacrificing myself if I had to.

CHAPTER FORTY FOUR

Aaron

Having my parents home fucking sucked. Especially after everything Rhys and I had gone through over the past week. We didn't need further shit happening. I already missed him even though he'd only been gone for an hour. I'd said hello to Mum and Dad, but we'd not had any interaction other than that. They seemed to be busy dealing with something now they were back home. It was always like this. No doubt they'd want to speak to me later. That's why they were here after all.

I slumped on my bed, stroking my hand across the pillow where Rhys had slept. It still smelt of him. I might be crazy, but I loved that boy more than life itself. He meant everything to me. Giving him my virginity last night had felt so natural. So perfect. Whilst it had hurt at first, it had felt incredible after that. It made my heart swell to think I'd got to make a choice in the matter and have it be the love of my life. We'd shared all our firsts together. First kiss. First love. Losing our virginity. Everything about Rhys and I was fucking magical.

My phone rang. I reached over and grabbed it off the bedside table. Frowning when I saw it was Steph calling me, I answered it.

I wonder why it's her and not Rhys.

"Hi, Steph."

"Oh, Aaron, I don't know what to do. Rhys is in so much trouble."

I froze. Dread made my skin prickle all over. This couldn't be good at all.

"What?"

"The police are here... they've arrested him. They suspect he murdered someone... that boy who's been in the news. The one they found on the canal path."

My entire world went down in flames. Rhys had been arrested. My boy had been arrested for Valentine's murder.

What the fuck?

"What do you mean? Why would they arrest him for that?"

"I don't know, but I'm going down to the police station with him. He's underage so he needs a guardian. Aaron, he didn't do this, right? You've been with him for days. Please tell me my son didn't kill this boy."

I shook my head.

No, I did. I killed Valentine.

"No, Steph, he didn't." My voice came out all shaky and I tried to keep myself under control, but I was falling apart on the inside. "Rhys would never do anything like that."

"I don't know what to do. I've never been in this situation before."

Neither had I. What the fuck did we do? Rhys would need legal help to get him out of this, wouldn't he? And he needed me. I had to make sure he didn't get charged with murder. It would be selfish of me to let him take the fall for it.

"Just go with him to the police station and find out what's going on."

"Okay, love. I thought I'd let you know as Rhys would want that. I'll call you later when I know what's happening."

"Thank you… and tell Rhys I love him if you can."

"I will, love."

We hung up. My hand dropped down beside me. Rhys had been arrested. How could this have happened? He didn't do anything wrong other than help me get away from the scene. There was no way in hell I could allow him to get in trouble for me. I didn't have time to think about the consequences. I had to get to Rhys now and make sure they didn't charge him with murder.

Jumping up from the bed, I stuffed my phone in my pocket and headed out of my room. I ran down the stairs and was at the front door, pulling my shoes on. Mum came out of the kitchen, frowning when she spied me.

Great, just what I need.

"Aaron, where are you going?"

"Can't talk right now, Mum. Rhys has been arrested. I need to go to him."

"What?"

"Rhys got arrested by the police. They think he killed someone, but he didn't. I have to go."

Mum put her hand on my arm, stopping me in my tracks.

"Hold on, he was arrested for murder?"

"Yes, Mum! Let go. I have to set them straight."

She put her other hand on my shoulder.

"Aaron, I think you need to come and speak to me about this properly with your father."

I stared at her. Didn't she understand? This situation was urgent. I couldn't let him get charged with murder. Rhys hadn't done anything wrong.

"But Mum—"

"No, come into the kitchen now."

I didn't have any choice but to follow her. My dad sat at the breakfast counter with a newspaper. He raised his head and frowned when he saw me.

"What's going on?"

"Aaron says Rhys has been arrested for murder," Mum replied.

Dad's eyebrows shot up.

"I knew that boy was nothing but trouble."

"No, Dad, he didn't do it. It wasn't him. And they only suspect it, he's not been charged. I have to find out which station they took him to. I have to go."

"You are not going down to the police station, Aaron. There is no need for you to get involved in this."

I stared at him. How could he not see this had everything to do with me? I'd killed Valentine. Not Rhys. He was innocent.

"I have to go!"

Mum put a hand on my shoulder.

"Listen to your father, Aaron."

My parents were fucking stupid. They had no clue. No idea. The very thought of how distressed Rhys would be right now killed me. How he'd protect me at the expense of himself. I'd never allow that. I couldn't.

"No. No! You don't get it. I can't let him go down for this. I can't."

"Shh, it's okay, Aaron. I know it's upsetting—"

"Upsetting? It's not fucking upsetting, Mum. He didn't kill Valentine. He didn't!"

"Valentine Jenkins? Howard's son? He's dead?" my dad exclaimed.

My hands shook. All of my emotions pulsed through my veins, making me absolutely crazy. They weren't listening to me.

"Yes, he died, but it was an accident."

"What do you mean? How would you know that?" Mum asked.

My hands curled into fists, my blunt nails digging into my skin. There was nothing for it. The only way they'd let me go is if I told them the truth.

"Because I did it. I pushed Valentine down the stairs and he died. It's my fault. He attacked me… he tried to… he tried to assault me…" Tears welled in my eyes at the memory. "It was an accident, but it was me. Rhys didn't do it. The only thing he did was take me home after it happened. I told him we couldn't report it… I made him promise not to tell anyone."

The reality of what I'd done crashed down on me. Seeing my parent's shocked faces brought it all home. I'd made a huge mistake.

"Why would he attack you, Aaron? That makes no sense."

I took a deep breath, the violence of my emotions making my entire body shake uncontrollably.

"He was jealous of me and Rhys… because… because we're in love."

I don't think my dad's expression could have got any worse at that moment. The anger in his eyes made me take a step back.

"What did you say?" The venom dripping from his tone had me wanting to run.

My nails dug harder into my palms.

"We're in love, Dad. I'm… I'm gay."

You could hear a penny drop in the silence which followed my declaration. In those moments I knew my dad would never accept it. The way his lip twitched and the level of rage simmering in his eyes had me flinching. As did Mum rubbing my shoulder with her hand. I glanced at her. The look in her eyes made my heart shatter. The disappointment was more than I could cope with.

"Aaron, why didn't you tell me?"

I couldn't help the tear slipping down my face.

"I was scared you wouldn't understand or accept me," I whispered. "And I know you don't approve of Rhys, but I love him. He's the only piece of happiness I have in my life."

Her face crumpled and then she took me in her arms, holding me tight against her chest.

"My darling boy, I'm so sorry you felt like you couldn't come to me."

Any hold I had left on my emotions snapped. Tears fell and I clutched her clothes, my body shaking violently.

My parents had never been there for me. Not once. Her apology was too little, too late, but she'd still said sorry. I'd never get that from my dad. Never. He wouldn't be sorry for the way he treated me.

"I have to help Rhys," I sobbed. "I have to."

Mum stroked my hair.

"Shh, it's okay, my sweet boy, it's okay. I understand. I know."

I shook my head. She didn't understand. Neither of them did. Rhys was the love of my life. The only person I wanted in this world. I'd do anything for him. He needed me.

"You are not going to turn yourself in to the police, Aaron," came my father's voice from behind us.

I flinched. That would be the only sure-fire way I'd get Rhys out of this situation. I should've taken responsibility the night it happened. I should've let Rhys call the police. My stupid decision not to had only got him arrested.

"You will ruin your entire future if you hand yourself in. I will not allow it."

I pulled away from Mum, unable to comprehend how he thought allowing someone else to take the fall for me was in any way acceptable. Then again, all he cared about was making sure I had the future he'd laid out for me. Doing things his way because that's what he expected of me.

"You can't stop me!"

He stood up, his eyes hard as steel.

"Yes, I can. You're not an adult, Aaron. You are my responsibility and you are not going to the police. I don't care if you caused Valentine's death. If this gets out, it will ruin you, me and your mother."

"I can't leave Rhys to take the fall for it. I won't! I love him. He's the only person in this world who gives a shit about me. He loves me and he will protect me at all costs, but I can't let him do that. I can't!"

My father was an absolute bastard. He didn't care about Rhys or me. He only cared about his precious fucking image.

He stared me down for a long minute before letting out a huff.

"I can see you won't back down on this. I will ring my solicitor and have him take on Rhys' case on one condition. There will be no negotiations on this point, Aaron. You will do as I say without any complaints or arguing."

My heart squeezed painfully.

"What condition?"

I knew what he was about to say would destroy me. Rhys needed our help to make sure the police wouldn't charge him with murder. I knew Dad's legal team were top notch and his offer of help was more than I could've ever hoped for.

"You will end this little thing you have going on with Rhys. You will end it and you will not see him again. I don't care if you claim to love him. He has been nothing but trouble since he came into your life and this latest incident just proves it. If you weren't so insistent on being friends with him, then you wouldn't have got into that situation with Valentine."

He shook his head, his eyes dark with anger.

"I am so disappointed in you. You let that boy lead you astray. You've brought shame on our family. You'll just have to live with the fact you caused someone else's death. And you are also grounded. I will allow you out to say goodbye to Rhys and end it with him once the police let him go, but after that, you will stay home and you will concentrate on doing well at school. I'm taking away your car and I will be asking Harriet to stay here with Ralph to keep an eye on you. Do you understand?"

My heart fractured a thousand times over. What he was asking of me was impossible. I couldn't break up with Rhys. It would ruin me. I'd never be the same without him. And I couldn't believe he had the audacity to insinuate it was Rhys' fault that Valentine had attacked me. Then again, my father was a terrible person who didn't care about anyone but himself.

If I didn't accept his stipulation, I couldn't help Rhys. Dad wouldn't let me turn myself in. This was the only other way I could make sure Rhys didn't get charged with Valentine's murder. My fucking father had me over a barrel and he knew it. There was no point objecting. He wouldn't listen to me. He didn't understand my feelings towards Rhys. Neither did my mother because she stood there, not saying a single word in my defence. She didn't care my father was ripping my heart right out of my chest and wrecking my life completely.

So even as my world broke around me and I wanted to bawl my eyes out, I found myself nodding.

"Okay, Dad, I'll end it, just please help him," I whispered.

He stared at me for a minute before pulling out his phone and wallet. He tugged out a business card, stepping towards me and holding it out.

"I'll call Henry Bartlett now. You better tell Rhys' mother and give her Henry's details so she can inform the police to get in contact with him."

I took the card on automatic. Despite feeling completely shattered on the inside, I knew I had to do this for Rhys. So I trudged out into the hallway, ignoring Mum's stare and pulled out my phone. Wiping my eyes, I dialled Steph's number. She picked up after two rings.

"Hi, Aaron. We're at the police station now and he's being processed as we speak."

"Oh… um, my dad has agreed to help Rhys with legal representation. Can I give you his solicitor's details to give to the police?" My voice was all high-pitched and shaky, but I couldn't help it. I was on the verge of breaking entirely. "Henry will help Rhys with everything. I promise, he's good at what he does."

"Oh, your father really didn't need to do that."

"I know, but please accept this, Steph. It's the least I can do to help him. I know he didn't do it."

"Well, tell your father thank you from me."

We spoke for a little longer after I gave her Henry's details. By the time I got off the phone, desolation began to set in. I turned to go upstairs but found Mum watching me.

"Aaron—"

"No, don't, Mum. Just don't," I choked out. "I'll never forgive him for this. You hear me? Never. And I won't forgive you either… you let him do this to me. You stood there and let him destroy me. So don't."

I trudged away upstairs, tears streaming down my face. When I got in my room, I shut the door and walked over to my bed. I curled up in a ball on it, holding the pillow which smelt like Rhys to my face, crying into it for all I was worth. This might be painful now, but nothing would hurt me more than when I had to tell Rhys I wasn't allowed to see him again. When I had to say goodbye. I could already picture the look on his face. The devastation he'd feel. I would have to hurt him. I'd have to walk away when I'd made a promise to him when we were kids I'd never leave.

I cried harder. I was going to break all the promises I'd ever made to him. The boy I loved more than life itself. Who'd put me back together so many times. He was my whole world. He was my everything. And now I had to destroy all of it. All my hopes and dreams about us spending our lives together.

Now more than ever I hated my father. Hated him for the decision he'd forced me into making. I'd never forgive him or my mother. They'd ruined everything. Absolutely everything.

Rhys wouldn't forgive me for this either. He'd hate me. He'd tell me I'd chosen my family over him. And the worst part… that was true. My parents had left me with no choice. They'd used my love for Rhys against me.

I'd protected him but it was at the biggest cost of all.

Us.

I'm sorry, Rhys. I'm so, so sorry. I know you'll never forgive me. I hate myself for this. I hate myself so much right now.

I'd never forgive myself for doing this. For ruining everything. I'd die a thousand times over when I ended it with him. It would rip my soul in half. And those pieces would never fit back together again.

I love you, Rhys. Please remember that when I end it. Please remember I'll love you for the rest of my life.

CHAPTER FORTY FIVE

Rhys

The whole time I'd been at the police station getting processed, I'd felt my heart fucking sinking with every moment. When Mum told me Aaron's dad had provided us with a solicitor, everything got so much worse. Patrick wouldn't ever willingly help me, which meant Aaron had to give something up to get his help. The question was what? Had he told them it was him? No doubt if he had, Patrick wouldn't want Aaron getting involved in this. His dad only ever cared about his self-image. Whatever Aaron had given up, it couldn't have been good.

Patrick's solicitor was called Henry Bartlett. He'd explained in detail to my mum and me how the interview process would go after he'd had an initial consultation with the officers. He said the allegations made against me were a little flimsy given the evidence they'd shown him, but he hadn't seen everything they had. He advised me to make no comment to all questions asked of me as he didn't want me incriminating myself. There were a lot of legal details he'd explained to me as well, which I didn't really understand, but my mum seemed to. The whole thing hadn't reassured me at all.

My skin prickled as I went into the interview room with them. My nerves hit an all-time high when all the recording equipment was turned on. Henry looked at me whilst I listened to them reading my rights. Mum was sat back from us. She had a right to be in the room as I was under the age of eighteen.

"So, Rhys, we know you were at Oliver Trenton's house on the night of the fourteenth of August. We have eyewitness statements placing you there and you had an altercation with the victim in question, Valentine Jenkins," Detective Sargent Mandrake said as he placed down various pieces of paper in front of me. "Would you care to tell me what your argument with the victim was about?"

I knew what I had to say and that was nothing.

"No comment."

The DS gave me a long look before he asked me some further questions related to the party, all of which I answered in the same way. Henry told me not to incriminate myself regardless of how much I wanted to tell them I had nothing to do with Valentine's death. My only crime was knowing who'd done it and helping that person escape prosecution. I would never incriminate Aaron.

The DS set out another piece of paper with blurry CCTV footage of a lone boy walking in a park.

"You were seen walking near where the victim was found at twelve sixteen after witnesses said you left Oliver Trenton's house. Care to tell me what you were doing here?"

I did not know they had footage of me. It made me nervous as hell. I glanced at Henry who gave me a subtle nod.

"No comment."

"Do you want to explain what happened between when you left Oliver Trenton's house and when you were next seen here at twelve forty-seven walking hand in hand with another boy?"

He set out another photo which showed me and Aaron together. It made my stomach twist in knots. I couldn't believe they had pictures of this. They'd clearly done a thorough job in investigating and that's why they'd arrested me.

"No comment."

"Can you identify this person in the photo here for me?"

He pointed at Aaron. No way in hell would I be telling him. Protecting Aaron from this shit is the only way I could get through it. I could deal with the police questioning me if it meant I kept the love of my life safe.

"No comment."

I could tell the DS was slightly irritated with my insistence on not answering his questions, but I'm sure he was used to it. Henry had assured me he advised a lot of his clients to respond with no comment during police interviews. He said they would be looking to trip me up as he suspected they did not have the evidence they needed to convict me of murder. I had to hold on to that no matter how much this whole process scared the hell out of me.

The DS looked at the officer next to him. That's when I knew. They hadn't been able to identify it was Aaron. They'd not caught his face on camera like they had mine. The relief I felt knowing that spread throughout my system.

They asked me some further questions. All in the same vein as the ones before, trying to get me to talk, but I kept responding the same way. By the time the interview was over, I felt on edge and completely overwhelmed. The evidence they had didn't look to me like it was enough, but I didn't know for sure.

When the officers had turned off the equipment and left the room, saying someone would be back to take me to the cell again, Henry turned to me.

"I do not believe they have enough evidence to charge you," were the first words out of his mouth.

"No?"

"They want a confession of guilt. That's why they were pressing you. Not answering was your best call. Now we just have to wait. They'll have to go to the Crown Prosecution Service with the evidence they have, regardless. They will decide whether or not you will be charged."

I nodded. Mum stood up and came over to me, giving me a hug.

"It'll be okay, love. You did nothing wrong."

I had done something wrong. I'd not told them who was with me that night. And I'd not told them Aaron responsible for Valentine's death. Those things couldn't be helped. Betraying Aaron was the very last thing I'd do.

When the police came to take me back to the cell, I didn't feel confident about what would happen next. Whilst I'd taken Henry's advice and he'd said he didn't think they would charge me, there was still a risk there.

Sitting alone in a prison cell made me think a lot about how I'd got there. The entire thing was insane. Aaron and I should have gone to the police that night. Told them the truth. But we couldn't take it back now. We'd made our bed. I had to hope it wouldn't completely backfire on us.

When two officers came to let me out of the cell, I wasn't sure how much time had passed. They took me to the front desk where Mum was waiting for me. She had a nervous smile on her face, which worried me. The officer at the front desk gave me a nod as I stood in front of it flanked by the other two.

"Okay, Rhys, I'm advising you no further action will be taken today. That means we won't be charging you at this time. You are free to leave. I need you to sign a few things for me then your mother can take you home."

My knees almost buckled with the relief I felt at hearing those words. I went through the process of them discharging me on automatic. They explained other things to me about why I was being released but I was hardly listening. All I could think about was seeing Aaron and holding onto him tight. I was so relieved. They couldn't charge me. I wouldn't have to go through a court case. And I'd kept Aaron's name from coming to light. All of those things shouldn't make me feel happy since someone had died, but they did.

Mum and I caught the bus home. She kept looking at me with concern and I felt bad, but I wasn't sure what I could tell her. She'd had to spend hours at the police station with me worrying I might be charged with murder. It couldn't have been easy on her. I was the one who'd had to sit in a prison cell and undergo an interrogation. We'd both been through it today.

I pulled out my phone on the way and sent a text to Aaron. Hopefully, he'd come over when he saw it. That's if his parents even let him out.

Rhys: They didn't have enough evidence to charge me. On my way home with Mum now. Love you x

I didn't get a response even though I saw that he'd read it. It was my first sign things weren't good. I had to hope when we saw each other, it would be okay. There was nothing I wanted more in the world than to hold him in my arms and never let go.

Graham still wasn't home when we got back, probably at the pub. I could only be glad about that. It was almost dinner time so Mum put some food on before she made us tea and we sat together at the kitchen table. She reached over and put a hand on mine.

"Are you okay, love?"

"Not exactly."

The whole thing had shaken me. Getting arrested for a serious crime I didn't commit was probably the most fucked up thing to happen in the last few years.

"You promise me you didn't hurt that boy."

"I didn't do anything, Mum, I swear. Valentine was a dick who bullied me and Aaron, but that doesn't mean I wanted to hurt him."

She stroked my hand.

"I know, love. I'm sorry I asked, you'd never do anything like that. This whole thing has put me on edge."

"Me too."

We lapsed into silence for a moment. I looked up at her. She seemed sad which broke my heart.

"Don't tell Graham about this, Mum. You know it will only make things worse."

She nodded which I hadn't expected her to do.

"Don't worry, Rhys love, I won't tell your father. You're right. He won't take that news well and we don't need any more trouble right now."

I felt relief at that. Now I had to wait for Aaron to contact me. It worried me no end he'd not responded to my text. If there was ever a time I needed him, it was right now.

Where is he?

CHAPTER FORTY SIX

Rhys

A whole day went by without a word from Aaron. It'd made me nervous and I worried what had happened between him and his parents. We'd rarely gone a few days without talking in the ten years we'd known each other.

I was just getting a glass of water from the kitchen to go to bed with when the doorbell rang.

"I'll get it, Mum," I called, carrying my glass out into the hallway.

"Okay, love," she called back from the living room.

Graham hadn't come home and I didn't ask her where he was. I didn't care to be honest. The longer he stayed away, the better. Then I wouldn't have to deal with his bullshit.

I set the glass down on the side table by the door and opened it. Aaron stood there with sad eyes and a tense expression on his face. It set me on edge but didn't stop me barrelling my way into his arms and holding him tightly. The relief I felt being in his presence flooded my veins, warming me from the inside out.

"Aaron," I breathed.

"Hi."

His voice sounded all quiet and laced with pain. That single word betrayed so much. The reason he was here wasn't a happy one. I didn't want to believe it. The only thing I wanted was for us to hold on to each other and never let go.

I dropped my arms from him and stepped back with some reluctance. His expression had fallen further. I had a feeling I knew exactly what was about to happen. So even as my heart constricted, I took his hand and led him inside. I shut the front door and snagged my glass before walking upstairs. Aaron followed me without a word.

When we got into my bedroom, I set down the glass on the bedside table before turning to him. He'd shut the door behind us. His blue-grey eyes were like storm clouds, filled with agony and brimming with tears.

"Whatever you're about to say, don't... just don't."

"Rhys..."

I put a hand up.

"Don't," I whispered, almost unable to get the word out. My throat constricted and my chest burnt with an intensity I'd never experienced before.

His expression grew ever more pained. The sight of it severed me clean in two and he hadn't even spoken the words yet.

"I can't see you anymore."

"No, don't say that."

"I don't want to do this, but I have no choice," his voice broke on the words. "He's making me, Rhys. God, fuck, this hurts so much. I'm so sorry."

Tears slipped down his cheeks and I realised they were falling down mine too. When had they appeared? The world seemed to swallow me up in a vortex of emotion. A sharp pain lanced across my chest, tearing my insides to pieces.

I shook my head. Those words were like icicles falling on me, piercing through my skin and shredding my soul.

"You always have a choice. He can't make you do this."

Aaron took a step towards me. The desire to let him hold me and take this away was almost overwhelming.

"I wish that was true. He forced my hand. I'm not allowed to see you. I had to agree to what he demanded so he'd help make sure you didn't take the fall for what I did. You didn't deserve to get arrested for something you had nothing to do with. I wasn't going to let that happen."

His hands came up as if he was trying to make me understand his predicament. I understood just fine. Patrick Parrish was a cunt of the highest order who didn't care an ounce about his son's happiness. Who did whatever he wanted because he was rich and powerful, including forcing his son to bend to his will. I understood. And I hated it and him more than words could say.

"I'm grounded. He's taking away my car and Harriet and Ralph are coming to live at the house until I finish school. They're basically my fucking gatekeepers. He left me with no choice. If I was eighteen, it would be different, but I'm not."

He sucked in a choked breath and took another step towards me.

"Don't look at me like that, please. I'm sorry. I'm so, so sorry. I don't want to do this. Fuck! You know how much I love you... you are my entire world, Rhys. You are my everything. I can't stand this. I won't survive without you."

My hands trembled at my sides, the violence of my feelings sucking me into a black hole of desperation.

"Then don't do this."

He closed the distance and brought his hands up, cupping my face. His touch seared into me. I loved and hated it at the same time. Aaron would always have this strange power over me. For the last ten years, he'd helped me see the good in the world. See I had things worth living for. Namely him and my mum. He'd taken my bruised soul and healed it. And now he was maiming me beyond recognition. He was undoing everything by ending not only our relationship, but our friendship too.

"Please don't," I all but whimpered.

"I love you," he whispered. "I will always love you."

I didn't want to hear those words from him when he was breaking my heart. Breaking my whole damn soul.

"Don't say that."

"I love you."

I shook my head even as I reached for him, unable to help myself. The moment my hands ghosted up his chest, I could no longer control the despair coursing through every part of me. My knees almost buckled under the onslaught.

"I can't live without you," I sobbed, the words coming out in a choked moan of pain.

Instead of answering me with words, he answered with his lips on mine. The bloom of torturous pleasure washed over me. My hands clutched his t-shirt, pulling him closer even as my head screamed at me to stop this. My heart wanted Aaron more. It drowned out the noise. The only sounds I could hear were of our desperation for each other.

The moment his teeth closed around my bottom lip, the sharp pricks of pain echoing the anguish in my heart, I lost all sense of control. I had to have him. Aaron was the air I breathed into my lungs. He was my oxygen and depriving myself of it would lead to my ultimate demise.

My hands were in his hair, tugging at the strands and no doubt causing him pain, but I wanted him to hurt. I wanted both of us to drown in misery and regrets. And when he pressed me down on my bed, I let him, not caring how much this would wreck me afterwards.

We fumbled with each other's clothes, tugging at zips to gain access to the parts we needed. The moment his hand wrapped around my cock, I moaned in his mouth. His touch was my kryptonite just as mine was his. We stroked each other, the harsh sound of our mutual breath echoing in my ears. Our eyes were glued to each other, foreheads pressed together as neither of us could look away. His conveyed all the horrific torment at what his father had forced him into. The sight of it ruined me. Knowing he was hurting as much as me was like knives against my skin.

"Do you still love me?" he whispered, his breath fluttering against my lips.

I didn't want to say those words, but they were ripped from me anyway.

"I will always love you."

It didn't matter we were ending. My heart would always belong to Aaron. He had the keys to it. And he'd take them away with him when he walked out of my life. The thought of it made more tears spill down my face.

"Don't leave me."

His tears fell on my cheeks before he kissed me again. We chased the high together. The bittersweet ending of pleasure and pain ripped through our chests when we came. There weren't any more words anyway. I couldn't keep begging him to stay and hearing him tell me he couldn't. There wouldn't be enough times we could say we loved each other even whilst everything crashed down around us. Our love had become a weapon his father had used against us. And I hated Aaron for going along with it. Hated him for doing this to us. Decimating everything we shared in one single moment.

We sat on my bed together after we'd cleaned up, both staring at the floor as if knowing this was the end. This was the final chapter. Our lives had been so entwined for ten years. They flashed before my eyes in an instant, reminding me of how beautiful our friendship had always been.

"I'm sorry," he whispered.

Sorry wasn't good enough. Sorry wouldn't bring back what he'd broken. Sorry only brought more pain. And sorry only reminded me of how vast the differences between us were.

He'd always come from privilege and I'd always come from nothing.

I turned my head towards him.

"Your dad is a cunt."

"I know."

His abject defeat only served to make me angry. Had he not fought for us? Had he not tried to tell his father no?

"Did you even try to stop him from doing this?"

He didn't look at me. I had my answer there.

"You didn't fight for us."

Aaron put his head in his hands, his shoulders shaking with the violence of his emotions.

"I wanted to, Rhys. I wanted to fight. He used you against me. And the fact it's my fault Valentine died... he has too much leverage over me. I had no choice. None."

My fingers itched to comfort him as I'd always done, but I was in too much pain. Pain he'd caused. So I stood up and walked away, unable to take the sight of his agony on top of my own.

"You could've said no, A. You didn't have to help me. They would've appointed me a solicitor, regardless."

"You don't get it. Even if I'd told him no, he'd still have grounded me and banned me from seeing you. He knows I killed Valentine by accident. Do you really think he wouldn't use it against me?"

My fists clenched at my sides. Patrick Parrish would stop at nothing to keep us apart. Aaron had fought against him so long as his dad had no reason to break us up. Now he had the biggest reason of all.

"Oh, I fucking get it. I get you won't stand up to your father. I should've known one day this would happen. You and I were always too good to be true. Especially since you come from a life of fucking privilege and me… I'm just a boy who grew up on a council estate. A boy who has nothing. No recourse to fight against the likes of Patrick fucking Parrish and his bullshit… you could've done that, you know. You could've said no and told him to go fuck himself, but you've spent your whole life trying to please him when he doesn't give a shit about you."

"Rhys—"

I put a hand up. I didn't want to hear any more excuses out of his mouth.

"You've said enough, Aaron. I think you should leave now. You came to tell me goodbye. You've said it. So just go… go before you break me further."

Despite my anger, tears still fell down my cheeks like a fucking tidal wave. I couldn't stop them. And what I hadn't expected was for him not to listen to a word I'd said. No, the moment I felt him wrap his arms around me from behind, my entire body shook with the effort of staying upright.

"I'll love you forever, Rhys King. Never forget that even when you hate me for this… remember this… remember us… remember we're soulmates."

He clutched me tighter, his tears soaking into the back of my t-shirt.

"Goodbye, my beautiful boy. You'll always be in my heart… forever."

Then he let go and walked out of my room. He walked out of my life. He left me with my heart in pieces on the floor.

I dropped to my knees, trying to hold back the weight of my emotions but failing miserably. I let out an agonising wail of anguish, not caring who heard me. Then I curled up in a ball on the floor, letting the pain overwhelm all of my senses.

Aaron had done the worst thing imaginable.

He'd broken all the promises he'd ever made to me.

He'd left me.

And by doing so… he'd annihilated me completely.

PART IV

restore

verb, re·stored, re·stor·ing.

to bring back into existence, use, or the like; reestablish.

CHAPTER FORTY SEVEN

Rhys

Seven Years Later

I leant back in my chair and rubbed my face before running my hand through my hair, knowing I'd left it sticking up. Didn't matter too much considering no one could see me. Working from home had its benefits. Three years of university earning my degree in graphic design followed by two years of working for someone else had allowed me to find my way in the industry. A year ago, I'd branched out on my own after bringing in more work part-time freelancing in book cover design and illustration than I earnt in my day job.

I'd started working in the evenings as I wanted to have the financial security to allow me to help Mum during her divorce. She'd finally got the courage to leave Graham two years ago. Something I'd been thrilled about. Now she lived in a one-bedroom flat twenty minutes away. Gaining her independence had done wonders. Whilst she still couldn't work in a regular job, she'd taken up knitting and crochet. I'd helped set her up online so she could sell her wares. For the past year, she'd gone from strength to strength, something I was immensely proud of her for.

I'd been working on the same project for the past few days and had finally completed it. I hoped the author who'd commissioned this illustrative work would be happy. They'd found out about me via my hobby, an online comic strip I updated twice a week. It wasn't something I charged for, but it'd brought in enough potential work that I was often turning down opportunities.

After I sent off the final version to the author along with the second part of my invoice, I checked my email. One sat there from a major publisher. I didn't pay attention to who exactly it was. Reading it over, I found they'd discovered me through my illustrative work and wanted to commission some art from me for a fantasy book. I checked the details, noting they wanted to offer me a contract for further work after this. Shaking my head, I replied stating I only worked on a commission basis as a freelancer and if they wanted to work with me, they'd have to accept those terms. Sometimes these companies tried to pull shit with artists and I wasn't having it.

I got up and went into my kitchen, flicking the kettle on for tea and sorting something out for lunch. Kicking back on my sofa, I put my feet up on the coffee table and switched the TV on. After ten minutes of watching a game show my mum had got me hooked on all those years ago, my phone went off.

I checked it, finding the publisher had emailed me back stating she accepted my terms and would love to set up a meeting.

I dumped my plate in the dishwasher and went back to my desk. There were other projects I had to get on with, but there would be no harm in setting something up. It would mean good money and I wasn't about to turn it down, having grown up with very little.

First, I'd do my research before replying. I looked closely at the publisher she worked for. My heart almost stopped in my chest.

Johnstone & Parrish.

I stared at the name, feeling sick to my stomach. Sitting back in my chair, I put my hand on my chest, rubbing it as pain blossomed. Seven years had done nothing to quell the feelings seeing that name brought on. I wished I could say I'd let it go and laid that day to rest. That it didn't still haunt me whenever I saw anything to do with that fucking family. Anything to do with… him.

The boy who'd ruined my life by almost getting me charged with a murder I hadn't committed. The boy who'd stolen my heart and hadn't given it back. The boy who'd broken my heart into tiny pieces, eviscerating my very soul when he'd left me, despite promising he never would.

Aaron Jackson Parrish.

I hated him. I hated him so much. And yet… despite that hatred, despite the intervening years, the biggest fucking kicker of all… my heart still yearned for him. It still fucking beat for him. My blackened, cold heart which had never healed from the way he'd broken it. It still belonged to him.

I got up from my chair and paced my living room, dragging my hands through my hair. This commission would pay a lot. I'd read over what they were looking for. It was right up my alley. Something I could do with complete ease and it would be beautiful. It could do wonders for my career. I'd wanted to get to the next level for a while now. Like I had some sick need to prove I was better than where I'd come from. That I could make it on my own and be successful. More successful than anyone else who'd lived on that shitty council estate.

Whilst I knew Patrick Parrish was no longer directly involved in running Johnstone & Parrish as he'd stepped back from it, his son worked there. His fucking son. The person I'd sworn I never wanted to see again after what he did to me.

I had no clue what to do. It's not like Aaron worked in the creative department, so I likely wouldn't even see him unless he knew they'd reached out to me. I hated knowing he worked in editorial, just like his dad always envisioned for him.

I needed some advice on how to deal with this shit. Pulling my phone out of my pocket, I sat down and dialled the one person who I'd become close to during university.

"All right, fuckface?" came the dulcet tones of my best friend, Meredith Pope.

"Well, hello to you too."

"Have I ever greeted you any other way?"

I snorted. Meredith had been nothing but real with me. Her blunt approach to life was refreshing. She was one of those marmite people. Either you loved her or you found her too in your face. I was firmly in the former camp.

"Maybe when we first met."

"True, but I was attempting to make a good impression then so you'd actually hang out with me. Anyway, to what do I owe this pleasure? You calling to say you're finally going to accept my offer to set you up with Jonah?"

I rolled my eyes. Meredith had been trying to get me to go on a date with her older brother for years. I'd met Jonah a few times and he was nice enough, however, I didn't date. Ever.

"That would be a large no, Mer."

"If you're going to start on about how you're demi and that makes dating impossible you can save it. I'd rather not have that lecture again."

I rubbed the back of my neck. Meredith knew all about my sexual orientation and how I used it as an excuse not to get close to anyone. The real reason had more to do with the fact my heart had never healed from the damage done to it when I'd been seventeen. I couldn't imagine feeling the way I did for Aaron about anyone else. And therein lay my issue.

"It wasn't a lecture."

"Right, so you didn't lament over it for three hours when we got drunk that night."

"Shut up."

I could tell she was smiling, even if I couldn't see her.

"So you going to fess up as to why you called? Some of us have work to do."

I didn't rise to the bait as I probably worked harder than she ever did. Meredith and I had met in my first year of university. She walked over and plonked herself down next to me in the union bar and that was how our friendship started. She'd been studying to get a degree in production design for stage and screen and now regularly worked in the West End as a set designer amongst other things.

"I had an email from the creative department from Johnstone & Parrish. They want to commission me for some illustrative work on a fantasy book and no, I can't tell you who it's for since that's confidential."

"Oh. My. Fucking. God. That's amazing! This could set you up."

I stifled a sigh. As much as I wanted to go ahead and set up this meeting, the fact remained the company contained the one person who had destroyed me.

"That's why I'm calling. I don't know if I can."

"Hold on, are you really telling me you're considering turning down an opportunity to work on a book from the publishing house who has your favourite author on their books? Are you mental?"

I bit my lip. My favourite author happened to be the person they wanted me to do the illustrative work for. Something which excited me no end.

"It's complicated."

"Well un-fucking-complicate it, Rhys. You cannot turn this down. Wait… is it for her? Is the work for her new book?"

"I can't tell you that."

"FUCK! It is! You have to do this. No excuses, fuckface, you're doing it."

I took a deep breath. It was time I told Meredith the truth. I had alluded to there being more to the story than I'd let on. She never pushed me to tell her. Besides, she had her own shit when it came to men. It had been a particularly unpleasant time for her back when we were twenty and in our second year of university. Meredith had told me she wouldn't have survived it without me. The two of us had become closer because of it. Honestly, if she ever saw Cole again, I might punch the guys lights out and I wasn't a violent person.

"You know how I told you I don't date because I'm demi?"

"Well yes, but I don't see what this has to do with it."

It has everything to do with it sadly.

"The person who broke my heart when we were seventeen and the reason I don't date works for the editorial department."

You could hear a penny drop with the silence ensuing from my revelation. The only person who knew what happened that day was my mum. And it's only because she'd picked up the pieces in the wake of my heartbreak.

"I knew it! I fucking knew you had to have a better reason for why you don't date. You sneaky little fuck, Rhys. That's it, meet me at our place for cocktails later. You're going to spill every damn detail of this sordid affair to me."

"What? I don't have time for that."

"See you at eight."

She hung up.

Typical.

The girl could be determined as hell when she wanted, but I loved her for it. Meredith was pushy and opinionated, such a contrast to me. Probably why I liked her so much. We bounced off each other. A bit like chalk and cheese. Meredith had been my rock for the past few years and I couldn't do without her.

I guessed I was going out tonight, getting drunk and telling her about Aaron. There were things I couldn't say. Like the real reason we'd ended. Even though Aaron had broken his promises to me, I'd kept mine. No one would ever find out from me about his involvement in Valentine Jenkin's death. A death that had gone unsolved all this time.

Meredith would likely persuade me to go after this commission from Johnstone & Parrish. Would it really do me any harm to set up a meeting? I could always back out if I changed my mind.

So I set about responding to Diana Merry. Turning down a job like this because of something which happened seven years ago seemed stupid. This had nothing to do with *him*. He wouldn't be at this meeting. There was no way he even knew Diana had contacted me. I was in no doubt Aaron wouldn't have deliberately found a way to contact me after all this time. If he'd not tried when he'd turned eighteen, why the hell would he have decided to now when we were twenty-four?

CHAPTER FORTY EIGHT

Rhys

I felt the slap on my back before I heard her voice.

"All right, fuckface?"

Meredith plonked herself down next to me at the bar and put her hand up, signalling the bartender. I'd already been nursing a caipirinha for the past ten minutes.

"What time do you call this?"

She waved me away as the bartender joined us and she ordered a margarita. Meredith was notorious for being late to everything. When she said eight, she meant more like eight-thirty. I was lucky she'd only been ten minutes late today.

"So, did you pussy out of taking this job?"

I shook my head and rolled my eyes.

"Not exactly… I set up a meeting for next week, but that doesn't mean I've said yes yet."

"You *have* to say yes. It's only E. R. fucking Davidson."

"Shh, keep your voice down."

The bartender, Dan, deposited a drink down in front of her. He was used to us by now. Meredith grabbed her purse and paid, giving him a wink.

"I never said it was her."

"Whatever, I know it is. You are taking this job because you'd be a fool not to. Now tell me about this boy who broke your heart."

I took another sip of my drink and stared down into it. Talking about that time in my life was never easy. Mum didn't bring it up. She knew how much it hurt me.

"He didn't just break my heart... he eviscerated it," I said, my voice so low I wasn't sure she heard it over the music playing in the background.

When I didn't hear a peep out of her, I glanced to the side. Meredith looked at me with such a sad expression, I almost called her out for it. Except this time I knew it was genuine. She knew exactly what it was like to go through a heartbreak. She'd had to suffer it twice with the same person.

"Rhys…"

I let out a lengthy sigh. Aaron had destroyed me. The last year at school had been hell for me. Whilst I'd got good grades for my A-Levels, the rumours going around that I'd been responsible for Valentine's death had run riot amongst the kids. I'd been completely ostracized. It didn't matter since I never intended to see any of them again, but even Becky and those girls had given me a wide berth. I'd been glad when it was over and I went off to university. Meeting Meredith had been a lifesaver.

"It's okay. Well, it's not, but there's nothing I can do to change what happened."

She put her hand on mine, which was resting on the bar, giving it a squeeze. When it came down to it, Meredith was a good listener and gave pretty solid advice. She might push me, but it was out of love and wanting me to experience life. This girl had been through enough herself, but she'd pulled herself out of the black hole and decided not to allow someone to ruin the rest of her life for her. I admired her courage and strength.

"You don't have to tell me."

I smiled. Meredith was in for a shock.

"You might want to get another drink."

"Why?"

"Mostly because the boy who broke my heart is none other than Patrick Parrish's son."

Meredith stared at me.

"Hold on, what? *The* Patrick Parrish, husband of Kellie Parrish, the world fucking famous director, Patrick the fucking owner of Johnstone & Parrish."

I nodded before downing my drink. Putting my hand up, I waved Dan over and ordered two more drinks for me and Meredith. Dan rolled his eyes and set to it.

"Yeah, that Patrick, Mer."

"Well, holy shit."

The two of us lapsed into silence. Dan put our drinks down, eying us with a raised brow.

"You two aren't normally miserable."

I got my wallet out and paid him.

"Just one of those days I guess."

"Well, make sure that one doesn't get wasted. Last time you had to carry her out."

He walked away before I could respond. Meredith was known for drinking too much and relying on me to take care of her. Since my place was around the corner, more often than not I ended up taking her there to sober up. Meredith and I had no qualms about sharing a bed. We'd become close enough for it to be a non-issue for me. I wouldn't allow it with anyone else.

Meredith might not have her shit together all the time, but she was coping the best way she knew how.

"You know, it occurs to me I don't even know their son's name. Didn't they raise him out of the spotlight?"

I almost snorted. Patrick and Kellie had left raising Aaron to other people.

"If you call dumping him with nannies as raising him."

Meredith blinked and nudged me with her shoulder.

"And you know that for a fact?"

"He was my best friend for ten years."

I couldn't bring myself to say his name. I hadn't spoken it out loud for years. Too painful for me to even see it written down.

"Okay, you have to spill now, Rhys. You had a whole other best friend before me who you were in love with. That's huge. Besides, you know my sob story when it comes to men, isn't it only fair I know yours?"

I sipped my drink. She had a point. Maybe telling her would be cathartic in some way. After all this time, I hadn't spoken about what Aaron did to me. Opening up about it could do me some good.

"We met when we were seven after he saved me from a bully. We became best friends somehow, even though he had everything and I had nothing. I relied on him for everything… we knew each other inside out. He helped me gain confidence in myself… he saved me."

My heart tightened painfully at the memories flashing before my eyes.

"Then ten years later, during the summer holidays before the last year of school, he kissed me out of the blue. And it was all kinds of fucked up. It's like how I told you I struggled with my sexuality… well, that was because of him. He awakened something in me. It was kind of like a fairy tale love story, except this one doesn't have a happy ending."

It had the worst ending possible. Nothing good had come out of my relationship with Aaron.

"We had four weeks of bliss… we were so in love, you know, completely inseparable. I mean, we always had been, but it was different. Then everything went wrong and he broke up with me. His dad found out we were together and banned him from seeing me. And that's it really… we've not seen each other since."

There was so much more to the story than that, but I couldn't tell her those things. No one could find out.

"What's his name?"

My hand tightened around my glass.

"Aaron."

Hearing it out loud from my own lips tore into my already shattered soul. How did he still have the power to hurt me all these years later?

"Shit, Rhys… and he's why you won't date?"

"He's why I will never allow anyone else close to me like that. I can't go through losing my best friend and the person I love all over again. Being demi doesn't even factor into it. I don't want to risk everything for love when it destroyed me."

Meredith wrapped an arm around my shoulders and half hugged me.

"I get it. Fuck knows, I understand more than most what a broken heart can do to a person. I'm sorry I tried to set you up with my brother so many times. Won't happen again."

I almost rolled my eyes.

"Also, you can't let Aaron stop you from following your dreams. You get to illustrate a fucking book for your favourite author. Don't let anything ruin that."

Meredith was right. This wasn't about the past, it was about my future. I would not let myself get sucked back into the vortex of emotional turmoil that came with Aaron Jackson Parrish.

"Thanks, Mer."

"Anytime. Now, let's get fucked up and I'll be your shoulder to cry on for life, yeah?"

I groaned but joined her in downing our drinks and signalling for more. This would probably get messy, but with Meredith, I wouldn't have it any other way.

CHAPTER FORTY NINE

Rhys

I checked myself in the mirror one last time, making sure I looked smart enough for this meeting. To say I was nervous would be an understatement. Not when it came to my ability to do the job the publisher was asking of me, but of the risk of seeing *him*.

I fiddled with the curls in my hair again, making sure they sat just right. Then I straightened my black shirt.

You look fine. You don't have to worry. Even if you see him, you know you look good.

I glanced back at the blue hair sticking out from my covers and rolled my eyes. Meredith had come around last night. We'd got a takeaway in, watched a film, laughed and drank a lot of beer. Her way of giving me moral support for today. We'd talked a lot about how I'd approach it if I saw Aaron today. I had no idea how I would feel if it happened.

"Mer, I'm going now. Let yourself out, hey?"

"Good luck and don't let him bring you down," came her mumbled response.

Grinning, I left the bedroom and grabbed my jacket on the way out. The entire journey over on the tube had me tapping my bag, which contained my sketchbook and tablet. I'd already done a couple of sketches even though I didn't have the full brief yet. Maybe I was more excited about working on an Emily Davidson book than I realised. She went by the pen name, E. R. Davidson and was my favourite fantasy author. Whilst she wouldn't be at this meeting, I hoped I might get to meet her or even get her autograph at some point.

Johnstone & Parrish had their building in Central London, whilst Mum and I lived close to Richmond Park. I'd left the flat early to get there on time. Why did I arrange this meeting in the morning? I wasn't usually up before ten.

I hadn't told Mum about this meeting, nor that I might see Aaron. She would only worry and I'd rather not put her through it. She'd dealt with enough throughout her life without getting concerned over her son's heart yet again. And I knew picking up the pieces of it when Aaron had shattered it had taken a lot out of her.

I glanced around the modern interior of the building as I walked in. The place was all straight lines and edges, not a curve in sight. The front desk was white with chrome accents and the lady behind it gave me a bright smile.

"Good morning, welcome to Johnstone & Parrish, how can I help?"

"Hi… Rhys King, I have an appointment with Diana Merry."

She looked down at her computer for a moment.

"Of course. If you'd like to sign in here, I'll get you a visitor pass and let Miss Merry know you're here."

I filled out my details on the tablet she handed to me before she gave me a lanyard. I pinned it to my shirt pocket.

"If you just wait here, someone will be down to get you soon."

She waved her hand towards the seating area. I gave her a nod and strode over, setting myself down in a rather square-looking white chair. Ten minutes passed before a lady approached me.

"Hello, you're Rhys, right?"

I stood up and shook her outstretched hand.

"Yes."

"Xanthe Henslowe, I'm Diana's assistant. Please come this way."

I followed her into the lifts. The longer I stood in this building, the sweatier my hands got. I could be in the same place as *him* right now. The one person who had the ability to rip open the carefully crafted stitches I'd applied to my heart and let me bleed out on the floor all over again.

"We're very excited you might be working with us. Emily absolutely loves your comic strip."

I glanced at Xanthe, raising an eyebrow.

"She does?"

"Oh yes. Some publishers don't give their authors input into their book's aesthetic, but Emily is one of our best sellers. When she mentioned it to Diana, she just had to check you out."

Xanthe had a very laid back approach to smart casual. Her hair was up in two buns on top of her head and she wore a vibrant, almost neon patterned blouse.

"I had no idea."

And I didn't. My favourite author liked my comic strip. That was insane, wasn't it? Especially considering who it was about. I guess you could say I may have carried on drawing the same character over and over since I was a teenager. It evolved into the story of a teenage boy and his many trials and tribulations. I'd called it *Kingston Kidz* since that was near where I'd grown up.

Xanthe continued talking all the way up to the fifth floor and down the corridor until we hit the meeting room. There were three people in the room. The first one to stand was the blonde-haired lady who introduced herself as Diana Merry. The green-eyed man was Paolo Cortez, the cover artist, and lastly, the lady from the marketing department, Betty Wendel.

"I'm afraid Emily's editor is unable to attend today but we're all very excited you're here," Diana said as we sat down.

"Oh, that's absolutely fine."

The meeting got started. Emily was branching out into urban fantasy in her latest novel. They wanted to commission artwork from me for the hardcover edition and for their marketing campaign. I could see why Emily wanted me when they showed me their plans and ideas. It matched the style I used for my comic. My mind whirled with possibilities and I knew then and there, I couldn't turn this down.

When everything wrapped up an hour later, I grinned from ear to ear, excited to get started. Working on this would be a dream come true.

"Well, we'll get the contract over to you as soon as possible, if this all amenable to you," Diana said as the others were packing up their things. "We just need to run this by Aaron, Emily's editor first."

My heart froze in my chest. Hearing his name made me sick to my stomach.

"Aaron… as in Aaron Parrish?"

Diana raised an eyebrow.

"Yes… do you know of him?"

I stuffed my tablet back in my bag and shifted in my seat.

"You could say that."

I had no idea he was Emily's editor. It meant me working on this project hinged on him signing off on it.

Well, fuck.

"Now you have me intrigued."

What did I say to that? There was one thing I had to know before I decided how to answer.

"Does he know you arranged this with me?"

She smiled.

"Well, not yet. We have a few options to present to him but making Emily happy is our goal and she wants you."

"I see."

The others left the room, saying goodbye to me on their way out.

"Do you and Aaron know each other?" Diana asked me as I stood up to go.

"Um, we went to primary school together, but we haven't seen each other in a long time."

I hoped it was a safe enough statement. No need to go into how close we were. Not with one of his work colleagues.

"Tell you what, why don't I take you up to his office? I bet he'd love to see you."

I swallowed. The thought of seeing Aaron gave me heart palpitations.

"I'm sure he's too busy for a reunion."

"Nonsense. Who wouldn't want to see a childhood friend?"

I rubbed the back of my neck before slinging my bag over my shoulder. Diana looked so eager and it made me queasy. I shouldn't have said I knew him. How had I gotten into this mess?

He would find out about me regardless of whether or not I saw him today. Perhaps if I got this over with now, he might not screw me over by blocking their request to have me work on Emily's book. Meredith would tell me to suck it up and not allow anything to ruin my opportunity.

"Well, okay."

Diana clapped her hands together and gathered her papers before taking me over to the lifts. We rode up to the sixth floor. She chatted to me along the way, but I hardly listened. My blood pounded in my ears and my body felt stiff as a board.

You're going to see him. Fuck. How did this happen?

I didn't know how to feel about him not knowing they'd contacted me. Would he have let them if he knew? Aaron had never been a vindictive person, so I couldn't imagine why he'd say no. There was still the real possibility he wouldn't allow this considering what happened between us all those years ago.

I shook myself as we approached his office and turned to Diana.

"Would you be totally put out if I did this alone? It's just been a long time and I'm a little... nervous."

Diana gave me a knowing smile.

"Of course, I'll just let him know he has a visitor."

We stopped outside the open door and Diana stuck her head in.

"Aaron, honey, are you busy?"

"Always. Why?" came a voice from inside the office. A voice which chilled me to my fucking bones.

"Oh, well, you know we had a meeting today with an artist for Emily's book. Turns out they know you from school and would love to say hello."

"I guess I can spare a few minutes. Who is it?"

Diana pulled back without answering and gave me a nod.

"I'll be in touch."

She waved and walked away with a giant smile on her face. I watched her go before wiping my sweaty palms on my trousers. Then I tried to hold my head high as I walked into his office and pushed the door shut behind me. It was all chrome and glass with black accents everywhere. Sat at the desk with his eyes on a computer screen was the person who I never thought I'd set eyes on again.

His blonde hair glinted under the strip lights, the shade a little darker than when we'd been teenagers. Those blue-grey eyes were the same as I remembered. The sight of him had my heart in a vice. He was still just as beautiful as he'd always been, if not more so now.

Why does he have to look so good? I feel so inadequate right now.

Sucking in a breath, I decided I had to get on with it. There was no going back now.

"Hello, Aaron."

His eyes flicked to me and all the blood drained from his face in an instant.

"Rhys?" his voice came out in a hushed whisper.

I gripped my bag strap as an anchor. The world seemed to freeze around us as we stared at each other. All those feelings rushed back in an instant. Ones of lust, desire, love, hurt and betrayal. They whirled around inside me, shattering any sense of self-control and pride I had left.

A part of me wanted to walk out and never see him again. Another wanted to rain down hell on him for what he'd done to me, to us. And the last part wanted to go to him, hold him close and tell him how much I'd missed him… and how I still loved him after all this time.

I did none of those things. No, I stared like an idiot who'd got all tongue-tied. The boy I'd fallen in love with had grown up into a man. The only person in this world who'd known every inch of my body just as I knew his. My first kiss. My first love. My first everything.

It didn't come as a surprise he recognised me. All those years ago he'd said he'd love me forever. He wouldn't have forgotten me because I could never forget him. I could feel the pulse of connection between us, hanging in the air like it always had. And it made me want to break down into floods of tears because I never imagined for a moment seeing him again would force my cold, dead heart to beat so violently in my chest.

"I can't believe it's you," he said after what seemed like an hour of us just staring, but really, it'd probably been a few minutes.

"Surprise."

He let out a little forced laugh before standing and coming around his desk. I tried to stop my mouth watering. His clothes fit him to perfection. His white shirt was crisp and his navy trousers clung in all the right places. I felt stupid in comparison even though I'd been happy with the way I'd scrubbed up when I left my flat earlier.

Cut it the fuck out. Remember what he did to you. You cannot be lusting after him.

I couldn't help it. The years had done nothing to dull my attraction to him. And it made me pretty fucking angry. My own body and mind were betraying me. Aaron had destroyed me. Utterly. I shouldn't feel this way.

Fuck. How am I going to get through this when all I want to do is kiss him, pin him down on his desk and show him exactly how much he'd hurt me all those years ago?

CHAPTER FIFTY

Aaron

The very last person I thought I'd ever see again stood in front of me. When Diana had stuck her head around the door, I'd been reading over a contract which was giving me a headache. I should've realised when she said the artist Emily wanted was someone I knew from school, it would be him. There was no one else I'd known or been close to who'd been into art or design.

Rhys King is in front of me. What the actual fuck?

Very few times in my life had I been left floundering, not knowing what to say. All of those times had been when I'd been in the presence of this boy... no, man. Rhys was a man now. And he looked it. He had a well-trimmed beard. His inky black hair fell in waves, hiding one of his dark eyes from view. It was a little longer at the sides than it had been when we were teenagers. His skin was still tanned and he wore all black.

His beautiful hands clutched the strap of the brown satchel he carried.

Nothing could prepare me for the way my heart clenched and my skin prickled. I couldn't believe how fucking incredible he looked. He always had, but now, he was so handsome it almost killed me. Every part of me itched to reach out and touch him. To confirm he was real and not some apparition.

I'm not dreaming, am I?

How could Rhys King be here? It'd been seven years since I'd laid eyes on him. Since that fateful day when I'd wrecked us and broken his heart. The pain of that experience had never left me. Of what I'd done to him. It haunted me like a fucking black cloud hanging over my head. There was nothing I regretted more in my life than breaking the promises I made to Rhys. And I felt fucking guilt and regret over a lot of things.

The past seven years had been filled with living up to my parent's expectations. Just like working for Johnstone & Parrish was. I never thought I'd enjoy being an editor, but when I got to help bring to market books like Emily's, there was nothing better I could think of doing. The person I had to thank for encouraging me to read was right here. Rhys' love of books had somehow become mine. And maybe, just maybe, I wanted to put out ones I knew he would like.

It's not like Dad immediately stuck me in this role. I'd worked as a junior editor for two years after university. And I'd earnt the promotion by working hard. Besides, he no longer ran the business. His partner, Jeremy Johnstone did and I was thankful for it. He was a good guy who cared a lot about the publishing industry, unlike my father who only cared about image and money. He and I were no longer on speaking terms for a multitude of reasons anyway.

I couldn't keep staring at Rhys like a fucking lemon even though every part of me craved him like nothing else. It'd been so long. Too long. My heart had been buried beneath so many layers of pain and suddenly it was full of life again just by seeing him.

I'd never stopped loving Rhys King. Never stopped wishing everything had been different.

"I had no idea you were who Emily wanted to work with," I blurted out, unsure of what else to say.

He let go of the strap of his bag and rubbed the back of his neck.

"I didn't know you were her editor."

Did that mean if he'd known, he wouldn't have accepted a meeting with Diana? I couldn't ask. He didn't owe me an explanation. If anything, I owed him one for everything I'd done. For the way I'd hurt him.

Fuck, I've missed you.

It was like finally being able to breathe again after years of drowning in self-pity and hatred. Funny that when I'd met Rhys, he'd been in a similar state. How the tables had fucking turned.

"You look good… really good." *For fuck's sake, don't say that!* "I mean… Jesus, it's been forever. What are you doing now? I know you're doing art, but…"

He didn't look put out by my question, but who knew how he really felt. His emotions weren't clear on his face. All those

427

years ago I'd been able to read him so well. Now, I was completely in the dark. And it didn't sit well with me at all.

"I freelance in cover design and illustration for the most part. I set up my own business and went full time a year ago. And I produce a free bi-weekly comic strip. Kind of unpaid advertising I guess."

He smiled and shrugged, the gesture a little rueful.

"That's great… really great. And Steph?"

You sound like an actual fool right now. Get a fucking grip!

"She's great, actually. Has her own online business knitting and crocheting. Her and Graham got a divorce so that was good. I don't know what he's doing."

"Wow… who'd have thought."

His smile grew wider.

"Yeah, I guess she finally had enough, you know."

This didn't feel like a comfortable conversation for either of us. We used to have such camaraderie. Now we were strangers. It didn't feel right at all. He'd been my best friend for ten years. We'd always been something more than that though.

Soulmates.

So why did this feel so awkward now? My fault, I guess. I'd ruined us. I'd destroyed everything we had together.

Does he still feel what I feel?

You'd have to be blind to fail to recognise the connection which still remained. As if the cord binding us together had never broken despite our demise.

Does he care or is he angry?

428

I wouldn't blame him if he hated me or harboured resentment.

"You look like you've done well for yourself," he said with a glance around the room.

"I guess so."

"Don't be modest, it's not every day you get to be an editor for an author like Emily Davidson."

Something in the way he said it made me think he liked Emily a lot more than he was letting on.

Is that why he went ahead with the meeting?

He stuck his hands in his pockets and looked away.

"Anyway, I'm sure you're busy. I should get going... it was... um... I guess I might see you around."

I didn't know what to say. Every part of me screamed to come up with an excuse to keep him here, but I couldn't. I didn't deserve that from him.

He looked at me again, his eyes growing darker as they flicked down to my mouth for the briefest of moments. Then he turned and walked away, opening the door of my office and heading out.

I stood still for all of thirty seconds after he left the room. Then my legs carried me outside and I called his name.

"Rhys!"

He'd got a few feet down the corridor but he stopped and turned, raising his eyebrow. I swallowed hard.

"Do... do you want to work on Emily's book?"

He bit his lip. My pulse spiked further and heat flooded my body. That fucking lip. I hadn't been seeing things when he looked at my mouth. I saw it in his eyes. He remembered all too well what his gesture meant.

"Yeah… I do. She's my favourite author."

I had a feeling that was the case. And I wanted a reason to see him again. Desperately. Somehow, I knew Rhys was the right person for this anyway. I remembered his skill from when we were younger and I could only imagine how much he'd improved since.

"Then I'll sign off on it."

"You don't want to see what I can do first?"

I shook my head.

"I remember."

He stared at me for a long moment as if trying to work out what my game was. I hoped he did. Nothing in this world would make me happier than to have him back in my life. Wishing for that would be futile nor did I deserve it, but it wouldn't stop me wanting it. Needing it. Needing him. The reality was… I'd always needed Rhys King. That would never change.

"Well, thank you… I guess. Um, I need to…"

He pointed towards the direction of the lifts and I just nodded. Then I watched him walk away from me, my heart singing with each step even though it meant he was leaving. But he'd be back. I'd make sure of it. Any damn excuse I got to ask him to come into the office, I'd take it. I shouldn't because I'd hurt him so much.

The heart wanted what it wanted.

My heart had always been his. It belonged to him. And I'd do whatever it took to make up for the past because I was fucking damned if I was going to lose him all over again.

I hope you remember when I said forever, Rhys, I meant it.

CHAPTER FIFTY ONE

Rhys

I kept it together all the way back to my flat. Kept a lid on the emotions swirling around inside me. I was not about to let myself break down in front of other people on the tube. I'd already suffered enough today as it was so further embarrassment was not on the cards. Only when I unlocked the front door, walked into my living room and sunk down on my sofa did I allow myself to feel it. Everything I'd held back the moment I saw him.

"Fuck!"

I dropped my head into my hands. A confusing mess of anger, desire and everything in between coursed through me. The delicate stitches holding me together burst at the seams, allowing it all to bleed out. Every last piece of me shattered.

"God fucking damn it. Fuck. I hate you. I hate you so fucking much."

It wasn't as if I could say it to his face. We were going to be working together. I had to remain professional, but by fuck did I want to rage and scream at him. I wanted to hurt him. I wanted him to understand he couldn't just walk back into my life and expect me to be friendly. I wanted him to suffer as much as I had over the past seven years. Worst of all, I wanted to pin him down, tear his clothes off and fuck him for all I was worth. And I had the distinct impression he'd let me. My skin crawled from the knowledge and the way he'd looked at me. As if he still cared. As if he wanted me. As if he still fucking well loved me.

Why did it feel so damn good?

I not only hated him for making me feel anything for him, but I also hated myself for it. Why was I such a mess over that fucking man? Hadn't he done enough to me already? Hadn't I been tortured by this shit for too long?

My phone started ringing in my pocket. I threw my bag away, tugged off my jacket and pulled it out, checking the caller ID. I had no interest in having a conversation with anyone right now.

Meredith.

The thought of telling her what happened made me sick so I dumped my phone next to me and allowed it to ring out. Better she thought I was busy. Busy falling into the abyss of fucked up shit seeing the only person I'd ever loved had sucked me into. I really fucking hoped she didn't try again. And I didn't want her turning up here either. No one could see me like this. Not even my best friend.

434

Why does he have to be Emily's editor? Why did I say I wanted the fucking job?

The obvious answers to those questions made me want to smash something.

Because the world hates you. And you said yes because you want to work with Emily so badly, you don't care that you have to deal with him.

I did care. I cared a great fucking deal.

My mind kept fixating on the way he looked at me. Those damn blue-grey eyes having the ability to steal my breath at every turn. The beautiful boy who'd grown into a man. And how he was everything and more to me.

"Fuck you, Aaron. Fuck you," I shouted at the air in front of me.

I got up and stalked into my kitchen, ripping open the alcohol cupboard and grabbing a bottle of tequila. As much as I hated the stuff, I had to take the edge off somehow. Not bothering to find a glass, I unscrewed the cap and swigged directly from the bottle, almost choking on the liquid burning its way down my throat.

I slammed it down on the counter and put my hands either side of it, panting. It hadn't taken the edge off at all. If anything, it made it so much worse. My defences were down. He'd torn apart my walls and forced me to see the truth.

Memories flooded my vision. The way Aaron smiled when I called him, prince. Us running along the promenade on Brighton beach, laughing and chasing each other. The first time he'd kissed me during that freak storm. The first time I realised I loved him more than life itself. The day I'd told him. The first time he told me he loved me. The growl of his voice when he had me pinned down on the bed whilst he fucked me.

That one played over and over on repeat, flooding me with unwanted arousal. My breathing became heavy and my body wanted everything he had to offer.

This cannot be happening.

Except it was. Just because I hadn't been with anyone in the intervening seven years, didn't mean those urges went away. They'd come back in full force, knocking the wind out of me.

I wanted Aaron with a desperation it bordered on madness.

So much madness it had me stumbling out of my kitchen and finding myself in my bathroom the next minute. I tugged on my zipper, groaning in anticipation until I freed my cock and wrap my hand around it.

"I hate you, Aaron. I fucking hate you."

His name sliced into my heart, making me angrier and hornier than ever. I hated myself for stroking one out to him, but I couldn't help it. Nothing could stop the one-way train I'd inadvertently jumped on.

My laboured breath was harsh to my ears. Self-loathing filled me as I stood there over my sink thinking about my ex and how much I hated and loved him at the same time. How much I wanted his hands all over me and mine on him. My mouth watered at the thought of being on my knees for him. The rough way he always handled me.

"Fuck," I whimpered, coming violently as waves of horrific bliss washed over me.

I gripped the sink with one hand, staring at myself in the bathroom mirror. Hating my flushed face and the wild look in my eyes.

"What is wrong with you?"

Everything was, clearly. I'd lost the plot and it was all because of him. His stupid damn blonde-hair, blue-grey eyes and mouth-wateringly hot body.

I washed away the evidence in the sink and cleaned up, despising every sickening moment. The proof I was still insanely crazy over Aaron.

You know why that is. You've always known. Nothing he did all those years ago changed that fact.

Yeah, I fucking well did and it sucked. It sucked so fucking much. I guess I would have to live in hell for the rest of my life now. The torment of knowing what he meant to me would never end. I didn't want this. I didn't need this. He was the very last person I wanted to see again.

Fate was having a huge fucking laugh at my expense.

Aaron Jackson Parrish is my soulmate and I hate him for it.

CHAPTER FIFTY TWO

Rhys

 loud sound blared in my ears. I didn't like it. It hurt my head. It needed to stop. Right now.

"Go away."

The sound came again, making me groan in frustration. Why couldn't it leave me alone? I was happily buried in my covers. Sleep was far nicer than reality right now.

The sound stopped.

Finally.

I pulled the covers higher over my head and drifted off again. At least I tried. My phone started buzzing loudly near my head.

"Fuck."

I fumbled for it under the pillows where I'd shoved it last night and put it to my ear.

"What?"

"Open your damn door, fuckface."

"No. Go away."

I hung up and slapped the phone down next to me. Meredith had been bugging me for days but I didn't care. Bed was warm and my head felt fuzzy. It wasn't long before sleep dragged me back under.

The damn phone was ringing yet again. Why couldn't she leave me alone? I grabbed it, stuffing it against my ear.

"What part of go away did you not get, Mer?"

"Um... Rhys?"

I sat up abruptly, tearing the phone away from my ear and looking down at the caller ID. That was not Meredith. No, that was Johnstone & Parrish. And the voice on the end belonged to none other than Aaron. The sound of it sent chills racing down my spine.

Fuck. Shit. Why is this happening to me?

I held the phone to my ear again, wondering how on earth to explain why I'd answered it like that.

"Hi... um, sorry about that, I didn't look before I answered."

Now you sound like a complete fool. Who doesn't look at their phone first?

"Have I caught you at a bad time?"

I think I could describe the past three days as a bad time. The day after the meeting, the contract was sent over. I duly signed it, hating myself even more for doing so and promptly drowned myself in a bottle of vodka for the rest of the day whilst trying to work on another project due next week. The same happened the next day. Yesterday had been even more day drinking followed by crying into my takeaway pizza like a baby. More crying into a tub of ice cream. And more drinking. I think I passed out after breaking into a bottle of scotch Meredith had got me for my birthday.

"No, no, now is fine."

It is not fine. Why are you lying to him?

I was hanging like a bitch, my mouth felt dirty and I hadn't showered in three days.

"Are you sure? I can call back later."

I hauled myself out of bed, inwardly cursing my pounding head and padded out into the kitchen. Tucking my phone into my shoulder, I grabbed a glass and filled it with water.

"I'm good to talk… what can I do for you?"

I downed the glass, knowing I needed several more, tea and a bacon sandwich to cure the overwhelming hangover I was currently sporting.

"Okay, well, I just wanted to let you know the contract is all sorted and Diana will send you the full brief as well in a few weeks once we've finalised everything with Emily."

I blinked. He could've told me that in an email. Maybe it was the fact I felt like shit so my walls were down and I couldn't seem to find my filter. I had to have some explanation for why the next words I spoke came out of my mouth.

"Is this really a business call, Aaron?"

I swear I could almost hear him fidgeting.

"No."

"Then what do you want?"

"Have dinner with me."

I almost hung up the phone. Doing that would be childish. I had to be an adult about this. Especially since I was now technically working with him.

"Why would I do that?"

"We need to talk… and… I want to see you."

I gripped the counter for support so my knees wouldn't give out. My heart went full-on batshit crazy. The sound echoed in my ears over and over.

He wants to see me? What does that even mean?

Considering I'd spent three days drinking myself into oblivion over him, I wasn't sure seeing him outside of a professional capacity would be a smart move.

"I don't see how there's anything to talk about."

"Okay, let me put it another way. I know I don't deserve it, but I'm asking you to give me a chance… please. It's just dinner and a conversation. That's it."

He was deluded if he thought it would be just dinner and a conversation. I knew better. Hell, the temptation for more would be staring me right in the face. Part of the reason I kept drinking so much had everything to do with not wanting a repeat of the day of the meeting. I refused to have sexual thoughts about him. They messed me up too much.

"I don't think that's a good idea. I'd prefer to stick to this being about business."

"I know you're probably still angry with me, but—"

"Angry? I don't think that's the right word for how I *feel* about you."

Don't say it. Don't you dare have a go at him down the phone during working hours.

Apparently, my mouth didn't get the memo.

"Angry doesn't cut it. Not by a long shot. I *hate* you. You ruined my life. I had to live with a cloud of suspicion over my head for the entire last year at school. Everyone thought I was a fucking murderer thanks to you. So don't you tell me to give you a fucking chance. We were done seven years ago and we're done now. Nothing you say or do will change that."

I put a hand over my face, unable to believe those words had left my mouth. The resentment I harboured towards him had clearly got the better of me. And his silence spoke volumes.

"I shouldn't have said that."

I wasn't going to apologise as I meant every word but it was highly unprofessional.

"I'm pretty sure I deserved it," he murmured.

"I'm not saying sorry for it."

"The only one who should be sorry is me… and I am. Not that it'll mean anything to you probably, but I really am sorry, Rhys. I don't think you'll ever know how much."

I had a pretty good idea. Aaron wasn't a dick even if he'd behaved like one that day. When he came to say goodbye, he should've said his piece then left me. But no. He had to kiss me and touch me, making it ten times worse when he did eventually walk away.

"Sorry won't change what you did."

"I know."

"I don't want to see you."

"I get that."

"I want to hurt you."

443

"Then hurt me."

His voice came out all quiet and breathy. The sound made my insides tighten.

"You want me to?"

"I want you to do whatever it is you need so you'll let me talk to you."

This is what I'd meant by temptation. His voice dripped with the insinuation he'd let me take out my anger on him... sexually.

Had he been with another man since we broke up? I couldn't imagine why not. Aaron had always been incredibly charismatic and charming. He could have anyone he wanted. And I did not like the irrational stab of jealousy filling my bones at the thought of someone else having touched him. Tasted him. Loved him.

He's mine.

Where the fuck had that come from? I needed to get a grip and end this conversation before it got out of hand. Let's face it. It already had. And I was about to make it so much worse.

"Come over tonight at ten. There'll be no dinner, talking or asking questions. If you want to see me, this is your one and only chance. I'll email you the address."

"Okay."

Absolutely zero hesitation on his part.

"I'll see you later."

"See you tonight."

I hung up and placed the phone on the counter. Then my knees gave out. I sat with my back to the cabinet after I slid to the floor, banging my head against it.

What did I just do?

Why the hell did I tell him to come over?

I have actually fully lost the plot.

I couldn't take it back. This almost felt inevitable after we'd seen each other.

Shit, I need to go out and get supplies.

What the hell was I even saying? I wasn't going to actually go through with this, was I?

Yes, you are. You're going to fuck him out of your system so you can move on.

The rational part of me knew this was a mistake and that moving on from Aaron would be impossible. He was drowned out by irrationally horny Rhys who had apparently decided on the course of action called fuck the consequences.

There was only one way this would end.

And that was badly.

CHAPTER FIFTY THREE

Aaron

id I think going around his and letting him do whatever he wanted to me was a terrible idea? Well, yes. But this was Rhys King. I didn't care what I had to do to have him back in my life, including allowing him to take out all of his anger and frustration on me.

I wasn't sure I was prepared for what he'd do. The way he'd spoken to me earlier put me on edge. Yes, I completely deserved what he'd thrown at me. I probably shouldn't have called him and asked him to go to dinner with me. It'd been stupid, but I'd spent the past three days going back and forth with myself over it. Then I'd snapped. I had to speak to him. Had to hear his voice. Had to know how angry he was and whether he still had feelings for me. The fact he'd said he wanted to hurt me made it clear he did.

He would make me work hard to earn his forgiveness. And I would fucking well do it. I didn't care what he threw at me or how long it took. Speaking to him earlier only made me more determined. I loved him. I'd loved him for seventeen years. He was the sole reason my heart still beat in my chest. It would take everything I had to prove to him how much. To show him I still belonged to him just as he'd always belonged to me.

I'd tried, albeit unsuccessfully, to flush him out of my system. The dates I'd gone on over the past seven years only led me to one conclusion. Rhys was it for me. And how I'd come to that realisation? Talking to guys was all fine and good, but the moment they initiated anything remotely physical, I recoiled from it. I'd once tripped over my own front door mat in an effort to get away from a guy who tried to kiss me. All of it felt like a huge fucking betrayal of my relationship with the boy from my childhood. So I'd given up.

No one had touched me, kissed me or fucked me nor the other way around since Rhys. No one. And if that didn't tell me exactly how much I needed him and only him, I don't know what else would.

So yes, I was incredibly nervous about seeing him because I knew what he wanted. I'd seen it in his eyes the day he'd landed back in my life. He wanted to punish me for hurting him. He wouldn't be gentle. And he wouldn't care if I enjoyed it or not.

I wanted him that much, I didn't care either despite the trepidation inside me. Probably why I'd spent an hour preparing myself mentally and physically before I took the tube to his. I didn't feel remotely at ease or ready when I stood outside his building. Nor when I pressed down on the buzzer. And definitely not when he answered and let me up.

What am I doing here? This is such a bad idea.

I had come to the conclusion I'd lost all sense of rational thought. Coming here and letting him fuck me was probably the worst idea I'd ever had. Knowing I'd have his hands on me only filled me with red hot desire. And that's what kept me from chickening out.

His front door was open by the time I'd ridden up four floors. Rhys stood there with his face half-hidden in shadow and his eyes dark with repressed anger. He hadn't calmed down in the intervening hours. If anything, his rage burnt hotter. And I knew any preparation I'd done wouldn't be good enough.

Rhys stepped back without saying a word. He'd already told me there'd be no talking so I wasn't expecting a hello or a conversation. I swallowed hard before walking in. His hallway was dark and it made me nervous as fuck. And I should've been as the next thing I knew, he'd shut the front door and had me pinned against it with his forearm across my chest. His other hand rested next to my head.

"I want you to listen carefully. There's only one way this is going to go and it's my way. There will be absolutely no kissing and if you try to touch me, I will kick you out."

"Okay."

He stared at me for a long moment. The burning rage in his eyes had me flinching. Why had I decided to do this again?

You love him and you want him to forgive you.

"Good. Come with me."

He let me go and grabbed my hand instead, dragging me through his dark flat. I didn't get a chance to look around before he pulled me into a room and shut the door behind us. The only light source in here was from a single bedside table lamp.

Oh shit… I'm in his bedroom. This is where he sleeps.

From what I could make out, all the furniture was black and he had dark sheets on the bed.

My attention was dragged to him as his hands were on me, pulling the coat off my shoulders and discarding it before his hands went to my shirt buttons. I sucked in a breath, watching him almost tear them open without much care. His desperation showed in the way his eyes roamed over me when he'd tugged it from my trousers, undoing the little buttons at my wrists. My shirt was pushed from my shoulders and it fluttered to the floor. His hands traced a line down my bare chest. I tried not to make a noise, but my skin burnt where he'd touched it. The low hiss escaping my lips was involuntary.

I wanted to fall to my knees and beg him to forgive me, but he wouldn't appreciate that right now. No, he wanted one thing and one thing alone. An outlet for his anger towards me.

"Fuck," he muttered. "I hate myself for wanting this… for wanting you."

His words made my heart squeeze and I fought against the urge to comfort him like I'd always done. Despite his statement, he unbuckled my belt and tugged open my fly. I stared at his hands and let out a strangled noise the moment one of them stroked down my cock. It strained towards his touch like it was starving for him. And it was. Starved of this man who I loved and desired more than life itself.

"You still want me."

"Of course, I want you. I wouldn't be here if I didn't," the words were out of my mouth before I could stop them.

His eyes flicked up to mine. The unadulterated lust and hatred in them almost made me take a step back. His hand slid between the fabric of my boxers and my skin. I panted when his fingers enclosed around my cock, his grip borderline painful. I don't know where this assertive and dominant Rhys had come from but it only aroused me further. It'd been too long. Far too fucking long since I'd felt his touch.

"This isn't about you," he outright growled, his face drawing closer to mine. "I don't care if you want me. The only thing I care about is you doing what I tell you. And I'm telling you now so we're very clear about what will happen next. I'm going to *fuck* you as much and as hard as I want and you're going to take it no matter how much it hurts. Right now, you're fucking mine to do what I want with."

There was literally nothing I could say to that. Anything I could think of sounded stupid. I didn't want him to stop. Especially not now he'd touched me.

"I'm yours, I'll do what you want," I whispered.

I think it made him happy as his lip twitched. Then he dragged me closer to his bed by my cock and I could do nothing about it. He had all the cards here. He'd made it clear he was in complete control. I was at the mercy of his choices and decisions. The desire coursing through my veins was almost violent in nature. I wanted everything coming my way. And I wanted it right now.

I toed off my shoes as he tugged the rest of my clothes off me. Rhys pressed me face down on the bed with his hand on the back of my neck.

"Stay."

I dared not move as he let go and I heard him moving around behind me. I felt him next when his hand landed on my lower back, pressing me against the bed whilst his slick fingers delved between my cheeks and brushed against my hole. I shuddered in response and whined the moment his finger slid inside me.

"You came prepared."

"Yes," I murmured.

I'd known exactly what I was walking into. When he said he wanted to hurt me, I knew how this would go. So I'd made sure I was ready.

I felt him lean over me as his finger slid out of me. His breath fluttered across my shoulder.

"Prepared enough to take me?"

"Yes."

He ran his nose up my shoulder and breathed me in. I craved more of his touch. More of him.

"Do you want this? Do you want me to fuck you?"

I felt him press against me, the hardness of his cock digging into my skin. A clear indication I still turned him on as much as he did me.

"Yes… please."

He pulled away, making me pant. I needed him so fucking badly, it burnt. This would hurt and I knew that, but it didn't stop me from wanting it. The delicious yet painful ecstasy it would bring.

I heard the rip of foil and had to bite down on my lip to stop from telling him I didn't want that. Right now, I was in no position to make demands of him. He didn't know I'd not been with anyone and who knew if he had. I hated the thought of it. Of him being with another man. I had no right to feel that way, but I did. Rhys was fucking well *mine*.

His hand curled around my hip and his cock pressed against me. I fought hard not to tense up. I'd only been fucked once in my life and that was a long time ago. The experience had been magical. This time it would be very different.

I choked out a grunt of pain when he slid inside me. It only burnt a little, but the suddenness took me off guard.

"Fuck," he groaned above me.

Rhys didn't let me adjust, he kept pressing forward, making me take him no matter how much I struggled. I gripped the covers, panting as sweat beaded across my back. When I'd taken him halfway, he pulled back and pressed inside me again, starting to gain a rhythm. The warring sensations of pleasure and pain drove through me.

The moment he buried himself completely inside me, I moaned because fuck did it feel so good knowing it was him. Rhys. The man I fucking loved with everything I had.

He leant over me again, his bare chest brushing against my back. Nothing else felt as good as having him skin on skin.

"I hate you for making me want you like this. I hate it so fucking much." His hand wrapped around my shoulder and he started to move inside me. "I hate you, Aaron. I fucking hate you. You ruined us. You hurt me so fucking much. You broke my fucking heart."

Each word was punctuated by a hard thrust which only made me moan all over again. He could fuck me as hard as he wanted, I didn't care. He could hate me too, but he'd said it himself. He wanted me.

I gripped the covers tighter in my fists, taking him deeper and harder as his movements grew more erratic with his anger.

"God, I fucking well hate the sight of you. I hate how you look so fucking good. I hate how you still have this fucked up power over me. Why are you doing this to me? Why are you fucking back in my life?"

I didn't answer him. Who knew why fate had brought us back together. I could only say I was glad of it even if he was fucking me into oblivion right now. Fucking me so hard, the need to come pounded inside me. He had to know because he was hitting me at just the right angle.

"I. Hate. You."

I whimpered, trying desperately to hold back.

"Rhys."

"Fuck you."

"Please."

His hand tightened around my shoulder. He didn't let up and I knew if I came right then, he'd only make it worse for me. This was a fucking punishment, but of the best kind.

"No, don't you fucking well beg me. You don't deserve my fucking mercy, *prince*."

That name. The way he'd used it as a taunt rather than the term of endearment it had been between us almost outright destroyed me. The only thing I could do was hold on and let him decide when he'd punished me enough.

The sound of our skin slapping together and our harsh breath filled the air. It echoed the ferocious passion between us. You couldn't fake the connection we shared. He might hate me right now, but there were so many years between us. Years of friendship, love and being everything to each other. If Rhys didn't still feel something for me, he wouldn't have asked me here. He wouldn't be fucking me right now.

Abruptly, he pulled away from me. I felt bereft of his touch, unsure of what he wanted next.

"Turn over," he grunted.

I let go of the covers and struggled to obey him. When I was on my back, he shoved my legs up on the bed and fit himself between them. He entered me again, his hands banding around my legs and pressing them to his chest as he pounded into me. The wild look in his eyes set my skin ablaze. My hands curled around the covers again so I wouldn't touch myself.

He slightly adjusted his angle and every stroke brushed up against my prostate. It made it harder and harder not to come. And by the way he smirked at me, I was pretty sure it's what he wanted.

"You want to come, don't you?"

I nodded, biting down hard on my cheek to stop from begging him to let me. It only made him let go of one of my legs and wrap his hand around my cock. A whimper escaped my mouth despite my best efforts not to make a sound.

"Go on, fucking show me how much you love this."

I did love it. Mostly because it was Rhys doing the fucking and even though he was punishing me right now, it still felt incredible. And it only took a couple of strokes from him for me to erupt all over his fingers and my stomach.

"Rhys!"

"Fuck," he ground out. "Fuck!"

He thrust inside me impossibly hard before his face contorted and he groaned, emptying himself inside me. I watched with rapt attention as my cock pulsed in his hand. I didn't think I'd get to see pleasure and pain written all over his face like this.

Fuck, he's so beautiful it almost hurts to look at him.

He leant his head against my calf, panting as he let go of my cock. The sticky mess I'd made pooled on my stomach, making me very aware of how despite the pain, he'd brought me such pleasure too.

Rhys pulled out of me and walked away, disposing of the condom. Next thing I knew, he'd chucked a box of tissues at my head. I sat up and cleaned myself off before getting up and throwing them in the bin.

I stood there, unsure of what to do. Did he want me to leave now he'd had his fill of me? The thought of it cut me. I didn't want to leave him. I wanted to stay right here where I could be close to the man I loved so desperately.

"Do... do you want me to go?" I all but whispered.

He turned and stared at me for a long moment. Then he pointed at his bed.

"I'm not fucking done with you yet."

I swallowed hard not knowing what that meant. Even so, I walked over to his bed and laid down on the side he'd indicated. Satisfied I'd obeyed him, he nodded and walked out of the room. I didn't know what he had planned for me or what this even meant, but I wasn't going anywhere. If I could, I'd stay here forever in his space. Nestled on his bed with sheets that smelt of him.

Whatever Rhys wanted when he came back into the room, I'd give it to him. I'd spend eternity making up for everything I'd done to him if he let me remain with him. If he stayed in my life.

I love you, Rhys. I'll never stop loving you. No matter what you do to me, I'll keep coming back for more because that's what you do for the person you love more than anything in the entire universe.

CHAPTER FIFTY FOUR

Rhys

armth and contentment flooded me when I
floated back into the world from what felt like the
deepest sleep I'd had in a long time. My arms
were wrapped around a solid body who smelt like home. A
sense of belonging washed over me. After years of emptiness,
I felt complete.

Then I opened my eyes and realised who the fuck I was
holding onto. Whose chest my head was resting on. And
everything came rushing back.

What the fuck? Why the hell did I let him stay the night?

I extracted myself from his grasp. Sitting up, I stared down
at him. My very naked ex who I'd had very angry, vigorous sex
with last night. I couldn't help the way my insides clenched at
the sight of his bare chest and the peaceful look on his
sleeping face.

You fucking idiot, Rhys.

I should never have told him to come over yesterday. All my common sense fled the building. Desire, anger and need were the only driving factors in my decision making. Fucking him out of my system seemed like a good idea, but really, it made everything worse. Now, I craved him more than ever.

I couldn't face him or myself right then. Sickness coiled in my stomach knowing what I'd done. How fucked up I'd become since the moment I'd laid eyes on him again.

I crawled out of bed and quick-walked out of the room, going into the bathroom. Flipping on the shower, I desperately needed to wash away the lingering smell of sex and him from my skin. I stood under the scalding hot spray, hoping he wouldn't still be there when I got out.

Wishful bloody thinking.

The memory of last night branded itself on my retinas. It wasn't the angry hate sex I'd had with him which tormented me. It was after that. When I'd told him to get in my bed and stay there. That had been my biggest mistake.

He'd been there when I got back with two glasses of water, one of which I handed to him. Then I got under the covers and turned out the light. He hadn't asked any questions. I didn't have any answers for him either. There was no rational thought process behind why I wanted him there. I just did. And the sound of his breathing had lulled me to sleep.

When I woke up in the middle of the night, fear had gripped me because for a full minute, I thought he'd left me all over again. Then I'd heard the toilet flush. The relief I felt when he reappeared and crawled back into bed had me doing something stupid. I'd reached for him. I'd pressed my face into his neck and breathed him in. And I'd held him, allowing him to put his arm around me too.

Then… then I'd whispered those fucking disastrous words to him.

"I've missed you so much."

He'd let out a long breath.

"I missed you too."

The words hung in the air between us. I didn't let go and neither did he.

Why did you tell him that?

I scrubbed my face with my hand before slamming it down on the tiles in front of me. Frustration with myself and him exploding in my blood. He didn't deserve to know how being apart from him had been hell for me. He deserved nothing from me after he'd ruined us.

The shower door opened. I turned at the sound. Those stormy blue-grey eyes seared into me. I didn't tell him to stop when he walked in, closing the door behind him. We stood inches apart under the streaming water. My skin prickled. My hands twitched with the effort of holding back. I hated it. Hated how seeing him made my heart fire on all cylinders. How he felt like home.

Why do I still love you, Aaron?

I sucked in air when he leant closer and rested his forehead against mine. Did he have any idea how close I felt to breaking down? Having him right there made the two warring sides of me clash violently. Love and hate. When it came to Aaron, they were two sides of the same coin. I'd felt so adrift for seven long years. He had been my anchor to the world. Keeping me secure and safe.

"Don't," I whispered as his hand rose and cupped my face.

"I'm not going to kiss you. I know I don't deserve to… yet."

It didn't fill me with relief. Quite the opposite. Kissing him would be too intimate. It's why I'd stated last night it wouldn't be happening. Yet wasn't fucking the most intimate thing you could do with another person? No, that was making love. And we definitely had not done that. You could hardly call the shit spewing out of my mouth last night in any way loving or romantic.

"I want you to know no matter how hard you try to push me away, I won't stop coming back. I won't leave you again."

He'd known last night when I reached for him, it had everything to do with me being terrified of him leaving. I didn't have to voice it. Aaron knew me. He recognised my needs. It's part of the reason we worked so well together.

"I don't want you to do that."

"Yes, you do. You want me to fight for you."

"I don't want anything from you."

"You do."

I didn't get a chance to respond. He pulled me closer and wrapped his arms around me. The gesture broke through all my defences. Being held by the one person my entire world had revolved around for so long made every part of me ache. The dam broke and the tears came as I clung to him. I was grateful for the water beating down on us, washing the evidence of his effect on me away.

"I hate how you make me feel," I whispered through a broken sob.

He didn't need to say he was sorry again. I could feel it in the way he held me. How he regretted the way we ended and the distance between us. The years without each other. Sorry didn't mean anything anyway. It was just a word. I knew what he was trying to do. Give me what I needed. What I asked him for without words like he'd always done. And it annoyed me. It made it so much harder to hold all this hate towards him in my heart.

I don't know how long we stood there not speaking. He pulled away and grabbed the shower gel. I watched him lather it up in his hands before he touched me. My breathing became erratic as he washed me with such fucking reverence, it damn near broke me. And I let him. I allowed him to take care of me. Just like he always had. Because it felt so fucking good. I didn't have it in me to tell him off for breaking the rule I'd laid out last night. The one about not touching me.

When he was done, I stepped away and he let me leave without saying a word so he could clean up too. I grabbed a towel off the rail, drying myself before slinging it around my hips and padding out into my bedroom. I found he'd picked up our clothes from the floor and had left them in neat piles on my bed.

I pulled some clean ones on, a t-shirt and a pair of shorts and fiddled with my hair for a minute so it wouldn't dry in a wild mess of curls. Rubbing my face, I went into the kitchen and stuck the kettle on before I sat at my desk and stared out the window.

A few minutes later I felt his presence behind me. My skin raised up in goosebumps. He leant over my shoulder, making me let out a choking sound as he grabbed my sketchbook and the pencil resting next to it. I daren't look at what he did when he straightened. Only when he leant over me again, placing both items back down did I try to formulate words. Tried and failed.

His hand landed on my shoulder and he pressed his lips to the top of my head before resting his cheek against it.

"If I have to spend the rest of my life making up for what I did to you, *knight*, I will," he whispered.

My heart. My god damn fucking heart. It ached and squeezed hard. So fucking hard. I'd taunted him with the nickname I'd given him last night, but the way he said mine with such tenderness had me in bits.

Do not break down in front of him again. Do not do it.

He kissed the top of my head again before he let me go. I listened to his footsteps as he walked away and the slam of the front door when he left. My breath whooshed out of me. I leant forward and picked up the sketchbook. He'd turned it to the last page where he'd written me a note.

Call me if you need me. Day or night. Any hour. Even if it's just to punish me again, I'll be there. A x

He'd followed it up with his personal phone number.

I swallowed hard. The memory of the way he'd moaned my name last night slamming into me. I got up and made myself a cup of tea along with a bowl of cereal. Then I grabbed my phone from my bedroom and put his number in my contacts even though I should've torn up his note and thrown it in the bin. No, stupid me ripped out the page and pinned it to the whiteboard next to my desk with a little magnet. I kept track of my projects on there so looked at it regularly. Why I wanted a piece of him close to me wasn't much of a mystery, even if I despised myself for it.

I ate my breakfast and sat back, fiddling with my phone. Then I stuck it against my ear and let it ring.

"You finally ready to talk?" Meredith said when she answered.

"I'm sorry."

"Don't apologise. I know you, Rhys, you never drop out of contact unless something really fucked up happened. So, what's the deal?"

I stared at Aaron's note on my whiteboard.

"Do you want the long or the short explanation?"

"The short one. Hold on, before you start, can you video call me? I got called into work because someone messed up the fucking sets for the promo shoot on Monday so I've only got the weekend to fix it."

I rolled my eyes but hung up and grabbed my tablet, setting it up on the desk in front of me before calling her back. Her face appeared on the screen a minute later, her blue hair up in a messy bun and her green eyes glinting. She wore jean dungarees with one strap undone and a bright purple t-shirt. Meredith was nothing if not quirky.

"You look different."

I frowned.

"What do you mean?"

"All glowy and shit. Anyway… tell me what happened."

She'd know soon enough why I looked glowy.

Meredith moved away from her phone and grabbed her paints, starting to work on the set backdrop behind her. She was working on some low budget theatre production whilst she was in between major jobs.

"Okay, the short explanation is… at the meeting on Monday I found out my ex is the author's editor. We saw each other. It was weird and uncomfortable, but it brought back all my feelings from seven years ago. I signed the contract with Johnstone & Parrish the next day and then spent three days drinking and eating junk food whilst crying on and off over him. Yesterday he called me and asked me to go to dinner with him, I refused, shouted at him and then told him to come over. He did. We had what I can only describe as hate sex, I let him stay the night and he just left like ten minutes ago."

There seemed no point in sugar-coating the truth with her. Meredith had always confided in me about her love life. I didn't have one to speak of until now. Not that this was anything. Just a fucked up mess with my ex-boyfriend, ex-best friend and soulmate.

"Holy. Fuck."

"Welcome to my very own version of hell."

"Well, shit, Rhys. I mean, shit. When you said you had hate sex, did you fuck him or was it the other way around? Like did you two have a defined top and bottom when you were together?"

I stared at her. Meredith had never held back with me. Ever. I knew more about her sex life than I ever wanted to.

After everything with Cole, she'd sworn off relationships so for her, it'd meant she dated but it never went any further or got serious. Giving her heart to another person was something Meredith had proclaimed she'd never do again. And honestly, I couldn't blame her. I was just as bad, what with the shit with Aaron.

"What?"

She glanced at the screen.

"I need more of an explanation than that. This is the first time you've got laid in... forever. So, give me something, please."

"I didn't realise the fact I had sex was the most important part about what I said."

"It's not."

I rolled my eyes.

"Fine. I fucked him and that isn't how it was when we were together. In fact, the only time I topped him before was like two days before he broke up with me. Make of that what you will."

"Was it good?"

My skin prickled. It had been more than good. Being with him again after all this time could only be described as bittersweet ecstasy.

"I haven't had sex in seven years, Mer, what do you think?"

"I think that's why you're all glowy, so it must've been good."

I snorted. And then self-loathing washed over me at the realisation I wanted to do it again. I needed to. Once wasn't enough. I didn't think any number of times with Aaron would be enough to satisfy me. To rid myself of this innate craving I had for him.

"So, what are you going to do now? Did you two talk about things between you?"

"No, we didn't and I have no fucking idea."

"Are you telling me you literally asked him to come over so you could fuck him?"

I rubbed the back of my neck.

"Pretty much. I wanted to… punish him for what he did to me. I told him there'd be no talking and he didn't object. He let me do what I wanted, which included me telling him how much I hate him."

Meredith smiled and bit her lip.

"Oh boy, you are a dark horse. This I was not expecting. I'm actually impressed. I mean, I'm not saying I think it was a good idea or anything. Speaking from experience, sleeping with your ex isn't something I'd recommend, but it's a bit too late for that now."

I couldn't take back what happened last night or this morning. I could, however, not do it again. Except I knew that would be impossible. The pull I had towards Aaron hadn't dulled. My whole being cried out for him. Staying away wouldn't work, but I had to try. I had to do it for me. Because I couldn't forgive him for hurting me. The wounds he inflicted were too deep.

"I don't know where my common sense went, but it happened and I can't go back and change it."

"Do you really hate him?"

I looked at the note he'd left me again.

"Yes and no. I hate him but I love him at the same time."

Admitting it out loud cut me deeper than I expected it to.

"Then I think you should talk to him."

"I don't think I can forgive him… or let him back in."

"I hate to break it to you, Rhys, but it's been seven years and clearly you haven't let go. I think you owe it to yourself to, at the very least, have a conversation with him."

"You're right."

There would be no point denying it. Aaron and I did need to talk. I had no idea how it would go, but if I was ever going to move forward, then I had to do this. I had to talk to him.

"Listen… I really need to get on with this, but we should do drinks and pizza on Monday, yeah? Then you can cry on my shoulder if you need to or whatever."

"Okay, I can do Monday."

She glanced at the screen and winked at me.

"See you then, fuckface. Love you."

I smiled.

"Love you too."

I hung up the call. Talking to Meredith had helped me a little. Unburdening myself felt like a small weight had been lifted off my shoulders. It didn't stop me being all kinds of messed up over Aaron. I could fix this somehow, couldn't I? Fix it so I could walk away for good and not feel this way any longer.

That's what I wanted… wasn't it?

CHAPTER FIFTY FIVE

Aaron

hen I got home, I was glad I'd showered at Rhys' flat or I'd have still smelt like sex. It wouldn't have been a good thing since I'd agreed to babysit this weekend. I'd just got done changing when my doorbell rang. Walking down the hallway, I reached my front door and hit the buzzer to let them up. When the knock came at the door a few minutes later, I opened it. Two small children slammed against my legs in an instant.

"Uncle Aaron!"

"Hello, girls."

Hetty and Harmony, my five-year-old twin nieces, curled themselves around my legs. Harriet stood on the threshold, giving me a soft smile.

"Thank you so much for this, you're an absolute lifesaver."

Sarah Bailey

Harriet and Ralph were having marital issues and with our parents being out of the country, she'd asked me to help her out.

"It's okay. The girls and I will be just fine, won't we?"

I patted their blonde heads as they stared up at me.

"We always have fun with you," Harmony stated as if it was a dumb question.

They pulled away from me and gave their mother a hug before rushing by my legs into the living room. Harriet rolled her eyes and handed me their bags.

"They've been acting up all week so if they give you trouble, I'm sorry. It's unsettling for them not to have Ralph at home."

"I hope you two sort things out."

I didn't because I still hated Ralph and thought he was a twat, but I wouldn't voice that to Harriet. Being a supportive brother was the only thing I could do in this situation despite our thirteen-year age-gap. Harriet and I had grown closer over the years whilst I'd only drifted further apart from my parents. I just about tolerated speaking to my mother and she knew better than to bring up anything about my father to me. As far as I was concerned, he was fucking dead to me. Especially after our last argument where he'd said he was disappointed in me for turning out gay. Like it was my fault for being born this way.

"Yes, well, we'll see."

She leant forward and kissed my cheek.

"I'll pick them up before you go to work on Monday."

Then she turned and left. I shut the door behind her and walked into the living room. The girls had taken up residence by the window where I'd already laid out colouring books for them last night. I watched them for a moment before taking their bags into one of the spare bedrooms they always stayed in whenever I took care of them.

I padded out towards the kitchen and poured apple juice into two cups before taking it through to them and setting the cups down on the side table near to where they were colouring.

"Uncle Aaron?" Hetty piped up.

"Yes, sweetie?"

The girls had just started full time at school this year and had been adjusting well until their parents had decided they needed to take time apart.

"Are Mummy and Daddy going to get divorced?"

I froze. Harriet hadn't yet mentioned the divorce word to me or the girls. I didn't think she wanted it to get that far.

"How do you know what that is?"

"One of the boys in our class said his mummy and daddy are divorced. He says they're always shouting and are really nasty to each other. We don't want Mummy and Daddy to fight. We don't want to live in separate houses."

I walked over to them and squatted down, stroking her head.

"Mummy and Daddy are just taking a little time apart, sweetie. It doesn't mean they're going to get a divorce, okay? Just remember they love you both very much."

Two sets of blue eyes stared at me with sadness in them and it made my heart hurt. They didn't deserve to go through this shit.

"Daddy said he doesn't think Mummy loves him anymore."

"That's not true, Hetty. She loves him very much, but sometimes adults go through bad patches and they have to fix what's gone wrong."

"I don't want to be an adult."

"Well, lucky for you that's still years away."

I didn't blame her for not wanting to grow up. Sometimes I wished I could go back to when I was younger. When everything had been simpler. And I hadn't hurt the person I loved. If I could do it all again, I would change so many of my decisions. The first one being never agreeing to go to that fucking party with him. Then we might not have crashed and burned the way we had. And I wouldn't have Valentine's death on my conscience.

I'd made peace with it over the years. It didn't absolve my guilt, but it had been a tragic accident. I couldn't take it back or make it right. Moving on from it had been difficult since my feelings about it were all tangled up with my feelings towards Rhys. However, I'd learnt how to separate them. It was the only way I'd been able to carry on living after that fateful day where everything had changed and not for the better.

The girls went back to their colouring. I rose to my feet and walked over to the sofa, taking a seat so I could still see them but also get on with some work. Grabbing my laptop off the coffee table, I booted it up. I'd just opened up the document I needed when my phone buzzed. Pulling it out, I stared down at the text, my heart doing a backflip in my chest.

Rhys: Come over later?

I honestly had not expected to hear from him today, if at all. Leaving him my number had been a gamble. The way he'd cried on me in the shower earlier broke my heart clean in two. I hated I was the reason for his torment. My need to make it better for him drove me. I couldn't give up no matter what he threw at me. And it really fucking killed me, I had to say no to his request. Especially when I'd told him I'd be there no matter what.

I eyed the twins, wondering if I could get away with inviting him here instead. There was no way in hell I wanted to turn down the opportunity to see him.

"Girls."

Hetty and Harmony popped their heads up, looking over at me.

"Would you mind if I invited a friend to dinner tonight?"

"A friend?" Harmony asked with wide eyes.

"Yes. He's very nice."

"Is he your boyfriend, Uncle Aaron?" Hetty probed.

I almost choked on my own breath. Kids really came out with such blunt statements sometimes. Harriet hadn't hidden my sexuality from them. She wasn't ashamed of me, unlike our father.

"Um, no… he isn't."

But I wish he would be again. Fuck, do I wish he'd give me a second chance.

"Oh. Well, we don't mind. Can we show your friend our colouring?"

"If he says yes. I'm sure he'd love to see."

The girls gave me a smile and went back to their books. I should've known they wouldn't be bothered either way. So I typed out a response to Rhys, mentally crossing my fingers in the hope he'd say yes.

Aaron: Wish I could, have my nieces staying this weekend.

Aaron: You could come over for dinner and meet them. We can talk after I put them to bed.

I noted he'd seen the messages a minute later. And it took five more to get a response. In that time I'd gone back and forth with myself several times over whether or not I should tell him to forget it.

Rhys: Harriet had kids?

Aaron: Yes, twins.

Rhys: Are you sure they'd be okay with that?

Aaron: I already checked with them.

Rhys: What time?

Aaron: Six.

Rhys: Okay. Text me your address.

My heart thumped against my ribcage as I typed it out. He'd said yes. He was going to come over. We could talk after I put the girls to bed or if he just wanted sex, I would let him have that too. I didn't care. I wanted to see him.

Now I had to work out what to make. The girls tended to be picky, which drove Harriet crazy. She disliked how they'd be good for me about food, but not her. Maybe they'd behave today. I never knew with them. I could take them to the supermarket with me. They'd like that. If you made them feel included, they were more likely to eat what I'd prepared.

"Girls, can you put your shoes on? We're going shopping."

"We are?" Hetty asked, setting her red pencil down.

I stood up, dumping my laptop on the sofa.

"Yes, you can help me choose what we're going to make Rhys tonight."

"Can we help you cook later?" Harmony put in.

"Of course you can."

The girls jumped up from where they were sitting and grabbed their shoes, which they'd left next to them. I went into the kitchen to check what I did and didn't have first. The girls and I would make sure Rhys enjoyed himself tonight. And hopefully, I could fix what I'd broken between us all those years ago.

CHAPTER FIFTY SIX

Aaron

The buzzer went at five to six, right after I'd checked the chicken cacciatore in the oven. The girls were setting the table for me. The two of them were excited about having a guest and had asked me all sorts of questions about Rhys. I'd attempted to answer the best I could considering I didn't know much about his life now.

I walked out into the hallway and buzzed him in. Sticking my head back in the kitchen door to check on the girls, I found them placing napkins down carefully beside the plates. It had me smiling. If I could give them one weekend of normality, I would.

The knock at the front door had me pulling back and walking over to it. I checked myself in the hall mirror.

You look fine, stop worrying.

Rhys stood there with his hands shoved in his jean's pockets, his curly hair a little wind ruffled. And shit if it didn't make him look sexy as hell.

"Hi, come in."

I stepped back. He hesitated for a long moment before walking in. After I shut the front door, he slid off his coat and I hung it up on the rack next to me.

My fingers itched with the need to run them through his hair. My eyes fixated on his lips, desperate to kiss them. My entire body craved his with such an intensity, I had to dig my nails into my palms to stop from acting on my impulses.

"I don't know what I'm doing here," he murmured.

"Dinner, you're having dinner."

"I know but…" He waved a hand at me. "This isn't me forgiving you. We're not suddenly friends again."

My heart lurched. It would take time for him to trust me again. If he ever could. It didn't stop hearing him say that from hurting me.

"I don't want to be your friend."

His eyebrow shot up.

"What?"

I took a step forward, making him back up.

"I have no interest in being just your friend."

Another step brought his back flush with the wall. I had no idea what I was doing. Only the need to make him understand I wanted him back as my everything drove through me.

"You know as well as I do that ship sailed years ago."

He stared at me, his eyes unnerving in the way they darkened to almost black.

"Friends don't fuck the way you fucked me last night," I murmured, keeping my voice low so the girls wouldn't hear.

"Are you saying you want a repeat?" he asked, his voice equally low.

"You already know the answer to that question."

The thought of his brutal pounding only made me want him more. I couldn't allow myself to get carried away. He was here for dinner. So no matter how much the sexual tension brewing between us grew closer to exploding, I had to stay calm. Stepping back, I turned towards the kitchen.

"Come meet my nieces."

Thankfully, he followed me without a word. Hetty and Harmony were stood by the dining table. Both their eyes fixed on me and Rhys when we walked in.

"Girls."

The two of them came around the table and stared up at Rhys.

"This is Rhys." I turned to him. "These are my nieces, Hetty and Harmony."

I indicated them each in turn. They were almost identical except for one notable difference. Harmony had a beauty spot right over her left eyebrow.

"Hello," Rhys said, giving them both a smile.

"Hi," Hetty said.

"Uncle Aaron said you were friends when you were at school," Harmony added.

Rhys glanced at me.

"That's right. We were best friends."

My heart tightened. Nothing would make me happier than to have my best friend back. But I wanted more. I wanted Rhys mine for life. Doubts about him being my one had never entered my mind. It'd been love at first sight for me, even if I hadn't understood that when I was seven.

"Did you know our Mummy too?"

"Yes, she constantly said your uncle and I were joined at the hip, but that was a long time ago."

We had been. It'd taken a tragic accident my father had used to his advantage to drag us apart.

"Uncle Aaron said you draw. Can we show you ours?" Hetty asked.

"You can show Rhys after dinner, okay? Why don't you show him where to sit?" I said, waving a hand at the table. "Do you want something to drink? I have wine, beer, spirits or juice?"

Hetty and Harmony each grabbed one of Rhys' hands and pulled him with them. He glanced back at me.

"Beer's fine."

I wandered towards the fridge, eying the girls as they made him sit down and started asking more questions. Grabbing two beers out, I set them on the counter and popped the caps with the bottle opener. Next, I checked the rice and took the chicken out of the oven. Once I'd served everything up on plates, I brought them all over to the table and went back to get the beers.

The girls had sat Rhys next to me with them across from us. As I handed him the beer, I took a seat and nodded at the girls. I'd already put juice out for them earlier.

"Well, tuck in."

I sipped my beer, eying the girls to make sure they started. My attention drifted to Rhys. Him being so close to me made my skin burn with need. I wanted to touch him so fucking badly. Doubt he'd appreciate it, so I refrained.

As kids, we'd had constant physical affection between us. My body remembered it. It didn't feel normal not to reach for him. To feel him against me in some small way. Perhaps I deserved this. The torment. Since I'd brought him so much of it. Didn't make me feel any better.

"Uncle Aaron," Hetty's voice floated over the table.

"Hmm?"

My eyes stayed fixed on Rhys, who'd raised his beer to his lips. How could I do anything but stare at him? He was so fucking handsome.

"We know you like boys, but does Rhys too?"

Rhys choked on his beer. My head snapped to the girls. In all honesty, I should've expected it considering they were far too curious for their own good.

"You cannot ask people that, Hetty."

"Why not?"

"It's inappropriate."

"But why?"

"We're not starting the why game at the table. You don't ask people outright about who they like. If they want to share it with you, they will, okay?"

Hetty looked put out, but if you weren't strict with the girls, they would run riot all over you. I'd got wise to them.

"Now, apologise for being rude."

"Sorry, Uncle Aaron. Sorry, Rhys," she said with no hesitation.

"It's okay," Rhys said, glancing at me.

I couldn't stop the girls from asking questions. At least they listened to me when I told them off. They weren't so good for their parents. Maybe since I refused to let them get away with anything, they were better behaved with me.

When the girls' attention was back on their food, I leant closer to him.

"Sorry, they're kind of blunt sometimes," I murmured.

His lip curved up.

"Aren't kids always?"

"They're just going through a difficult time. Harriet and Ralph are separated at the moment. That's why I have the girls, they're working on their marriage."

His eyes met mine and the understanding in them had me remembering what he'd gone through all those years ago. Rhys understood the pain of trouble between his parents.

"That's rough. So, they know you're gay, huh?"

I swallowed my mouthful.

"Uhuh, Harriet doesn't have any issues with it, unlike their grandparents."

Rhys snorted.

"Well, that's hardly surprising."

I almost slapped myself for bringing up my parents. Rhys was not their biggest fan. In fact, he probably hated my father as much as I did. He was partially to blame for the breakdown of mine and Rhys' relationship.

"I don't mind them knowing I'm gay," he murmured. "Unless you do."

"I don't."

Rhys had never shied away from being open about it. I didn't want to confuse the girls after I told them he wasn't my boyfriend, so it was probably best not to bring it up again.

"What kind of things do you draw?" Harmony asked, making me pull away from Rhys.

"I draw fantasy scenes for books mostly, and I make book covers. I also have a comic strip," Rhys replied, smiling at my niece.

I wish you'd smile at me like that again.

"Will you show us?"

"I can… if that's okay with your uncle."

"Is it child friendly?" I asked, trying not to grin.

Rhys would never show them anything inappropriate, but I had to check, nevertheless. Harriet would kill me if they saw something they weren't supposed to.

"Not all of it, but the latest update would be okay for them."

His dark eyes sparkled like something about it was funny and I wondered why.

"I'm okay with it."

I didn't stop him slipping from his chair whilst he pulled his phone from his pocket. He fiddled with it as he rounded the table and squatted down by the girls. We were all still eating, but my curiosity about this overrode telling the girls they'd have to wait until dinner was over.

Rhys showed them his phone screen, pointing something out to them. The girl's eyes flicked between me and the screen at least five times. Harmony leant closer to Rhys.

"Why does the boy in the comic look like Uncle Aaron?" she whispered.

I blinked.

Wait… what?

"Because I started drawing these when I was fifteen and your uncle was my muse."

"What's a muse?"

"Someone who inspires your art."

Rhys' eyes flicked to mine. My heart constricted and everything narrowed to just him. I didn't think he'd still be drawing the same character he'd based on me. Nor that he'd share it with the world.

What do I say to that? What does it mean?

"Can you draw me?" Hetty asked.

Rhys smiled.

"Maybe one day, but not tonight. You two need to finish your dinner so you can show me your drawings."

The girls instantly went back to their food. Rhys rose to his full height and came back around the table. He sat down and placed his phone between us on the wooden surface. I stared down at the screen. There, clear as day, was his comic strip. Harmony hadn't been wrong. The main character looked exactly like me. And I remembered his sketchbook full of these drawings of a cartoon version of me he'd done when we were teenagers.

Holy. Shit.

"Why?" I whispered.

"You already know the answer to that question," he replied, echoing my exact words from earlier.

Do I?

Rhys couldn't forget me. Not even after I'd broken his heart. And this was the comic strip which had made Emily want him to illustrate her book. Did she recognise it was me?

I had to go back through all of them and read each one when I was alone. Maybe then I'd understand why. Maybe it'd give me some insight. Who fucking knew. This felt surreal.

I went back to my food, unsure of what else to say. By the time we were all done, I sent the girls into the living room to choose a film whilst Rhys offered to help me clean up. We didn't speak as I filled the dishwasher and put the leftovers away. He kept watching me, which had my skin itching with the need to have his hands all over me instead of his eyes.

The girls had chosen *Beauty and the Beast* since it was one of their favourites. I got everything set up on the TV whilst they showed Rhys their drawings. He made appropriate noises, smiling at the two of them the whole time. I made them get changed into their pyjamas and brush their teeth before I put the film on.

The girls insisted on sitting in between us. I didn't put up a fight even though I wanted to be closer to him. Halfway through the film, they fell asleep on us. I paused it and Rhys helped me carry them to the spare bedroom. We put them in the double bed together and crept out.

We stared at each other in the hallway. I was in half a mind to throw myself at him and beg him to let me love him again. Having him here tonight meant everything to me.

"Maybe I should go."

Those were not the words I wanted to hear. I would do anything to keep him here.

"Don't... please, stay. We haven't talked yet."

CHAPTER FIFTY SEVEN

Rhys

My emotions were a complete and utter fucking mess. I'd come here tonight so I could have a conversation with him about the past. Fuck knows we needed to. Moving on would never happen unless I got a sense of closure. Except being around him only made me want him all the more. And meeting his nieces had been an unexpected joy. Seeing how good he was with them even as he made sure they didn't step out of line. Aaron would make an amazing parent one day if he ever wanted that.

His blue-grey eyes pleaded with me not to leave, breaking through all my defences, just like he'd always been able to. I took a step towards him, unable to help myself. My body wanted his touch. I wanted him. Us being alone without his nieces as a buffer only stoked the flames.

"Where's your bedroom?" I murmured.

He glanced back at the door at the end of the hallway. I took it as a sign he wouldn't stop me. Stepping towards him, my hand landed on his chest and I pushed him backwards. Aaron stared at me, wide-eyed and stumbling a little on our path towards where the inevitable would happen. Nothing about this decision could be called rational. I had to have him again. Nothing else would do. Talking be fucking damned right at this second. Anything we had to say could wait.

I shut the door behind us when we got into his room. Not bothering with the lights as the curtains were wide open, I shoved him towards his bed. He fell back onto it and I was right there with him, pinning him down with my body on top of his. The temptation to kiss him had me in knots. Feeling his mouth on mine would be bliss. But I wasn't going to do that. Instead, I buried my face in his neck, my tongue flicking out and running over his pulse point.

I trailed a path towards his ear with my lips, kissing just below it. He panted, spurring me on. My teeth grazed along his earlobe. Between us, his cock hardened, matching my own, which already throbbed in anticipation.

"Rhys," he moaned.

His hands landed on my thighs, gripping tightly as if he needed to anchor himself. I rocked my hips, making him squirm beneath me. Aaron wanted me. He wanted me as fucking badly as I wanted him. It should make me stop. It would be more of a punishment if I denied him this, but I couldn't stop now.

"I clearly need to shut you up before you get too loud," I whispered in his ear.

Pulling away and sitting up, I fumbled with my jeans, getting them open and tugging my cock out. I might want to fuck Aaron into next week, but I also wanted his mouth on me. I missed the way his tongue felt and the warm wetness encasing me.

Shifting off him, I stood up and stared at him with my cock in my hand. My eyebrow quirked up. He lay there with wild eyes and if the bulge in his jeans was anything to go by, just as turned on and ready for this as me.

"On your knees, *prince*."

Aaron pushed himself up and off the bed, dropping to his knees in front of me. I cupped his face, running my thumb along his bottom lip before pushing it inside his mouth. His eyes burnt with need as he swirled his tongue around the tip.

"You want this?" I asked, stroking my cock right next to his face.

He nodded. I popped my thumb out of his mouth, brushing the wetness along his lip.

"If you want my cock, you know how to ask for it."

I understood why he'd always got off on control when we were younger. This power I had right now felt freeing. Like I could give in to these dark urges I had when it came to Aaron. I could do what I wanted with him and he'd let me without reservation or hesitation.

"Please give me your cock. I don't deserve it, but I want to give you pleasure. I want to make you come." He reached for me, his hands curling into my jeans. "I want you so much, Rhys. Let me suck your cock, please."

I hooked my thumb in his mouth again and pulled it open. Even if he hadn't begged, I would have given it to him anyway. He'd been good for me, so I wouldn't tease him. Wrapping my hand around the back of his head, I pulled him closer and slid the head of my cock in his mouth.

Fuck me. Just as I remembered. So fucking good.

Aaron didn't try to direct proceedings. He let me press my cock deeper into his waiting mouth. His eyes betrayed his need for this. This beautiful man who I still loved with every inch of my fucking soul would let me do exactly as I pleased to him.

"You want to make me come, *prince*? Come right down your fucking throat?"

He hummed his agreement around my cock, the vibrations sending shivers up my spine.

"Go on then… you're going to have to work for it."

No hesitation. His hand left my jeans and gripped the bottom of my cock. Aaron worked me, his mouth suctioning around my shaft and driving me fucking crazy. My fingers tightened around his head, digging into his scalp. I panted when he took me deeper, my other hand landing on his shoulder. He was still amazing at this. He knew exactly how hard to suck me, to stroke me with his hand. He knew everything about me and it was equal parts incredible and damning. I hated and loved him knowing how to please me.

"Oh fuck," I groaned. "Yes, like that. Don't stop! Fuck, that's it, A."

My slip of the tongue registered with me the moment I felt everything inside me tighten. This situation was far too fucked up for words. Aaron somehow chipped away at my walls in the brief time he'd been back in my life. Almost effortless on his part. You couldn't erase our past. The friendship we'd forged. The love between us. It all still remained. Clear as fucking day.

Aaron might not have told me he loved me, but I could feel it from him. His heart crying out for mine. His soul bleeding for me. Just as mine did for him.

I didn't want this to end. Didn't want to walk away. But how could I trust him again? How could I forgive him? We hadn't even talked things through. Being alone with him made it hard to concentrate on anything else but having him against me. Touching his body and sating the overwhelming desire I had to fuck him. This wasn't just about my anger or my hate. Being close to him soothed my shattered soul.

I stared down at his blue-grey eyes, the part of him I'd always adored the most. Every inch of me melted for him. I didn't have it in me to deny him anything. Not when I could see his feelings for me written all over his features and in the way he touched me.

"Shit, Aaron," I moaned, erupting in his mouth as the sensations washed over my skin.

I couldn't look away, watching him take everything I had to give and how some of it spilt out over his lip. Seeing him take it was so fucking hot. Pulling my cock free of his mouth, I breathed deeply. Aaron swallowed and licked his lip, cleaning the cum from it. I let go of him, the urge to reward him for being so good overwhelming all my senses.

"Get on the bed."

He scrambled to obey, shifting backwards. I didn't bother putting myself away. No, I just dropped to my knees and crawled between his legs, running my hands up his thighs. Lifting my hand, I pressed it against his chest and shoved him down. Then my hands were at his jeans, tugging open the zip and pulling him out. He let out a choking gasp when I wrapped my mouth around him, my tongue circling the crown of his cock. His hands flexed by his sides and his breathing grew erratic.

I loved the feel of him in my mouth. I revelled in making him moan and struggle not to reach out to me. Fuck knows I shouldn't be doing this, but the consequences of my actions weren't on my list of priorities. Was it so wrong of me to want to just feel right now? To remember how good it was when we were together.

Damn it, Aaron, I love you so much and it kills me. It fucking decimates me.

"Oh fuck," he panted. "Rhys, fuck... please."

My hand curled around the base of him, stroking as I sucked his cock exactly the way I knew he liked it. Forgetting how to please Aaron would be impossible. It was almost like muscle memory for me. We'd been so in sync with each other, so in tune. Seven years hadn't changed that in the slightest. My body knew his just as his knew mine. It remembered everything. Every dip and curve. The dusting of blonde hair leading down to his cock. The slight curve to his hard shaft. Everything. And I fucking adored it. Adored him.

I got off on his moans and pleading. Watching him come apart right before my eyes as if he could never get enough of me. Of this. Of us. And when he came, groaning my name, I took every last drop, swallowing it down when I pulled away.

I shifted up on the bed and flopped down next to him, watching his chest rise and fall as he tried to catch his breath. My hand reached out without me thinking, stroking down the centre of it. Every part of me wanted to be wrapped up with him. I stared hard at his mouth, trying to quell the urge to kiss him.

"Do you want to stay?" he whispered.

"I shouldn't."

"I have no right to say this, but I want you here." He turned his head towards me, his eyes full of emotion. "I need you, Rhys. I don't function right without you."

My heart constricted in my chest, the ache driving right into my bones. He placed his hand on top of mine on his chest, right where his heart sat.

"This belongs to you. It always has and it always will. If you want to keep punishing me, you can… just stay with me. Please give me one chance to show you how sorry I am. To prove to you I'll never leave again."

If only it was that easy. The pain of being apart from him overwhelmed me. Made me want to give in. To allow him back in my life so I no longer had to live with this anguish. I wanted to let Aaron take it all away. To let him love me again. Except there were so many things holding me back, preventing me from allowing him back in.

"I don't know how to trust you," I whispered, hating myself for admitting the truth.

He shifted on his side and reached for me, cupping my face.

"You don't have to do anything. I'll do it all. I'll fight for you. Just let me, please. I don't care if I have to beg because I fucking will, okay?"

All the sincerity in his voice made me crumble.

"Okay. I'll stay tonight, but don't expect anything from me, Aaron. Don't think this is going to be easy. I don't even know if I can forgive you or move past what happened. You really hurt me... I did something stupid because I couldn't handle being without you."

His eyes grew concerned.

"What happened?"

I didn't want to tell him about this, but perhaps he'd understand why this wasn't a simple case of me forgiving him. It couldn't be. Not after everything I went through.

"The week after school started, I had people calling me a... murderer under their breath. I ignored it at first, but it kept getting worse. It was enough my heart was broken, then I had to deal with that bullshit on top of it. I didn't want to go on any longer, I'd had enough. Everything hurt too much."

I swallowed, my eyes darting away from his and focusing on his chest instead.

"I ran a bath, locked the door and got in with all my clothes on. I didn't care any longer. Without you and the shit at school, I had nothing to live for. So I held myself under the water, wanting it to be over, wanting the pain to just fucking well end."

Aaron's hand around my face tightened.

"The thing is… Mum came upstairs to check on me because she knew how much I was struggling. I could sort of hear her banging on the door, but I couldn't bring myself to care. Under the water was so still and peaceful for the longest time, even as my lungs constricted, I kept myself submerged. The next thing I knew, Graham ripped me out of the water. I choked and struggled to breathe again. Turns out, Mum had got him to kick the door in. She wasn't very happy with me for obvious reasons, but she understood. I put her through a shit time during that year. I hated myself for it and I hated you for making me want to end everything."

When he didn't say a word for several minutes, I got the courage to look up into his eyes and found he had tears in them. Not an unexpected reaction. I had admitted I'd almost ended my life over him and the shit at school. Didn't stop me hating the sight of him crying. So I reached for him, pulling him against me and letting him cry on my chest.

"I'm sorry," he whispered through choked breaths. "I'm so sorry."

I stroked his hair, unable to say anything else. It already hurt enough telling him about that awful day. It's why I couldn't just forgive him. Why I harboured all this hate for the boy I loved in my heart. The pain of the day he'd ended everything had driven me to an extreme measure to stem my bleeding heart.

Aaron raised his head, staring at me with watery eyes and a broken expression on his face. I couldn't take it any longer. My hands curled around his cheeks and I tugged him closer until our lips met. The kiss was gentle at first, but it didn't stay that way. It became hard and messy, so charged with the violence of our emotions. We clung to each other. His tongue clashed with mine, making me drunk off him and the relief I felt at finally giving in to the urges overloading my system.

When he put inches of space between our mouths, I felt bereft. I wanted him right there again.

"I'll never hurt you like that again," he whispered. "I swear. You are my everything and I'm so fucking sorry. I love you. I've never stopped loving you."

My heart clenched hard.

"I know you do."

I let him pull off our clothes and tuck us up under the covers. It was still early, but honestly, after all of that emotional shit, I was exhausted. We held each other tightly and kissed again, but it was more out of comfort than anything else. Reassurance. I had Aaron. The man who enabled me to breathe easy.

I still had no idea if I could forgive him or trust him, but I'd taken a giant leap of faith today in admitting just how much he decimated me all those years ago. I came here hoping to find closure so I could move past him. Now I knew better. There would be no moving past Aaron, walking away or saying goodbye. My heart and soul fucking belonged to him.

I love you more than life itself, Aaron. I want you to fight. I want you to show me I can trust you.

Please… never leave me again.

CHAPTER FIFTY EIGHT

Rhys

I'd left Aaron's early yesterday before his nieces woke up. He didn't want me to go, but I had to put some distance between us. Especially after what I'd admitted to him. It didn't feel right to give him hope things would eventually be okay between us. I didn't know if they would be or not. I could allow him to try to mend my heart and regain my trust, but I couldn't make any promises he'd succeed.

Walking away from him might be impossible, but I needed time. Burying myself in work helped keep my mind off it all. I had a lot to do anyway having neglected stuff last week. Well, it did until he started texting me around lunchtime today. I hadn't responded yet. Instead, I'd read them over and over, obsessing about what he'd said. They'd arrived at hour intervals as if he was trying to give me space but failing miserably.

Aaron: I started reading your comic strip last night. Your artwork is stunning. I can see why Emily likes it.

Aaron: I can't wait to see what you come up with for her book.

Aaron: I missed you sleeping next to me.

Aaron: Honestly, I just plain miss you all the time.

Aaron: You're my home. Everything feels empty without you.

Aaron: I love you x

The last one made my heart melt into a puddle on the floor. He could see I'd read them. Who knew if it was driving him crazy, me not replying. Probably. But Aaron wasn't giving up on me. He wanted me back. If I had to let him sweat a little, so be it. I told him it wouldn't be simple or easy.

The buzzer went and I got up to let Meredith in, opening the front door and leaving it for her. I went into the kitchen and grabbed two beers from the fridge, popping the caps. Then I took those back to the sofa and set them on the coffee table.

"Pizza has arrived!"

Meredith flounced in with two pizza boxes and jumped onto the sofa next to me.

"Hello to you too."

She grinned and shoved a box at me.

"All right my bestest friend in the whole wide world?"

I narrowed my eyes.

"What do you want?"

"What makes you think I want something?"

I opened my box and gave her a look. Meredith would only ever be over the top nice when she wanted a favour. And usually, it was something I didn't want to do.

"Okay, fine, I need you to help me."

"With what?"

"A guy at work asked me out for drinks and I said yes thinking it was a group thing but it's not."

Considering Meredith hadn't been out with anyone in weeks, I was a little surprised.

"Just tell him if you're not interested."

She shook her head.

"I am, but he's too hot for me. Like he's a twenty out of ten."

I raised an eyebrow as I stuffed a slice of pizza in my mouth. The melty, cheesy goodness made me groan. Meredith grabbed one of the beers I'd left on the coffee table and took a swig.

She had leftover hang ups from when she was a teenager so I wasn't exactly taken aback by her comment.

"Mer, no one is too hot for you. You're stunning."

"You're my best friend so you have to say that, not to mention being as into dick as me."

"Being into dick doesn't disqualify me from being able to appreciate female beauty."

There was only one dick I had any interest in other than my own. One I'd worshipped on Saturday night even though I shouldn't have. I tried not to shiver at the memory of the mutual pleasure I'd shared with the owner of said dick.

"I need you to come with me."

No way in hell I wanted to be a third wheel on her date.

"I'm sure he'll appreciate your gay bestie crashing the party… not."

The twinkle in her eye told me that wasn't everything.

"I was thinking more like a double date."

"Firstly, no and secondly, hell no, and thirdly, just no."

"But Rhys—"

I shook my head.

"Meredith, I love you, but no way. You promised you wouldn't try set me up with Jonah again and, did you conveniently forget, I do not date."

No doubt that's who she had in mind. I grabbed my beer and knocked half of it back. She really had no fucking shame at all this girl.

"I wasn't going to suggest Jonah, I swear."

I didn't want to know who she would have suggested. It didn't matter. I was not going to double date with her. Just because I'd got myself involved with some fucked up mess with my ex, didn't mean my love life had suddenly kick-started into high gear or anything.

"Even so, it's still no. Just go on the damn date and stop being a baby about it. Why would he have asked you out if he didn't like you?"

"God, fine, you're such a spoilsport."

I stuffed another slice of pizza in my mouth so I wouldn't say something mean back. She hadn't had a ton of luck with men. She needed to stop getting involved with dickheads and emotionally unavailable men. I knew where her shit with them stemmed from. Fucking Cole Carter. Bringing him up would only upset her so I refrained. She didn't mention him unless she was wasted and then it only resulted in her crying over it. In so many ways, Meredith and I were alike. We still had feelings for the people who broke our hearts. And that just plain fucking well sucked.

"How was your weekend anyway?"

I swallowed and looked away.

"Okay."

"Just okay? What happened?"

I fiddled with the cardboard as Meredith opened her own box. It made little sense for me to be nervous about telling her. She had told me to talk to him. My relationship with Aaron was just all kinds of complicated.

"I saw Aaron," I mumbled.

"You did?"

"I went to his for dinner and met his nieces."

"Did you two get to talk?"

I was about to open my mouth to reply when the buzzer went. Meredith raised an eyebrow.

"Expecting someone?"

I dumped my pizza box and beer on the coffee table before getting up.

"No."

Probably one of the neighbours forgetting their key again. Kenny on the third floor was notorious for it. Whilst I'd never actually met the guy in person, he'd ended up introducing himself down the intercom after the third time he'd misplaced his keys.

I trudged out into the hallway and pressed down on the intercom.

"Hello?"

"Hi… I'm sorry to turn up like this. I need to know you're okay."

My heart did a backflip and somehow, I found myself smiling.

"Is this your idea of proving to me you're not giving up?"

"Sort of. You didn't reply to my texts. I got worried. I just… damn it, Rhys, I can't help it. I need to see you."

I didn't reply, pressing down on the buzzer instead. If he was that desperate, I'd put him out of his misery. To be honest, I was secretly happy he'd turned up here.

"Who is it, fuckface?" came Meredith's voice from the living room.

I stared at the wall, unsure of whether to admit my ex was on his way up here or not. No doubt if I did, she'd be all over Aaron asking questions. Not sure I wanted her up in his face. Not when I'd only given her very minimal details about what happened with him.

He knocked on the door before I had time to decide. I opened it finding him looking effortlessly handsome in his work clothes.

I waved a hand at myself.

"As you can see, I'm alive and well."

He took a step towards me.

"I was going to reply, but I was focused on work."

And another step, his blue-grey eyes full of determination.

"And you could have called me. I would—"

Aaron grabbed my face, tugged me towards him and kissed me. My body reacted on instinct, clinging to him as waves of relief and desire flooded me. He nibbled on my bottom lip reminding me how obsessed he was with it. Then he put precious inches between our mouths.

"I needed to see you," he murmured. "I couldn't wait any longer."

"So I see."

His hand drifted down to rest on my chest where my heart thumped against my ribcage.

"You're not mad at me for turning up unannounced, are you?"

I smiled.

"No… but I do already have company."

He stiffened, his eyes growing darker as the grey became more pronounced.

"Oh."

I pulled back from him and took his hand, tugging him inside so I could shut the front door and stop giving my neighbours an eyeful. He clearly thought I meant male company. And I kind of liked him being jealous. I hadn't told him about me not being with anyone else in the time we were apart. Wasn't sure if I wanted to open that can of worms considering he might have done. Anyone else having touched what's *mine* would not sit well with me.

And here you were getting all happy about him being jealous when you're just as bad.

"Meredith is here."

His eyebrow raised.

"Meredith?"

"Uhuh. Come, I'm sure she won't mind you gate-crashing our pizza and booze night."

Aaron looked puzzled as I dragged his coat from his shoulders and hung it up. Then I took his hand and pulled him along into the living room with me.

"You took your damn time, fuckface..." Meredith's eyes went wide as soon as she spotted Aaron behind me. "Oh... is this...?"

"Mer, this is Aaron, who apparently couldn't wait to see me." I glanced at him, stifling a smile when I noted his face had gone red. "Aaron, this is Meredith, my very annoying best friend."

"Hey, I'm not annoying!"

I raised my eyebrow as I tugged a bewildered Aaron over to the sofa.

"Don't listen to a word she says, she has zero shame and will tell you explicit details about her sex life despite you not wanting to hear them if she gets half a chance."

"I so do not do that. You've never complained about it before."

I grinned as I made Aaron sit next to me on the opposite side from Meredith who stared at him with unnerving intensity as if assessing every inch of my ex and sizing him up. She leant over me and put out her hand to him. He took it with some reluctance.

"It's nice to meet you. Rhys has told me a little about you, but he failed to mention you look exactly like Alex from his comic strip." She eyed me with a smile, telling me she was on to me. "Can I get you a drink?"

Aaron looked at me as he withdrew his hand, confusion painting his features.

"Mer treats my place like her own." I turned to her. "You can get him a beer if you really want."

She grinned, jumping up and walking away into the kitchen.

"Best friend?" Aaron blurted out, his voice laced with hurt he had no right to feel.

"Yes, best friend. We met at uni like six years ago. You do realise I have a life outside of whatever this is, right?"

He looked stricken.

"I didn't mean to. I just…"

I patted his thigh.

"Don't worry, A, you're still the only person who knows me inside out."

No one else would ever know me the way he did. We'd grown up together. He'd seen me at some of my worst moments. That forged a closeness which couldn't be replicated.

He didn't get a chance to respond as Meredith came back and handed him an open beer bottle which he took whilst still staring at me with wide eyes. Leaning forward, I picked up the pizza box, settling it on my lap again.

"Hungry? You can have some of mine considering Miss Disgusting over there likes pineapple on hers."

"Don't diss the pineapple."

"Fruit does not belong on pizza."

Meredith rolled her eyes before tucking back into her own food. Aaron leant closer to me.

"Are you sure it's okay for me to be here?" he whispered in my ear.

I nodded and stroked his thigh again. Now he was here, I didn't want him to go. It'd be useless to deny how much more at peace I felt when he was near me.

"I want you to stay," I whispered back.

And that's the moment I realised a small window had opened inside me just for him. All Aaron had to do is climb in if he dared.

I hoped he noticed. I hoped he worked out how to heal the rift between us. There was no doubt in my mind I needed him to break down all my walls so I could learn to trust him. I would not survive losing him all over again. Not at all. Not one little bit.

CHAPTER FIFTY NINE

Aaron

A s happy as I had been spending all the time I could with Rhys for the last two weeks, not knowing what we were actually doing here was getting to me. The day I ended up on his doorstep and met his friend, I should say… best friend, had left me feeling all kinds of fucked up jealousy. Not to mention not knowing if he'd been with anyone else whilst we were apart. We weren't even together now.

Fuck.

I could see why Rhys liked Meredith so much. She was fun, brash and quirky. The evening I'd spent with her and Rhys showed me he'd grown so much without me. It cut deeper than it should have. The way he laughed and joked with her was like knives digging into my skin. We'd been like that once. Constantly winding each other up. Being able to talk about anything under the sun. Free and open. And I fucking hated seeing him be that way with another person.

I shouldn't complain since when she'd left, he'd pushed me down on the sofa and shoved his tongue in my mouth. We'd left a trail of clothes from his living room to his bedroom, unable to keep our hands off each other. He'd fucked me on my back whilst we kissed, our hands roaming across each other's bodies, rediscovering every inch.

The one thing that hadn't changed from when we were teenagers. Our insatiable lust. The desire constantly pulsing between us. There was no doubt I loved sex with him, but it wasn't enough. I wanted my Rhys back. All of him. Everything we'd shared when we'd been younger. I knew for a fact he would never allow me to top him again until he learnt to trust me with his heart.

I'd finally persuaded him to let me take him out on a date tonight. We'd been back and forth on this for two weeks. I needed us to sit and talk about everything without it escalating into sex. Something he kept initiating and I found it impossible to say no.

He'd avoided having conversations about us since he'd told me about his attempt on his own life. It just about fucking killed me. The huge role my decisions and actions had played. I'd driven him to those depths of despair.

How the fuck did I even make that up to him?

Rhys was so full of life now. He'd picked himself back up and carved out a place in the world. Seeing how successful he'd become and how much he'd grown up made me feel so inadequate.

What did I have to give him now?

The only things I had to offer were myself and my undying love.

Would that be enough?

Was *I* enough for him?

I had to talk to him about this. Had to know what he was thinking when it came to me and him. For the past seven years, I'd just been surviving. Now, I had the love of my life within reach and yet he still felt so far away.

I stood outside his front door after he'd let me up clutching a bouquet of flowers, having put on a suit even though I felt ridiculous about this. We'd never been out on real dates as teenagers. He opened the door and stared at me without talking for a long moment. Since I'd told him I was taking him to dinner, he'd put on a dark grey shirt and smart chinos. And he looked fucking sexy. I wanted to push him back into the flat and strip those clothes from his body. Instead, I stood there awkwardly, trying to think of what to say.

"Are those for me?"

I nodded and shoved the flowers at him. He took them and smiled in that heart-stopping way of his. The first time since we were teenagers I'd seen it directed at me. It made my heart hammer wildly in my chest. God, I loved this man so fucking much.

"Well, thank you. I'll just put them in water. Do you want to come in for a minute?"

I followed him inside, still unable to speak. He went into the kitchen, filled a jug with water, popped them inside and placed it on the counter whilst I stood in the doorway. Rhys turned to me, his dark eyes assessing my appearance. He closed the distance between us and stroked a hand down my arm.

"You look good," he murmured. "The suit is hot."

"Thank you," I managed to say.

"Are you okay?"

I flexed my hand at my side, trying not to reach out to him.

"I'm just… nervous."

He cocked his head to the side.

"Why? We're only having dinner."

"This is the first time I've taken you out properly."

My eyes landed directly on his bottom lip as he bit down on it.

That damn fucking lip.

I reached up and pulled it out of his teeth on instinct. His pupils dilated and he let out a breath.

"Did you forget that's mine?"

"How could I forget? You going to reclaim it?"

His taunt had me tugging him against my chest and running my thumb along his lip.

"Why? Did someone else try to take it from me?"

Those dark eyes assessed me for a long moment.

"No."

As if my heart couldn't pound any harder inside my chest.

"Does that mean what I think it does?"

"There's never been anyone but you in my eyes, A. I've not been with another man."

I leant closer, staring at him with a newfound understanding. It's not as if I'd forgotten about him being demi. I knew dating would be hard on him. This proved something significant even if he hadn't said it.

Rhys still loves me. He's never stopped.

"Neither have I."

His eyes widened a fraction.

"What?"

"I won't lie and say I didn't try dating other people, but it was just that... dates. Nothing physical ever happened. I haven't even kissed or touched anyone else. The thing is, Rhys, none of them were you. I told you I'd always love you. You're my one."

My mouth was only inches from his now. I could feel his breath fluttering against my lips.

"The thought of someone else kissing you made me ridiculously jealous," he whispered. "In my head, you're still mine."

God, I fucking love how you're jealous over me.

"I've always been yours... what I don't know is if you're still mine."

"Maybe I'll tell you the answer if our date goes well."

I should've known he'd come out with something smart. Stepping back, I took his hand and pulled him towards the door.

"Wouldn't want to be late for our reservation."

"It's like that, is it? You going all out for me?"

"You have no idea, *knight*."

Tonight had to be special. He deserved all of my care and attention. All the effort I'd gone to planning this. I wanted him to understand I'd give him the world if I could. Hell, I'd bow down and worship at his feet if he asked it of me.

He didn't let go of my hand the whole way to the restaurant except when we were going through the barriers to the tube. It made us feel real even though I had no fucking clue if we were or not. I gave my name to the host and we were led over to a table in the back. I'd asked them for something intimate and this definitely was. There were extra candles on the table and we were slightly hidden from view from the other diners.

We sat down across from each other and looked over the menu. After ordering, Rhys smiled at me, his eyes twinkling.

"This is rather romantic."

I reached across the table and took his hand, stroking my thumb down his.

"Well, I wanted it to be, to show you I'm serious about treating you right."

"A…"

"I love you. There's nothing I wouldn't do for you. What I did to you in the past was unforgivable. I know that. Trust me when I tell you I wish I could take it all back."

His fingers tightened in mine.

"You're here now, isn't that what matters?"

"Is it? We've not moved beyond what happened yet."

He shifted in his seat, staring down at our hands.

"I blame him just as much as I do you."

My father. The man who'd forced me to cause this rift between us. If we hadn't been seventeen, things would've been so different. My hands had been tied because of our age.

"He's dead to me."

Rhys raised his eyes back to mine.

"He is?"

"He never accepted me for who I am, so I told him where to go. I did it for me... but mostly, I did it for you even though you were no longer in my life. I never stood up against him in the way you needed, so I changed that. I made him understand he was no longer in control of me or anything I did."

Rhys' eyes softened and it made me feel as though I might have dug my way past another one of his walls.

"I don't stay at Johnstone & Parrish for him. I actually like my job. You taught me about the beauty of books. Everything I do in life is influenced by you, Rhys. I can't help it. You told me once I saved you, but the reality is, you saved me every single day even when you weren't here."

We were interrupted by the waiter bringing over drinks, but it didn't matter. Rhys' expression said everything words couldn't. He wanted me to know he was still right there. Maybe we could get through this. Maybe he could learn to forgive me. And let me back into his heart. Although, I was pretty sure I still resided in there, regardless.

When the waiter left us, he reached out and took my other hand, squeezing both of them.

"I'm still yours, A... I never stopped being yours."

"You sure about that? Don't want to wait until the date is over?"

He smiled and shook his head.

"You still need to give me time, but I can't lose you again. So yes, I'm sure. I'm yours."

I dropped his hands and scrambled out of my chair, rushing around the table and pulling him into my arms.

"I'll give you all the time you need. All of it. Just stay with me, *knight*. Please stay."

I didn't care if I sounded like I was begging. Knowing he still belonged to me gave me hope we could fix our relationship. We could mend it all if we tried.

"I'm not going anywhere. You have me. I promise, *prince*. You said you'd fight for me. I want to fight for you too."

And really, I couldn't ask any more of him than that after everything I'd put us through.

CHAPTER SIXTY

Rhys

I'd known I couldn't keep avoiding the subject of what we were with Aaron. It's why I'd agreed to go on a date with him in the first place after initially refusing. It'd taken me spending all this time with him to realise I couldn't keep hiding behind all my walls. Having Aaron back made me happy. The way he gave me everything I needed without question. Even the nights I'd wanted to get lost in his body and not have to think about anything else.

Aaron had proved to me he deserved a second chance. I could try for him just as he kept doing for me. He'd been so patient with me these past two weeks. I owed it to him to stop fighting against my need for him. I owed it to myself most of all.

Forgiving him wouldn't happen overnight, but we had made progress. I no longer held onto that hate in my heart. Letting it go was the first step. Learning Aaron had stood up to Patrick and told him where to go had been the catalyst. It made me confront reality. Aaron had never had a choice. We'd been too young to do anything about the events leading up to our destruction. Only now as an adult did I see the truth behind all of our secrets and lies.

What happened with Valentine wasn't Aaron's fault. He'd been afraid and distraught over it. Patrick took advantage of the situation. Used it to drive a wedge between his son and me. But Patrick no longer held any power over us. He no longer mattered. Just Aaron and I did.

So giving us a chance even if I still had reservations about how it would work now we were older was the only way forward. I already knew I couldn't live without him. It would annihilate me all over again. It's why I'd told him at dinner I'd stay. I'd be his. I always had been.

Aaron had brought me back to his after our romantic dinner. We'd spoken about less charged topics, like my ideas for Emily's book now Diana had sent me over the full brief. And how his nieces were doing with their parents' separation.

"I have a surprise for you," he said as he tugged me into his living room.

Sitting on the coffee table was a wrapped box. I raised an eyebrow. He had gone all out with this whole date business. Not that I didn't appreciate it.

Aaron sat me down on the sofa and indicated the box with his hand.

"You didn't have to get me anything."

"Well, I know but this isn't just anything. Open it."

His smile made me a little suspicious.

What have you got up your sleeve?

I reached out and unwrapped the box. It was pale green and had a forest pattern all over it. When I flipped the lid open and stared down inside, my breath caught in my throat.

A full set of hardbacks sat staring at me. All of Emily's books.

Reaching out, I picked the first one up, running my hand over the cover. Turning it to the title page, I just about died. It was signed with a personalised note from her.

Rhys,

Aaron told me how you loved to get lost in books and fantastical worlds when you were kids. I hope this inspires you in some way.
Love
E. R. Davidson

"She's signed them all for you."

I carefully placed the book back in the box and turned to him. His eyes were full of love and adoration.

"I can't believe you got these for me."

"Emily was happy to sign them, especially after I told her about us... not everything obviously, but so she'd understand why. And when we do her book launch, she would love to meet you in person."

I had no words. He didn't have to do any of this for me. This damn man knew exactly what would bring me the most joy. I'd never lost my love of books. My phone was full of eBooks since I rarely read physical copies any longer. Didn't stop me collecting my favourites. Now I could put these on my shelves.

"I don't know what to say… thank you so much."

"I could say it's because we all believe in your ability at work but really, I did this to make you happy. Getting to see you smile is all the thanks I need."

If I was a more cynical person, I'd have thought Aaron was doing this to win me over. Aaron never did anything for other people out of selfishness. He might have been raised with privilege, but he still had the biggest heart of anyone I knew. I never took his over the top gestures as anything but a need to make me happy.

"Do you have any more surprises? You know, just so I can prepare myself."

He grinned and shook his head.

"Didn't want to scare you away."

I reached for his tie, loosening it so I could tug it from his shirt. Aaron eyed me, his eyes growing stormy the way they always did when he got aroused.

"I don't want sex," I blurted out, making his eyes go wide.

"What?"

"I mean, it's not that I don't want to have sex with you. I definitely do… like you look so damn hot tonight. I just… god, this is coming out wrong." I slipped his tie from his shirt and placed it on the coffee table before running my hands along his shoulders. "I feel like I've been using it to avoid my feelings and I don't want to do that tonight. Can… can we just like cuddle? Or is that way too lame?"

He bit his lip before reaching out and running his fingers through my mop of curls.

"I'd like that."

I leant towards him.

"I'm still going to kiss you."

His smirk made my blood pound.

"No objections here."

Our lips met and my hand curled around the back of his neck. Love flooded me. Love for this beautiful man who owned my heart and soul even if I'd not told him that yet. Saying I love you again would take me a little more time. I wanted to know we worked now we were older and no longer had anything holding us back. I wanted to trust Aaron again.

My phone buzzing in my pocket made me pull away. Noting it was Mum's part-time carer, I answered.

"Hi, Daria."

"Hi, Rhys. I'm afraid I have some bad news."

My blood ran cold.

"What is it? What's happened to Mum?"

"I came to check on her like I usually do at the end of my shift, but I found she'd taken a really bad fall. The paramedics are here and will be taking her to A&E. They want to have her ankle x-rayed as they're worried it's broken. She's in a lot of pain and I'm not able to go with her as I need to get home for my kids."

I stood up abruptly.

"Oh god, shit. How did she fall?"

"She tripped over the rug in the hallway. I've told her we need to get rid of it."

I rubbed my face.

"So have I. I'll deal with it. Thank you for letting me know."

"Of course, do let me know how she is. I'll find out where they're taking her and text you, okay?"

"Thank you, I will do."

She hung up. I'd told Mum a million times she couldn't have rugs in her flat as she wasn't always steady on her feet. Hating I'd been proved right, I rubbed my face again. The last thing I needed was her breaking her ankle.

Aaron put a hand on my arm, getting my attention.

"What's wrong?"

"Mum's had a fall and they're taking her in to have her ankle x-rayed. I need to go be with her. Daria, her carer, can't as she's got to be home for her kids."

He stood up, his eyes growing concerned.

"Do you know where they've taken her?"

"Daria's going to text me."

He reached for me, wrapping his hand around the back of my neck.

"Will you let me drive you? If she's broken her ankle, she'll need help getting home."

I nodded, feeling my phone buzz in my hand. I checked the message and noted the hospital they were taking Mum to. Aaron hadn't even hesitated to offer help. And really, I needed him. Seeing my mum hurting killed me every single time.

I showed him the message and he took my hand, giving me a sad smile.

"Let's go, hey?"

I let him lead me from his flat and out to his car. The whole way to the hospital, my leg bounced in the footwell. It's not like I could help being worried about her. She still had good and bad days. This latest incident just about killed me since it happened needlessly. If she wasn't so stubborn about that damn rug. As soon as we got her home, I'd be rolling it up and taking it away with me. She needed to stay safe.

Aaron parked and got a ticket before taking my hand and following me into the hospital. I couldn't see her in the waiting room so I went straight to the front desk. The lady manning it looked up from her computer.

"Hello, how can I help you?"

"My mother was brought in a little while ago, Stephanie King."

Mum had never bothered to change her name back after the divorce.

"Hold on, let me have a look…" She tapped on her screen for a moment. "Ah yes, she's been taken through." The lady looked at Aaron sceptically. "She's in bed six through the double doors there."

"Is my partner allowed through with me?"

I needed Aaron. Panic I didn't want to feel had started to set in. My stomach got all twisted and I wanted to be sick. Aaron's presence grounded me.

"Yes, I'm sure that'll be fine."

"Thank you so much."

My hand tightened around Aaron's as we made our way through the double doors and down the beds until we found Mum. My breath whooshed out of me all at once when I saw

523

she was sat up in bed whilst a nurse was checking her over. I waited a moment until they were finished. The nurse looked over and raised his eyebrow.

"Can I help you?"

My mum looked up and broke out into a smile.

"It's okay, Dale, this is my son, Rhys."

"Mum." I was by her bedside the next moment, dragging Aaron along with me. I reached out and touched her cheek with my free hand. "Are you okay?"

"Yes, love. They've given me something for the pain."

The nurse, Dale, smiled and shook his head.

"She's been telling me all about you for the past ten minutes. They'll be along to take her up to x-ray soon, but you're welcome to sit with her."

"Thank you," I replied with a nod.

He left, pulling the curtain over to give us some privacy. I dropped my hand from her face and shifted on my feet.

"You look very dressed up, were you out somewhere?" she asked, her eyes roaming over me.

That's when Mum noticed I had someone with me. Her eyes widened and her mouth went a little slack.

"Um, yes, I was."

"Aaron? Is that you?"

I glanced at him and his flushed face.

"Hi Steph," he replied, rubbing the back of his neck.

She looked between us, confusion written all over her face when her eyes landed on our joined hands.

"What's going on, Rhys?"

I hadn't mentioned Aaron to her at all, wanting to be sure this was the real deal between us before I opened that can of worms. She'd picked up the pieces after our breakup and had to go through hell on earth with me. It concerned me how she'd feel about me getting back together with Aaron. And I hadn't considered that when I'd rushed over here with him.

"Um… well… Aaron and I are kind of back together."

Kind of? You are back together, aren't you?

I glanced at Aaron whose eyes were on me and full of hope. We hadn't explicitly stated we were boyfriends again, but it's what I wanted.

"Back together? When did this happen?"

"The getting back together part?"

Her brows turned down.

"All of it."

"Maybe I should…" Aaron started, pointing towards the curtain.

I'd promised him I'd fight for us. It included telling my mother we were back together and not shying away from a tough conversation. Aaron's presence gave me courage. I took a step back from her bedside and looked at him.

"No, I need you here."

Those blue-grey eyes spoke volumes. The affection and love grounded me. He wouldn't leave me to flounder on my own.

My eyes fell on Mum again who was watching us with cautious eyes.

"We saw each other again three weeks ago when Johnstone & Parrish offered me the opportunity to illustrate an urban fantasy book. Aaron had no idea the creative department had contacted me so it wasn't on purpose or anything. We've spent a lot of time together since then. He understands he hurt me and we're trying to move beyond what happened in the past. I know it might be hard to understand, Mum, but our feelings are still there. You know I haven't dated and well, he's why. It's always been Aaron."

Aaron's hand tightened around mine. Mum's eyes flicked to him.

"Does he know what you did?"

I knew exactly what she was referring to.

"Yes."

She leant forward.

"Do you realise I almost lost my son because of you?"

Aaron flinched. This wasn't how I expected her to react to the news of our reunion, but then again, she didn't understand everything Aaron and I had gone through together. She didn't know what really happened with Valentine. How it'd affected our relationship in ways I never expected. Despite everything, going through that shit together had brought us closer even as it ripped us apart. If his father hadn't interfered, Aaron and I would've only gone from strength to strength. I would've helped him heal from it. Instead, we had to do that by ourselves. And perhaps it had been better for us in the long run.

Aaron and I had learnt how to be without each other. How to stand on our own two feet. So us coming back together was on even ground this time. I was successful in my own right. His privilege no longer hung over us like a black cloud. His father no longer had any power here. We were equal and it showed.

"Yes I do, Steph, and I'm sorry," Aaron said, his expression falling. "If I could take it all back, I would. Rhys means everything to me. I never wanted to hurt him. I'll spend the rest of my life making it up to him. I love Rhys more than anything."

"I'm working on the forgiveness part, Mum. We both are," I added.

She sat back and crossed her arms over her chest.

"I'm not going to say I'm happy about this, but I trust you know what you're doing, Rhys."

I looked at Aaron. He made my heart fucking swell. He'd been my entire world when we were younger. He was still my entire world now even though that world had expanded. Aaron took up the most space in it. That would never change no matter what happened between us.

I can't stop loving you even if I try. And I don't want to try. I just want you, Aaron. You… forever.

"I do. I promise I know exactly what I'm doing."

The porters came then to take Mum down to x-ray. Even if she didn't understand right now why I'd agree to get back together with Aaron, she would eventually. He'd show her just as I would.

I felt stronger with him next to me.

My anchor. My soulmate. My everything.

CHAPTER SIXTY ONE

Aaron

I couldn't say I exactly blamed Steph for reacting to the news of Rhys and I getting back together the way she had. It made me more determined to prove I would do anything for him. That I deserved this second chance he'd given me.

Whilst Steph had been at the hospital, I didn't leave Rhys' side knowing he needed me there. Thankfully she hadn't broken her ankle, it was just a nasty sprain, not that it made Rhys feel any better. I'd taken them both back to Steph's flat after she'd been discharged and helped get her upstairs with Rhys. We got her settled in bed for the night. Rhys let Daria know what was happening for when she came to see Steph in the morning.

We'd gone back to his for the night as it was closer in case Steph needed anything. Rhys had fallen asleep tucked up against me out of sheer exhaustion. I'd lain awake watching him. My beautiful man who'd begun to let me back in despite everything I'd done. He gave me meaning. And he'd shown me without words how much he wanted this to work between us.

When I awoke, I found him laid out on his front, the covers half falling off him as if he'd kicked them away in the night. His back was bare and made my mouth water. The temptation to touch him overrode everything else. I moved closer and ran my fingers down his spine, revelling in the softness of his skin. He mumbled something I couldn't hear and shifted a little, but it didn't stop me. Leaning over, I pressed kisses down his back. I didn't want him to think I was being a creep or anything, touching him in his sleep, but I'd not had a chance to do this so freely.

My hand curled around the covers, pulling them lower so I could take him in fully. I felt like a right fucking perv staring at him like this. Especially since my eyes were on the curve of his behind and the memory of the way he'd let me fuck him assaulted my senses, making my cock stand to attention.

You are not going to ask him about that. If he wants it, he'll tell you. He'll ask you.

I hated feeling this way. Like it wasn't enough we'd come back together. He always made sure I was satisfied when we were intimate.

"Don't stop," came his muffled voice, startling me.

"Kissing you?"

"Mmm."

I continued my path down his back, carefully shifting over him so I straddled the backs of his thighs. My fingers followed my mouth. He shifted under me, pressing back against my touch. When I met the base of his spine, my hands drifted lower, splaying out over his cheeks tentatively. It made my cock throb. I wanted him so fucking much.

"Take them off." His voice had a commanding note to it, making me shiver.

My fingers curled into the waistband of his boxers, tugging them down his legs. He didn't try to turn over or stop me when I touched his bare skin with my fingertips. He shivered and let out a little pant.

"A…"

I snatched my hands back, scared I'd gone too far.

"Sorry, do you want me to stop?"

"No. Touch me. I know you want to."

Apparently, I wasn't the only one who could read him. He read me like an open fucking book. Then again, I wasn't trying to hide my feelings or emotions from him.

I leant over him again, trailing my tongue down his back this time. He moaned in response, arching up against me. It made me brave. Braver than I'd ever been before. My hands splayed out over him again and I spread him open for me. The moment my tongue brushed across him, Rhys jerked in response.

"A… what… fuck…"

I shifted, using one hand to keep him spread whilst the other slipped beneath him, wrapping around his hard cock. He let out a strangled moan as I tongued him. He rocked back against me, encouraging my exploration, which only made me eager to please him further. I concentrated on stroking him, feeling him throb harder under my fingers.

"Aaron," he groaned. "Fuck, fuck. God."

I pulled back slightly.

"You like this?"

"Can't you tell?"

I grinned, watching him strain towards me as if he couldn't get enough. So I gave him what he wanted, loving the way he panted and moaned as I brought him closer to the edge.

"Please," he breathed. "Please, A, fuck, please… please fuck me."

I thought I'd misheard him. Pushing myself up, I stared down at him.

"What?"

"I want you to fuck me."

"Are you sure about that?"

He looked back at me, his dark eyes wild with need.

"Please, I want you."

Who the fuck was I to deny him? I wanted to do this, but I'd been scared to ask, wanting it to be his choice. Reaching over to his bedside drawer, I tugged it open and grabbed what I needed. Then I worked him with my fingers, opening him up to me whilst he panted, moaned and writhed beneath me.

"A, please."

I pulled off my own boxers, ripped open the foil packet and rolled the condom on. Whilst we'd not been with other people, we'd not fucked bare yet like we had done as teenagers. Making sure to use enough lube, I pressed against him, taking a deep breath before sliding inside. He was exactly as tight and hot as I remembered. So damn perfect around my cock.

"Fuck," I groaned. "You feel so good."

"I want to see you," he whispered as I leant over him.

Pulling out of him, I let him turn over on his back. His eyes were so full of desire and affection as he reached for me. I settled back between his legs and slid inside him again, building a steady but slow rhythm, knowing if I went too fast, I'd blow my load. My hands were planted by his head as he held my face, his other hand resting on my shoulder.

"Thank you for yesterday."

"What part?"

"All of it… the date, being there for me at the hospital. It made me realise something."

"Yeah?"

He nodded, tugging me closer until our lips brushed.

"I forgive you."

I swear my heart just about stopped.

"What?"

"I don't want to live in the past. I can stand on my own two feet, but I don't want to be without you. You bring me happiness. You know me inside out. You give me everything I need without me having to ask for it. My world is a better and brighter place with you in it. I choose you, A. I choose this. I choose us."

I pressed my lips to his, sealing away his words because they made me feel too many emotions.

"I love you so much," I whispered against his mouth.

"I know."

It wasn't an *I love you* back, but it was enough for me. Whatever Rhys chose to give me would always be enough.

I kept kissing him as my thrusts grew harder and more erratic. All my love poured out of me with each kiss. Each touch. We lost ourselves to each other. To this moment where nothing else in the world mattered but us. Loving Rhys was the only thing I wanted to do for the rest of my life. Showing this man he was the single most important person to me. Giving him my all.

Seventeen years ago I'd fallen in love with him. I'd known then I wanted him forever even if I'd not dared to hope he would ever reciprocate my love. Having him with me now made me more certain than ever.

I want you to be my husband, Rhys. I want to marry you and take your name.

My own name had brought me nothing but heartache and pain. Being Rhys' meant more to me than anything else. So if he said yes, I'd take his name and we'd be each other's for life. Our love was once in a lifetime and one of a kind.

I knew he wasn't ready for that yet. I'd just got him back so scaring him away was the last thing I wanted to do. I'd continue to show Rhys he could trust me with his heart. Prove we'd work now we were adults, something I knew he was worried about. I'd wait until he could tell me he loved me too.

For now, I'd love him the only way I knew how. Just like this. Us locked together in ecstasy and bliss. And when we crested the wave together, both panting and out of breath, peace washed over me. Rhys had chosen me. He'd picked us. He'd fight for this.

"Fuck, I needed that," he murmured after I rolled off him and disposed of the condom and he cleaned up the mess on his stomach.

"Is that so?"

"I missed it."

I shifted and laid my head on his chest, letting him stroke my hair.

"I missed it too."

He snorted.

"Of course you did. Don't think I've forgotten how much you loved to fuck me when we were younger."

I ran my fingers along his stomach.

"I did. I still do, but I love you being inside me just as much."

"I'm aware, you're very vocal when you beg me to fuck you harder."

I dug my fingers into his ribs.

"Shut up."

"Ooh, touchy, are we?"

"Fuck off."

I looked up, finding him grinning. He wasn't wrong. I did like it when he got rough and ordered me around.

"As much as I'd love to lie in bed with you all day, we need to go see Mum and make sure she's okay."

"Do you think she'll eventually accept this?"

He poked my nose with his free hand.

"Yes, she used to adore you, I'm sure you can charm your way back into her good books again. You are my Prince Charming after all."

"I hope so."

His eyes grew concerned.

"I don't need anyone else's approval to be with you, okay? This is my decision and she respects that even if she's still upset with you right now. She had to see me go through my very worst when we broke up, so you have to give her some time, just as you did with me."

I reached up and stroked his face.

"I'll prove to her I'm worthy of you."

I shifted off him and got up, stretching.

"You're lucky Mer already approves of you or you'd have an uphill battle with that one."

I glanced back at him, watching as he got up and walked towards the door.

"She does?"

"Yes. She's a hard one to please, but you are terribly charming when you want to be."

He winked at me as he left. I couldn't help following, tugged by the cord binding us together, noting him disappearing into the shower. I hoped Steph wouldn't mind us being a little late. There was no way I was passing up the opportunity to get wet and soapy with my boyfriend.

I could prove to Steph I deserved her son even if it meant I had to do a little grovelling. Our past had been laid to rest. Now, we were moving forward. And we'd do it together. Just like I'd always wanted when we were kids.

CHAPTER SIXTY TWO

Rhys

With the passing weeks, Aaron and I grew ever closer. It felt like we'd got back to where we'd been before everything fell apart. Except this time we were so much stronger. It's as if going through our breakup and living without each other had only made it even more imperative we made this work now. We knew what being away from each other felt like. And neither of us wanted that again.

I'd finished up the final illustrations for Emily's new book a couple of days ago. They were perfect. A part of me knew they'd love the images whilst the other had my nerves tingling in anticipation of them hating everything about them. Aaron hadn't seen any of it because I wanted to unveil it to them at the same time. I needed to see their reactions, which is why I was now sitting across from Diana, Xanthe and Aaron at Johnstone & Parrish.

"Are we allowed to turn them over now?" Diana asked with a smile.

"Go ahead." I waved at the packs I'd made for them. "Just be honest with me."

I watched them look through each drawing, wiping my sweaty palms on my thighs as I tried not to say a word. Knowing Aaron so well, I could see his reaction written all over his face. Pride shone in those blue-grey depths.

"These are stunning," Diana said after a few minutes. "Emily is going to love them so much." Her eyes flicked up to me. "Honestly, thank you for this. It's been an absolute joy to work with you."

I smiled.

"The pleasure is all mine. I didn't think I'd get to illustrate for one of my favourite authors."

Diana's eyes moved toward the door.

"Well, we can do one better than that."

I glanced back to find Emily Davidson walking in, looking a little harassed.

"I am so sorry I'm late, the bloody train got delayed. Did you start without me?"

"I'm afraid we did, but come take a seat."

I watched the brunette Emily breeze in and take a seat next to me. My eyes remained glued on her, feeling a little star-struck.

"Emily, this is Rhys."

Diana indicated me with her hand. Emily turned to me with a bright smile on her face. And before I knew it, she'd reached out her hand to me. I took it despite not really liking human contact if I didn't know a person. It was something I'd just had to get used to over the years.

"It's so nice to meet you." She gave me a little knowing look. "Aaron has told me so much about you."

I glanced at Aaron who'd gone red and was shifting in his seat.

"Has he now?"

"All good things." She lowered her voice. "He's rather smitten."

I let go of her hand and felt a little awkward. As far as I was aware, he hadn't mentioned our relationship to his work colleagues.

"Yes… well… um…"

"Did you want to show Emily what you've done for her?" Diana piped up, saving me from drowning.

I slid the drawings across the table to Emily. Her eyes lit up as she looked through them.

"Oh my god. You've captured my characters so well. Honestly, they're brilliant." Her hand pressed to her chest. "I've been so nervous about this new direction, but this makes it all so worthwhile." She turned to me. "I cannot thank you enough. I've been reading your comic since the beginning and getting to have your artwork for my book is just such an honour."

What do I even say to that?

Having her like my work was totally crazy.

"The honour is absolutely all mine."

She waved me off, her ears going pink.

"You are going to give him an early copy, right, Aaron?"

"As long as you sign it," he replied with a grin.

"Wouldn't have it any other way. And you *have* to come to the launch party. This one has never brought a plus one." She waved at Aaron.

I noted the way Diana and Xanthe looked between me and Aaron with confusion.

Aaron rubbed the back of his neck.

"I hadn't asked him yet."

"Well, consider this an official invitation."

I looked between them. Aaron had clearly worked his charm with his authors. No one could resist that boy. Not even my mother who, after a few weeks, had finally come to accept Aaron back into the fold. She saw how happy he made me. How he supported me in my work and always made sure he consulted me about anything involving the two of us. When I told him I had to work late, he never complained about it. To be honest, he spent more time at my place than his own even though it was a longer journey to work for him. I had to admit, I liked he was there when I came to bed even the times he'd already been asleep. His presence helped me sleep easier.

"I'd love to come."

Emily smiled wide.

"That's settled then. Right, are we going to approve these or do I have to strong-arm you into it?"

My heart swelled as Aaron gave me one of those secret smiles of his. The ones where his eyes softened and his adoration shone through. He wanted me with him. To make it public knowledge we were together. Aaron had never let me doubt his feelings for me. And he never made me feel pressured to admit my own.

I think I'm ready, A. I want to tell you how much I love you.

I'd tell him later when we were alone. Right now, we still had business to conduct.

The rest of the meeting went well. Emily had a further meeting with Aaron to discuss her next book. Aaron stood next to me by the lifts as they waited to go up and I waited for one to go down. Reaching out, he brushed his fingers over mine.

"I'm so proud of you," he murmured.

"Thank you… you coming over later?"

"Can't keep me away."

I bit my lip, watching his eyes fall on it and darken.

The lift to go down arrived. I smiled at Emily.

"It was so nice to meet you. I guess I'll see you at the launch."

"You definitely will."

I stepped forward into the lift but Aaron grabbed hold of my arm and spun me around. Next thing I knew, he'd kissed me. It was only a brief kiss, but I was startled all the same. Aaron didn't shy away from public displays of affection, but we were in his office. Apparently, he didn't care about that.

"See you later, *knight*," he whispered against my lips.

He let me go and I backed away, pressing down on the button for the ground floor. My hand raised to my lips as I stared at him. His eyes held a promise of later and he mouthed the words *'I love you'*. My eyes remained fixed on him until the doors closed and the lift moved.

Now I was surer than ever I wanted to tell him how I felt. I ran over how I'd do it in my mind all the way back to mine, but every idea I had seemed stupid.

After I got home, I changed into something more comfortable and got on with some work as I had more projects due. My mind raced with all the possibilities of what would happen when Aaron got home.

Home? Since when did you start thinking of your place as being his home too?

We were here more than his considering I had my home office in my living room. Aaron's flat might be bigger, but mine was more homely. We spent some weekends at his when he was taking care of his nieces, which had become a more regular occurrence whilst Harriet and Ralph worked on their marriage. Aaron and I didn't mind as the girls were good for us and had been rather excited when he told them we were together. They'd immediately taken to calling me 'Uncle Rhys' and pestering me to teach them how to draw comic characters. Hetty and Harmony were sweet girls so I didn't mind too much. And I knew it made Aaron happy to see me becoming part of the family.

I must've got so lost in work and my thoughts, I barely noticed anything around me. The front door slamming shut made me jump and spin around my chair. I'd given Aaron a key a week ago, but I'd not got used to him coming and going on his own quite yet.

"I come bearing gifts," Aaron said as he walked in, holding up a bag from my local Thai place.

"You spoil me."

He grinned and shook his head, dumping the bag down on the coffee table. Then he came over and leant down to give me a kiss.

"I like looking after you."

He pulled away and walked out, leaving me staring after him. Aaron did everything in his power to make sure I wanted for nothing. Whilst he was trying to make up for the past, it's just the way he was. He wanted to take care of me.

I got up and went into the kitchen, grabbing a couple of beers from the fridge before getting plates and cutlery. Carrying them out into the living room, I got everything set up and started dishing up when Aaron walked back in having changed out of his work clothes. He'd left a lot of his stuff here out of convenience and I didn't mind one bit.

He jumped on the sofa next to me and picked up his plate whilst I put the TV on. The two of us ate in a companionable silence with *MasterChef* on since we were obsessed with it.

"How was the rest of your day?" I asked after I'd come back from the kitchen having put the plates in the dishwasher and cleaned up.

I sat down and Aaron leant closer, putting his head in my lap as he stared up at me. I stroked his hair on automatic.

"Good. Emily and I were discussing the sequel and how she wants you to do the artwork for the rest of the series."

"Meeting her was crazy for me, you know. Her words make me feel so many things and to have her like my art is just… mad. Also, since when did kissing at your workplace become acceptable?"

He grinned, his blue-grey eyes twinkling.

"You're mine and I want the world to know."

"Even though it will get back to you know who?"

He rolled his eyes.

"I don't give a shit what he thinks. I told you, I made it very clear his opinions don't matter. Don't need his toxic bullshit and disappointment in my life. Besides, Mum called earlier... Harriet told her about us."

"Oh?"

Aaron and Kellie had a very shaky relationship, but he didn't want to cut her out of his life completely.

"She said she's happy for us and apologised again for her part in the breakup. I don't think she'll ever leave him, but it doesn't matter. She's trying to be there for me and that's all I can ask for."

I leant down and kissed his nose, stroking his cheek with one finger.

"I'm so proud of you for not taking their crap any longer. You deserve better."

"I have you, Harriet and the girls, that's all the family I need."

I sat up again and rested my arms over the back of the sofa. It'd been a long time since I felt so at ease. Having Aaron back in my life had brought me the utmost joy even though it'd been hard in the beginning.

"I wanted to ask you something..."

I glanced down at his face finding worry there.

"What is it?"

He didn't meet my eyes and it concerned me.

"I want... I want to move in with you."

I blinked, having not been expecting him to say that at all. "What? Here?"

He nodded, still staring at my chest rather than my face as he fiddled with his t-shirt.

"Is that even practical, A? We don't have space for the girls and it takes you longer to get to work. Plus I rent and you own your flat."

"You don't like working at mine. Besides, I can sell it and maybe we can get somewhere bigger so we can have the girls over still, but in this area so we're close to Steph."

It's not that I didn't want to move in with Aaron. Nothing would make me happier than to have him with me all the time. I didn't want it to be impractical for him. I could work anywhere. He was right though. I preferred being surrounded by my things when I was working. I'd just got my space exactly how I liked it.

"A..."

"I've thought a lot about it, Rhys. The longer journey doesn't bother me. Getting to come home to you every night would make me so fucking happy. Please say you'll at least think about it. You don't have to decide now or anything."

"You'd really want to sell your place and move here?"

He smiled, finally meeting my eyes.

"Anywhere you are is home, *knight*, so yes, no doubt about it."

"Okay. I'll think about it."

Though honestly, there wasn't much to think about. Aaron basically lived here as it was. And he said he'd get us a place of our own close to my mum. He really was too bloody perfect and it made my heart sing.

"Now, move, I want to spoon you."

He snorted but did as I asked, shifting off my lap and letting me lay down behind him with my arm slung over his chest. I rested my head on my elbow as I stroked my fingers along his body. He snuggled back against me, turning his attention to the TV. I loved holding him like this and he knew it.

"*Prince.*"

"Hmm?"

I leant forward, brushing my lips up against his ear.

"I love you."

He almost knocked his head into mine with the way he turned it up so fast towards me. Aaron's eyes were wide with shock.

"What?"

"I love you."

Tears welled in those blue-grey depths. I reached up and stroked his cheek.

"No crying. You're supposed to be happy right now."

"I am," he whispered.

I leant down and kissed him. He turned over so he could tangle his hand in my hair and press himself against me. My hand drifted down his back, landing on his beautiful behind and curling around it. Aaron let out a moan as he started grinding against me, making it very clear what he wanted. I kissed my way up his jaw towards his ear.

"I want to take you to bed and show you how much I love you," I murmured before biting down on his earlobe.

He let out a strangled groan of pleasure, his fingers gripping my hair.

"Please," he breathed.

"I better hear more begging tonight, *prince*. I want to reward you for being so patient with me."

I pulled back and stared at him. His flushed face and his stormy blue-grey eyes. This man was all mine and I loved him with my whole entire fucking soul.

"Take me to bed and fuck me, *knight*... please."

I smiled.

"Gladly, my love, fucking gladly."

Maybe if he was good for me tonight, I'll tell him exactly what he wanted to hear.

I wanted him here every day so I never had to be without him again.

CHAPTER SIXTY THREE

Aaron

The last four months with Rhys had been more than I could've ever imagined. I'd moved into his place not long after he told me he loved me for the first time as adults. And I'd just completed the sale on my flat since we'd finally found the perfect place for us. It had three bedrooms, one of which we could turn into Rhys' office and was very close to Steph's flat. We'd just had our offer on it accepted so we had a lot to celebrate.

The drive down to Brighton reminded me of when we'd driven down here together all those years ago. We had the windows rolled down and the music up loud. Rhys' tanned skin had darkened in the sun over the past month. He had his sunglasses on and his hand tapped on the outside of the car door in time to the music. I'd never get over how handsome my boyfriend was.

No matter how many times I told myself not to be nervous about today, it didn't stop my skin prickling all over. I had no idea what I'd do if he said no but asking Rhys to marry me had been on my mind for months. Now we were moving forward and planning a future together, it felt like the right time. Taking him back to where this relationship had begun was only fitting.

After I parked up, we strolled down the shopping streets to the beachfront hand in hand. The smile on his face lit my skin on fire.

"Are you going to make me go on the teacup ride?"

I raised an eyebrow.

"Our day out wouldn't be complete without it."

"Oh right, I forgot, you're too scared to go on the rollercoaster."

I shoved him with my free hand.

"Shut up, I am not."

"Don't worry, *baby*, I'll hold your hand so you don't get scared."

He always gave me shit about it. I didn't get scared, I just wasn't a huge fan of heights.

"I'm not your fucking *baby*."

He leant over and kissed my cheek. I couldn't help the smile gracing my lips. Being with him always made me happy. Especially with how free and open we were with each other. I'd been damn happy when my father hadn't attended Emily's launch party for her new book. And getting to show off Rhys was the icing on the cake. He got a bit embarrassed about me gushing over how he'd done all the artwork but I was so damn proud of him. He'd been so inundated with work recently, he'd had to hire a virtual assistant to help him manage everything.

"No, you're my Prince Charming."

"I'll take that."

I dug my hand in my pocket, running my fingers over the little box in it. It'd taken a considerable effort on my part to find out his ring size without giving the game away. I'd resorted to wrapping a piece of string around his finger when he was asleep. It'd been damn a miracle he hadn't woken up since sometimes he could be a light sleeper.

As much as I wanted to take him straight down the beach and propose to him, it'd have to wait. I wanted him relaxed and happy before I took the plunge. That and I was nervous as fuck. My palms were already sweating and I hoped Rhys assumed it was the heat of the day.

We got down to the pier and Rhys turned to me, his eyes twinkling. He'd shoved his sunglasses up on the top of his head so I could see them now.

"Let's get doughnuts. I've been dying for these all week."

I shook my head but let him drag me over to the booth. We got twelve sugar-coated ones and took them with us as we strolled along the pier. Rhys leant on the railing and stuck one in his mouth, getting sugar all over it. I shook my head, grinning as I reached over and brushed it off.

"What? Not going to lick it off?"

"I bet you'd like that."

He leant over and kissed me.

"I'd love it… though I'd love it more if you licked me all over."

"There's always time for that later."

And if everything went well, I'd want to pin him down when we got home and make love to him, showing him how much I adored him with every kiss and every touch.

God, I fucking hope he says yes.

For the rest of the afternoon, we spent our time going on the rides, including the teacup one and playing in the arcades. I felt like a teenager all over again. Rhys made me feel on top of the world and spending the day together like this without any worries or cares was more than I could ever ask for. But I had a very important question to pose to him. And I intended to make sure he answered the way I hoped.

I gripped his hand tighter as we walked down the promenade together away from the crowds out for a day in the sun. The closer we got to where we shared our first kiss, the more I wished I wasn't so scared of doing this. Rhys had repeatedly told me he wanted forever with me, but marriage had never entered the equation. I had no idea if he even wanted it. Nothing would hold me back though. Rhys was my one and I wanted to be his husband. The two of us had been through so much together. I wanted to cement forever with vows and promises I'd never break again.

"You remember when we were here last time with that freak storm? It was crazy."

I jumped at the sound of his voice, glancing at him. He frowned when he took in my face.

"Jesus, A, you're a bit skittish today. Is something wrong?"

"No, no, nothing's wrong. Everything's perfect. Just perfect."

His eyebrow shot up and he stopped us in our tracks.

"Okay, now I know something is up."

I had to just bite the bullet and ask him. I pulled him towards the stones even as he kept frowning at me.

"Aaron, what's going on?"

We stopped on the pebbles. I took both his hands and held them tight.

"I remember that day very well. Every second is branded in my memory. I could never forget it, Rhys. It's the first time I kissed you."

"Well yeah… though I still feel bad about the way I told you off over it."

"Don't. I deserved that even if I don't regret doing it."

He tried to let go of my hand so he could reach for me, but I held on tight.

"You're being really weird right now, A."

I shifted on my feet.

"I know. I just… I'm nervous and freaking out, but I have to do this."

He began to open his mouth, but I let go of his hand and shoved mine over it.

"Just let me talk, okay?"

He nodded and I dropped my hand. I stared into his dark eyes, noting his concern. Rhys had no fucking idea what I was about to do.

"You mean the world to me, Rhys. The whole entire world. I brought you here today for a reason and it's not because we're buying a flat together. This is where it all started for us. It's where everything changed and that makes it special to me."

His eyes softened and I almost lost my nerve.

Suck it up and say the words. Just do it, Aaron.

I dug my hand in my pocket, curling it around the box.

"Rhys… I… I have a very important question to ask you and I want you to consider it very carefully before you answer, okay?"

A little furrow appeared in his brow but he nodded all the same. So I took that as my cue, watching his eyes widen when I dropped down onto one knee. There were a few people near us, but I only had eyes for him. My beautiful man.

"I fell in love with you seventeen years ago. The moment I saw you, I knew you were the one. We have been through thick and thin together, ups and downs, heaven and hell. There's no one in this world I want to spend my life with other than you. I love you so much, Rhys. You are my soulmate and my best friend. And nothing would make me happier than if you did me the honour of becoming my husband."

I tugged the box out of my pocket and dropped his other hand, opening it and holding it out to him.

"Will you marry me?"

I watched him swallow hard, his eyes pinning me in place with their intensity. Then they flicked down to the box where nestled inside was a plain palladium band. I knew for a fact, he wouldn't want anything fancy. He wasn't that type of person.

"You want… you want me to marry you?"

"Yes, *knight*. I want to be your husband more than anything else in the world."

He swallowed again. The pebbles were digging into my bare knee but I didn't care. I'd wait here forever for his answer.

"You're fucking crazy, you know that, right?" he said, his voice low as he ran a hand through his hair.

"You wouldn't have me any other way."

He reached out and wrapped a hand around my bicep.

"Damn it, A, get off your knee and come here."

He tried to tug me up but I wouldn't budge.

"You haven't given me an answer yet."

"You're such a pain."

Next thing I knew, he'd launched himself at me, pushing me back against the pebbles as he straddled my waist. His mouth brushed against mine as he stared down at me.

"You're fucking lucky I love you so much, *prince*."

"Is that a yes?"

"It's a put this damn ring you went out of your way to get me on my finger and kiss me."

I grinned and he put out his hand for me, letting me slide the ring on awkwardly from our position. Then before I had a chance to do anything else, his lips were on mine and we were practically dry humping each other in public.

We were interrupted by some clapping and whooping. Rhys raised his head and stared at the people nearby who were making all the noise.

"Congratulations!" someone called.

"Oh Jesus," Rhys muttered. "We have a fucking audience."

"You did just pounce on me after I asked you to be my husband."

He looked down at me.

"Can you blame me? You're like the hottest guy ever and you asked me to marry you. I think that calls for pouncing."

I snorted and pulled him down towards me again, kissing him, albeit more PG this time around. He rolled off me and reached out, entwining our fingers together.

"Just so we're on the same page, that was a yes, right?"

"Yes, Aaron, I'll marry you."

Relief flooded my veins and my heart squeezed. He put a hand over his eyes. I adored the fact my ring sat there now, showing the world he was mine.

"Oh god, Mum is going to freak out and be a nightmare. She'll want to help us plan the whole thing. Please tell me we don't have to have some big ceremony with a ton of people there. I don't want that. At all."

I laughed.

"No, it can be as intimate as you want it to be. I don't care, as long as I get to promise myself to you."

"Oh good, you know I hate being the centre of attention."

I reached out and stroked his cheek.

"Don't worry, I'll make sure their eyes are on me."

He dropped his hand and turned to me with a grin.

"How could they look at anyone else? Prince Charming is the main event."

"Well, this Prince Charming only gives a shit if his knight in shining armour is looking at him."

Rhys rolled on his side and leant down until our lips almost met.

"I've only ever had eyes for you, A. You're the only one I want to wake up to every morning and fall asleep with for the rest of our lives. I love you forever, *prince*."

He kissed me, making me melt for him entirely. I was so fucking happy. Rhys was going to be my husband. Nothing in this world could top that.

"I love you forever too, *knight*."

EPILOGUE

Rhys

Was it normal to be this nervous on your wedding day? My palms were all sweaty and I kept adjusting my suit every two minutes. Maybe it was the months of planning that had gone into this. Or the fact I was going to be standing up there and declaring my undying love to my soulmate. Either way, I couldn't help feeling like I was about to faint.

"You look like a ghost right now," Meredith said as she patted my arm.

She looked absolutely stunning in a dove-grey dress which complimented her now natural strawberry blonde hair.

"You're not making me feel any better. Isn't that what a best man is supposed to do?"

"Best woman and yes, I'm sorry. You're going to be fine. You love Aaron and he loves you. So don't be getting cold feet right now or I'll have to beat your skinny arse up."

"I do not have a skinny arse!"

She leant back and looked at it.

"No, you're right, it's perfectly proportioned. Nice and muscly. I see why your husband-to-be keeps staring at it."

I nudged her with my shoulder.

"Oh, shut the fuck up already."

Aaron did have an unhealthy obsession with staring at it but then again, I had an unhealthy obsession with staring at him too. I guess we were both completely crazy about each other and it showed.

"Language," she hissed.

I glanced over at Hetty and Harmony who also had matching dove-grey dresses with white flowers entwined in their blonde hair. They weren't looking at us. The twins took their roles as flower girls very seriously. They were waiting for the music to start.

"They've heard me and their uncle say the word fuck before… by accident."

Meredith raised her eyebrow.

"Do I even want to know?"

"When do you ever not want to know about my sex life?"

Her green eyes lit up.

"Spill right now!"

Meredith was so fucking predictable.

"Okay, so there I was, riding Aaron hard with my hand on his back, pinning him to the bed. He's moaning and telling me to fuck him harder. The girls walk in just as I'm saying, 'that's it, fucking take my cock,' and Hetty pipes up going 'what does fuck mean, Uncle Rhys?'. I swear Aaron and I have never scrambled to hide ourselves under the covers so fast. Aaron practically died trying to tell them it was a bad word they shouldn't use. We got an earful from Harriet over it since they asked her why I was on top of him when they went home."

Meredith shook with her attempt to hold back her laughter and I was trying not to join in myself.

"Oh my god, you two are like horny rabbits. Did you forget they were staying?"

"No, but we thought they'd gone to sleep. They don't normally wake up in the night, but Hetty had a nightmare."

Telling Meredith that story had loosened me up. My best friend was right. I loved Aaron and becoming his husband was what I wanted.

"At least you'll have no interruptions tonight. And I still can't believe Aaron invited Emily Davidson here. Isn't that like fucking huge?"

I grinned. Having my favourite author at my wedding? Pretty damn amazing. Emily and Aaron were close, which is why she was here.

"Uhuh, that man certainly knows how to make me happy."

Meredith didn't say anything else as the music started. The girls walked into the ceremony room and Meredith stepped forward. She glanced back, giving me a wink. I hadn't wanted to be given away or anything so Mum was sitting up at the front. We hadn't invited our fathers to the wedding since neither of them deserved to be here. We only had about thirty guests. I'd been insistent on keeping it small.

Meredith walked into the ceremony room and I stepped forward, wiping my sweaty palms on my trousers. I looked down at myself. My blue suit moulded to every inch of me, as Aaron had insisted we have them tailored specifically for today. His matched mine. He wanted our wedding to be perfect.

I shook myself and took a deep breath before walking in. I couldn't help the smile gracing my face when I saw him waiting up there for me at the end of the aisle. Our guests paled in comparison to my beautiful blonde-haired, blue-grey eyed man who held my heart and soul in his palm. I walked up towards him, loving the way he smiled back at me, his eyes shining with happiness. When I reached him, he took my hand and squeezed it.

"Hi," he whispered.

"*Prince*," I murmured, making his cheeks redden.

We turned to the registrar, who began proceedings and I half-listened, completely captivated by the man who was about to become my husband. We went through the various legal declarations we had to make before the registrar, Lydia, spoke to our guests.

"Aaron and Rhys have chosen to write their own personal vows to one another. Aaron, would you like to begin?"

He turned to me, clutching my hand tightly as he pulled out a small piece of paper.

"Rhys, I have loved you since we were seven-year-old boys who had no idea of the trials and tribulations we'd go through in life. You have taught me how to be brave and stand up for myself. Today, I give myself to you completely. I promise to love, care and support you in all our future endeavours and to cherish every moment we have together. Whatever life throws at us, I know we'll fight our way through it, just as we've always done. I love you, *knight*."

I bit my lip which made his eyes darken. His words made my heart swell. No one understood our nicknames for each other but us.

"Thank you, Aaron. Now, Rhys, would you like to say your vows?" Lydia said with a smile.

I'd thought long and hard about what I wanted to say to him. There didn't seem words to express my feelings, but I'd tried my best. I pulled out my own sheet of paper even though I'd memorised everything I wanted to tell him.

"From the day we met, you had me captivated by your blue-grey eyes and your smile. No one else has managed to challenge, frustrate and push me out of my comfort zone the way you always have. And for that, I am eternally grateful. You saved me, *prince*, every single day of our lives. I promise to love you, to support you and encourage you as we continue to grow stronger together with each passing day."

The tears in Aaron's eyes said it all. I reached up and brushed the one which fell from his eye away. He gave me a watery smile. The two of us were it for each other. There was nothing in this world which would keep us apart ever again.

After we'd exchanged rings, we had to sign the registry book and finally, we were able to walk down the aisle together as husbands. My heart was so fucking full to bursting. And as Aaron looked over at me, his blue-grey eyes shining with adoration and happiness, I knew then and there, I'd got my fairy tale ending. My happy ever after. Something I'd never dared to hope for.

When we stood outside the ceremony room together, I reached up and held his face whilst his fingers tangled in my hair. We pressed our foreheads together, breathing each other's air.

"We're married," he whispered.

"Fuck yeah, we are."

He laughed and kissed me as his arms came around my back and he held me tight.

"You are the best thing that ever happened to me, *knight*," he whispered when I pulled back.

"So are you. You promise you're not leaving this time?"

He smiled, his eyes so bright with love.

"I promise… I'll follow you to the ends of the earth if you need me to, Rhys. You are my soulmate. My happiness. My home."

"I'm so going to hold you to that, *prince*."

"I hope you do."

I stroked his cheek, staring at my handsome husband who meant everything to me. We'd finally made it. After all these years with nothing standing in our way and only hope and happiness for the future. We'd grown from boys into men. One day we'd grow old and grey. And we'd do it together.

"I love you, Aaron Jackson King. You're my forever."

ACKNOWLEDGEMENTS

Thank you so much for taking the time to read this book. I really appreciate all of my readers and hope this book gave you as much joy reading it as I did writing it.

There's only one person I have to thank for this book and that's my critique partner, podcast co-host and the best writer friend I could ever have, Sab. Your encouragement when I was writing this story got me through all the pain and heartache I had to endure. You demanded chapters like never before and I could do nothing but pour the words out onto the page. Rhys and Aaron's story took the both of us by storm. I would not have been able to do them justice without you helping me when I got stuck, listening to my plans for their story and generally insisting I get the book written. This is the longest book I've written to date and in that respect, the fastest. You lived and breathed their story right alongside me. And pretty much told me if I didn't give them the happy ever after they deserved, I'd be in the doghouse for god knows how long after everything these two boys went through. Believe me when I say this book would not exist without you even though

I was the one who wrote it. I needed you there to keep me going even when I wanted to throw in the towel. This book forced me to go to some pretty dark places in order to get it written. Made me dig deep inside my emotions and pour out a story unlike anything I've written before. To tell the story of these two boys who became best friends and fell in love only to have it ripped away in the most devastating and painful way imaginable. I bled out on the pages and you were there to patch up my broken heart every single time. This was *the* book I knew would change everything for me and you were by my side as I delivered this emotionally hard-hitting and painful experience. Words cannot express my deep and profound gratitude for having you in my life. I love you so much. Never stop being you or I'll have to come and 'Quinn' you... and we both know how that will end! But in all seriousness, you are an amazing, kind, caring and incredible soul who I have the honour of calling my best friend. Just remember I'm always here for you in return, my savage partner in crime!

ABOUT THE AUTHOR

Sarah writes dark, contemporary, erotic and paranormal romances. She adores all forms of steamy romance and can always be found with a book or ten on her Kindle. She loves anti-heroes, alpha males and flawed characters with a little bit of darkness lurking within. Her writing buddies nicknamed her 'The Queen of Steam' for her pulse racing sex scenes which will leave you a little hot under the collar.

Born and raised in Sussex, UK near the Ashdown Forest where she grew up climbing trees and building Lego towns with her younger brother. Sarah fell in love with novels when she was a teenager reading her aunt's historical regency romances. She has always loved the supernatural and exploring the darker side of romance and fantasy novels.

Sarah currently resides in the Scottish Highlands with her husband. Music is one of her biggest inspirations and she always has something on in the background whilst writing. She is an avid gamer and is often found hogging her husband's Xbox.

Printed in Great Britain
by Amazon

78538046R00328